"Once again Chan Ling has prod
fifth, to delight her many fans. H
with Dick Francis and Jeffrey Archer, even if the context is totally different. The backdrop is Malaya (where the sunrise can be red) in its twilight years as a British possession, and Malaysia at its dawning, with the cruel Emergency period between as centre ground. As ever, the author tells it how it was, with complete objectivity and fairness where concerns the evanescent expatriate Brits, the aristo Malays and the thrusting Chinese. A tangled web of love stories it may be, yet there is suspense on every page. But whatever else is suspended, it is never our belief in the characters or the action. An excellent, enjoyable read."

—Bill Jackson,

Editor, *The Corporal and the Celestial*

"Chan Ling's latest novel begins in Somerset in 1950 and ends there fifteen years later – with the intervening years taking place in Malaya as it moves towards independence. Although Chinese May and English Ruth become close friends, there were many misunderstandings and intrigues along the way. What at first appears to be a conventional love story soon develops into one of intrigue, sexual tension and tragedy. There are racial and societal differences, with rich and poor all added to the mix. The pace is fast and there is plenty of action to keep you reading. Post-war Malaya is brought to life with its mix of crowded cities, steamy jungles, white sandy beaches, and the heady scents of the flowers and spices. You also get glimpses of a different life in 1960s London. This book enthralled me. I could not put it down."

—Julia Appleton

President, Princes Risborough Morning WI

Where the SUNRISE *is* Red

CHAN LING YAP

Cover designed by Lynn Chin, photo of lady by Skeronov/Shutterstock.

Published by Marshall Cavendish Editions
An imprint of Marshall Cavendish International

Other Marshall Cavendish Offices:
Marshall Cavendish Corporation. 99 White Plains Road, Tarrytown NY 10591-9001, USA • Marshall Cavendish International (Thailand) Co Ltd. 253 Asoke, 12th Flr, Sukhumvit 21 Road, Klongtoey Nua, Wattana, Bangkok 10110, Thailand • Marshall Cavendish (Malaysia) Sdn Bhd, Times Subang, Lot 46, Subang Hi-Tech Industrial Park, Batu Tiga, 40000 Shah Alam, Selangor Darul Ehsan, Malaysia

National Library Board Singapore Cataloguing-in-Publication Data

Name(s): Chan, Ling Yap.
Title: Where the sunrise is red / Chan Ling Yap.
Description: Singapore : Marshall Cavendish Editions, [2017]
Identifier(s): OCN 1004681154 | ISBN 978-981-47-9400-8 (paperback)
Subject(s): LCSH: Malaya--History--Fiction. | Malaya--History--Malayan Emergency, 1948-1960–Fiction.
Classification: DDC M823.92--dc23

Printed in Singapore by Fabulous Printers Pte Ltd

To Tony

I lay my cheek on yours
You were still warm
Tears flowed sealing mine to yours

Acknowledgements

I would like to thank Sue Porter, Angela Wall, Bill Jackson and Julia Appleton for reading my draft and giving it their time. Their comments and suggestions were invaluable and much appreciated. Thanks also to all those who have encouraged me to continue writing and the love and support of my children, Lee and Hsu Min.

Part One
Somerset, England
1950

Chapter 1

RUTH DUG DEEP into her pockets. Her fingers were frozen with cold. She stamped her feet and huddled her slight body further into the sheepskin coat. She loved the coat. Worn and almost bare in patches, it smelt of wood smoke and reminded her of the fire she would light when she returned home that evening. She cast her eyes in search of Buster. She called his name loudly, palms cupped round her lips to give her voice weight. She knew she should hurry, for dark comes suddenly in December. From a distance black clouds loomed; streaks scuttling towards her like a lion's mane flowing wild. A sudden wind whipped up. She shivered. The air had turned distinctly cold. She reached up to touch her nose. It was numb and she imagined it looking red. Not your best feature, her mother had told her solemnly when she was a child. But her mother was no more. They said that a bomb dropped on Liverpool Station had killed her instantly.

A lump formed in her throat. Ruth swallowed and brushed the damp from her cheeks. She searched in her pocket for the letter. She had used the excuse of walking Buster to leave the house to read it in private. She had read it over and over again, examining each word, each line, in search of a deeper meaning in them. The words seemed distant. Did he not wish her to come, she asked herself. It had been almost a year since Mark left for Malaya. She had wanted to go with him. "No, Ruth," was his answer, whispered in her ear. He had nuzzled her neck, his breath warm with a hint of tobacco. "Plantation policy does not permit it. I need time to settle and get to know the job. It would not be prudent for you to come. Things don't look too good over there." Mark had stopped short then. She could see that he did not wish to talk about his work in Malaya. "Anyway, what about your father?" he had challenged after a moment's hesitation. "He has not recovered from the loss of your mother. He needs you." Ruth could still see, in her mind's eye, the flecks of light in Mark's hazel eyes; eyes that commanded her to see sense, to yield to her responsibility to her father.

With a sigh, she called out loud for Buster again. He came bounding up the hill wagging his tail. His tongue hung out in breathless pleasure and his eyes were full of joy, the joy of running in the wild and the joy of chasing rabbits. A joy that she could not share.

"Come! Time to go home," she said, ruffling the hair on his head.

***

"So what did he say?" her father asked the minute she stepped into the kitchen. He was seated hunched by the hearth. His face was wan and his cheeks bristly. The bags under his eyes told of sleepless nights and worry.

"Nothing much," she replied hiding her face which had turned a deep red. She piled the wood high in the hearth and began twisting and knotting old newspapers to start the fire.

"Nothing much?" John's voice was gruff in disbelief. "It's been three months since he last wrote! I see you wring your hands each time the postman comes."

"The mail is slow," she replied lamely. "Mark said that security is tightening up in Malaya. It would not be a good time for me to join him."

"*Huh!* Excuses! If security *is* being tightened up, would it not make it safer for you to go? You can't remain apart forever. Since you married, Mark has been away for most of the time. I won't be here forever. The farm has to be sold. I can't run it, not even with your help. Labour is difficult to come by. All the lads have left for the city. And, my dear daughter, I don't want you to waste your life sitting by me when I know you are pining for your husband."

She knelt down and placed her head on his lap. "I love you Dad. I am not wasting my life. Mark knows best. I am sure he has good reasons for my not joining him."

John laid a hand on his daughter's head and ran his fingers through the blond curls that refused to lie flat. He could not bring himself to tell Ruth that the creditors had been. The farm had to be sold sooner than he had anticipated. He knew that he had himself to blame. He had allowed himself to wallow in the loss of his wife and had done little to redeem the situation after the war. First he lost the wheat crop in 1946 as a result of incessant rains. Then the following year, the potato crop had failed because of hard frost and snow. The little he had set aside for rainy days had all vanished. Now, with the farmhands almost all gone and no land girls to call upon, it was mechanisation or sink. Investing in machinery was not an option he could afford.

***

Ruth opened her eyes and pulled the blanket right up to her chin. She wriggled her toes to get some warmth into them. In the silence of the night, an owl screeched. A silvery beam of moonlight peeked through the gap between the curtains. She shivered. A little warmth would be lovely, she thought. Shadows played in the room, shifting with the movement of the curtain. The room was draughty. Mark had told her about the heat in Malaya. She could not imagine such heat. Relentless, he had said. She didn't quite grasp what that meant. She had never been abroad. The nearest to being hot was that one sunny day they had had in Brighton. Lying on the beach with the pebbles and fine sand round her, it was the nearest thing to heaven. She had been so in love. She remembered licking ice cream from a cone. She could even taste it now. Yes, a little warmth would be wonderful.

Perhaps she had imagined it all. Perhaps she had read into the letter something that was not there. Mark must just be busy. After all, his job was a difficult one. He had hinted at dangers that he might have to encounter but had never elaborated on them. She had tried to find out more about the situation in Malaya, 'The Emergency' they called it. She had failed. All news seemed focused on the situation in England itself. The war had virtually bankrupted the country. Just getting bread, meat and enough to eat, became an all-consuming activity. Feelings ran high and people vented their pent-up frustration through strikes and demonstrations. Page after page of news was devoted to the never-ending problems in England. What news they had of the colonies was few and far between and centred mainly on India and Burma. Their demand for independence and subsequent gaining of it caught the attention of the media as did the turmoil and massacre that followed the partition of India. Malayan news seemed, however, to be buried somewhere, inaccessible. Perhaps she just didn't know how to find it.

Ruth turned on her side dragging the blanket around her shoulder. She wanted desperately to know more; she wished not to show ignorance when she wrote to Mark. She wished he would talk to her, write more. She wished that she was with him.

Chapter 2

Tanjong Malim

SWEAT DRIPPED DOWN his forehead and gathered at his collar, turning it a dirty brown. The shirt clung to his body tenaciously. Mark caught a whiff of himself. With an impatient move of his shoulders, he shrugged his shirt off and threw it into the woven basket in the corner of the bathroom. From the corner of his eye he caught sight of a gecko scrabbling on the wall. Mosquitoes buzzed. He leaned forward to look into the mirror. In the harsh neon light, his skin was a deathly pallor despite his dark tan. He turned on the tap. The pipe clanked in protest. A trickle of brown rusty liquid flowed, followed by a gush of clean, clear water. He dipped his head under the tap and allowed water to fall on his head and face. Then abruptly, he turned off the tap and straightened up.

"A clean shirt," May said handing him a dazzling white shirt starched and ironed. She had come in without his knowing. It always amazed him that she could move so quietly.

May smiled and two tiny dimples deepened on her cheeks. Mark felt his heart skip a beat. He could hardly describe the effect she had on him.

"Let me," she said. Gently she patted the towel around his head, then face and then his shoulders. He let her, standing mutely, submitting to her ministration. He could smell the scent she used. He had asked her once what it was. She had smiled her enigmatic smile. "A secret handed down from my mother," and said no more.

He gathered her in his arms, his fingers spanning her waist. He marvelled at her slenderness even as he drew her urgently to him. She let him, her body moulding into his.

"I have a wife." Mark could feel May stiffen at this reminder. He knew he was at fault by not telling her earlier. "You must understand that I love her and that when she comes, this cannot continue." He placed a finger under her chin and tilted her face to him, forcing her to look him in the eye and understand what he was trying to say to her.

"Yes," her voice almost a whisper. He had to bend low to hear her. She looked away. "I understand. I now know that is how it would be. My friend Su Yin said the same. When her master's wife came, she became once more the maid, no longer mistress in her master's bed. Ah Lan fared even worse. When her master's wife came, they threw her out. She had nowhere to go. Now she works in knock-knock shop, so many men. She cried so hard."

A glimmer of tears threatened in the corner of her eyes. She buried her face in his chest. He could feel the dampness. She had not reproached him for not telling her earlier that he had a wife and he was filled with guilt.

"But must it be so for me, for us?" she asked.

Mark took some time to answer. The silence hung over them like a hot cocoon. He had never planned this to happen, never planned to have a mistress. He had not wanted to take advantage of May. Beneath his breath, he cursed the loneliness of his posting in this god-forsaken part of the country. Stuck out in the sticks with no one to talk to and with nothing to divert his attention, all he had was the all-embracing heat, the jungle, the flies and mosquitoes, the noise of feral beasts, of wild boars snorting and monkeys cackling, and rubber. Rows and rows of the dratted tree, that white gold that had once attracted him to the country now bound him like a snake, choking the life out of him. When May took on the job as his housekeeper, it was like a godsend. The Office had sent her over; they had said that they had vetted her and she was clean. Her Chinese name was Ling Mei, a mouthful, so they shortened it and anglicised the spelling. "She has," they said, "no connections whatsoever with the insurgents." Within days he was smitten. She was beautiful, young and gentle. She spoke English. He began to stay at home more and more. He looked forward to the evenings when he could be with her. He wooed her; it was not his intention to do so. He just did; it seemed the most natural thing to do. Young, innocent and pliable, May responded. He could tell that she liked him and was flattered by the attention he showered on her. He remembered the first night when they came together. It was a hot sultry night. He had gone to her bed and lifted the thin cotton sheet that covered her. Slipping beside her he drew her close to him. He told her that he just wanted to hold her. He had convinced himself that that would suffice. She had been frightened and had tried to push him away. But the contact had been electrical. It opened up in him a torrent of passion that he had never felt before. He had drowned in it. Tormented afterwards, he tried to explain over and over again that it should not have happened; that it could not and would not continue. Yet it did. Each time he was filled with remorse. He could not write to Ruth and explain. All he could do to postpone the separation from May was to remain separate from Ruth.

"No," he whispered back in reply, "no knock-knock shop of course." He mustered a confidence he did not feel and laughed aloud as though amused. "Perish the thought. I'll think of something. I'll ask the others what they do." After all, he was not the only one. There were others who successfully kept separate their wives and mistresses.

***

May folded the last of the shirts and placed them in the drawer. She had lined the drawer with paper and had wanted to place sachets of dried jasmine in them. She hadn't. She had grown to love the way Mark smelt even when he was musty and sweaty. Just thinking about him made her tingle with expectation. She had never fallen in love before. She didn't have a boyfriend. Her parents' marriage had been arranged. She had not thought it possible to fall in love with someone so totally. It consumed her. Her mother had warned her about the dangers of being isolated from the outside world with a total stranger, a *qwei loh* at that. "Remember child," her mother warned, "you are only sixteen. Do not let him touch you. You have no future if that happens. No man will want you."

May smiled. How could she explain to her mother that she had fallen in love with Mark?

Unwilling to let May take the job, her mother had spoken of the danger of being alone in a house situated right in the middle of a rubber plantation, edged all round by the jungle where communist insurgents hid. "You know you can be killed by one, or even worse, bombed by the British. Many innocent people have been killed despite not being communists. If you must work in that place," her mother finally relented, "at least stay away from the jungle and remain in the house. Even then, you may not be safe."

May knew it was not safe. She had no choice but to take the job. They had no money. Now, she also had no option but to stay. How could she leave Mark? He was everything to her. She loved him. No place was safe. Being Chinese was perhaps the most dangerous, and how could she help being born as one? Every Chinese was a suspect insurgent. She recalled the searching each time she visited the New Village where her family had been recently confined along with hundreds and thousands from other areas. The village was fenced with triple rows of barbed wire. Guards searched her each time she entered. They searched when she left. She retched the first time. The probing and touching of her most intimate places made her skin crawl. She was allowed only a couple of hours to see her parents. The New Village was under perpetual curfew. To call it a village was abomination. People were confined under inhuman conditions. They were allowed to leave the compound in the day to work in plantations, paddy fields or tin mines; each movement out was monitored; each movement in was similarly checked. No, she counted herself lucky to be here with Mark.

***

"Could you find out why May's parents were moved into this New Village? Damn it! Could you do something to move them out again?" Mark demanded, his voice clipped and impatient.

Mark was in the military base of the Royal West Kent Regiment near Tanjong Malim. He had gone straight to it after leaving May.

"My friend, you ask the impossible." Major Hugh Anderson let out an exasperated sigh. "Suspects or not, we are to treat all Chinese squatters the same. That is the new policy. They are all deemed potentially dangerous. The arrangement helps to deter those so inclined from helping the insurgents but look at it this way. It also protects them from being intimidated into doing so. You know what insurgents do to those unwilling to help them. Let us hear no more about this. Your May might still be rounded up so keep a lid on your temper."

"Surely not! She has been cleared. That was why she was sent to me," Mark blustered.

"I am telling you this as a friend. The killings in the neighbouring estate have prompted this response. Two Chinese plantation assistants decapitated! Their boss, an Englishman like you and me, shot in both legs. What do you expect? The order from above is that we have to shut off the insurgents' lifeblood. We suspect that they could not have lasted without outside support. Their food supply would have run out if people had not been supplying them on the sly."

"Is that why the rice rations to these settlements have been cut off? So many innocents suffering just because of a suspicion. Do you not feel guilty?"

"Orders," Hugh replied sheepishly and went back to his desk, "and you know that it is not just a suspicion."

Hugh sat down. He waved Mark to a seat. He did not like the policy any more than Mark but there was nothing he could do. It was a case of a few rotten apples infecting the majority. "Listen! Things will get worse. This is only the beginning; more and more Chinese squatters will be rounded up into settlements under General Brigg's plan. You cannot fight it."

Mark plonked himself on the chair, energy seeping out of him. He could feel the cold metallic seat pressing against his buttocks, which were already wet with perspiration. In fact there was not a single part of him that was not wet.

"About May," Hugh continued eyeing Mark sternly. "I was not joking when I said that she too could be rounded up now that her family is resettled and held in suspicion. It was all right before because they were living in Malacca town. That was why she was given a clean bill of health. I do not know why the family decided to move to this area to become squatters. Tanjong Malim is hardly an attractive place. How could any person with common sense wish to move here! The minute they made the move, they were classified as suspects. They should know that Tanjong Malim is a hotbed of terror."

"They moved here because May was posted to me!" Mark spluttered with exasperation. "They wanted to be near their only daughter. Look! After the Japanese left, May's father was too ill to look for another job. He was tortured and imprisoned during the Japanese occupation. After the war, the family had no means of looking after themselves. May was sent out to work. She was sent to me. Soon after, their landlord in Malacca kicked her family out because of their arrears with the rent. They ended up as squatters. You know as well as I do that under the new laws, which may I remind you the British helped to formulate, many Chinese would find it difficult, if not impossible, to buy land even if they had the resources."

"Well, what can I say," Hugh replied, "except that we can only act according to orders. We cannot make special preferences." He was as frustrated as Mark about the entire situation. He had seen May once, a young slip of a girl. He remembered her. She was beautiful.

Mark got up and, without a further word, left the room. He walked quickly, kicking up dust with each stride, taking his anger out in the only way he could for the moment. If he could he would have shouted out his rage. He knew Hugh's hands were tied. That did not stop Mark's anger. Waiting outside was Amat, his driver. He got into the jeep. "Back to the plantation," he ordered.

The driver stole a sidelong look at Mark. "Yes Sir," he said.

They drove out of the military camp, leaving a trail of yellow dust. Mark kept silent, a whirlwind of thoughts churning in his mind. He took little note of the heat, the pungent smell of oil from the engine, the dust and the constant humming of insects. He did not wish to disappoint May but there was little else he could do for her family. Hugh made that amply clear. He had to find another way. He would drive to Kuala Lumpur and talk to his superiors. He reached into his pocket. With a guilty start he remembered the letter. He had left it on the dresser when he was about to leave. It must be from Ruth.

"Drop in at my house first," he said.

Amat swerved and turned into a side road. Ahead the road forked into two, one leading to the west and the other to the east. Jungle loomed on both sides.

"Sir, look! Check point?" Amat turned urgently to his master for confirmation. Mark looked towards where Amat was pointing.

Barbed wire and crates barred the road just before the junction. Two uniformed men with rifles stood behind the rolls of wire. Amat slowed down to a halt and wound down his window. Suddenly from behind the two uniformed officers, a band of men and women surged forward. Dressed raggedly in khaki shorts, trousers that were ripped and torn, and an assortment of headgear, they opened fire. The two officers fell, one clutching his arm and the other spurting blood from his neck. Amat slumped forward, hitting the horn. Mark reached for his pistol. Faces pressed onto the windowpanes and arms reached into the jeep. Someone grabbed Mark's pistol and smashed its butt onto his temple. They yanked open the door. Two men got hold of his ankle. Mark felt the kicks; his ribs burned and blood squirted from his nose. Then darkness.

***

All was quiet in Mark's bungalow. At the back of the house, next to the kitchen, stood an altar. A figurine of the Goddess of Mercy, no bigger than a foot high, looked benignly down from her perch. Her forehead was smooth and between her fingers prayer beads flowed. May knelt before it and bowed low. Her lips moved in silent prayer. "Please," she prayed, "keep us safe. Please keep us together. Please keep our child safe."

She had not told Mark. She wanted to be absolutely sure. Her aunt had lost two babies in the initial months of pregnancy. She must wait for the critical months to pass before telling him. Her hands went to her tummy. It hardly showed. When she first realised that she was carrying Mark's baby, she was frightened. Now she thought of it as a blessing; everything would be all right. Mark had promised that he would find a way. He would look after her. She trusted him. She got up and went into the living room. The ceiling fan turned slowly, stirring air somnolent with the heat. The hibiscus and oleanders picked in the morning were already wilting. She must replace them with fresh flowers. Hastily she went to the dresser where the vase sat. Next to it was a letter addressed to Mark. She saw the stamp. Her heart stood still. Mark's words came back to her. "Was this it?" she asked herself, "Was his wife coming?"

Chapter 3

Singapore

THE SKY WAS a clear bright blue. Ruth stepped off the gangway clinging on to her hat. A gust of wind threatened to dislodge it. She tightened her hold and hugged the suitcase to her side with the other hand. Tendrils of hair clung damply to her cheeks. The heat struck her with a force she could not describe. The journey on the cargo ship had taken almost a month. During that time, as the ship skirted the Indian Ocean to make its way to Singapore, she had thought she had become acclimatised. She was mistaken. The sun was red hot on her skin. She placed one foot carefully in front of the other. The earth beneath them seemed to roll and waver. Someone caught hold of her elbow.

"Steady on. Hold my hand."

Ruth turned.

"Is someone meeting you?"

Ruth searched through the crowd. Doubt crept into her eyes. She shook her head. "I am not sure. I wrote to my husband. I left without waiting for his reply. He should have received my letter by now but I don't see him."

She stood on tiptoe hoping to see beyond the throng of people bustling on the dock side. Bare brown bodies carrying heavy sacks and crates on their shoulders moved with dogged purpose. Men in suits, sailors, women in long skirts holding on to their children; a multitude of people of all colours, dress and walks of life. "I don't know if I am going to be met," she confessed. She was frightened and excited at the same time. She did not know if she had made the right decision. In truth she had had no choice; she had to come. There was nowhere else to go. The farm was gone. Overcome by grief and loss, her father had passed away suddenly. She remembered that day as if it were yesterday. She was washing up in the kitchen when she looked out of the window. Her hands were full of soapsuds. She saw her father walk towards the barn. Halfway there, he staggered, reeling like a drunk. His hand went to his chest and the next minute he was on the ground. She ran to him, her feet still shod in house slippers. She recalled her feet sinking into soft mud and the smell of soap on her cheeks. She tried to revive her father, slipping her arms around his shoulders in a desperate attempt to lift him. But he was gone. With her father's death and the loss of the farm, there was nothing to keep her in England.

"Well, let me help you with this." Bill reached out to take her suitcase, brushing her hand as he did so.

"Thank you," she said shyly. He had been very attentive during the journey. She was not used to the attention he gave her but was grateful for it. Everything seemed strange and alarming. She didn't know any of her fellow passengers. She had never been abroad before, not even across the Channel and found herself at a loss at the dining table with little to contribute to conversations.

"No problem. Let me lead the way." Bill walked ahead. He was in luck, a lone lady whose husband had not turned up to meet her. He threw another quick glance at her over his shoulder. He had learnt a lot about Ruth during the voyage. He remembered every detail and filed it in his mind. It was his way, to record every minute detail that could be useful.

***

Ruth watched as the last of the passengers left the dock. The immigration office was almost empty. Only a handful of officers remained. They hovered at the far end taking an inventory of trunks that were to be collected the following day. Ruth scanned the docks again.

"It looks like your husband will not be here. What do you want to do?"

Ruth couldn't hide her dismay. "I'll have to find my way to my husband's office in Kuala Lumpur. I'll have to take a bus. Perhaps I should find a telephone to call his office."

A young boy with a turban came over and handed Bill a telegram before retreating to the side. Bill read it and stuffed it into his pocket. He made no reference to it, except that he waved the young boy over and scribbled a note before whispering into his ear. The boy ran off with the note and Bill walked to a notice board hung on the wall. "You won't have time to look for a telephone if you are to catch a bus. There is only one more today." He looked around the near-deserted depot. No telephone booths could be seen. "According to this schedule, buses do not run very frequently," he continued, "the curfew makes it difficult. Perhaps the train might be more comfortable. One will be leaving in thirty minutes."

"Does it cost more?"

He nodded.

"I'll take the bus." Her lips trembled. Suddenly she was afraid. Mark was not expecting her. He hadn't got her letter.

"I'll take you to the bus stop." Bill took her suitcase and they walked out of the immigration control into the bright sunshine. A group of people stood across the road. "There it is," Bill said. He walked quickly over, leaving Ruth to follow.

"I expect you don't speak any of the local languages," he said over his shoulder. "It is difficult for newcomers. There are many dialects and languages to wrestle with."

The dismay in Ruth's face deepened. She was not sure she could cope in this strange country. How could she, if she couldn't even communicate with people?

"You'll get by though," he added more kindly seeing her panic. "Most people speak a smattering of English. What you need to prepare yourself for is the bus ride."

"Why?" she asked, alarmed.

"Riding a bus here is not the same as in England. It is the cheapest way to get to Kuala Lumpur though not the safest. The train would have been better. Although in fairness, any form of travel in Malaya at the moment is not safe. The threat of ambush by outlaws is always there, whatever means of transport you take."

Ruth's heart sank with each piece of information that Bill gave her.

He ushered her to a tree with spreading branches heavy with bright yellow blooms. "Here, stay in the shade. The next bus is due soon. Even then it is not worth the risk of standing in the open under the sweltering sun on your first day."

Ruth wiped her forehead. Underneath her hat, her hair was sodden. She was nervous. She had gathered from other passengers on the ship that a full-scale war was being fought in Malaya. Mark had never said anything in his letters beyond a clipped acknowledgement that it was not safe. They had described with relish the atrocities that insurgents inflict on victims. She remembered the woman from Kent on her way to rejoin her husband. The woman, a mother in her mid-forties, had declared calmly as though it was the most ordinary of events that she would shoot insurgents willingly to repay what they had done to her friends. The other passengers had cheered her on. Ruth shuddered and tried not to think of them.

Slowly her ears adjusted to the voices and chatter around her. Perhaps the dangers were exaggerated. There was so much laughter. She could not believe that anyone in the throng of people surrounding her could commit violence. They all looked gentle and amiable. While in England, people would not stare, people here made no attempt to hide their curiosity. They stared openly, often giggling with a hand poised in front of their mouths. Men and women squatted by the road, some with their sarongs hitched high while others rolled up their trouser legs to reveal bare brown feet shod in rubber slippers. Ruth could not help smiling back at them. Surely, no guerrilla would dress in such a manner.

Bill watched her. He took care not to be observed. He could see that she was captivated by everything around her.

Ruth threw him a quick glance and nodded towards a hawker selling sugar cane juice by the wayside. She watched with fascination when the man hacked each cane into shorter lengths and fed them into a metal roller. He discarded the cane debris carelessly on the ground. Bees hummed and buzzed around the jugs of rich pale green liquid. Next to him a vendor, with nothing on him except a thin singlet and a sarong, sold young coconuts. He slashed one open and offered it to Ruth. His eyes, bright with expectation, coaxed her to take it. He laughed when she hesitated, revealing toothless gums stained by betel nuts. She looked to Bill again.

He nodded. "It should be safe. It is best to drink while you can. No liquid is allowed on board." Gratefully, she reached out and took the coconut. She gulped the juice, not caring that some spilled on to her cotton blouse.

"The bus will take you to Kuala Lumpur. It will be a long ride. You should arrive before dark. Travel is forbidden at night under the new laws."

Fear returned to Ruth's eyes, fear that had been temporarily laid aside because of the novelty of the scene in front of her. She would be on her own from then on.

"Once there, get in touch with your husband's employers. I am sure they would help take you to your husband." He took her hand and gave it a squeeze. "Remember, you have my telephone number. Call me."

Ruth was nervous. She could not muster a smile. He saw it.

"I have written in Malay the address of your husband's firm. The telephone number is at the bottom. It is a small world here. Our paths will cross I am sure." Of that he was absolutely confident. He would make certain of it.

The bus arrived. It grunted to a halt. A cloud of dust rose, dust the colour of paprika. People rushed to clamber on board. Bill pushed Ruth forward and helped her up. She could feel his hand on the small of her back. She turned to say goodbye but he was already swallowed by the crowd of people behind her. There was no time to say more. She walked down the narrow aisle looking for a seat. An Indian woman pointed to the empty space next to her, gathering as she did so her bright turquoise sari to make more room. Ruth sank gratefully on to the plastic bench, thankful to rest her aching feet. She waved to Bill. The bus lurched forward, its wheels protesting against its load. Bill stood by the wayside, his eyes watchful. Then he gave a small, almost indiscernible, nod. A man jumped on to the bus, his foot catching the step just in time as the bus picked up speed.

The bus was packed. Many stood like sardines in a can, lined up against each other, swaying with the motion of the vehicle. Ruth could feel the rumbling in her stomach. She had not eaten since she left the ship. There would be no food until she reached Kuala Lumpur. The carrying of food and drinks was prohibited in case bandits waylaid them. The bus rolled and swayed. By and by Ruth fell asleep, overcome by heat and fatigue. When she woke, she found the lady beside her had also nodded off. People had wound down the windows and a hot breeze blew in dissipating the smell of body odour and spice. Lush green paddy fields and plantations rushed by. She looked across the aisle; between the gaps of swaying bodies, a man was watching her. She looked again. He had turned away. Mindful, she glanced nervously again in his direction. He was bowed low and she could see only his dark hair. Ruth chided herself. Her imagination must be running wild. Surely no one would be interested in her.

Chapter 4

Kuala Lumpur

IT WAS ALMOST nightfall when the bus approached Kuala Lumpur. “Go to the hotel opposite the railway station. It is called The Majestic,” Bill had advised. “It is better than the Station Hotel. Planters go there. You are bound to meet someone who might help.”

“Very good hotel,” the Indian lady said flashing a bright smile when Ruth mentioned it. “For white people, rich people,” she added wagging her head, like a doll’s head pivoting on its neck, tilting to the right and then left and back again. “Other hotels not good, too low class for a lady like you.” She looked Ruth up and down. “Maybe dangerous even.”

The Indian lady draped the end of her sari around her head and whispered conspiratorially. "Not many hotels in town. Nice ladies stay with friends or relatives. No stay in hotels." She looked pityingly at Ruth, her gaze on Ruth's ring on her fourth finger. "Where is your husband? No meet you?"

Ruth pretended not to hear. Well the Majestic it has to be, she thought. She just needed to have sufficient money left over to go to Mark.

"Don't worry, Ma'am. I show you the way. Not far from bus stop. We get there before dark. Everyone knows the railway station. It's beautiful like a palace." She rolled her kohl-lined eyes in an exaggerated fashion.

Ruth thanked her. She looked across. The man was not there. A woman sat where he had been.

***

It was half past nine in the morning when Ruth arrived at Mark's firm in a trishaw.

A group of young women giggled and spoke amongst themselves the minute she stepped out of the vehicle. Some eyed her with open astonishment. Blood rushed to Ruth's cheeks turning it an even brighter red. She should have expected that. The hotel footman had tried to persuade her against the use of a trishaw. "No, Madam, no good. Trishaws not for you." His eyes darted to the left and to the right and his voice dropped to a whisper. Apparently no self-respecting women, certainly not a European woman, used trishaws to travel, a privilege reserved principally for ladies of the night.

Ruth had refused to budge from her decision. She thought of the bill she would have to pay staying at the Majestic. She had to make economies. Now, confronted by smirks, she was not sure she had taken the right decision. She put on a brave face and hoped that her nervousness was not obvious. She had travelled all that distance to be with Mark. She was not going to be defeated by a bunch of ridiculous young women. With a pounding heart, she climbed up the flight of steps into the reception area and declared her desire to see Mark. "I am his wife, Ruth Lampard," she added.

Behind the thick black spectacle frames, the receptionist's eyes widened in shock. "Wait please," she said and rushed out from behind the desk. Within minutes she was back with a grey haired gentleman in a dark suit.

"Mrs Lampard? I did not expect you. Welcome to Harrison and Crosfield. I am Andrew Clark, the Manager."

Ruth took his extended hand. It was clammy. She noticed the nervous tick at the corner of one of his eyes. "I am sorry. I didn't call. I wanted to be here first thing in the morning."

"Come with me to my office. This way." Ruth felt his hand on her elbow, urging her along the narrow corridor. They went into a large room with maps and photographs on all four walls; he motioned her to take a seat. They sat facing each other, he behind his desk, she in a high backed chair. Between them stretched a vast expanse of dark wood. A young attendant brought tea. Ruth wondered at his agitation. She waited impatiently for the girl to set the cups in place. The process seemed to take an infinitely long time. The manager coughed discreetly and waved the girl away. Once she left the room, he began rubbing his temple. He wouldn't meet Ruth's eye. His reticence alarmed her.

"Is anything wrong? Where is my husband? Can I go to him? Today if possible."

"*Umm!*" His eyes met Ruth's for the first time since they entered the room. "You should stay in Kuala Lumpur for a few days. It can be arranged." His voice was grave. His eyes darted to the door as though he wished to make his escape. Andrew Clark was sure that Ruth would not last in the heat and certainly not out in the remote area of Tanjong Malim. He thought her completely unsuitable for a life in the tropics: her slenderness, her paleness with the dusting of freckles across her nose and total naivety. The receptionist had told him about Ruth's mode of transport. Certain standards of decorum had to be maintained as a planter's wife and she had shown her total ignorance of it. There was no way he could tell her that, not with the bad news he was about to deliver.

Through the gap of the slightly open door, Ruth saw the receptionist pass by.

"But I am not interested in staying in Kuala Lumpur," she said. Her voice cracked and she crinkled her forehead in exasperation.

"You must. Rather you should. The Majestic is a pleasant retreat for most of our staff. Planters and their families use it. You will be comfortable there."

"Why can't I go to my husband? I was told that he is in a place called Tanjong Malim. You mean he is here in Kuala Lumpur?"

Ruth recalled the anxious looks of people at the hotel when she mentioned Tanjong Malim. She hadn't given it much heed then. She had been too awed and surprised by the hotel the previous evening after the uncomfortable bus ride. She had never come across anything like The Majestic before. In the dining room, white-uniformed waiters scurried between potted ferns and tables laid out splendidly with silver cutlery, fine porcelain and crystal glasses. She had never seen so many starched white tablecloths. Suspended from high ceilings, fans whirled slowly forming a backdrop to the clinking of glasses. Piano music floated across the room to mingle with the modulated voices of well-dressed women and men in evening attire. The scene dispersed the sense of danger she had gathered from fellow travellers on the ship. Bathed and changed from her travel-worn clothes she had felt a new person last night. Her sense of well being, however, was now fast dissipating. She watched the beads of perspiration gather on Andrew Clark's brows.

"Is something wrong?" she repeated.

He took both her hands in his. "The telegram we sent you obviously did not reach you before you left. I am sorry," he said, his eyes looking right into hers. "You have to be strong. Mark is missing."

Chapter 5

Tanjong Malim

"MADAM, WE ARE TO return to Kuala Lumpur immediately after you've seen the bungalow. We have to be quick. We can't stay here. Please," the driver's voice was almost pleading, "nightfall is just a few hours away. We are not allowed to travel once it gets dark. I am to take you to a rest house if we can't return to Kuala Lumpur."

"A rest house?"

"There are no hotels in the area."

The driver held open the door for Ruth. A guard with a pistol in the upholster on his hip and a rifle over his right shoulder, stood just two feet away from the car. His eyes roamed the surrounding area.

She stepped out. For a moment, all she could do was to stare at the bungalow in front of her. Mark's bungalow. The windows were open. There was a desultory air about it, as though it was lost and did not know what to do with itself. Like me, Ruth thought, a disembodied spirit. She made herself walk towards the bungalow, one foot forward then the other. Her legs were heavy. She turned back to look at the driver. He stood as still as a rock. The expression on his face was unreadable. She turned once more towards the bungalow. A curtain lifted. She saw a movement behind them. Mr Clark had mentioned that there was a cook and a housekeeper. Ruth quickened her footsteps. Perhaps they could tell her more. She would like to know everything, even things not directly connected with Mark's disappearance. She wanted to know how Mark lived, the food he ate, the things he liked; little things that she would be able to connect with. It had been so long since she had seen him. Had he changed? It was suddenly important to know how he was before he was captured; she needed the threads of normality she could cling to.

She pushed open the door. It swung open, its hinges creaking in protest. There was no one in the hallway. Sunlight streamed in from windows on all sides of the bungalow. She had noticed, when she was driven here, how houses had big open windows, quite unlike those in England where thick walls and closed windows were needed to keep the warmth in and the cold out. Here windows were flung open to the elements, open windows, however, that were heavily barred.

She stepped into the house. It was cool relative to the scorching heat outside. A woman, small like a gnome, appeared. She spoke with her eyes cast down. The words tumbled out in rapid succession. Ruth did not understand her. She turned and was relieved to see the driver behind her. He must have changed his mind and followed her into the bungalow.

"Can you tell me what she just said?" asked Ruth.

"Ma'am, she is Fu Yi, the cook and general housemaid. She said no one else is here. Everyone has left, even May the housekeeper."

"Tell her please that I would like to go round the house alone. Then I would like to speak to her. Would you help interpret?"

"Yes, Ma' am. I can do that. Fu Yi speaks English though you might not understand her. She spoke English just a moment ago. I'll wait outside. Call me when you're ready."

Ruth waited until they left. Her head throbbed. There were so many questions she would like to ask. She switched from fear for Mark to sadness and disbelief. She did not know which came first. How could it have happened? Of all the things she had thought could happen, this was not one of them. She walked further into the house. The hallway led into a living room. It was sparsely furnished, like a bachelor-pad. A rattan sofa and a couple of armchairs, a coffee table and a side table were all there was in the room. She saw a photograph. It was the one taken by Mark of her when they were in Brighton. It seemed a lifetime ago. She walked quickly towards another corridor that branched off from the living room. It led to a bedroom. The door was ajar. She pushed it open. A bed stood in the middle. Over it was a mosquito net, coiled into a loop. She went to the bed and stood hovering above it. She did not know how long she stood there before she sat down on its edge. The mattress sank slightly under her weight. She ran her fingers along the bed sheet, smoothing it as she did so until she reached the pillow. It still had the imprint of a head on it. With a sob she clasped the pillow to her. She held it to her face and inhaled. She could smell

Mark; she recognised him just from that. She clasped the pillow to her chest and rocked, finding comfort that it was Mark's pillow, her connection to him. Yet as she breathed deeply into it, there was something else, an undercurrent scent that was undeniably feminine. She dropped the pillow. She was imagining it, she told herself. She got up and went to the adjoining bathroom. She turned on the light switch. A flourescent strip sprang to life. A shower, a washbasin and a toilet occupied three corners of the tiny area. By the basin were a shaving kit and a bar of soap. She caught her breath at the sight of them. Her chest felt so tight, she had to concentrate on each breath.

Listlessly she opened the cabinet over the basin. A jar of Ponds cream stood in solitary isolation. She closed the cabinet door quickly. In its mirror she saw a face so pale and drained that she could hardly recognise herself. Behind her stood the lady who had greeted her earlier. Before Ruth could speak, the woman had rushed out.

***

"Ma'am, Fu Yi says she knows nothing. She just cleans and cooks. It is May, the housekeeper, who manages the house. The master gives his instructions through May. She does not know where May is. In fact the police have been. They too asked for May. Perhaps they might know a bit more."

Ruth tried to catch Fu Yi's eyes but the cook refused to look up, leaving Amat to translate.

"Does my husband have any friends around here? Surely he must have some friends?"

Ruth was desperate. She had learnt no more than what she had gleaned from Andrew Clark. As yet there was no ransom note, no body. "If he was dead, we would know," Clark had said. "Insurgents normally make an example of their captives to drill fear into people."

"Who was the last person to see him?" she pressed.

"The cook said that the master left with his driver to see Major Hugh Anderson."

"Then take me to him."

"Ma'am, we don't have time if we are to return to Kuala Lumpur today. Rest houses are not safe. I much prefer we return to Kuala Lumpur. Mr Walker, one of the company's manager was killed in this very state at his plantation."

"I am not going anywhere until I see the Major. I must know what is happening. No one seems able or willing to tell me anything."

From behind the kitchen door, May heard everything. She slipped out of the back door and hurried out through the backyard.

***

"Mrs Lampard, Mark and I spoke just minutes before the incident. He was here in this very room. The thing is I can add little to what you have been told."

Hugh closed the file. He sat down to face Ruth. He could see the desperation and sadness in her face. Her eyes were red-rimmed and swollen. He could not make himself add to her grief by repeating his conversation with Mark. Mark had only spoken about his concern for the girl May. He had made no mention of his wife during it. Now May, it would seem, had run away and left no trace. Was she involved in Mark's disappearance? Or did she take flight because she was frightened? Hugh did not know the reasons for her disappearance and would not judge without further investigation. However, as it stood, it certainly did not look good for the girl.

"There was a housekeeper, May," said Ruth breaking into his thoughts.

"May?" he asked as though he did not know the name. "*Ahhh!* May! What do you want to know?"

"Can I reach her?"

"We haven't been able to find her. We thought she might have gone back to her family. Apparently they have not seen her either."

"How strange that she had not made contact with them. Her husband and children must be worried," Ruth was of the impression that May was a middle-aged woman. The word housekeeper conjured up such an image in her mind. She had not known many housekeepers in her life except Mrs Lawn in the neighbouring farm and she certainly was middle-aged. "If only we can find her. She could tell me more about Mark's friends, acquaintances, perhaps even enemies. Is Mark in dispute with any one? Could his kidnap be an act of vengeance?"

"This is nothing to do with dispute. It is an act of terror. Planters are easy targets. We are searching the jungle for Mark. A helicopter is surveying the entire forest even now as we speak."

"About May," Ruth persisted.

"I'll take you to the settlement. You can meet her parents. She is not married."

Ruth looked past him. The wall behind was plastered with notices and photographs. A picture of a young woman caught her eye. Next to it someone had penned in a big question mark in red. Below her picture was one of Mark wearing a hat and leaning on the bonnet of a jeep. His shirtsleeves were rolled up and he had a grin on his face. He looked happy.

Hugh turned and followed her gaze. He cursed himself. He should have removed May's photograph.

"When was that taken?" Mark seemed so carefree and happy. Ruth had not expected that. From his letters, she had imagined that he hated it here in Malaya. That was the impression he had given when he told her not to come. The photograph showed a completely different Mark.

"That was taken when we first recruited May."

Ruth's eyes darted back to the photograph of the young woman. She had meant Mark, not the girl whom, until then, she had not associated with May. Her eyes were drawn initially to the picture because of the big question mark. Ruth leaned forward, her chest touching the edge of Hugh's desk to take a closer look at the photograph. The woman was beautiful, more beautiful than anyone she had met since her arrival in Malaya.

"Yes," she said, "I would like to meet May very much. If not her at least her parents." Ruth took a deep breath, willing her heartbeat to slow down. She clenched her hands hard, so hard that her nails bit into her palms. She felt her scalp tingle. She recalled the jar of cream she had seen and the scent on Mark's pillow.

"Very well, we'll arrange a meeting with her parents," Hugh relented, not quite meeting Ruth's eyes. Ruth was bound to find out about May and Mark sooner or later. He told himself that he was not going to be the one to tell her. She had to find out for herself. "Stay at the rest house tonight. I'll arrange for you to be picked up tomorrow morning."

He stood up and walked round to her.

"Stay within the rest house compound. Do not walk on your own, even in the garden."

"Has it always been like this?" Ruth asked as she rose to her feet. "The tight vigilance, the danger and the sense that one is being watched all the time?"

Hugh shook his head. He looked out of the window. It was lush green outside. Picasso would have found it a painter's paradise. Wooden houses on stilts dotted the landscape. A wild orchid plant hung from a tree. Below it grew red cannas and hibiscus. It was hard to imagine that a war against communist insurgents was being fought.

"No!" he replied. "I was here before the Japanese occupied the country, as was Mark briefly. Malaya is beautiful. It gets under your skin like a drug, heady, exotic. Like the *toddy* that people drink. Mark loves it here. When we parted company before the Second World War, he vowed to come back. He did not expect," Hugh sighed, "*we* did not expect to come back to a country beset with problems."

He turned to face Ruth. "The Japanese occupation tore the country apart. It split the population. While we won the war in Europe, we did not quite do the same here. We were routed. After the war, the Malayan people's view of us changed. As their colonial masters, we had promised them protection and safety. We failed. We left the fight against the Japanese to the Malayan People's Anti-Japanese Army. That army was principally filled with ethnic Chinese. They went underground to conduct guerrilla warfare against the Japanese. I suppose it was not unlike the French resistance army in France, except that when the war was over, the MPAJA was not given the recognition it sought. These are the people we are fighting now. People we had trained and who had supported us during the war. No doubt they had their own agenda in doing so. Many owe allegiance to China. Their aim being to bring the whole of Malaya under Communist rule and to oust the British. Malaya is now in a state of turmoil. Mark's disappearance is a drop in the ocean of carnage and bloodshed that now afflicts the country."

Ruth could not digest all that was said. What she learnt was that they were surrounded by danger. If she had any inkling at all about these dangers, she would have tried her hardest to dissuade Mark from coming here. Now it might be too late.

"Perhaps, with your permission, I'll accompany you to the rest house." Hugh was embarrassed. He had said too much. "It is the least I can do."

Chapter 6

MAY SLIPPED INTO the hut, a tiny featureless single-storey one-room building with a zinc roof, grey cement flooring and an outside toilet. A woman was kneeling on the floor, bent over a pile of ironing. A basket, half-filled with freshly laundered shirts, stood to her left. At the far end was a stove, blackened by a coal fire. A plastic washing basin stood on the floor beside it. She glanced up, saw May and continued her ironing with not even a nod as her greeting. To the right of her, suspended from the ceiling, a faded brown sarong swung gently. A wail rose from it and a dimpled fist, the size of a chestnut, appeared above the sarong's opening. Another cry followed. Bee Ying propped up the iron and reached out to jiggle the sarong. The crying stopped. Bee Ying returned to her ironing. Throughout, she ignored May completely.

"*Piu soh*," said May with as much respect as she could muster. She addressed Bee Ying as 'cousin's wife'. She knew Bee Ying would consider her impudent if she were to address her by name. "Is Chun here?"

The corners of Bee Ying's fleshy lips curled. "Can you not see? Look around. It is not as though this is a house with many rooms."

"Will he be back soon?"

Bee Ying knelt back on her heel and glared. She touched the small of her back. It was sore with the hours spent ironing on the floor. She did not like May and made no attempt to conceal her dislike. She suspected her husband's concern for May was more than cousin's love.

"How would I know about his comings and goings?" she hissed.

"I need to ask him if he could help me find my master. He is missing, probably kidnapped."

"Master? *Huh!* You mean your lover! Well then," replied Bee Ying returning to her ironing, "too bad. I don't know where Chun is. I can't help you."

"Please, I must speak to Chun. I need his help."

"And do you think I would tell you even if I knew where he is? It is your fault that he has disappeared."

"Why is it my fault? Why has he disappeared? Please *piu soh*. Please help me."

"You come between my husband and me and dare ask me for help?" Bee Ying snarled, baring her teeth. Spittle flew out of her mouth. Tiny pinpoints of bubble landed on May. She set the iron down with a bang. The iron sizzled, sending heat and steam into the air. The baby wailed. His piteous cry pierced the air. "Get out! Get out before I take the broom to you."

"I have nowhere to go. I can't go to my parents and get them involved."

"Get out!" Bee Ying screamed. "I don't care. Get out I say!"

***

Poor, poor Ruth, thought Hugh. She had looked wretched when they met earlier in the day. He hated covering up for Mark.

Hugh crossed his legs and leaned back on the over-sized stuffed armchair. It smelt of dank cotton. Overhead, the ceiling fan droned. The sitting room in the rest house doubled as a bar. All the guests, it would appear, were male and were seated at the bar at the far end of the room. Ruth would be the only female guest in the rest house. Another reason, he thought, why she should not stay in this place for long. He would tell her so gently when the time was opportune.

He rose to his feet when he saw Ruth enter the lounge. With her hair tied back into a ponytail and the scattering of freckles on her nose, she looked younger, more vulnerable than she had done earlier. Heads swivelled to stare. Hugh pulled a rattan armchair out for her. She gave him a weak smile.

A boy in a starched white uniform and with black hair sleeked behind his ears came bearing a tray. On it were pale blue teacups and saucers, a mismatched teapot, a milk jug, a sugar bowl, its rim slightly chipped, and a plate of sandwiches.

"I have taken the liberty of ordering sardine sandwiches if that's all right with you. It is the safest option. They are canned sardines," he apologised. "Food is still short. Mashed up with a squeeze of lime and tomato ketchup, it is palatable." Hugh picked up the plate and offered it to Ruth. She seemed not to have heard. Her hands lay immobile on her lap. There was not a flicker of response or interest. Embarrassed, Hugh returned the plate to the table.

The boy poured out the tea. The sound of liquid pouring into cups bridged the awkward silence.

Ruth watched silently at the golden brew spouting from the brown earthen teapot into the blue cups. Without warning, a surge of anger rose in her. What did it matter what was in the sandwiches? What mattered was finding Mark. And so far this man had nothing positive to offer. Why was he telling me about sardines? She felt the air squashed out of her lungs. Two red spots appeared on her face. She placed her hands on her ears. She heaved; she couldn't breathe.

Aghast, Hugh half rose before settling back to his chair. He didn't know how to comfort Ruth. "I am sorry," he said. "Forgive me for rambling on. I was just trying to help. The driver said you have had nothing the whole day. You have to eat. At least drink something. You won't be able to cope if you do not eat and drink."

Ruth lips lifted minutely at the corners. The concern in his face touched her. Her anger subsided as fast as it rose. It was not his fault.

Hugh coaxed her to breathe deeply. "Are you all right?" he asked after a while. Many of the other guests were looking their way.

Hugh followed her eyes. "Planters and visitors from Kuala Lumpur mainly. No women amongst them, I am afraid."

Loud voices intruded. Two men were having an argument at the bar. Red faced, their voices grew louder and louder. The bartender tried to usher them out of the room. They turned on him, shouting abuses at the bewildered young man.

"Too many gin and tonics. Hard drinking is a problem amongst many planters and tin miners," Hugh explained apologetically without being prompted.

"What about Mark? Was it his problem?" Ruth's question took him by surprise for she had not spoken since she sat down.

A shadow crossed Hugh's brown eyes.

"No, he didn't have a drinking problem. Not as far as I know."

"Did he have any other problems?" Ruth could feel the dampness in her hands. She was sweating.

Hugh took a moment and then shook his head. He could see that she was worked up again. "Have you decided what you want to do?" He did not want Ruth to continue with a line of questioning that would force him to lie.

A flicker of life rose in her eyes. "I would like to stay on. I want to be here when they find Mark."

"It is not safe."

"I am not leaving. I would like to see the place where he was taken."

Hugh saw the determination on her face. A sigh of exasperation escaped him. "Tanjong Malim," he said with as much patience he could muster, "in fact the whole of the state of Perak is not a safe place for a woman, especially a white woman. The first act of war by insurgents was committed in this State. Three European planters were killed in Sungai Siput, just north of here. Please, for your own sake, return to Kuala Lumpur. I will keep you informed of developments. The company will, I am sure, take care of you."

Ruth shook her head. She squared her shoulders and lifted her chin defiantly. "No, I am staying."

"Where would you stay?" he asked, surprised by her doggedness. He saw the set of her chin and lips. "In the rest house?"

"No, not here. I will call Mark's boss tomorrow. I will ask if I could use the bungalow. Mark is still an employee and the bungalow is still his for the time being."

"What would you do while you wait? It might take a long time."

"I need to find a job to pay my way." Two bright spots reappeared on her face. "I don't have much with me and I cannot access Mark's bank account."

"What sort of job?"

"A teaching job." Ruth recalled Bill's words at the bus stop. According to him, the education system was in a shambles after the war and good teachers were needed.

"Have you taught before?"

"I can teach English to the small ones."

Hugh saw the desperation in her face. He knew there was nothing he could say that would dissuade her.

***

May hid behind a tree. She sighted Fu Yi several times in the back garden. Once she came out with a knife in hand to cut a papaya from its tree. Another time she came out to collect the washing. Still May didn't venture near the bungalow. Instead she waited till the sun dipped into the horizon like a red ball of fire in its last throes and darkness threw a dark inky veil over everything. Slowly with stealthy steps she crept to the back door. She knocked, once, twice and then a rapid succession of small staccato raps. She saw a movement behind the curtain in the adjacent window. May saw Fu Yi and beckoned her to open the door. A flurry of noise followed. The door opened an inch.

"You shouldn't be here. The Master's wife asked for you. The police have been as well. Please don't get me into trouble. You promised you would not come back after this morning. You will have to go to the police and tell them what you know."

"I don't know anything. I can't go to the police. They won't believe me. They torture you if they don't believe you. Remember the number of people put in jail and then never heard of since. Please let me in. I have nowhere to go."

Fu Yi hesitated. Reluctantly she stepped back and allowed May to enter. With a quick glance around the backyard, she bolted the door and drew the window curtains shut. Fu Yi did not want to be party to this but she owed May. May had arranged for her employment when Fu Yi was down and out. She had been kind. Fu Yi knew about May's relationship with the master. If the master returned, he would want to know that the cook had stood by May in hard times, that was if May was not involved in his disappearance.

"I went to see if my cousin Chun could help find our master."

"Chun?" After that one involuntary word of surprise that sprang out of her mouth, Fu Yi kept silent. She had heard about Chun, the union man. Tanjong Malim was a small town, more a village really. Everybody knew what the others did. She wondered if May could be really so naive that she had no suspicions whatsoever about her cousin Chun. Under her lowered eyelids, she examined May's face when May was not looking but averted her gaze when she sensed May looking her way.

"Chun knows many people. In the past he proved himself adept in helping others. He helped find our neighbour's son when he went missing. If I am to have his help I cannot go to the police or the military."

"Why?" the question shot out of Fu Yi's mouth before she had time to think.

"Chun has always warned against going to the police. My parents trust him; they have often said that Chun would look after me when they are gone and that I am to do his bidding. In any case, the police have not been helpful in the past."

Fu Yi had nothing to say in response. She agreed with May about the police. Still, she thought, May was too trusting. And May's parents were old fools. Knowing May she would inevitably do as her parents told her. Fu Yi muttered under her breath. She did not want to be involved. What good would it do? She kept quiet, filing away this piece of information.

"Chun is family. So I chose to rely on him instead of the police. Am I wrong?" May raised her eyes. They were clouded with doubt. "Would it be better to talk to the police? I thought Chun could use his connections to track Master Mark far better than them."

Fu Yi grunted and walked to the stove. She began to stir the contents of a pot burnt black from the charcoal fire. "Eat something," she said. "You cannot think on an empty stomach."

***

A thud woke May up. The window shutters were closed even though it was stifling hot in the room. Another thud. She gathered the blanket that had fallen around her feet and sat upright.

"It's me, Chun."

May stood up; the blanket fell to the ground in a heap. She opened the shutters and peered through the bars. Chun's face was in the shadows. Behind him moonlight lit up trees and turned leaves and branches to silver.

"I was looking for you," she whispered.

"I know. We have him. What do you want us to do with him?"

May froze. Her hand went to her heart. She could feel it beating wildly. "What do you mean? You have my master?"

"Yes! You didn't think I would let him drop you like a dead carcass after he had had his way with you? Bee Ying told me you are carrying his child, a half-caste that would smear your name forever. He will not marry you. You know that?" Chun's voice rose to a furious whisper. "The best he would do is to give you a fistful of dollars. They treat our women like whores. They breed here and then return to their own country. Well, I won't have it. I have him. We'll dispose of him. Then we'll rid you of the baby."

"No! Why are you doing this?"

"To help you? Save your honour. If you didn't want me to know about the baby, why did you tell my wife? You should know that I would not let any man sully you without punishment."

"I didn't tell Bee Ying. I was just holding your baby when I ... I whispered to it that I am also expecting. I was so happy. I didn't realised that Bee Ying was standing behind me. I begged her not to tell you. She laughed and called me a harlot."

"I'll kill him for what he did to you."

"No! Please no! I love him. Let me go to him. I shall beg him not to tell if you let him go. Is he hurt?"

Chun growled. "You stupid girl! He will promise you anything to be free. Once he is free, he will come for us."

"Please, please let me go to him."

"I have to go. I will speak to you when you talk sense. I could have had him killed immediately and perhaps that is what I should have done."

"No! No! Please..."

But like the shadows on the wall, Chun had vanished.

***

Mark lay trussed up with his wrists and ankles bound tight. A dirty piece of cloth was stuffed into his mouth. Blisters formed like red-crusted beads around his lips. A tape, used to bind his mouth, had cut into it. His forehead and cheeks were a crazy mosaic of wounds inflicted from fists and boots and streaked with blood that had long dried. Flies hovered around his wounds. He could not move; every time he struggled, the chain that secured him tightened him further to the tree trunk. At times he could hardly sustain the pain. They had not given him any water to drink nor food. They had not even allowed him to relieve himself. Mark watched as ants marched up his forearms and legs. He could smell the rank odour of urine, blood and sweat.

From the other end of the camp, coarse laughter rose. Someone threw a stone at him. Powerless to defend himself, Mark could only screw shut his eyes and pray that they would miss.

"Not so grand now. Not so handsome." Chortling and obscenities followed while yet another stone pelted on Mark's face.

A young man rose and walked to Mark. Mark opened his eyes. From under his swollen eyelids, he saw the man, smooth of face, slim and about five feet six. Before Mark could blink, a foot swung his way. He had hardly time to register the kick when another followed, followed immediately by yet another and another. One connected his temple. Mark blacked out.

The young man turned away. "We have to move camp and disperse; go our separate ways. Remember! Cover your tracks. Leave nothing and conceal everything."

"What about him?" asked one pointing at Mark, lying slumped on his side.

"We'll leave him. When they find him, the wild animals will have got to him first. By morning he will be dead. I can tell my cousin with a clear conscience that I did not kill him."

Chapter 7

RUTH WOKE UP to bright sunshine. It streamed through the thin curtains into the room and lit up a haze of dust motes dancing in the air. She had slept fitfully, tossing and turning on the hard bed. Questions and thoughts tumbled through her mind throughout the night. The photographs of May and Mark haunted her. At intervals an owl screeched and an elephant trumpeted. Mosquitoes buzzed round the net hung over her bed. Geckos chirped. Strange sounds that became oddly comforting as the night wore on and sleep eluded her.

She moved the mosquito net aside and swung her feet on to the mosaic floor. It felt oddly cool, for the air was already warm and sultry. She made her way to the bathroom and stripped off her nightdress. She stepped under the cold icy shower. No hot water. None was deemed needed in the hot climate. Ruth shivered and made short work of her wash.

Towelling her hair dry, she changed quickly into a cotton frock and went out to the dining room. She had made a list of things she would do. She would breakfast quickly and wait for the car that Hugh had promised to send her.

The breakfast room, where she had dined the previous evening, was almost full. The chatter stopped when she entered, a lone woman in a room full of men. An Indian boy in white addressed her as 'memsahib' and showed her to a table. She sat down. Self conscious that her every move was observed, she pretended a nonchalance that she did not feel. She became aware that someone was watching her intensely. She looked up to see Bill sitting at the next table. Before she could exclaim her surprise, he was already standing before her. "May I join you?" he asked, pulling back a chair.

For a moment she was speechless. The moment passed. She smiled, delighted to see a familiar face. "How ... why are you here?"

"Harrisons and Crosfield sent me. It was a last minute decision. I heard about your husband. I am sorry."

"I didn't know that you worked for the same company. You didn't say," she accused. She blinked and swallowed hard. Her earlier joy in seeing a familiar face dissipated. Nothing seemed as it was. The truth, it would appear, was a very rare commodity. It was her own naivety. He had volunteered hardly any information about himself, always steering their conversation towards her. She should have shown more interest in him rather than talk about herself. But even so he could have said something.

"I don't, not really." He made a rueful, apologetic face. "I ... am with the Government. I have been sent to Harrisons for the moment to sort out some problems. Until yesterday, I didn't know that I would be posted here."

He saw the doubt in her face and the hesitation that could mean questions, possibly awkward ones. "More importantly, how are you?" he asked quickly. "What are you going to do?"

"I plan to stay on. I hope that the company will allow me the use of Mark's bungalow until ... until we find him." Her voice broke. She didn't want to contemplate the possibility that Mark could not be found. She found Bill's penetrating stare too much and looked away to collect herself. "I need a job. Major Hugh, he is Mark's friend, is going to look into the possibility of my taking a teaching post." She paused; her cheeks grew a bright red. "I don't have enough to live on without a job. I can't access Mark's bank account."

Bill reached out and took her hand in his. "I don't think it would be safe for you to stay alone in the bungalow."

Ruth removed her hand, disconcerted by his familiarity. "I have no choice until I know where things stand and where Mark is. You can hardly expect me to return to England without trying to find my husband." She bit her lip; she did not wish to break down, not now, not ever.

"When will you move?"

"This afternoon," she replied.

***

Ruth heaved the suitcase on to the bed, Mark's bed. The sheets had been changed. The room dusted. She could smell polish and the remnant scent of mosquito spray. She opened the drawers. Mark's shirts remained neatly folded. She took one up and placed it to her nose. There was no trace of Mark there, just a hint of soap. Impatiently she went to the bathroom and flung open the cabinet door. The jar of Pond's cream had disappeared. She turned round. Fu Yi stood by the door observing her. Taken by surprise, Ruth could only return the stare. The diminutive cook turned and walked away.

Ruth stood for a moment in the room wondering what to do. Then she hurried out of the bedroom. "Fu Yi," she called after the cook's retreating back. Fu Yi stopped. Reluctantly, she turned to face Ruth. Her eyes hooded over like a glaze.

"Yes, Ma'am," she replied.

"Tell me about May. Where is she? When did she leave? Why did she leave?"

"No speak good English. Sorry, can't tell you." She bowed and prepared to turn away.

"Please," Ruth pleaded.

Fu Yi shook her head. She did not look up; instead she stared at the floor. Ruth followed her eyes. The floor was shiny clean. Yet at the corner, where a skirting board met the floor, a swarm of red ants marched in a single file as though in a drill.

"I know nothing, Ma'am. Sorry. I woke up, she gone. I take orders. I, very low, not important. I take orders from May and May from Master. I stay in kitchen. I see nothing and hear nothing."

Ruth watched helplessly as Fu Yi retreated back to the kitchen. Once in the kitchen, Fu Yi heaved a sigh of relief. She was happy that May had gone before dawn, before the madam came. At the market, the rumour was that the Master was probably dead. Insurgents were not known to keep their captives alive, unless they wished to trade them for something. Chun too had disappeared. It appeared that he had been under suspicion for a while. Fu Yi let out another sigh. There was no other way she could reduce the tightness in her chest except to dispel a loud sigh of frustration. She wondered again at May's guilelessness. How could she have trusted her cousin? She should have gone to the police instead of trying to get her cousin to help even if the police had been unhelpful in the past. It was too late now. "The error of youth!" she muttered in Cantonese. May was inexperienced in life and followed her parents' instructions as though they were gold, as though whatever they said would be correct. And how could they have such trust in him? Fools! Chun was a troublemaker. He stirred up discontent. Tin mines closed down because of it. People claimed that he always wangled his way out. Not this time. Not when the life of a white man was involved. The disappearance of May and Chun immediately after the capture of Mark made him a wanted man, and her, a wanted woman. When she went to the market, she saw posters with their faces plastered on the walls of the Post office. Fu Yi decided then that she would not get involved any further; she would not try to reach May to warn her about the Mistress taking occupation of the house. May would have to find out for herself.

***

It was almost mid-day when Ruth arrived at the spot where Mark had been taken. The road was deserted. Bill jumped out of the jeep and helped her down, his hands clasping her waist to lift her to the tarmac. They lingered a fraction longer than necessary. Ruth did not notice. She was on edge, eager yet dreading at the same time, to see the place. The soldier that accompanied them stood a short distance behind, his rifle ready at hand. Everyone, including Hugh, had advised against coming but she had been adamant. She wanted to see for herself.

Ruth walked towards the spot where a big cross had been marked on the tarmac. A stain surrounded it like a flower in bloom; dark, metallic, menacing, bloodstains dried by the sun and wind. There were tyre marks near it. Ruth looked around her. Tall grasses, coconut palms and trees with huge buttress-roots grew on either side of the road.

She clenched her hands, digging her nails into her palms until she felt pain. Somehow, the physical pain helped relieve the pain in her heart.

"Mark, Mark," she whispered to herself, "where are you?"

Bill came up close. "We have to go now. There is nothing to see. Nothing here will give you an inkling of where he has gone or where they have taken him. The police have combed the area. They have found nothing."

She turned, her face ashen. A tear spilled out despite her desperate attempt not to cry. Bill drew her to him. She rested her head on his chest. She could feel the thumping of her own heartbeat, a heart that had been pierced a hundred times, a heart filled with pain, pain for the loss of Mark and pain because of her suspicion that Mark had been unfaithful. She was not aware of how tightly Bill held her.

***

In the lounge at the rest house, Hugh was growing impatient. The evening was drawing near. Hugh had been reluctant to come to meet Bill. He did not like Bill's bullying manner or the way he was summoned. But the instructions from the top were that he was to assist Bill in whatever way he could.

"Tell me," Hugh said as soon as they were seated, "why are you here. What do you want from us?"

Bill cast his eyes around the room before finally resting his gaze on Hugh. The warmth he projected when he was around Ruth was completely gone.

His cold steely eyes bored into Hugh's. "I am here to put right what has gone wrong, to do what you people have not been able to do. You should know even without my prompting the worsening situation in Malaya." He leaned back and tapped his fingers impatiently on the arm of his chair.

Hugh remained silent. He was fuming.

"Perhaps not," said Bill. "You are a soldier. Perhaps the wider agenda of our government escapes you. How long have you been here?" he asked, the note of sarcasm deepening in his voice.

"Since the insurgency," he continued in the same breath without giving Hugh time to answer, "no new tin mines have been discovered. People are just too frightened to venture out to the jungle to prospect for tin. New mines are vital as existing ones are used up or on strike. The output of rubber has also fallen. The disruption of these two exports has affected the sterling and Britain's economy. Britain would not be able to pursue the recovery it sought without these two exports, at least not easily. Yet the army here pussyfoots around the insurgents. You people just don't understand the importance of getting this country quickly back on even keel."

"Why don't you get to the point?" asked Hugh in exasperation, irritated to be talked down to.

"Of all the states in Malaya, Perak, your patch, presents the most problems," Bill continued as though he had not heard. "Two years ago, Harrisons and Crosfield's manager at the Ephil Estate was murdered. Now the manager sent to replace him disappears, one who has come under our radar of surveillance. I am here to investigate him and others like him; we have to wheedle out the worms amongst us, the traitors. When we find them and dispose of them, we'll cut off the insurgents blood supply and the economy will return to normality."

Bill settled back in his armchair. He raised one eyebrow. The look he gave Hugh was pitying, scornful even. "I hope this is a sufficient answer to your question. I called you here this evening to demand your full cooperation and support. Obviously I need your promise not to divulge my role here to Mrs Lampard."

Hugh was startled by Bill's pronouncement that Mark was under surveillance. He didn't believe a word of it. His dislike of the man deepened. His insolence aside, there was something about Bill that aroused in Hugh a deep sense of distrust. The man was too sure of himself. Hugh did not like the way he was always around Mark's wife.

"I am surprised that you were chosen to investigate when you have never been to Malaya before," he said bluntly, casting caution to the wind.

"I served in Kenya. I don't have to know Malaya. I know how insurgents operate. Blacks, browns, they are all the same. One has to counter insurgency simply with a terror that they understand. And this is what I am here to advocate. We'll bomb them out of existence. I think the army here is too soft."

Hugh quelled the desire to explode. He was irritated to the core by Bill's smugness, his disdain for the Malayan people and his assumption that one size fits all. He could hardly credit what he was hearing. He took his time to respond. He faced a dangerous man, a chameleon, changing to whatever suited his purpose. He had observed how gentle Bill had been with Ruth and the kindness he seemed to radiate when she was around. Hugh acknowledged that he too had been taken in initially. Not now.

"Did you know," Hugh said in a quiet voice, "that we had trained these same insurgents to let them fight our war against the Japanese when we ourselves were routed? Did you know," he said quickly before Bill could respond, "that we had promised them citizenship after the war? Did you also know that under the new legislation of 1948, most of the people who fought on our account have not been given citizenship and are unable to own land? Many were forced to become squatters. It is these people, caught in the middle and who are not insurgents that I am concerned about. We should not tar everyone with the same brush."

A glimmer crossed Bill's eyes. "I see. You sympathise with them. You too! We have a name for sympathisers." It was a statement, not a question.

Hugh shook his head. "No! Not for insurgents. Just the innocent caught in the middle. I don't think atrocity against atrocity works. I believe one should also look at the causes for dissatisfaction and address them."

"Well, I have another theory. These yellow bastards are not working on their own. They have connections and carry out orders from China, their motherland. And some of our own people are helping them."

Hugh did not respond. It would be useless, he thought. Dangerous, even to expand on what he had said. He had already said too much. He would dig a deeper hole for himself. He should bide his time before saying anything more. In any event, what Bill said had an element of truth. Hugh's quarrel was that all were made to suffer similarly even when they were not involved. He picked up his tumbler and gulped down the liquor. With a curt nod, he stood up and left the room.

Chapter 8

RUTH WOKE UP very early the next morning. She lay quietly on the reclining chair listening to the morning sounds: a cacophony of frogs croaking, cocks crowing, dogs barking and then, from a distance, the *Adhan,* the Mosque's call for prayer. Inch by inch light began to filter through the thin curtains. She wasn't going to get much sleep. She got up and walked to the back of the house. She could hear faint sounds from the kitchen. Fu Yi was up. Ruth stood outside the kitchen for a moment and then pushed open the door. Fu Yi was squatting down in front of a pestle and mortar, pounding. The smell of onions, chillies and the strong aroma of *belachan* hit Ruth's nose. "Fermented prawn paste," Fu Yi had explained the previous evening, "a local ingredient added to most Malay cooking. Master likes it very much. I cook it for you too?" she had asked.

Quelling her initial reaction to the pungent fumes, Ruth decided there and then that she would like it as well. "Let's have it tomorrow," she had said.

The sight of Fu Yi bent over a mortar and pestle so early in the morning touched her. "I didn't expect that you would have to wake up so early to prepare this," Ruth apologised, stricken that once again she had made a faux pas.

"No Ma'am. I do everything early before sunrise. It is not so hot. Breakfast?" she asked, rising to her feet. She took the bowl of chilli mixture that she had scraped from the mortar and placed it on the wooden counter. Then she grabbed a papaya from a basket nearby. "Papayas and lime from the garden. If you wish, also toast with *kaya*. It is a jam made with eggs, sugar and coconut cream. Master likes it too."

"Thank you. That would be lovely." Ruth was beginning to see Mark through these small domestic arrangements. It would appear, as Hugh said, that Mark was truly adapted to the local way of living. She must do the same. He would expect it when he returned. She had always thought of her husband as a quintessential Englishman. She was being proved wrong. She sat on a wooden stool to watch the cook. Fu Yi was beginning to open up. There was so much Ruth wanted to ask. She refrained; she shouldn't force the momentum by pressing for information as she had done the first evening. She bottled her impatience. The sound of cabinets opening and cups clinking floated around her. Gradually, her mind turned once more to her worries. Her resolution to be positive fell by the wayside. Where was Mark? How was she going to find him? What if he could not be found? She took a deep breath and forced herself to push aside these thoughts. She tried to focus on problems that she could and should address. How was she going to pay Fu Yi's wages at the end of the month? Could she ask for help from the Company? Almost a week had passed and she had not been able to find a job. "Not here in Tanjong Malim," she was told, "perhaps in Kuala Lumpur and other bigger cities. No schools here would be able to afford to employ a white school teacher." She might have to let Fu Yi go. She might not be able to stay on in this house for much longer. Her head grew heavy. She did not notice the sliced papayas set before her.

"Ma'am, eat! Don't worry," said Fu Yi setting a steaming cup of black coffee and a small tin of condensed milk on the table.

Ruth realised that she had been frowning and that her jaws were hurting from being clenched tight.

Fu Yi went back to the washbasin. She pitied the young mistress. It couldn't be easy to be alone in a strange land and to find her husband vanished into thin air. No wonder she did not sleep night after night. She could hear her prowling around the house and pacing up and down in her bedroom. What good would it do to tell her about May? Fu Yi shook her head. She shouldn't load her young mistress with more worries.

***

People were queuing up to leave the New Settlement. Rolls of barbed wire rose six feet high, isolating the camp from the outside world. May crouched down behind a bush. She waited to catch a glimpse of her parents and to see if Chun would be amongst those lining up to leave for work. She would plead with him again to release Mark. This time, she would go to the police if he were to refuse.

Four armed guards stood at the gate. A wooden sentry box rose high above the barbed wire fencing with another armed guard within it. The workers were meticulously searched. They thrust their hands up in the air as guards groped through their clothes and belongings. No food was allowed out of the camp or into it. To stop food finding its way to insurgents, rice rations for New Settlements had been reduced by forty per cent. Who, May asked herself silently as the gaunt half-starved faces of her parents came to mind, would have any food to give to others? The thought of food brought her own hunger pangs to the fore. She had not eaten since leaving Mark's house; she wanted to go back to Fu Yi but the sight of a white woman stopped her. Instinctively she knew it was Ruth. So she stayed on the fringe of the estate, hiding her face from the world with a scarf tied round her head and a wide coolie hat, just like those worn by other coolies. She became one of the faceless people in the rubber estate.

The queue moved slowly; people shuffled forward with faces devoid of expression. All emotions had to be curbed, resentment bottled inwards and tempers held. The sun rose high up in the sky. A warm breeze stirred up leaves and yellow dust from the dirt road. There were still no sign of her parents. Suddenly she spotted Bee Ying. She was hunched forward with the baby strapped behind her back and a basket of laundry in each hand. Guards began to rifle through her laundry, crushing the freshly ironed sheets. May saw Bee Ying open her mouth to protest only to close it immediately when the guard scowled at her and pushed her back into the compound. "Go back! You can't leave," he shouted as he shoved her once again.

May shifted on her haunches. Her legs were sore and she was thirsty. People were passing her now. They whispered amongst themselves. May stood up and joined them, shuffling forward like they did. No one looked at her; they did not wish to see anything. She heard a couple whisper. "They won't let her come out of the camp now. Her husband is wanted. Soon they will cart her away for questioning. What will become of the baby? The whole family will be arrested. That young woman May who worked for the estate manager is also wanted. I saw her picture on the Post Office wall."

May shuddered. This was news that she did not know. She bowed even lower, hiding her face under the coolie hat. She had been wrong. By disappearing she had become a suspect. What should she do? Would the authorities believe her if she gave herself up now? She was torn. To give herself up would implicate Chun. She would have to tell the authorities about him. To implicate Chun, would drag her innocent parents into the mess. To anger Chun further would definitely mean Mark's death. Despite Chun's threats, she had hoped and prayed that he would spare Mark once he came to his senses. For hadn't she explained that she loved Mark? How she wished she had not made the blunder of revealing her pregnancy to Bee Ying. She blamed herself for the mess, for getting Mark into trouble. Never in her wildest dreams would she have imagined that this would happen.

***

"Let me have the file on May." Bill was curt with Hugh. "How is it possible that you had no idea of her connection with this guy, Chun? There must be a connection between the two."

"I did not vet May personally. The highest authority recommended her to us. She worked as clerical support staff in the Malacca office and was found efficient and loyal. There was nothing to suggest that she was subversive."

"*Huh!*" snarled Bill. "Don't you think it strange that she took a job as housekeeper."

"I believe she was desperate. The post she held in Malacca was a temporary one; she was filling for someone on maternity leave."

"And her relationship with Mark?" Bill lifted one brow in question. His nostril flared with disapproval. Hugh did not answer. Bill tapped his fingers on the table. He reached into his shirt pocket and fished out a pack of cigarettes. He lit one up, the end flared red like a warning to Hugh. He dragged deeply on the cigarette and then blew out a smoke ring. Through the cloud of smoke, he appraised Hugh in silence. His eyes were thoughtful, weighing Hugh's discomfort. To him, Hugh's silence said it all. Bill did not approve of inter-racial relationships. The outcomes were half-breeds, 'stengahs' they called them here. Neither of one race nor of the other and always with these half-breeds bearing English names. The fathers were inevitably Englishmen rather than the other way around. He wondered if Ruth knew about her husband's relationship with May. He would bide his time; he would choose the right moment to tell. He should not reveal everything up his sleeve. He hid his smile. He was attracted to Ruth. She was an interesting woman. Beneath her naivety was a headstrong character. He was always partial to strong-willed women with a bit of fight in them.

He picked up the files and riffled through the papers. The file on Chun was thick. Chun Yee Poh, a union man responsible for a series of strikes in tin mines and unrest in Perak. Born in the province of Fukien in China and educated in Chinese, he moved to Malaya when a child. He disappeared during the Japanese occupation and went underground as a member of the Malayan People's Anti Japanese Army, an organisation now regrouped as an anti British organisation, the Malayan National Liberation

Army. How, he wondered, could the British army, Major Hugh in particular, miss this? Or had they? Had he?

Bill was certain that Hugh was not cooperating fully with him. He could feel it in his bones. His eyes narrowed as he took another drag on his cigarette. If he could find evidence of negligence, he could have Hugh dismissed, court-martialled even. He picked up the files and flipped through the papers. He couldn't find any connection between Chun and May from the papers. She was born in Malaya. Both parents were Hakkas; the father had come from Guangxi twelve years ago and her mother was local born. Before the Japanese occupation, the father had been a teacher. During the war, he was imprisoned in a camp. They lived originally in Malacca, moving to Tanjong Malim after May took up employment here. Whatever contact they had with this Chun must have started when they were rounded up and put into the New Settlement.

Bill rose from his seat and went to the window, leaving the files opened on the table. He stood with legs astride and both hands clasped behind his back. Someone must know. He was frustrated. The harder he pushed, the more resilient the squatters became, resilient and silent.

Hugh watched. He sensed Bill's anger and waited. He had already said too much. He must keep his personal feelings and his antipathy towards Bill quiet. He had Chun on their radar for some time, even before Bill's arrival. He had not arrested Chun because he had wanted him to lead them to Chin Peng, the leader of the insurgents. He had not known of May's connection with Chun, if indeed there was a connection.

Bill spun around. "Over the next few days, we will be bombing north of this area, deep into the jungle. Our reconnaissance points to two guerrilla camps within a five-mile radius to the west. We'll be using five-hundred-pound fragmentation bombs and equal-sized nose-fused bombs. You should make sure that your officers stay clear of the area. We'll flush those bastards out or kill them."

"What if Mark is in one of the camps?"

Bill strode to the desk and picked up his hat. "Then he will be collateral damage." He had no sympathy for a Commie lover.

***

The body lay inert on the ground. Seven men clustered around it, wiry men with loincloths that barely covered their buttocks. They talked amongst themselves; their voices rose like the shrill chatter of birds in the forest. One, no taller than five feet, stooped down. Feathers hung like a garland around his girth partially covering the loincloth beneath. His chest was dark, smooth and bare and his hair reached his shoulders. Holding a blowpipe with one hand he prodded the inert body with his bare feet. He sprang back. His bare feet sank deeply into the soft rain soaked soil as the body rolled over, revealing wounds and cuts that covered almost every inch of the bare torso. The face was covered with open sores. The man's eyes, sealed by the pus oozing around the rims of his eyelids, were swollen and bruised.

"He is alive!" he pronounced. "*Orang putih,*" he said gesturing at the blond hair matted with blood, "a *tuan* that must have incurred the wrath of the Chinese fighters. What shall we do?"

"They must have left him to die."

"Shall we warn them that he is alive?" another asked.

"No. We'll take him back with us. Our chief will tell us what we must do."

"What about the Chinese fighters?"

"Let them believe that the *tuan* is dead. At least until our chief decides which side of the war we should be on. We have helped them enough. The tide is changing. The white man might be useful."

Chapter 9

THE LAST STREAK of sunlight disappeared into the horizon. Without warning, the jungle was thrown into darkness. May shivered. She squatted down by the stream and splashed water on to her face. Then she cupped her palms together and scooped up the water to drink. Hunger gnawed. The night sounds of the jungle increased in intensity. She jumped at every movement and every sound. Shadows lengthened and waned; wind howled. She couldn't stay in the jungle. She would have to make her way back towards the plantation. Gingerly, she placed one foot in front of the other. Each step was an agony. Her shoes had worn through and the sharp blades of *lalang* were cutting into her soles, turning the blisters into bleeding open sores. She stumbled. Instinctively she placed her hand on her tummy. What would happen to her and to the child within her? What had happened to Mark? Was he dead? "Please, please," she beseeched, her face turned upwards to a sky as dark as ink, "let him live."

She pushed through the thick undergrowth towards Mark's house. Bright light beckoned from within. May leaned forward, straining to see if Mark's wife was there. She thought of the letter left on the mantelpiece. She made her way towards the backyard. She remembered the gap in the fencing. With infinite care, she angled herself into the gap, her body jammed half in and half out, when suddenly a slim silhouette of a woman appeared at the window. Light turned the woman's hair into a halo of gold. Unlike the previous day, she could see her face. May gasped. It was Ruth, Mark's wife. May had not expected Ruth to be so young and pretty. In the flesh, Ruth looked vulnerable and sad. Bewildered, May sank down on the ground wedged between the fences. She had always thought Ruth to be older, much older. She was a fool. Before Mark had told her he had a wife, she had imagined the woman in the photograph to be his sister. He did not clarify when she asked. She remembered the night when he had told her that he was married. It was a week after he first came to her bed. After that she had assumed the photograph of Ruth on the shelf was an old photograph of a young Ruth. She had imagined Ruth to be dour. She had believed that Mark's marriage was over, no matter that he had said that their affair would have to stop when Ruth came. She wanted to believe that Ruth was old and dour. Why else would he take May as his lover? Perhaps she had deluded herself to assuage her guilt. When Fu Yi learnt of the affair, she had been furious. May remembered the two words Fu Yi used to describe her – 'young' and 'stupid'. May had retorted that she was nearly seventeen, and not a child. Perhaps Fu Yi was right after all.

May crouched, jammed in between the planks in the fence. She was not sure if she should go into the backyard. Ruth's presence changed everything. She had hoped to catch Fu Yi on her own and beg for some food and perhaps a blanket. A car turned into the drive. She heard the engine of the car switch off and a door slam shut. May slunk back. She pushed the fencing together again. She couldn't go into the backyard. She'd wait.

Footsteps followed. Through the slit between the fence, May could see a man and a woman come out to the terrace. She pressed her ears to the gap between the fences. She recognised the man. He was Major Hugh, Mark's friend.

***

"I am glad to see you settled." Hugh steered Ruth to a chair on the terrace. He lowered himself on to a seat opposite her.

"Any news?" Ruth's eyes were bright with expectation.

"I am sorry. I'm afraid not. I came not because I have information about Mark's disappearance. I just wanted to see if you are all right. The situation is deteriorating rapidly in this area. We are telling everyone not to go out unnecessarily. I have said this before but thought I should say it again. Please stay away from the plantation. Do not step near the jungle. Don't go anywhere near the New Settlement, no matter how tempted you might be to investigate on your own. It is not safe. I can't tell you more."

Ruth could not contain her disappointment. She hardly took in Hugh's warnings. For a moment she had allowed her hopes to rise. Why else, she had thought, would Hugh come to see her at this late hour if not for news about Mark? She didn't know him well enough to expect a social visit from him. Dampness gathered in the corner of her eyes. She brushed it away fiercely. She had kept herself in check even when she had discovered May's belongings. She was not going to cry now, not in front of someone she hardly knew. She saw Hugh watching her apprehensively. It struck her then. Hugh was Mark's friend. He must know of Mark's affair. He was hiding it from her. She must have the truth about May.

"About May," Ruth's cheeks were a bright pink, "the cook would not tell me much about her. Is she ... is she Mark's lover?" It was a relief to say it out loud. A part of her wished to be contradicted. "Mr Fletcher, Bill hinted. He ... he said that it is strange that she should disappear on the same day Mark vanished. That their disappearance could have been pre-arranged, a lovers' flight. That Mark," her lips trembled in her recollection, "was assisting the insurgents."

"Damn the man! I know Mark. He wouldn't enter into any arrangement that would cost a life! His driver was killed! Mark is not a traitor. He does not support the insurgency. You should believe in that, Ruth, and hold on to it, for others will use his disappearance to distort the truth. According to Bill, even I, perhaps even the whole British regiment in this district, is in cahoots with the enemy. Only he and his men could save the British Empire."

"Please tell me. Is May Mark's lover?" Ruth's stoicism left her. Her eyes once more glistened.

Hugh was pushed to a corner. He had vowed not to be the one to tell. Yet, there was no escaping from such a direct question.

"Men sent out here on their own are lonely." His voice was quiet and measured. "If it makes you feel better and if indeed he had an affair, he would not be the only one that had strayed."

The pool that had gathered in Ruth's eyes spilled over. A drop splashed down on to her blouse. Hugh leaned over and took Ruth's hands in his own. They felt small and helpless in his. He cursed himself. His words sounded hollow even to himself.

"Please," he continued hoping to dissipate his own words, "I am not saying that they were lovers. He has never said."

He realised that he had dug a hole for himself. Ruth withdrew her hands from his clasp.

"Sorry, I am so sorry. I am just making things worst. Everything we say or Bill says is conjecture. No one knows the truth except for Mark. Let's concentrate on rescuing him. I'd rather you did not go by my words. It is only fair that you wait for Mark to explain. Ignore what I said."

"What happens if we don't find him?"

Hugh could not reply; he did not know what to say, for what could he say that would bring her comfort? This limbo of not knowing was much worse than knowing for certain.

"I went to May's room. I searched her belongings. They were all hung out neatly in the cupboard."

Ruth did not mention that she could smell the scent May used in her clothes, the same scent she had found on Mark's pillows. She knew then, though she fought against the knowledge, that her suspicions were correct. She had also found the missing jar of Ponds cream on May's dressing table. Fu Yi must have retrieved it from Mark's bathroom.

"Surely that meant that she had not planned to disappear with Mark? Their disappearance at the same time must be pure coincidence." Ruth clung to this fragment of evidence. It was her only hope that Bill's cruel supposition of a lovers' flight was untrue.

"Don't take notice of Bill. He is a dangerous man. Be wary of what he says and what you say to him. He is not what he claims to be. Try to get some sleep. I'll come by tomorrow."

On the other side of the fence, May heard it all. Her cheeks were wet with tears. She did not know if they were prompted by compassion for Mark's wife or sorrow for herself. Perhaps both. May was ridden with guilt. Ruth clearly loved Mark, as she did. Was it true that Mark had turned to her only because he was lonely? That he had not loved her as she had thought. Was she like the other women? Like Ah Lan to be used and then discarded? She got up and ran. Tears blinded her. She did not feel the blisters and the cuts on her feet and arms, the hunger that gnawed and sapped her strength. She tripped, fell and picked herself up. She ran as though she was running for her life.

***

Two sentries stood outside the New Settlement. In the sentry box, a guard lit a cigarette. The red glow of his cigarette end sparked and ebbed. May could smell the pungent smoke from where she squatted. It would not be possible to get into the Settlement. The barbed wire fences were too high. It was quiet, the silence interrupted now and then by the shrill wails of babies or the harsh coughing of the elderly. May waited. She hoped for a glimpse of her parents. She needed to be assured that they were all right. She was worried that they had been taken on account of her. Suddenly dogs began to bark; their yelping grew to a frenzy and as suddenly as they had started, they stopped. May tensed up, every fibre in her body was drawn like strings on a harp. She rose on her haunch, a sprinter ready to run. A hand grasped her mouth from behind, clamping it tight.

"It is me, Chun."

May's feet slipped from her and she fell back.

"*Shhh!*" Chun released her. "Come. Move away from here. They will find out soon about the dogs. I have poisoned them. Quick!" He pulled her urgently deeper into the jungle. She followed without thinking. They moved silently and quickly. They reached a stream and waded across, heading still deeper into the jungle. "My men are waiting for me." She stumbled. He grasped her hand and pulled her urgently forward. "We cannot slow down. We have to make haste."

May stopped. She tugged her hand away from his. Her breath came in great gulps. "I can't run any more. I don't want to run. I don't want to join you. I have my parents to think of. If I go with you and Mark is found, I will not be able to go to him. I will be cut off from him and from my family forever."

"You fool! He is dead. You will never be with him. You are a wanted woman; they believe you are one of us. You cannot go back."

May's legs collapsed under her. Dead! How could that be? She had been so sure that Chun would spare him after she had pleaded for Mark's life. That was why she had not gone to the police. Wasn't he a relative? Wasn't he supposed to look after her? Chun's face loomed, dark and imperious, as he bent down towards her. His cheekbones stood out from his hollowed cheeks like the cropped wings of a bird. She shuddered. She had not known Chun until recently when, out of the blue, he had appeared at her parent's house and persuaded them that he was her cousin. He seemed to know their relatives from China. From then on, her parents had urged her to look to him as a brother. He persuaded them that he would look after her when they were gone. Neither she nor her parents knew that Chun was an insurgent. She knew that he was active in the trade unions. But wasn't that true of many?

"You, you killed him!" She lashed out. He caught her, deflecting her blow with his wrist.

"No. I did not kill him. I just know that he would not survive the jungle. The jungle is booby-trapped. Bombs placed by his own people. Bombs set by us. Wild animals would tear him apart even if he managed to negotiate a way around these traps."

"You dragged him there knowing full well what would happen."

"My men did it. In hard times, men act like they must." He hauled her to her feet.

"You took him because you found out about the baby!" She lashed out again landing a slap on his face.

Chun brushed his cheek; he felt the sting where the slap landed. His ears tingled. Without a word, he grabbed her and hoisted her up on his shoulder. "I have no time for hysterics," he hissed. He ran sure-footed into the jungle.

Chapter 10

AFTER HUGH LEFT, Ruth went into the bedroom and lay on the rattan reclining chair. The chair had served as her bed since she arrived. She could not lie on the bed. Mark had slept with May on it. Images of the two entwined tortured her. She flitted between anger and sorrow. She grieved for Mark, for what they had been and what they could have been, had he not taken this job, had he not been infatuated with this country, so far and so different from the world that was theirs in Somerset. Here in Malaya was a Mark she did not know, had never known. A secret Mark who loved fermented shrimp paste and a Chinese woman, so beautiful and exotic that she, Ruth, could never match up to her. Jealousy rose like bile, hot and rank; she could hardly breathe, it consumed her. Yet despite all the hurt and anger, she loved Mark. The Mark she remembered was not the one grounded here. The Mark she knew had been tender, gentle, honest and loving and remembering that had sustained her during his absence. Believing that made it possible for her to overlook the gradual decline in the frequency of his letters. She had made excuses for him. Never in her wildest dreams when she embarked on the journey to Malaya had she contemplated he could have been with another woman. So Ruth sat, her thoughts flitting from one to the other; from anger to grief and back; from worries about the future to the uncertainties of the present. She was filled with hatred. She hated May, hated her for stealing her husband, and hated her for the situation she was now in. This hate sustained her when everything was falling apart.

The first hint of dawn rose when a shaft of golden sunshine seeped through the window. A cock crowed. The *adhan* call soared, towering above all other sounds. Ruth pulled a shawl around her. The morning air was damp and surprisingly cool. Fu Yi knocked on the door. She came through with a tray. On it was a pot of coffee, a cup and saucer, milk and sugar, a plate of toast and a can of butter. Fu Yi took one look at her mistress and knew that she had not slept. But it was more than that. Something had changed. There was a hardness in Ruth's demeanour that had not been there before. She set the tray down carefully, unloading its contents on to the small coffee table by the chair. She glanced quickly at the bed. As on previous days, it had not been slept on. The mosquito netting was still tied to one side and the sheets remained smooth.

"I know about the Master and May."

Fu Yi pretended she did not hear. She bowed and turned to go.

"Are you going to tell me?"

Fu Yi did not move. Her back was still turned away.

"Please," said Ruth more softly this time, "tell me."

Fu Yi turned to face Ruth. "May a good girl. She only sixteen when she came here last year. She not what you think. She never been with anyone."

"Not too young to steal my husband," said Ruth dryly. She wanted to retort that she had been eighteen when she met Mark and twenty when she married him. At twenty-two, she felt old compared to a seventeen-year-old slip of a girl. She wanted to ask if Mark loved May. How could she ask such a question? Where was her pride? Did she expect answers that would soothe her pain? What answers could possibly do that?

"May not out to seduce the Master. Master make mistake. It just happened. Such things happen in the tropics between white masters and local girls."

Ruth snorted. Then she laughed. She shook with laughter. She laughed without mirth. It bounced off the walls. "But she did seduce him," she said, her lips stretched in a macabre grin. "Things do not just happen! People make them happen."

Fu Yi looked bewildered. She could not catch what Ruth said. It was said too quickly for her to understand.

"Did May leave to join the Master?" Ruth asked.

Fu Yi shook her head. "May look for Master; she not know his whereabouts."

At least, Ruth took comfort from knowing that their disappearance was not a lovers' pact.

"Will you tell me, Fu Yi, if you hear anything at all? It is important. Master is in danger."

Fu Yi nodded. She kept her eyes down and, after a moment's hesitation, left the room.

"Where are you, Mark?" Ruth whispered to herself.

***

Bill stood with his shoulders thrown back and legs astride. Behind him a huge map of the state of Perak hung on the wall. The room was packed. Soldiers dressed in khaki green sat, attentive, on metal chairs, faces agog, uncertain as to what would be forthcoming from this new man from Kenya. He wore civilian clothes yet was rumoured to wield more power than their own commander.

"We have a three-pronged strategy in this war against the commies." Bill paused and looked at each and every individual in the room to let his words sink in. "We round up squatters and put them into settlements. Then we starve and isolate them. This will stop them from being conduits for the insurgents. You have seen both strategies enacted in the past months. Now we begin our next phase. We bomb them. To start with, here, here and here," he pointed to the various points marked out in red in the map.

"We will be engaging in this in the months to come. More camps will be identified and all will be similarly bombed. We will also sabotage them from within. We will infiltrate their ranks and supply them with self-detonating grenades and bullets. The users will be instantly killed."

A buzz went round the room; everyone spoke at once. At last there was to be action. Hugh looked on at his men and saw their excitement. He felt cold.

"We'll match their atrocity," Bill said, his voice rising as he caught the men's excitement. "They use fear to force squatters to supply them with food; they use fear to drive planters out of the country; and they use atrocities to weaken us. We'll do the same to them. They cut off a head; we'll match it. They cut off a hand;

we'll cut off theirs. We will judge our success by the numbers we kill. I urge you to make a chart of the killings. Shoot to kill! We'll dispel any notion that they are invulnerable."

Bill's eyes challenged Hugh to say different. He knew he wouldn't. He had the backing of the highest authorities and Hugh knew that.

"The tide is changing," Bill continued, his cold grey eyes still on Hugh. "We are also winning the jungle people to our side. In the future they will not supply food to our enemies. They will fight by our side. On our part we will not curb their practice of decapitation."

Someone laughed in response. "Maybe we should encourage it."

Bill did not reply, his left eyelid closed and opened in a wink. The grin that followed said it all. The men had little doubt as to what they should do.

So, Hugh thought, the rounded-up squatters, squeezed in the middle, suffer. He wondered where May was. Where Mark could be. Was he dead? Would he be numbered among the casualties to come?

***

Mark lay delirious. People floated in and out of his vision. He could not tell if he had imagined them or if they were real. Everything was a blur. He couldn't move; he burned, sweated and shivered in turn. He did not know where he was or who he was. He drifted in and out of consciousness; his world was a fantasy of moving shadows, of tree branches swaying overhead, of monkeys clambering on trees, of insects and bare-bodied people hovering by his side spilling words he could not decipher, their voices so shrill that he felt his ears hum. At times, they came and opened his mouth and tried to force-feed him. He was too tired to resist; too tired and weak to swallow. Food and water dribbled out from the corner of his mouth; the burning continued.

Chapter 11

CHUN DROPPED MAY unceremoniously on to the ground. They had been running for almost an hour and he was panting with his exertion. His men crowded round him. They glared at May with open hostility.

"What shall we do with her?" they demanded. They moved closer together joining ranks in their defiance of Chun. They did not want May with them. She was a hindrance. They needed to be back in their camp and to move on. If they were to remain too long at any one place, the British army would be on to them.

The air turned hot and musty with their anger and fear. May felt it and instinctively drew her legs up, clamping them tight.

"We'll take her back with us."

"No!" the men cried. "You were supposed to bring your wife and child out from the Settlement. We waited for you. That was already a concession on our part. You bring, instead, this *chow hai!* Cunt! A string of obscenities followed.

"My wife and son have been taken. Your parents too," Chun said to May. "I dug a tunnel under the barbed fencing and got into the Settlement and came out the same way. I killed the dogs. I poisoned them or they would be following us. The guards would have found out by now. We don't have time to stop here to argue."

"I am not going with you. Leave me here. I won't tell," cried May.

"No! We can't leave you here alive," said one of the men, "and we certainly would not want to take you with us." He drew out his revolver and pointed at May. He cocked the gun. Chun sprang forward and caught his hand, forcing it down.

"Shoot and they'll hear us. Go! Leave her with me. I'll do the deed. Go now. I'll join you when I have finished the job."

The men stood their ground. They did not believe Chun. "Do it! We'll stay and watch."

Chun grabbed May's arm and pulled her roughly to her feet. He slapped her hard across her mouth with the back of his hand. It drew blood. Then he whacked her again sending her head spinning to one side. He spun her around and with one arm across her neck twisted as though he was wringing a chicken's neck. May blacked out, a stain appeared on her trousers as her bowels emptied. He threw her down.

"Go! We must not lose time. I'll make sure she is truly dead." Chun drew out a knife. The men saw him bend over the inert body, his knife poised above her stomach. They turned and ran.

***

Ruth sank her teeth into her nail. A searing pain went through her as she tore at it. Incredulous at what she had done, she stared at her fingers. They were pink and raw and the nails chewed to ragged bits. She was half crazed with anxiety and was barely conscious of what she was doing. No one had been in touch, nor had any ransom notes been received. Each time soldiers passed by the bungalow with a body or bodies slung on poles, she would rush out to see only to be restrained by Fu Yi. When Fu Yi came back with news of killings and bodies found, her whole being shook. At times her heart would beat so fast, she felt she could hardly breathe. She grew thin and restless. Sleep evaded her. They heard nothing about May. May's parents and Chun's wife had been taken for further interrogation alongside dozens of others. Ruth wanted to see them. She was refused.

The sitting room with its barred windows seemed increasingly like a prison. She imagined the walls closing in on her. She had to do something. Yet what could she do?

Impatiently she went to the cabinet and took out the letter she had received from Harrison's and Crosfield. The firm agreed that she could stay on. They had enclosed Mark's wages. It was a thoughtful gesture. She could now pay Fu Yi. However, they warned that they would not wait indefinitely for Mark's return. The situation was being reviewed and another manager was likely to be posted to take Mark's place. The estate could not run on its own. The lines in the letter were like squiggles that went on and on. She couldn't bring herself to read any further. She crushed the letter and stuffed it into her pocket. She could hear Fu Yi at the door.

Fu Yi came in with a tray of food in her hands. In the past few days she had brought tray after tray, only to leave with each barely touched. This time, it was chicken soup. She prepared it using a whole fresh chicken bought from the open market. A whole chicken was a luxury during a time of shortage, a luxury she had obtained through trading some of the fruits grown in the garden. She laid out the bowl and spoon on the table.

"Eat something! *Aiyah!* How you deal with problems if you starve and fall ill?" She stood waiting for Ruth to eat. She was not going to leave until the mistress made an attempt.

Ruth sat down and forced a spoon of the broth into her mouth. 'No more! I just can't," she said.

Fu Yi knelt by her and took the spoon from Ruth. She began feeding Ruth as though Ruth was a child, opening her own mouth to urge Ruth on. "You must," she insisted.

"Any news?" Ruth asked with weary eyes as she forced herself to eat. She was too tired to refuse Fu Yi's ministrations.

"May still not found. The police took her parents and Chun's wife away. No one see them since. *Alamak! Chan hai cham!*" In her excitement Fu Yi began mixing her English with the vernacular. She recalled the stories she heard. Some of Fu Yi's own family had been rounded up and moved into the Settlement.

"I don't think May's parents *boleh tahan*. Very hard one you know?" Fu Yi opened her eyes wide to demonstrate how she felt. "Questions no stop. They ask, ask until you mad. Prisoners *tangkap* two years without trial. They sure die. Chun's wife will be sent back to China. Don't know what would happen to the child. He born here. *Yam kong!* "

"And yet they say nothing," Ruth muttered to herself, marvelling at their resilience. "Surely they must know."

"May don't know. She tells me. So how her parents know anything? What can they say? She ran because she frightened. Poor girl! She not want to be..." Fu Yi clamped her hand to her mouth. Her eyes were round with fear.

"So you spoke to her!" Ruth exclaimed.

Fu Yi cowed. Her hand shot up to shield her face as though she expected to be slapped. "So sorry Ma'am. I want to hear no evil, speak no evil, and see no evil.

"When did she come here?" Ruth clutched Fu Yi's arm. Her fingers dug into the flesh. She shook her violently. Suddenly aware of what she was doing and aghast at her own action, Ruth released Fu Yi. She watched with dismay at the deep red print marks she had left on Fu Yi's arm.

"Sorry," Ruth apologised.

Fu Yi took a deep breath. Carefully, choosing her words and ordering her thoughts, she explained. "I saw May just before you came. She very worried about Master. She went missing because she looking for Chun. She wanted him help find Master. Then she got frightened. She *tahu* that because she went missing for a day the police would suspect her. You see, she related to Chun. But she no idea he is bad. She young, stupid! She thought he knew people that could help her find Master." Fu Yi dropped down on her knees and kowtowed. "Don't report me. Please, please! My whole family will be punished. That's all I know."

Ruth looked into Fu Yi's eyes. They were pools of fear. "You swear you have told me everything?"

Fu Yi cringed and nodded vigorously.

Ruth got up. She did not know what she should do. If she were to repeat any of the things divulged by Fu Yi, Mark's murky love affair would be made public. Telling wouldn't help find Mark. The police were already searching for Chun and May. It would just ruin his career, should he be found. How could she bear the scandal? More importantly, if Mark were to know that she knew about his affair, it might make their reconciliation more difficult. She was determined not to lose Mark. It was far better to pretend not to know. She turned to look at the cowering cook. Fu Yi had been kindness personified these past days, tending to her needs. She was her only human contact; Ruth needed her. Surely Fu Yi would not lie to her this time. In this atmosphere of distrust everyone was for himself. So how could she blame Fu Yi for doing exactly that? Ruth made up her mind. For the moment at least, she would not say anything.

***

Later that evening, Ruth made herself lie on the bed even when imagination played riot in her mind and even when jealousy and hurt tore her apart. Did Mark touch May as he touched her? How many times had they made love on this bed? Fu Yi said that May loved Mark. Did he love the girl? She turned to her side and curled into a tight ball. She willed herself to remain on the bed. She had to face her demons. She could not wish the past away. Not sleeping on the bed did nothing. She must accept the past and go forward, even if she could not forgive. She must if she wanted Mark. Did she want him? she asked herself. Could she pack up her bags and leave right now? She thought long and hard. She couldn't. She loved him despite everything. She could not contemplate a life without Mark. She tossed and turned. Where was he? Was he dead? With each passing day, her hopes dimmed a bit more. Then weariness caught up and she fell into an uneasy sleep.

Chapter 12

THE PLANES SWOOPED down. Treetops sprung to life, branches shook and leaves fell. One by one the bombs dropped; like Easter eggs. The air turned silent. Then a deafening explosion ripped through the sky. Huge clouds of smoke rose and the heavens turned black. The ground burst open. Screams rippled through the jungle. Birds screeched; they flew directionless, en masse, wings flapping, crashing into each other. Black debris rained down like confetti. Within seconds trees were flattened and plants scorched.

Hugh's platoon watched from afar. Their orders were to shoot any survivors fleeing their way. They knelt low, hidden behind bushes, their guns at the ready. Not many were likely to survive the bombing. Was Mark in the camp? Was he caught in the fire? Hugh had argued against the timing of the bombing. He requested that they wait a few more days until Mark was found. His arguments were brushed aside. "This is war," Bill reminded him. "Believe me, he is already dead."

Hugh signalled his men to stay in position. He took three with him to patrol the rear. They could not afford to be surprised from behind. They moved quickly, crouching low. Hugh took out his pistol. They negotiated the thicket of secondary growth. The sun shimmered through the dense overhead canopy of leaves. They reached a river. Hot air rose like steam from the marshy swampland. The smell of decay choked the air. He signalled his men to drop to their knees. The insurgents were familiar with the territory. They knew the swamplands like the back of their hands and could cross them with far greater ease than his platoon. He waited.

From across the river, he spied a movement. Hugh and his three men stayed absolutely still. Time ticked by. They waited, motionless. After a while a head appeared followed by another and then many, many more. Bare-chested men with loincloths. They were men of the jungle, *orang asli* they called them. Hugh hesitated. He was uncertain of their affiliation. His finger tightened on the trigger. He gave a slight nod to his men to be at the ready. Many of the jungle people supported the insurgents; some, however, had turned. One of them stepped forward. He stood, his sturdy legs planted wide apart, his loincloth barely covering his lower torso, and looked directly at Hugh.

"I have the white man," he said in Malay.

***

Ruth wrapped a towel around her body and walked barefoot into the bedroom. She felt better for the shower. She went to the mirror. She had lost weight. Her eyes stared back at her, cornflower blue eyes that Mark once said he loved. Yet they were not the same. They had lost their innocence. Instead, a shade of darkness lurked within them, the darkness of pain. She dropped the towel. Her collarbones stuck out like wings but her stomach was taut and lean and her small breasts rose pert and high. She had never had a voluptuous body. Now she was completely devoid of superfluous flesh. With an impatient toss of her head, she picked up the towel and began to dry her hair, rubbing her scalp roughly until it tingled. She brushed her hair and then went to the cupboard. She picked up the prettiest of the dresses she owned, a white cotton dress with blue periwinkle flowers that brought out the colour of her eyes. The dress fitted snugly at the waist and the skirt flared out to reach below her knees. Last night she had vowed to pull herself together and to dress up in case Mark returned. Only by thinking that he was alive and would return, could she maintain her sanity and continue to live. She must not let him see her despair. She must be beautiful for him; she could not allow him to compare her unfavourably with May when he returned.

"Ma'am! Ma'am!" Fu Yi cried hurrying into the room without knocking. "*Aiyah,* a gentleman to see you. Must be important. He came with bodyguards."

Ruth rushed to the window. She saw Bill at the door. True enough there were a couple of bodyguards by his car. Her heart sang. Did he have news, good news for her? She rushed out, almost tripping over the clothes strewn on the floor. "Bill!" she exclaimed her face expectant; a smile on her lips. His grave face stopped her in her tracks. Her mouth became suddenly dry; like sand devoid of any moisture. Her hand fluttered to her chest.

"Hello Ruth," Bill's voice was solicitous. He steered her to a chair and took one opposite her. Solemnly, he waited until she sat down.

"Mark? You've found him?"

He reached over and took her hand in his. Ruth felt his large hand stroking hers in a manner that made her uncomfortable. It was not like how Hugh had held her hands. She remembered Hugh's warning.

"No! We have not found him" Ruth could hear the ticking of the clock on the wall. She wondered if he could hear her heart beat. Her lips parted. She wanted to ask...

"In all probability he is dead."

Ruth flung his hand away. She huddled forward and crossed her arms to hug herself. "No! No! I would know if he had died." She thumped her chest. "Deep down I would have felt something. Instead I felt hope this morning, the first time since I came."

"I tell you because it is best to be prepared. We have bombed three camps. He could not have survived the bombing. We have recovered many bodies, all burnt to cinders. They were unrecognisable. We suspect that Mark must be one of those."

"No! No! Without seeing his body, I cannot accept it."

"It is better this way."

Ruth looked up in shock. "Better?"

"I know you think me cruel for saying this." Bill composed his face. He looked earnestly at her and took a deep breath. "It hurts me to say this again. Mark is a sympathiser; he would be tried for treason if he were found alive. So it is better this way."

"What are you saying? How dare you?" She stood up. Bill stood up at the same time and tried to place his hands on her shoulders. She hit him, her clenched fists raining on his chest over and over again. "Mark is not a traitor! How could you? I thought you were my friend."

"I am your friend. As your friend, I have come to help you."

"Help me? How? By accusing my husband of treachery?"

"By telling you the truth. I have all the evidence. I have already told you that May was his mistress. She disappeared at the same time as he did. May is an insurgent. He has been protecting her all the while. There is not a shred of doubt as to his transgression." He caught hold of Ruth's hand and brought it down, forcing her to come nearer to him. "I could help cover his misdemeanour."

Ruth pushed him way. She recalled again Hugh's warning. Bill, he had said, was not what he professed to be.

"I like you. I don't want you to be hurt. I somehow feel you are my responsibility. If you do not believe me, come with me. I'll show you the documents and evidence of Mark's misdeeds. That was one of the reasons why the Company asked for my help. That was the reason the Secret Service seconded me for this investigation."

Ruth froze. All moisture in her mouth sucked out of her.

Bill stretched out his hand. "Come. It is only a short ride to the rest house where I left the documents."

***

They drove in silence to the rest house. Ruth sat slumped in her seat. She had her eyes tightly shut throughout the journey. Only when the car came to a stop did she venture to open them.

"Come up with me," Bill said as he opened the car door. "They are in my room."

The rest house was almost deserted. Ruth assumed that most of the guests must be out on plantation or tin mine business. A handful of staff members were listlessly going about their tasks of tidying and sweeping. Ruth recognised the boy who had waited on her when she first set foot in the building with Hugh. The boy stared at her with open curiosity. Ruth's cheeks turned a deep pink. He must be wondering why I came with a different man.

"Thanks. I'll wait here in the lounge," she replied.

"You wouldn't want anyone to overhear our conversation or set eyes on the documents," Bill advised. "Come," he insisted and headed towards his room, stopping on the way to speak to a man.

She couldn't hear what Bill said but was conscious of the round-eyed look of surprise and shock that appeared on the man's face. Reluctantly she followed Bill.

"Where are the documents?" Ruth demanded the minute she stepped into Bill's room. She remained near the door, unwilling to go further in.

"*Ahh!* The ever-practical Ruth. Relax! Don't look so uptight. Won't you have a drink?" He went to where she stood and placed a hand at the small of her back. It lingered. She brushed it away.

"No! I don't want a drink. Just show me the documents."

With a deft movement of his hand, Bill reached behind her and shut the door. He locked it. Pocketing the key he swivelled to face Ruth. He hedged up close to her, so close, she could see the hair in his nostrils. His eyes glinted. She took a step back. He came closer still.

"The thing is, Ruth, what are you willing to do to have the evidence quashed? What is Mark worth to you? Even if he is dead, you wouldn't want his name to be tarnished." He bent to brush his lips on hers. Ruth could smell the whisky on his breath. She pushed him away. He grabbed her. "Don't act high and mighty with me. I have waited too long. I have watched over you, taken care of you during the voyage, appointed someone to look out for you on the bus. You treated me like dirt. Not once did you return my affection. You were, however, quite willing to accept my help. Help always comes with a price." He placed a hand round her neck. "Such soft skin," he murmured. He trailed his fingers down her neckline until they reached her cleavage.

She backed away, stumbling as she did so. "I'll scream."

"You won't. Everyone saw you coming with me willingly. I took the opportunity of tipping the houseboy. I told him we were noisy lovers, that you liked a bit of rough play. It is the middle of the day. No one is around in this god-forsaken place except the servants. Anyway if you do scream, all I need to do is this." He clamped her mouth with one hand and pushed her, steering her towards the bed. Ruth kept backing away. She felt the edge of the bed pressed against the back of her knees. She fell backwards, hitting the mattress. Bill was on top of her immediately, one hand still clamped on her mouth, the other ripping the buttons of her dress. She struggled. He lifted her skirt and slid his hand up her thigh, his fingers probing, no longer gentle...

"Mr Fletcher," a voice called from outside the room, "Sir, a telephone call for you. She says it is urgent."

"I told you we are not to be disturbed," Bill growled, holding Ruth firmly down. "I'll call whoever back ... later. Do not disturb me again. Understand!"

A brief silence followed. Bill sneered; he turned his attention once more to Ruth. He caught hold of her knickers. She twisted and kicked. Loud voices sounded from outside. Someone kicked the door. It crashed open. Startled, Bill loosened his grip on Ruth. She screamed. With two strides Hugh was by the bedside.

He pulled Bill off Ruth and threw him to the floor. "Take him away," he commanded his men.

***

"*Shhh! Shhh!*" Everything is going to be fine."

"How did you find me?" Ruth gulped, wishing to quell the sobs that threatened to surge.

"I went to the bungalow to tell you that we have found Mark. Fu Yi said that you had gone to the rest house with a man. I knew immediately from her description that it was Bill. When we arrived here, the attendants told me that Bill had taken you to his room. They smirked and repeated what Bill said. The rest, you know."

"I am so ashamed." Ruth shuddered.

"Why? Bill has a lot to answer for. Not you."

"And Mark? He is here?"

"He is in intensive care." Hugh placed a glass of water in Ruth's hand and lowered himself on to the bench in the visitors' room. He had driven Ruth straight to the hospital.

"He is not dead!" Ruth' eyes brimmed. "Bill said he was incinerated by bombs. He said Mark would be tried for treason, for aiding insurgents."

"Mark is not dead and he will not be tried for treason. He is, however, seriously ill. Prepare yourself. He does not remember much. He does not seem to know me. Don't get upset should he not recognise you."

Ruth's mouth trembled. So much had happened in one day. But Mark was alive. It was all that mattered. "Can I see him now?" she asked. Hugh nodded and stood up. They walked out of the visitors' room into the corridor. It smelt of disinfectant.

Someone had slopped Dettol on to the long cemented walkway. It was wet. An Indian *amah* was busy mopping up the liquid. She smiled; her white teeth gleamed against dark skin that shone like ebony. Ruth smiled back. Her heart swelled with emotion. She was to see Mark, finally. They pushed open the door. Mark lay in a narrow cot. His face was almost hidden by swathes of dressing. His eyes were closed. Behind the swollen and bruised eyelids, she could see a flutter of eye movements. Nothing could be seen of his body and limbs; a starched white cloth covered them. Around him was a paraphernalia of tubes. Bags of fluid and blood hung overhead.

Ruth went to him. "Mark," she said softly. She bent down to kiss him. Her lips brushed lightly the swathing. He groaned. A nurse came in.

"Mrs Lampard, your husband will not be able to speak to you. It is best to let him sleep."

"Can I stay with him?"

The nurse looked doubtfully at her. She went out and returned shortly. "Doctor says that the patient is best left to rest. The doctor wants to speak to you. Would you follow me?"

Chapter 13

Port Dickson

RUTH TUCKED THE blanket round Mark's knees. It was hot, but the wind was strong, and Mark was still weak. His eyes were closed. He had not spoken the whole day, even when she prompted him. She watched his eyelids quiver. He must be dreaming, she thought. It was as though the eyes behind their lids were darting from one corner to the other, in search of something. Sometimes he jerked, his arms and legs flailing wildly as if to ward off blows. What disturbed her most was his silence. It had been nearly two months since his rescue. If only he would speak to her. It would give her an indication of how much he remembered. He did not recognise her. The doctor had warned her of it, as had Hugh. Mark remembered nothing of his previous life. His face was blank when he saw Fu Yi. He did not ask for May. For that Ruth was glad. She was not going to mention May. They could start with a clean slate again. She would pretend that the nightmare of the past had never happened. For now she would concentrate on Mark's recovery. Dysentery, malaria and the beatings had taken a heavy toll. The doctor said that only time would tell if he would fully recover his memory.

Overhead, casuarina trees swayed. Long branches, heavy with wispy needle like leaves, trailed down to brush the beach. A swirl of patterns formed in their wake. Ruth sat back on the deck chair and looked out to the Straits of Malacca. The sea was choppy. White flecks of waves rippled through the waters and crashed on the shore only to withdraw, leaving scatterings of seashells and white froth. It was high tide. Soon the sun would sink into the horizon like a big ball of fire, red, hot and fiery. She would stay on the beach; she would wait until Mark woke up. Would he show a flicker of recognition this time when he opened his eyes? One night, she had kissed him gently on the lips to stir up his memory. He had merely smiled, an apologetic grin that tore her heart. She was a stranger to him. Would he ever remember her? Could they be the same as before? Perhaps it would be for the best. If he didn't remember; then he would also not remember May.

She sat watching her husband, hoping, praying for the impossible. From a distance, she saw Fu Yi approaching. The Company had given them the use of the beach bungalow in Port Dickson for Mark's recuperation. Once he was sufficiently well, they would return to England. Ruth sighed. It would be wonderful to go home. But what would Mark do when he got home? How was she going to earn a living? There were so many things up in the air.

Fu Yi waved. She seemed in a hurry to reach them. She tripped; a flip-flop flew off her foot. She stooped to pick it up and then took off the other. Her bare feet sunk into the soft white sand.

"Ma'am," she motioned Ruth to come to her. "I have news. They've found May."

Ruth placed a finger to her lip. She glanced hastily back at Mark. He was still asleep. He had not heard. She could see his head roll and jerk before his chin dropped once more to his chest. She beckoned Fu Yi to follow her and walked ahead back towards the bungalow. Her face was drained of colour behind the tan. When she reached the flight of steps that led up to the house, she turned. "Where is she?" she asked.

"I don't know. Probably being interrogated somewhere."

"Who told you? Who else knows?"

"The kind major that helped us. The one that asked me to call and to insist on speaking to that awful bad man."

"You are not to say anything to anyone. Not even the Master, especially the Master."

"But..."

"Please, Fu Yi, " Ruth pleaded, "I will speak to Major Hugh. It is best that I take all calls from now on. You are not to trouble Master."

Fu Yi's lips folded into a thin line. "Yes, Ma'am," she said.

Ruth watched Fu Yi climb up the flight of steps to the front door of the bungalow. Behind her the sun was fast sinking into the horizon. Its fading heat caressed her, filling her with a warm glow, like a lover. It made her tingle. How she had longed for such warmth during those cold winter nights in the farm in Somerset. It was beautiful in this corner of the world. On a clear day you could see the island of Sumatra across the Straits.

The crashing waves, the blue sky and white sand, the riot of bougainvillea bushes that seemed to sprout in every nook and cranny, were hypnotic. It was like a painting of paradise. Being here with Mark these past weeks had been wonderful despite his illness. She felt a twinge of regret. She was beginning to understand Mark's love of this country. But she would leave all this to have Mark back.

***

Fu Yi and the houseboy had retired to bed. It was a calm night. No rain was forecast. The sea was a sheen of darkness. A mile away, on the promontory, the twinkling town lights beckoned seductively. Mark glanced sideway at Ruth, his brow a mass of vertical furrows. He searched deeply for something he could hang on to, which could remind him of this woman called his wife. He was frustrated by the blank wall in his mind. It refused to yield up to him any clue to his past. Ruth had shown him a snapshot of herself, the one she said she had found in the bungalow. He could not recall anything. Frustration made him angry; he dreaded her asking him what he remembered. His response was silence.

He sat facing the sea. From time to time he turned to examine Ruth's face covertly. He was ashamed of his behaviour. She had been so caring and gentle with him during his weeks in bed. He reached out and took her hand. Ruth smiled in response, a smile that lit up her face and made her beautiful. She was beautiful, he suddenly realised. He wished he could remember more. "Give it time," the doctor had advised. "Don't force yourself and be worked up about it. It will come eventually." Mark drew a deep breath and squeezed Ruth's hand.

Ruth got up and knelt by his chair. She leaned over and kissed him on his lips. She smelt of roses in a warm summer's evening. Something in him stirred. This was the first time he associated Ruth with anything. Summer, roses! Surely, it was a memory of sorts? He drew her down again, wanting more, needing to know more. This time he kissed her back; his lips pressed urgently on hers. Ruth's lips parted. Mark's heart quickened; he kissed her more deeply, drinking in the moistness of her mouth. He held her head with both his hands. He felt her softness yielding to his touch. He released her and looked into her eyes. In the soft light, they were almost violet in colour. He stroked her neck and was suddenly filled with a longing. It aroused something in him, a primeval feeling in his loins that was familiar and welcomed. He half rose and Ruth rose with him. They remained locked in each other's arms.

"I love you," Ruth whispered.

"I still don't remember. When we kissed, it rekindled something in me, something tucked deep inside. I feel I should know you; somehow that our kissing is right."

"Come to bed," Ruth said drawing him close, her body against his. Mark could feel her breasts melting into him through her thin cotton dress. Every fibre in his body tingled. He felt alive.

"Are you sure?" His voice was husky.

"Yes, I am sure." Ruth buried her face in the nape of his neck. "If you cannot remember, we can start anew."

***

Ruth arranged to meet up with Hugh the following day. She took the bus into town. The little bus crunched to a stop just outside Port Dickson's market square. It was late morning.

Traders were dismantling their stalls and packing goods away. Only a handful of shoppers remained. Soon it would be too hot to hawk fresh meat or fish. Baskets of green vegetables were beginning to wilt under the relentless heat. The smell of fast-ripening fruits mingled with the salty tang of sea breeze blowing in from the sea. Ruth inhaled and caught a whiff of the salted shrimps drying in the sun. She smiled. Everything pleased her that morning. She meandered through the stalls and headed for the coffee shop. Hugh assured her that she could not miss it. The town was tiny; a row of shops behind the market square was all there was to it. It had started out as a Malay fishing village. The Malays called it '*Arang*' then, because of the charcoal. Now, he explained, it was mainly a port named after its founder, Frederick Dickson, a British civil servant. With the discovery of tin in the surrounding area of Lukut, large numbers of Chinese had flooded into the vicinity. The shops, two-storey terrace buildings, each boasting a shop on the ground floor and a place of residence on the floor above it, were all Chinese-owned. "They are called shophouses in this region. The coffee shop you would be looking for is owned by a Chinese man, nicknamed Fei Loh, Fatty. You would not miss him."

Ruth headed in the direction she was given. She stepped out of the market square and spotted it immediately. She was aware of the curious stares of locals squatted beside stalls or chatting in the byways. Her hair, left free and flowing, fluttered in the wind, framing her oval face like a golden flame. Sitting daily with Mark on the beach had given her a tan and her blue eyes sparkled with renewed vigour. She thought of the previous night. A blush rose to stain her cheeks. I must be strong, she told herself, and I must protect the love we share.

Within minutes she arrived in front of the coffee shop. Hugh was right. She could not miss Fatty. The proprietor had positioned himself by its entrance. He was unmistakable; his girth was like a barrel and his legs were like tree trunks. He had tied a white apron around his waist. Stains of black wove into the white fabric of the apron like writhing serpents. Ruth recognised the stains from Fu Yi's cooking. It was black soya sauce, thick like treacle and used liberally to flavour food. Underneath the apron he wore a thin white singlet and a pair of equally thin white cotton shorts. Those too were stained. When he saw Ruth staring, he pointed to the huge wok on a stove placed by the entrance. "*Char kway teow*?" he asked, his eyes disappearing almost into the folds of his cheeks when he smiled. "Fried with lovely blood cockles harvested just this morning."

Ruth shook her head. She didn't quite understand what was said but guessed it was an invitation to eat. "Thank you. I am looking for an English soldier, a Major Hugh Anderson."

"*Ahhh! Yup bin.* Inside, inside," he pointed, flashing white teeth. The toothpick at the corner of his mouth wobbled in affirmation.

***

From the dark recess of the coffee shop, Hugh watched Ruth approach. It was a different Ruth from the one he knew a mere two months ago. This new Ruth looked determined. The dazzling smile she had on her face made her vivacious, a word he would not have used to describe her when they had last met. He wondered what she had in mind when she called him late last night. The call had come through when he was in bed. She had sounded breathless; she told him not to come to the house and that she would meet him in town instead. She asked him not to speak to Mark. He had explained that he had made the journey from Kuala Lumpur specifically to speak to both of them, particularly Mark. "Please," her voice barely a whisper over the phone, "your news about May would upset Mark's delicate state of mind; it could push back the progress we have made. Let you and me talk first."

He rose at her approach and drew back a chair. "Thank you," she said, "I appreciate your seeing me."

"You look well. How is Mark?"

"Physically, he is improving. Mentally..." she shrugged, "... he does not remember."

"I have to speak to Mark; you know that. I have to tell him we have found May."

Ruth fell silent. She became tense like a coiled spring ready to pounce, the smile banished from her face. It was a different Ruth from a minute ago.

They could hear Fei Loh calling passers-by to try his noodles. The sizzling of his hot wok was like the sound of electricity in the charged atmosphere of their table. The smell of fried cockles blew into the coffee shop. Ruth raised her eyes to look straight into Hugh's. They were pleading.

"Mark does not remember anything. Telling him about May would destroy our marriage. It would fill him with guilt. He might leave me. Is that what you want?"

"Of course not. I am, however, obliged to tell him about May."

"Why? At the moment he does not know of her existence and what she was to him. He may never remember it. Why do you wish to dig it all up and cause him pain and me, our marriage?"

Hugh sighed. He was caught in an impossible situation. "I am his friend."

"Aren't I your friend too? Does May need Mark's testimony on her role in his kidnap? He can't provide it. He doesn't remember. It would be useless and would not stand up to scrutiny. Meantime, our private lives are exposed to the world. The newspapers will make hay out of it."

A heavy silence fell between them. Hugh wrestled with his conscience. He was torn between doing the right thing as an officer, doing the right thing for his friends and the right thing for May. He had never had a real conversation with May until these last few days. He saw her in a new light now. She was a young girl who had fallen in love and had acted on impulse. She was a victim of circumstances, just like Ruth. There was something in May that touched him. She was like a wounded fawn. Mark should bear responsibility for her situation.

"The doctor says that we can leave Malaya as soon as Mark is able to travel. The company will release him. They do not think Mark, with his amnesia, will be ready to return to his job. This is our chance to start afresh. Remember, Mark's testimony at present does not count for anything because he cannot remember. He may never do so. No one knows about his affair with May. Only you, Fu Yi and me. And Fu Yi has promised not to tell."

Hugh could see that Ruth's arguments were compelling. Mark would not be able to help May even if she needed it because he couldn't remember. Telling Mark about May could do what Ruth had said. It could break up their marriage. Moreover May was no longer a suspect. Her injuries and her help in identifying Chun and the men involved in the raid had allowed her to be cleared. The Government had granted her an amnesty. It was part of its new policy to win the hearts and minds of the people. There was to be no trial. He remained silent thinking ... thinking. What would May want, he asked himself. She had not spoken about Mark nor had she hinted at a wish to be with him.

"How did they find May?" Ruth asked.

"A patrol found her in a ditch in the jungle. She was badly beaten up. They brought her back to a station further north. She said that she had been abducted and beaten by Chun. She gave us his whereabouts, at least up to the point where they abandoned her."

"They believed her?" asked an astonished Ruth.

"Yes. She was able to identify his other accomplices. She blamed Chun for causing the death of her parents. They died shortly after being returned to their settlement. Her father's heart failed. The interrogation was the last straw. May was distraught. He was already weak and sending him back to the settlement with its food-rationing programme hardly helped. Her mother died soon after. She couldn't sustain the harsh conditions they were kept in when they were interrogated. She died of pneumonia." Hugh remembered delivering the news to May. She had cried silently burying her face in the palms of her hands.

Hugh watched Ruth's face as he explained. He could see that she was not convinced of May's innocence.

"May said that Chun wanted her to be his woman and abducted her for that reason. Look, Ruth. She was very discreet. She did not mention her relationship with Mark. You should give her credit for that. She was protecting Mark. She did not disappear willingly. She had extensive injuries. Chun's wife told us that Chun was May's cousin. We discovered later, through our China contacts, that he made the story up to entice May's parents to entrust May to him." Hugh paused. "With Bill discredited, May will not face problems from that quarter. Bill has been sent back to England where he is likely to be court-martialled."

"So she is free." Ruth was incredulous. She was not ready to forgive May. Her face was hard. Hugh was keeping something from her. May had enticed him as she had Mark.

"Yes!"

"Then she does not need Mark's testimony." Ruth grabbed hold of Hugh's hand. "Please leave us out of this. Help us."

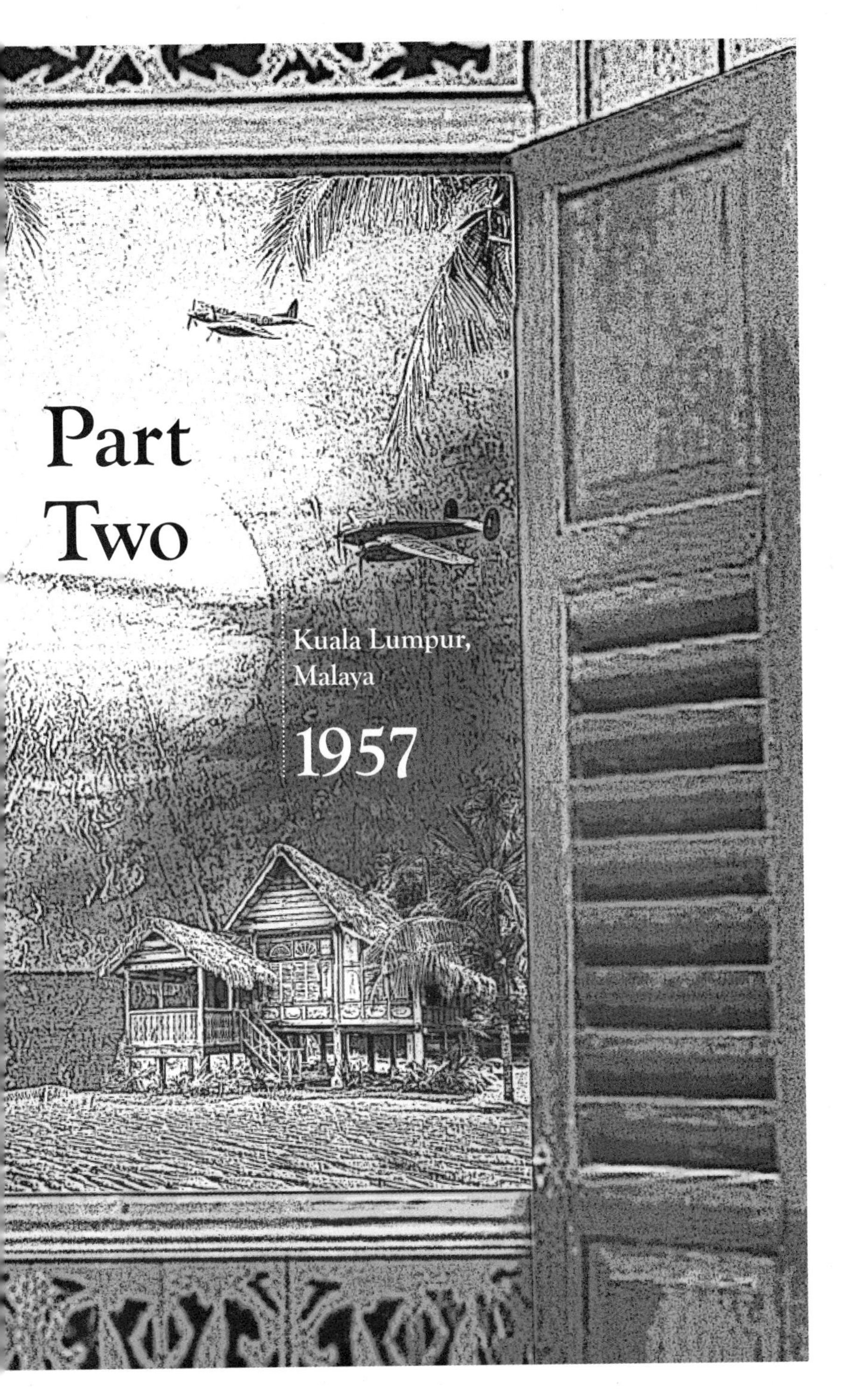
Part
Two
Kuala Lumpur,
Malaya
1957

Chapter 14

The room had no standing space. Under slow revolving ceiling fans, men in black-tied formal suits mingled with those in colourful long-sleeved batik shirts. Such shirts were fast becoming the norm in Malaya. It was a gesture of defiance, a break from colonial times. Suits and ties were history. They evoked too much of the past, of a country subservient to Britain. Some chose to wear short sarongs over silk trousers. Thus east and west stood side by side, incongruous in their attempt at harmony. A desperate air of gaiety filled the air. The men grouped together with drinks in hands. Glasses clinked. Conversations were conducted in urgent whispers; laughter was gruff and strained.

In the fringe, standing separate from the men, Malay women in long sarongs and diaphanous embroidered tops chatted alongside Chinese ladies in slim-fitting cheongsams with side slits that revealed shapely legs. Indian women wore silk saris and cholis showing bare midriffs. Fewer in numbers they were dispersed among the different groups that formed and broke-up. The women spoke with singsong cadence. Their tinkling laughter rose and fell. A band played sentimental songs. A Malay song was followed by a Chinese ballad and an English tune. It was necessary that each race in the room was equally represented. The women eyed one another, each not willing to be the lesser. The atmosphere was thick with suspense and rivalry. Already the swords were out amongst the men and the women knew where their loyalty lay.

May wove her way through the crowd, stopping to talk to one and then hastening to another. She eyed a waiter and indicated that he should refill the glasses. A boy stood at a corner with a tray of canapés. May made urgent gestures to him to distribute them. She beamed and nodded; glad that it would be one of the last, if not the last, cocktail party that she had to oversee. She was thankful for the time spent in mastering etiquette and elocution. She shuddered to think what she would be without them. At least now she could deal with diplomats and people from all walks of life without feeling shy. She squeezed through the throng of people and made for the terrace. The French windows were thrown open and some of the crowd had moved on to the paved area, spilling out to the garden beyond. A cool breeze stirred. She caught the scent of jasmine in the air. She inhaled its perfume, breathing deeply and expelling it slowly. She needed the calm. She needed to have a moment alone.

"Everything okay?" Hugh asked. "I saw you heading this way and wondered." He came to her side and touched her briefly on her bare arms.

"Fine. You go back to the guests and I'll join you in a minute. My feet are killing me." May looked at her feet shod in silver high-heeled sandals. Her toenails gleamed a burgundy red, the colour of her cheongsam.

"Such talk amongst our guests. Some speak as though we have already left. We have at least two months to go before Malaya's independence." A note of exasperation crept into Hugh's voice.

"Will the transfer of power be smooth?"

"The alliance between the Malays, Chinese and Indians will win, I am sure of that. In that sense, the transfer will be smooth. It will not be long now before we see them wield real power and who knows what will happen then? There has been such discord between them. Will they be able to mend their differences and work together? Have we been too precipitate in our decision to leave?"

May knew Hugh's anguish. She had no answers to the questions he raised. She could not concentrate on his words. All she felt was his presence and his breath on her neck. Her thoughts switched to Mark. She blushed with guilt. How could she think of Mark on a night like this? She berated herself. She must stifle all thoughts of the past. Mark was her first love and she would never forget him. It was Hugh, however, who had given her back her life. It was Hugh who had sustained her through those terrible months of suffering. She loved Hugh. She took his hand and pressed it against her lips. She forced herself to the present.

"It will not be your problem soon," she comforted. She ran her fingertips lightly on his cheeks. "Don't take it so hard. The tide is changing. India, Burma, now Malaya. Life goes on. It always does, perhaps not how we expect or wish it to be, but it works out itself. Sometimes it is even for the better. Like you and me.

At times, I still wake up terrified. The jungle and the horrors of the killings that I have seen crowd my mind. Then I look at you by my side." May sighed. "Everything becomes good."

Hugh beamed. May was always able to distil to the essence of things. "I'll circulate before the guests come searching for me."

"Yes, do. I shall go and check on Craig." May raised herself on her toes and brushed Hugh's lips with hers.

Someone guffawed loudly from across the terrace. "Such affection! I don't kiss my wife; kissing one means kissing all the others." Hugh's response was a strained smile. He knew the man's reputation. He had a harem of women. He would ignore the comment; the man probably had one too many.

May slipped back through the French windows into the crowded room. It was distinctly warmer in there. Some guests had loosened their neckties; others stood stoically, face flushed, with beads of perspiration on their brow and a sheen on their nose. A strong smell of alcohol rose to greet her, drowning the sweet undertone of boiled syrup flavoured with rose water drunk by the ladies. Perfume masked the muted odour of sweat. The level of noise grew; each person vied to speak above the other. The singer had given up belting out ballads and sat behind the band mopping her brow. May walked quickly through the lounge and made for the stairs.

***

Upstairs was quiet compared to the din on the floor below. May pushed open the door to the left of the landing. It swung open with a creak, like bones grinding together. It jarred her nerves. She made a mental note that something had to be done. Perhaps the amah could put some grease on the hinges.

With great care, she tiptoed into the room and closed the door behind her, wincing again at the sound it caused. In the quiet it seemed an exaggerated ear piercing noise.

"Mummy," cried Craig. He was still up with a blanket drawn to his chest. "I was waiting for you. Have you time to read with me?" He switched on the bedside lamp and flooded the room with light.

May sat down on the bed sideways and then turned to face Craig. Her heart melted at the sight of her tousle-haired son. "Yes! Just one chapter. I have to be with the guests." She slipped off her sandals and swung her legs up on to the bed. She took the book and settled down with one arm draped around Craig. At times like this, she felt her heart could burst with happiness. Without warning, she crushed Craig to her and kissed him soundly on the cheek.

Craig ducked. "Mummy! No! My friends don't allow their mummies to kiss them any more. Promise you won't do it when they are around."

"I promise. I'll only do it when we are on our own. Why don't you read to me and we'll see how well you do it."

"All right." He picked up the book and turned the pages until he found the chapter where he had left off.

May cuddled him closer, smelling the soapy tang from his bath. Her mind drifted as he read.

"Mummy, Mummy are you listening?" Craig shook his mother's arm. "I asked if Daddy was a soldier like the man in this book?"

"Yes, daddy was a soldier. Not any more. Not for a long while. Not after you were born. We came to Kuala Lumpur and he took a new job."

"A more important one than being a soldier?"

"Yes! Yes, I believe so, a more important job. Certainly a job he feels more comfortable with. You'll understand when you are older. Soldiering didn't suit him as much, at least when his heart was not in the policies that were being pursued."

"What policies? What do you mean?"

"I'll explain when you are older. For now, we have to close the book. I have to go downstairs. I'll come back again in a little while." She kissed Craig on his forehead and switched off the light.

***

It was well past midnight when the last of the guests left. The servants began clearing the room of glasses and bottles. Ashtrays filled with cigarette stubs were emptied and a semblance of normality returned. Tomorrow the chairs would be put away and the floors cleaned and the terrace sluiced down. Hugh sent the servants to bed. Linking arms with May, he stepped out in to the garden. It was too hot indoors and the air was stale with the aftermath of cigarette smoke, sweat and alcohol.

"We won't host any more parties after this one, at least not such a large one. The idea was to bring the various political factions together to talk more openly before full independence takes place. It will happen. Two months to go; 31 August is just round the corner."

"I am glad. What will happen to us?"

"Do you want to go to England?" Hugh held May's shoulders, marvelling at the smoothness of her skin.

"I want what you want. The British High Commission would be reduced in size wouldn't it? Isn't it possible that you might be sent back?"

"Yes," Hugh replied. "The opportunities for remaining in Malaya are limited. Expatriate presence in this country will be reduced substantially. This will happen even in the private sector. No one has told me directly. Malayans are very polite and rarely say things you don't want to hear straight to your face. It is clear from the political grapevine that Malayans will fill the posts vacated by expatriates, even in the private sector. Private firms, even Sime Darby, Guthries, the Chartered Bank have been told to reduce their expatriate staff. In one instance from a hundred to three! In this, the Tunku, the Prime Minister-to-be, has the support of the others in his party." Hugh's face became serious. "When these posts are vacated, knives will be drawn as to how they will be distributed amongst the different ethnic groups. The back-stabbing will begin."

May could feel the blood rushing to her head. She hardly registered Hugh's rendition of the political climate. The idea that they might have to leave Malaya came first and foremost in her mind. She had meant it when she said that she wanted what Hugh wanted. Yet she had never left Malaya; she had never been to England. Now that it is imminent, the thought filled her with trepidation.

"So it is likely that we would leave." It came out more a statement than a question.

"You will be fine in England." Hugh saw the doubt in her face.

"And Craig?" she asked.

"Craig will be fine too. He will benefit from schooling there."

"And Mark? Will we come across him in England? What happens if we were to meet and he sees Craig?" May's lips trembled.

"Craig is my son. Mark had no idea that you were carrying his baby when he left Malaya. Nothing since then has altered my belief that this is still true. Look, May, England is a big country. Our paths are unlikely to cross. Don't worry until there is something to worry about."

Hugh drew her into his arms. May's tininess never failed to astonish him. He could span her waist with the palms of his hand. It made him feel protective. When she had been found in a ditch in the jungle, almost dead and then subjected to harsh interrogation, he had sworn that he would make sure Mark took responsibility. Ruth had dissuaded him. Filled with guilt, he had looked after May; it had been his way of redressing his guilt. With time he had fallen in love with her. He might not be Craig's biological father but he was father to him in every other way. He loved Craig. He placed his chin on top of May's head. Moonlight lit up the garden and the scent of gardenias filled his lungs. He kissed May, tilting up her chin to do so. Her cheeks were damp with tears. "Everything will be fine," he assured her.

Chapter 15

HUGH AND MAY stood in the grounds of the Selangor Club squashed amongst the hundreds who had turned up for the ceremony. Across the field the Prime Minister designate, Tunku Zikri Rahman, arrived. He stepped out of the car. A cheer went through the jam-packed street. The lights went off and darkness fell like a silken screen. Absolute silence followed; people stood to attention. Hugh took May's hand in his. A lump rose in his throat. The clock struck midnight and the lights returned to flood every corner of the street. The Union Jack came down and the Malayan Flag went up. Shouts of "*Merdeka*" pierced the night sky! Independence! Freedom! The crowd went wild with jubilation. May threw a furtive glance at her husband. She saw the emotion in his face, the slight trembling in the corner of his lips. She squeezed his hand. "This is it," he said looking at her upturned face. "This marks the tide of change which will sweep us with relentless energy in the months and years to come."

They made their way back into the club, a mock Tudor building with white washed walls set in a wooden framework. The celebrations would continue till the early hours of the morning, when a formal ceremony would be held in the *Merdeka* Stadium. Britain would formally hand back power to the new Prime Minister, Tunku Abdul Rahman. Here in this club with its European members, the celebration would be muted, more commiseration than joy. Hugh looked at the glum faces of his colleagues. He understood their feelings. For many the future was uncertain. Years of negotiation for independence had dragged on with seemingly no end. People had got used to it. Then suddenly the end came upon them as if they had no forewarning. Typical, he thought bitterly. We always seem to underestimate the tide of feelings against us. He would like to stay on if possible. He had a lot of unfinished business in Malaya. He wanted to do more. He was sure he could serve Britain's interest if he stayed on. He remembered saying that Malaya was like an intoxicating drug. It was certainly so for him. Moreover, he knew May would like to stay on despite her assurance that she would live in England if he so wished. He knew his wife's love for her country of birth.

"Stay and mingle," he said to May. "I have to speak to the British High Commissioner. I'll come for you."

Left on her own, May was uneasy. She saw a group of acquaintances standing by the bar. They beckoned her over when they saw her. She hesitated a moment and then walked over to join them.

"Gosh, you look lovely this evening May," Andy said ignoring the sharp nudge in the ribs he received from his wife. Deborah was not pleased. She glared at May. May looked away. Deborah curled her lips in derision. A faint line of perspiration appeared on her upper lip. "May is always well turned out. She has to be. Haven't you?" she sneered forcing May to engage with her.

"What do you mean?" May asked. She was uncomfortable under the cold gaze of the woman in front of her. Deborah had clearly had one too many to drink. Her face was flushed and her half-exposed bosom heaved with the effort of speaking. It was not the first time that May had insults thrown at her. There was a clear demarcation between 'them' and 'us' amongst the wives of the Commission's staff. The 'us' were the pure undiluted English or at least Europeans; the 'them' would be non-whites married to Englishmen. May almost sighed in resignation with these thoughts. It was to be expected. A few years back, she might not even have been allowed into the club. Just five years ago the Malay Sultan himself was barred from attending a St George's Society dinner at the Lake Club in his own state. In Singapore, Committee members in the Tanglin Club were known to complain when European members brought in Asian guests.

Deborah sniffed and waved her whisky and soda at May. "*Stengah*," she drawled, which meant half-half, a term used to describe her drink in hand but also meant half-caste. "Don't you have to make an extra effort to keep your men ensnared?"

Andy took his wife's arm and tried to usher her away. "Enough! You have had enough!" He bowed apologetically to May.

Deborah shook his hand away and lurched to the side, spilling the drink on herself. Her cleavage glimmered with the drops that landed. "I am only saying what is true. Didn't you work for Mark of Harrisons and Crosfield before? You were a servant then, weren't you? Why do you steal our men? Why can't you go with your own?"

Blood rushed to May's head. Her face turned red. She couldn't speak.

"By the way," Deborah waved gaily, her plump hand raised high, spilling more of the liquor on the floor. "Mark is with his wife. I met them when I went to England on home leave. He made no mention of you at all. You are forgotten!"

May turned. She fled to the restroom. She went into one of the cubicles and locked herself in. She doubled over and retched into the bowl. She couldn't bring herself to go back to the lounge. A door slammed shut. Several women came in; they spoke loudly compelling her to listen. Spirals of cigarette smoke rose like whirls of clouds and flooded into her cubicle. She stifled her need to cough.

"Deborah has definitely overstepped herself. Her husband is furious with her."

"Well, it needs to be said. I don't know this Chinese woman. I dare say she deserves it. Fancy taking two of our men. If it was just one, perhaps one could overlook it. But two? What is there to stop her from pinching ours? Anyway, I don't like the idea of having them in our club. It would never have happened a year ago."

Hugh found May seated by herself when he returned. He knew that something had gone amiss. He glanced over his shoulder. He could hear sniggering. He got up ready to confront the men and women who had been whispering and glancing their way.

May stopped him. "Don't! Please! I would like to go home," she said.

***

Somewhere a clock chimed two o'clock in the morning. May couldn't settle down. Overhead the fan whirred laboriously creating shadow-plays on the wall. The women's words rang in her ears. She was not unfamiliar with prejudice. Nevertheless it still hurt. And it was particularly vicious tonight. Wouldn't it be worse if she went to England with Hugh? Wouldn't the prejudice be more widespread when English people outweighed the number of people like herself? Would Craig suffer because he had a Chinese mother? Perhaps she, May, should not return to England with them. If Hugh was adamant that Craig should receive an English education they could perhaps send him to a boarding school. No one need know that Craig's mother was Chinese. He looked English and unless he stood next to her, no one would know. Yet how could she bear to lose her son that way?

She turned on to her side and drew her knees up to her chest. Next to her Hugh slept on. His soft breathing filled the room. May crept closer to him. She wrapped her arms around him and snuggled into his back. She needed him. She needed his assurance that he loved her and that everything would be all right. Hugh snored and turned around to fold her in his arms. "Hugh," she whispered. He was in a deep asleep. Whatever she wanted to say would have to wait till morning. She stayed in his arms, breathing in his breath, feeling the warmth of his body until light streamed through the window.

***

"Are you going to tell me what happened?" Hugh pushed away the plate of fried eggs that the *amah* had placed before him. The sight of the yolks gleaming in oil made him nauseous. Instead he gulped down a cup of black coffee. May had not spoken a word all morning. He did not wish to make her uncomfortable by pressing for an answer. He flicked open the newspaper. He did not read it. Covertly he studied his wife under his lashes. She was beautiful even with reddened eyes. He had been upset to find her almost in tears at the Club, sitting on her own in a corner surrounded by a noisy loud-mouthed crowd. He should not have left her on her own. He should have anticipated that she would be subjected to snide remarks. Didn't they know that racial slights such as those that they had shown to May and others had been powerful goads to the nationalist struggle? Obviously not! Even after the lowering of the Union Jack! Thickheads. Not every one behaved like that but it took just a few to spoil it for everyone.

"I think I know what happened. They bullied you?" he said without taking his eyes off the newspaper headline: *Merdeka. A new nation was born on the stroke of Friday midnight...*

"They said some horrible things. I am frightened. I am scared to go to England. I... I know that I said I will but now..." She stopped unable to go on.

Hugh reached over and took her hand. It lay limp in his palm. He brought it to his lips. "We don't have to go immediately, at least for a while. The Commissioner has asked me to stay on. I'll stay if you wish to remain here. It will give us some reprieve to plan and think. I am to be the British planters' representative to take care of their interests in Malaya. Things are changing very quickly. There is talk that state-owned enterprises would be formed to buy us out. We will have to fight hard to maintain our interests. This post is a good opportunity for us. With the 'Malayanisation' of vital posts, others interested in staying on will work as subordinates to those whom they have previously supervised. Not in my case. As a representative, I will be pretty much my own man. I am lucky in that I speak Malay and Chinese fluently."

"And Craig?" May asked. Will he stay with us here?"

"I think it might be best if he goes to a boarding school in England. He will benefit from better schooling. It is best to prepare him young. In the end England will be his home, as I hope it will be yours."

May's lips trembled. She had thought about the very thing last night. Now that it was a reality, it hurt. Her heart felt as though a stone had been tied round it and she was drowning.

"He'll come back for his holidays and we will visit him." Hugh drew May to him. "Or would you rather we all leave for England?" he whispered in her ear.

May thought of the encumbrance she would be for her husband and son in England, of the prejudice they might face on account of her. She knew too that Hugh's career was better served in Malaya, where he was an important man. In England he would be one of the many returnees for whom a placement needed to be found. Most important, Craig would have a good education in England. "No," she replied, "let Craig go." She tried to rearrange her face and smiled. But her lips quivered.

Hugh held her close. He could hear her heart beat against his. He could not bear her suffering.

"We could of course leave the matter a few years. Craig is still very young. I suppose it might make more sense to send him when he is slightly older. We would know our situation better by then."

May looked up. Relief and gratitude shone in her eyes. "Are you sure?"

"Yes!" Hugh affirmed. "The more I think about it the more inclined I am to postpone the matter. So much uncertainty lies ahead for British expatriates in Malaya. Even British banks are having a hard time. Their attempts to expand operations into the smaller towns and outlying states have already been blocked. So who knows what the future has in store for us? So let's know where we will be before we make any major decisions."

Chapter 16

London

RUTH WAS EARLY. They had arranged to meet in Green Park. She spotted an empty bench and went straight to it. She sat down and placed her handbag by her side to discourage anyone from taking the seat beside her. She closed her eyes and raised her face. Dappled sunlight made its way through the overhead branches to touch her cheeks. Images of leaves flitted about on her skirt. Despite the warmth, she was chilled to the bone. Perhaps this would be the last time they should meet. She had told herself many times that she should end all contact with Steve. Yet they had continued meeting in secret. As time went on, she had found it more and more difficult to extricate herself. It would have been possible at the beginning of their affair. Now, she sighed, it had become impossible. Or was it?

She felt his hand on her shoulder, familiar and possessive.

"Sorry I am late. The students were particularly difficult. I am afraid I don't have as much time as I said earlier. One of the teachers was taken ill. I have been given charge of the after-school activities this afternoon." Steve bent to kiss her.

Ruth dodged. "Don't! Someone might see."

"I am past caring about other people. Maybe we should chuck the past away and start anew; as a couple, properly." He sat down beside her, her bag squashed between them.

"We have been through this many times. Would you leave your wife?"

"Would you leave Mark?" he retorted.

They avoided eye contact and looked ahead instead, watching yet not seeing the milling crowd. There were women pushing prams, women walking with children hand in hand and men clutching brief cases hastening to their next appointments. A group of teenage girls strolled by; one broke off from the rest and did a cartwheel; her skirt fell over her bodice revealing panties and stockings. Someone whistled. The girls giggled and hurried away. At a distance, a car sounded its horn and a red London bus ploughed through the busy street. An old lady dropped a scrap of paper into the litter bin; the wind caught it and it flew, rising and falling, rising and falling until it disappeared.

Ruth's thoughts were bitter. I would never be able to walk in this park or any park with Steve and our child. He must never know about Libby. Ruth folded her lips and glanced sideways at Steve. He was drumming his fingers and whistling a tune beneath his breath. How could he be so oblivious of my feelings, she wondered.

"My class is going on a school trip this mid-term. If you can arrange to have your class join us, we could carve out some time for ourselves. What do you say?" Steve did not like it when Ruth became pensive. He felt excluded. Life was too short to spend time on regretting. One should grab at life with both hands.

"I'll see," she replied. How different it had become. They had first met a year after her return to England with Mark. The affair had started like a whirlwind romance, exciting because it was forbidden; a secret. She was a new staff member in the school. Steve took her under his wing. Their coupling had been intense, a reprieve from the oppression she had begun to feel at home. Their stolen moments, secret rendezvous, candlelit dinners and short trips to the seaside gave her new life. She had craved for love; she had waited and waited for Mark; she had waited for him to remember her. But Mark remembered nothing of what she had been to him and showed little of what she meant to him at present. Despite her efforts he was distant. His initial attempts to start anew fell by the wayside. He was easily frustrated. His annoyance manifested itself in long spells of silence. He was morose one day and truculent on another. He retreated within himself. He drank. Yet she could not leave him, as Steve could not leave his wife. She needed Mark to be a father to Libby. Moreover, deep down, she still loved him.

"Try," Steve pleaded. He took her hand and surreptitiously hid it between them under the folds of her skirt.

***

The lights were on when Ruth reached home. She dropped the shopping bags at the porch and unlocked the door. She could hear Libby's squeals of laughter. It brought an immediate smile to her face. She picked up her bags and pushed the door open with her shoulder. "I'm back," she called. Libby ran out like a torpedo and clasped Ruth round her waist, almost knocking the bags off her. Her brown curls were like an unruly mop thrust into her mother's midriff. She jumped up and down unmindful of her mother's desperate attempt to hang on to the bags of shopping.

"Mummy, mummy I got my report card. Teacher says I am a good girl. I got an A for reading."

Ruth untangled herself. She squatted down and kissed Libby. "How wonderful! I am so proud of you. Let's see what treats I have in store. Come help me unpack these." She led the way into the kitchen. A dim light shone from the ceiling. Plates and cups lay unwashed by the sink. A stale smell of sausages and beans pervaded the air. The pan and saucepan were still on the stove. Thick streaks of tomatoes and grease covered them. The room had such a desolate air that she wanted to scream. She stood for a moment transfixed by the floral wallpaper greying at its seams and the linoleum floor patched in parts. Only Libby sustained her. Her thoughts went back to Malaya. Given half the chance she would go back there, a country that she was in such a hurry to leave.

"Where is daddy?" Ruth asked.

Libby lifted the carrots from the bag and put them in a basket. Then she took out the potatoes and placed them alongside. Her lips were pursed and her face a picture of concentration. She lifted her big brown eyes. "Daddy is not well. He is in the sitting room. I made him a mug of tea. He didn't want it."

"Stay here. I'll go and see him." Ruth wiped her hands on the kitchen towel and went to the sitting room. Mark was seated in an armchair in front of the television, a glass in his hand and a woollen blanket across his knee. Beside him was a half empty bottle of whisky.

"Are you not well?" she asked.

Mark didn't answer. He huddled into the blanket, drawing it closer around him. The pinched look on his face had become familiar to Ruth; it accused her of neglect. She resented it as much as she pitied Mark. She held her tongue to stop the sharp words that threatened to spill out. She walked briskly to him and placed a hand on his forehead. He smelt of alcohol. Mark flinched. He glowered at her. Anger made his eyes light up with sudden vitality. Then, as suddenly as it came, it vanished.

"Just bored."

She wanted to shake him. If he was bored why then did he not do something? Help with the housework at least. "Moping doesn't help," she said gently instead.

"I feel useless. I should be the one out working, not you. The company won't take me back. They have discarded me like a rag doll. I just can't seem to find another post. It would appear everything has moved on and I am left standing."

Ruth lowered herself until her eyes were level with his. She searched for something to say, something sympathetic that would comfort him. "I don't mind working. You have been unwell and jobs are difficult to come by. In any case you do help, you help with minding Libby." She stopped. Even to her own ears the words sounded banal and forced.

Mark turned away. "That is not a job." He could not recall what had happened in Malaya. It frustrated him. He was supposed to have spent the best part of his working life in that country. England with its cold dark days was alien to him. Yet the period leading up to his rescue was missing from his memory. When he asked Ruth, she was evasive and told him even less. He suspected she knew more than she divulged. There were no pictures or photographs of that time that could awaken his memory. Ruth assured him that everything was lost. She had been so happy and patient with him in the early days of their return. No longer! He knew he was at fault. He was often sickly with the recurrence of malaria. This and the frustration of being unemployed, of not remembering, of feeling unwanted made him difficult. It was a relief when she found a job. He couldn't stand her fussing around him. Then Libby arrived. With Libby, he had at least a role at home, of being a parent, the carer. Guilt washed over him. He was not much of a carer, not since she had started school.

"I am sorry. Leave me be. I'll be fine in a moment." Mark smiled feebly.

Ruth got up. "I'll make dinner," she said, turning away to hide her tears. Was this what she had fought so hard for? She had hated May. She had been so happy that Mark's memory of her was completely wiped away. It had carried with it, however, a penalty, a penalty that was becoming harder and harder to bear. For Mark was no longer the Mark she had once loved. In forgetting May, he had also forgotten her.

***

In Camden Town, Steve was washing up after dinner. He smiled broadly at Margaret beside him. "There," he said looking down at her, "we have finished. He handed her the last plate to dry. "I can tidy up here. Go to the sitting room and I'll bring a cup of tea in."

Margaret placed the glistening plate on the rack. She wheeled her chair around and went out, leaving ajar the adjoining door to the sitting room. Steve busied himself stacking the plates and dishes in the cupboards. Next he stored the pots and pans neatly on the shelves below the sink. The kitchen resonated with the clinking sounds of pots and pans.

"So what have you been doing today?" he asked. He filled the kettle and placed it on the hob.

"Nothing much. I knitted. Our neighbour Mary came over for a chat and a cup of tea. She bought milk for us and got you your newspaper. She is a dear lady. I do not know what I would do without her."

The kettle whistled; Steve jumped because his thoughts were far away. He was busy planning how to broach the subject.

"Would you mind if I took my class out on a school trip for the weekend during mid-term? Mary can come over and check up on you can't she? I will make a stew and leave it in the fridge. It will be just for a night."

Music floated in from the next room. Margaret had put on a record. "I hear the cotton woods whispering above. Tammy, Tammy..." Debbie Reynolds sang.

"Yes, of course. Enjoy yourself," shouted Margaret above the song. "Is that lovely young woman, Ruth, going as well? She went the last time didn't she? You said she was very helpful."

Steve could feel his heart pounding. The blood rushed to his face. He was thankful that they were not in the same room. Did she know, he wondered. Was that why she had mentioned Ruth? He could not speak for a moment, wondering if Margaret was just testing him, fishing because she was suspicious. He poured hot water into the mug. It splashed onto his shirt. "Damn!" he exclaimed. "Sorry dear. I made a mess in the kitchen. I do not know if Ruth is coming. She may. It depends on what the headmaster says."

He could hear Margaret humming to the tune. He sighed with relief. It did not look as though she was suspicious. He felt guilty for cheating on Margaret. He loved her. As for Ruth, he didn't know if he loved her except that he needed her, at least for now. She gave him what Margaret couldn't. If that was love, then he loved both, though in different ways. He stirred some milk into the tea and popping a custard cream on a saucer, he brought it to his wife.

Chapter 17

STEVE WAITED FOR about twenty minutes after the children had gone to bed. He eased open his bedroom door and went in search of Ruth. She was on the next floor. He hurried up the stairs. Her room was the first at the corner, just off the stair landing. A rubber band would be wound round the door handle if it were safe for him to go in. He stood for a moment looking left and then right and then back again. The coast was clear. Heaving a sigh of relief, he knocked, a hesitant rap.

The door opened. He slipped in and locked the door. Ruth stood slightly dazed. Not a word passed between them. Instead, he took her in his arms and kissed her urgently. Her body responded. She found herself drowning in the urgency of his kisses. He pushed her towards the bed, pulling her blouse off and then her skirt. The garments pooled round her feet. She reached down and rolled down her stockings, her movements frantic. He shrugged off his shirt and then his pants. They fell on the bed. A moan escaped her lips as he kissed her breasts. "Quickly," she moaned. She arched her back and pressed her body against him, relishing its hard muscular maleness. It was as if a void had opened up in her, a void that needed to be filled. She felt intoxicated, like a drunk, insatiable. Each thrust of his manhood, each touch, and each kiss an overwhelming balm to her loneliness. She bit her hand to stop her moans.

Much later they lay on the bed. They shared a cigarette. Steve blew smoke rings; his eyes were half closed and their lids heavy. Thick brown eyelashes cast shadows on his cheeks. The air was saturated with the smell of sex and sweat. Ruth pushed herself up. The sheet fell open exposing her breasts. She saw the teethmarks around her nipples. She looked around her; the clothes were in a tangle on the floor. The sheets were stained and crumpled. Her eyes fell on Steve. There was a satisfied knowingness in his face. He pursed his lips to draw deeply on the cigarette. The act jolted her. Disgust took over. She threw the sheets off completely and, still seated on the edge of the bed, began dressing. She ran her fingers through her hair. "You'd better leave. I can't do this anymore. We have to stop. It is not fair on my husband nor on your wife."

Steve reached over and grasped her shoulder. "*Heh!* What's got into you? Wasn't it good? I thought you enjoyed it. If you didn't then you were a pretty good actress."

She pushed him away.

"For goodness sake," he growled, taken back by the furious expression on her face, "you should have thought about them a long time ago."

Ruth shook off his hand. She was angry. He was right. Self-loathing and anger made her lash out at him. She swung round and pushed him on the chest. "It was a mistake. We should have stopped a long time ago. In fact it should never have started. I am sorry. Please leave. I don't want to see you again, not like this."

She walked to the pile of clothes and picked them up. She threw his at him. "Get dressed."

He got up and pulled on his clothes, first his pants and then his shirt. He grabbed the socks off the floor and stuffed them into his pockets. Throwing her a look of pure venom, he pushed his bare feet into his shoes. She waited until he finished. They did not speak. Then she walked with what dignity she could muster to the door and opened it.

***

Mark stared at his image in the mirror. His face was a maze of lines he had not noticed before. Deep ruts ran vertically from either side of his nose. How had he become this old man looking back at him? He not only looked old; he was unkempt. The beard and unruly hair turned him into a tramp. It made him far older than his forty years. What shocked him were his eyes. They were the eyes of a corpse, bereft of joy and distinguished only by the dark bags under them. He blinked several times willing them to show life. Self-pity, he realised, was the cause of it all. It had eaten into his soul. It had destroyed his self-esteem and his marriage. No wonder Ruth was disenchanted. How could he blame her? She disguised it well but he could see through her. He spied it on her face when she thought he was not looking. Ruth's absence had given him time to reflect. He must make a fresh start. He had made such resolutions before. This time he would see it to its end.

He ran hot water into the basin and began soaping his face. He shaved, systematically and meticulously removing all the hair on his face until his skin shone. He took a pair of scissors and began snipping. Hair fell in soft piles on the floor. His bare feet were covered with them. Still he kept on until he could see his neck and ears. He grinned at the face that looked back at him. Not perfect but much better. He stepped into the bath allowing the water to sluice over him, luxuriating in the heat. He watched the bath turn from clear to chalky grey. He felt reborn. It was the utter disgust on Ruth's face when she left for her trip that prompted him to search deep into himself. If he could not remember, he could at least start anew. That was what Ruth had wanted and what he had promised; he had failed her. He had failed Libby, their child.

He dressed with care. His eyes rested on the opened letter on the dresser. He had not told Ruth about it. He did not want to disappoint her again. He would tell her later.

***

It was grey and cold by the time evening came. What had begun as a lovely sunny spring day had changed dramatically. Mark did not notice. He headed home. His footsteps resonated on the cobbled path between the terrace houses. He had good news to tell Ruth and he couldn't wait. She should be back from school. Ever since the school trip, she had been returning home early. He scarcely took heed of the ominous dark clouds overhead or the pelting rain that had changed the path to a black sheen of slippery stones. He was unmindful of his squelching shoes.

Finally, a job, one that would take him back to Malaya. He was sure his memory would recover when he got there. He felt a sudden rush of adrenaline. The rain fell with increased intensity, hitting him on his face and running off his mackintosh. He pulled the hood tighter over his head and increased his pace. His heart pounded. His lips quivered and then broadened into a grin. People turned to stare. He felt obliged to tell them. "I did it," he shouted through the rain. "Well done!" they replied, not knowing what he meant yet eager to share his joy. He shouted again, pummelling into the air, and quickened his footsteps even more. By the time he reached home, he was breathless. He pushed open the front door.

"Ruth," he called. He shrugged off his soaking coat and hung it on a hook. With an impatient flourish he dropped his wet shoes into the basket by the door. He went into the sitting room. She was not there. He went into the kitchen, his socks still squelching with damp. Ruth was seated with her head clasped in her hands, her elbows on the table, her shoulders hunched. Overhead, the dim light flickered sending shadows to play on the yellow Formica tabletop.

It alarmed him to see Ruth like that. He went up to her and stroked her head. "What is the matter?"

Ruth's eyes were dull when she looked up. The lids were red and swollen. "I have given notice to the school."

Mark sat down. He was bewildered. "Why? I thought you enjoyed teaching?"

"Not any more. I need a break. I will look for another post, perhaps nearer this neighbourhood. I have some savings. We could draw on them."

Mark took her in his arms. "Don't worry," he murmured, his lips brushing her temple. "I know I have been a rotten husband to you. I will make it up to you." He held both her shoulders and pushed her at arms' length. He looked deep into her eyes. "I have found a job with Guthries. We can go back to Malaya."

Ruth was speechless. Malaya! She clutched her tummy. She could feel bile rise in her throat. She ran out of the room and up the stairs.

"Ruth! Ruth!" he called after her. "What's the matter?" He stood rooted to the ground uncertain if he should run after her. Would he make thing worse if he did? Should he give her time to collect herself?

***

Ruth locked herself in the bathroom. She was still reeling with shock. A job in Malaya with Guthries? How had that happened? She crouched down and hugged her knees. The cold tiles were hard against her buttocks. Overhead the bare light bulb gave out a yellowy dingy light. She shivered. It was damp and cold. She thought of Fu Yi and the luxury of having domestic help. The bungalows in Tanjong Malim and Port Dickson had been lavish compared to this. Only a week ago she had said that she would like to go back to Malaya. So why had she panicked? Her eyes travelled round the shabby bathroom. Damp patches stained the wall. Mark's job meant that she could leave all this drudgery for the comfort of a warm country. There was nothing left for her here. The break-up with Steve had been ugly. Last week he had confronted her in the school corridor. Oblivious of the curious stares of others in the busy passageway, he had pushed his face close to hers until her back was against the wall. She blushed to think of what the students must have thought. She recalled their giggling and whispering. A teacher passing by frowned and glared. Ruth could the feel the blood flooding into her face with shame. Steve stalked her relentlessly. At every opportunity he would sidle up and pretend that nothing had happened. Going to Malaya would give her the chance to be truly free from Steve.

She unclenched her fists. Her thoughts went to Mark. He was like a new man, more like the husband she knew of old. She owed it to him. She placed her head on her knee. Her head throbbed. "Mummy, mummy, I am home," she heard Libby's cry. "I'll be out in a minute," she managed to call back. Her limbs were heavy. She could not get up. She didn't want to leave the sanctuary of the bathroom. Soon they would knock and insist that she came out.

"Mummy, where are you?"

Slowly, with difficulty, she placed both hands on the floor and levered herself up. She splashed water on to her face and rubbed her cheeks to bring colour into them. Dead eyes looked back at her in the mirror. What about May? she asked her image. What if Mark remembered her? What if they were to meet? Would he forgive her for the cruel trick she had played on him?

Libby tapped on the door. Her little fists made staccato sounds. "Mummy, Mummy, Daddy says we are going to Malaya. Where is Malaya? Will I like it?"

Ruth leaned on the door pressing one cheek against it. She fumbled with the latch. The door swung open. She swept Libby up into her arms. "Yes," you will like it," she said nestling against the brown curls. Libby's body was warm and pliable. She clung to Libby; a cold fist of fear clamped her heart.

***

Ruth rolled over on to her side and drew her knees up into a foetal position. She closed her eyes, feigning sleep. A sliver of light peeped through the drawn curtains. She could hear Mark moving in the bedroom. His slippers made soft shuffling sounds. He got into the bed. It squeaked and sagged under his weight. She could feel his warmth. An arm reached over to draw her closer. He fitted his body to hers. She went rigid. She couldn't respond. All she could think of was May and the possibility that Mark would discover her deception.

"Ruth?" Mark moved closer, his lips brushing the nape of her neck. Ruth gritted her teeth. She was like a coiled wire, her body so tense that pain shot up her back right to her neck. She clutched the bed sheet tight.

"Are you asleep?"

She didn't answer. She made herself breathe deeply expelling the air like someone in sound sleep. After a few minutes, Mark moved away. Silence followed, interrupted by her feigned deep breathing and then that of Mark. She could not settle down. She tossed and turned, her mind in a whirl.

Chapter 18

Kuala Lumpur

THE CAR PARK was packed when Hugh's car swept into the gravel driveway. He got out. This would be his first meeting with the planters as their representative. The Club's conference room would be full. He straightened his tie and pulled his jacket into place. He took the steps two at a time, his feet light and confident. The massive teak door swung open as if by magic. A young Sikh, his gun slung on his back and pointing upwards, saluted and clicked his feet to attention. Hugh smiled. We have not given up our sense of formality and importance, he thought, perhaps not yet.

The interior of the Lake Club was luxurious. It had been built for British planters and colonial officers in 1890, long before him. He expected it to be the last of the British 'white only' strongholds. It would not be long before the Club would be forced to open membership to Asians. And it would not be soon enough, as far as he was concerned. Over the last month, his briefing had showed that there would have to be a complete change in attitude if planters wished to maintain their investments in Malaya. It was a message that he would have to drive home to them. Already, within months of independence, large numbers of expatriates had left the country. Foreign firms were required to introduce training schemes for Malayan managers and provide scholarships at Malayan universities and agricultural colleges to groom locals for the jobs hitherto taken by foreigners. He was not without sympathy to this policy. One had to be realistic. To survive in this political climate one had to go with the tide. It would not be a one-sided gain for Britain in the future. He was assured that residence permits for *bona fide* foreign directors would be automatically renewed. That assurance, he knew, meant that they had to play ball. He heard people say that the *Tuan Besar* could remain *tuan*, but perhaps not so *besar*. He grinned at the aptness of the expression: a 'sir' but not such an important one.

The conference room was packed. Despite the early hour, gin and tonics, whiskies and sodas were circulating freely. Young boys in uniforms with trays heavily laden with drinks wove their way through the crowd. Discussion was underway punctuated by indignant snorts of derision at yet another Malayan Government initiative. Hugh made his way to Reid, the Commissioner. He was talking to someone.

Hugh stopped. The man following him bumped into his back. Mortified, Hugh turned and apologised before returning his gaze to the Commissioner. He blinked. Next to him stood Mark, a much older Mark with streaks of grey in his hair. Nevertheless, it was unmistakably Mark. The Commissioner saw Hugh and waved him over. "Come and meet our newcomer, not quite new as he was here back in 1950. Mark Lampard, meet Hugh Anderson our newly appointed representative.

Mark turned to Hugh and put out his hand. He held it fast; a little frown appeared on his forehead. "Do I know you? Sorry. I lost my memory. I have not really recovered it. If I know you please accept my apologies for not recalling. It will come back now that I am back in the country. I am sure of it. I was surprised when I heard myself speaking Malay and understanding it. It was that knowledge that clinched my application for the post. Yet big gaps remain of my personal life."

"I am sure you are both acquainted," Reid said with a disarming smile. "Anderson was in Tanjong Malim around the same time you were there with Harrisons and Crosfield. Nasty business then. Mark was captured. I'll move on and leave you two to catch up. The gong will ring for lunch soon; we'll get down to business then." Reid moved away with a quick nod.

"Were we acquainted?" Mark was excited. At last someone from his past. "If you know me, then tell me. It would be a great help. I would love to know everything I can about my past."

"Yes! Of course! I would be delighted to talk about old times. But can we do it another day? I am sorry, I need to go now. My first speech and all that." Hugh looked desperately over Mark's shoulder hoping to catch someone's eye, someone who could rescue him.

"My apologies," Mark's face fell and his gaze turned flat, "I should not have bothered you at our first meeting. I'll let you get on with what you need to do." He was disappointed and embarrassed. He could tell that Hugh was not willing to renew their acquaintance. The excitement he had felt when they were first introduced left him. He turned to leave.

Hugh reached out and clasped Mark's arm. "Of course I know you. Don't fret. We'll definitely get together and talk about old times." He gave a sheepish grin. "Sorry I was not forthcoming earlier on. Didn't know what to do. Your memory ... I didn't know what to say."

Mark was delighted. His smile stretched from ear to ear. "It would help me tremendously if I could have a chance to talk with someone from my past. Here, take this card. I have your contact. Your card was the first thing my office at Guthries gave me. If I don't hear from you, may I call you?"

"I look forward to it. I have to leave you now. Several people are beckoning me and I must circulate."

***

The French windows were thrown wide open. A light breeze blew in perfuming the air with scents from the garden. Hugh was sitting in the sitting room waiting for May. She was upstairs putting Craig to bed. It was a beautiful room full of May's touches. Celadon jars, bronze statuettes, Persian rugs and teak furniture blended seamlessly. Hugh sighed. How was he going to break the news to her? He kneaded his brow.

"Bad day?" May asked. She walked to him and knelt at his feet. She placed her head on his lap. Her flowing silk batik top skimmed on the floor over her long sarong. Hugh was never tired of seeing his wife. He loved it when she wore her oriental dresses. Would Mark's return change everything? Mark was May's first love. Mark was also his friend.

"I saw Mark."

May's head shot up. "Where?" The atmosphere became charged with tension with that one sentence. He saw fear in her eyes.

"At the planters' meeting at the Lake Club. He has just arrived. He has joined Guthries."

"But that is not possible. You said that foreign firms are not employing expatriate staff."

"They can if they can prove that no local person can do the job and the expatriate has the local knowledge and experience to do it. Mark met all the criteria. That part of his memory seemed unimpaired."

"Did he recognise you? Does he remember?"

"No, he didn't remember me but it will be a matter of time. His memory, he said, is coming back. I cannot pretend that I do not know him, not when Reid told him I was in Tanjong Malim with him. I can't pretend, May. He was my friend."

"Did he mention me?" May's face was drained of colour.

Hugh shook his head.

May jumped up. "What if he remembers?"

"I have thought about it. In fact I have thought about it the whole day. If he does, what does it matter? He did not know about Craig. He will have to accept that you have moved on and love someone else, me." Hugh's voice faltered. "Unless you still love him. Are you afraid that you still have feelings for him? Are you afraid of seeing him and having these feelings rekindled?"

May put her arms round Hugh and hugged him hard. She could feel his heart pumping; hers too was going at a maddening rate. "I don't love him, I am just afraid of seeing him. I am frightened because of Craig. That he would recognise Craig as his when his memory returns."

Hugh wrapped his arms around her. "And I am afraid that you still love Mark."

She shook her head burying it deeper into his chest. "I love you. Mark was my past, when I was just seventeen."

Hugh crushed her to him. He couldn't let go. He was choked up with emotion and the fear of losing May.

"I am expecting our child," May whispered. "I went to the doctor today while you were at the meeting. He confirmed it. I am two months into my term."

Hugh lifted May off her feet and laughed. He bellowed with joy. "My sweet." He kissed her tenderly, making it linger, wanting the sweetness to go on forever. He traced the outline of her lips with a finger. "I am so happy. I thought for a while that it would not happen."

***

"This, Madam, is prime location, within ten minutes drive to the city centre, yet surrounded by greenery. Look at the trees around you. It would be difficult to find another rental property that could beat this. The owner built it for himself. Due to changed circumstances he is letting it out. Everything is beautifully and tastefully done. It comes fully furnished. Of course, the other advantage is that the majority of your neighbours, I would say over ninety percent, are expatriates, English mainly." The agent beamed. "You have at your doorstep, people from your own country."

Ruth walked from room to room, her hand caressing the walls, the curtains, and the sofas. It was indeed a beautiful house. Five bedrooms with an equal number of bathrooms! A far cry from the one they had to share in England. She popped her head through one of the doors. The bedroom had a balcony. A riot of colourful plants grew in metal baskets hung on the railings. She descended the stairs. Her fingers caressed the highly polished teak banister. The living room opened up to the left. Awed, she had to stop herself from tiptoeing on the black Italian marble floor. Teak panelled walls rose seamlessly to high ceilings from which hung chandeliers. A thrill went through her. Her first thought was that at last, there was to be no more mouldy wall papers. Why, however, she wondered, would they need so many rooms?

"Can we afford this?" she asked, certain that the price would be out of their range and that she would not need to make a decision. It would be taken out of her hands.

"Of course, Madam. If I could be so presumptuous. All foreigners out here have large houses. This house certainly meets the criteria. Quite a few expatriate employees from Guthries live in this neighbourhood. It would be a great social meeting place. There is a small parade of shops within walking distance catering to foreigners. Also a mini market that sells goods not easily available at the local market. They stock Marmite." He grinned. He had been told that was what the English liked and was proud to show off his knowledge. "There is a hairdresser and a general haberdashery store for linen," he continued, flashing his gold teeth. He saw the hesitance in Ruth's face. "Perhaps you need time to discuss it with your husband?" He twiddled his fingers. "I have to tell you that another family is also considering this property."

Ruth walked to the window. Tall trees skirted the lawn. A bed of orchids stood in the middle. Sprays of dark red orchids with spotted petals nodded their heads and swayed in the breeze. Mark had said he would go along with whatever she wished. She was overwhelmed by it all. She had been apprehensive that they would be sent out to the plantations immediately. She had dreaded that the posting would be in Tanjong Malim. When it was clear that they would be in Kuala Lumpur, she had cried with relief. He had gathered her in his arms and called her a silly goose, not guessing her anxiety. He told her he would be coordinating from the capital city. He would visit plantations as and when needed, for they were spread out over many different states. She prayed he would never need to go to Tanjong Malim. Surely there would be little chance of his stumbling on May if he was in Kuala Lumpur. She presumed that May would be in Tanjong Malim, or at least somewhere further north. Perhaps May was no longer in Malaya. The war against communist insurgents was fast coming to an end. Many people had been deported. May could have been one of those.

She could feel her heart beat. Whenever she thought of May, her mouth would turn dry. She had never met May. Yet her mind was besieged by that one image of May in the photograph she spotted on the wall. A smiling May that had filled her with jealousy. A jealousy so strong that she had done what she had done. She had hidden from Mark anything that she thought would trigger his memory of May. She had surprised even herself in her deviousness. That was then. Now she was weighed down with guilt. She was guilty for her willingness to sacrifice Mark's memory to be rid of a rival. She was guilty of adultery herself. She heaved a sigh as though by sighing she could rid herself of self-loathing. The faster she put out roots in Kuala Lumpur, the safer she would feel. Moreover, for Libby's sake, they should move out of the hotel as quickly as possible. As for the many rooms, she could turn one into a playroom; another could be a study. Then one could be a guest room. She turned to Ah Teck, the agent. "We'll take it."

Chapter 19

IT WAS ALMOST noon. Mark waited at the bar. He was to meet Hugh for lunch. Two weeks had passed since their first meeting. Hugh had not called. Mark had expected that. He knew Hugh had a busy schedule and when Hugh finally agreed to meet up with him at the Selangor Club, he was delighted. He swirled the orange juice in his glass packed full of ice. He had astonished the barman when he ordered a juice. The barman, a young Indian with well groomed whiskers, showed it by the slight lift of an eyebrow and a swift sardonic grin that he quickly hid. Gin and tonic or Tiger beer were what members normally favoured. Mark could see it for himself. He looked round the room and mentally counted the number of alcoholic drinks being consumed. Even the air was saturated with it. But he had vowed that he was not going down the route of gins, whiskies and brandies or even beer again. He was finished with that. He had sworn that he would pull out of the depression that had plagued him these past years. He gulped down the ice-cold juice and asked for another.

Outside the Club, the sky was a continuous expanse of blue with not a cloud in sight. It was blistering hot and a cricket match was being played in the manicured field separating the Club from the Government Offices across the road,

Mark leaned his elbow on the bar and crossed his ankles. Overhead, ceiling fans hummed. He was glad to be back in Malaya. He would rather be out in the plantations than in Kuala Lumpur but no doubt he would be visiting them soon enough. He was disappointed that Ruth had not shared his enthusiasm for returning to Malaya. However, things seemed to have settled down. The move to their new home was keeping her busy. Libby was settling into her new school. Even his work appeared to be going well. He had grasped automatically all that had to be done. It was as though he had never stopped working. He had no problems speaking Malay. Yet his memory of places and people remained tantalisingly vague. It would seem that his mind had deliberately shut down an episode of his life, an episode that he felt Ruth knew more about than she revealed.

He spotted Hugh walking towards him and waved. They ordered their drinks and walked over to a settee.

"Gosh, it is hot out there. Well over ninety degrees. Perhaps we'll have a thunderstorm. It would help cool things down," said Hugh. He sipped his drink and examined Mark covertly. May had begged him not to meet Mark. Yet how could he continue to avoid him? It would only arouse suspicion. The best thing was to let events take their course. If Mark was to remember, nothing could prevent it. So he sat waiting for the inevitable questions to arise, wondering if he should pre-empt them to avoid suspicion.

Mark too was thinking rapidly. He had made enquiries about Hugh. He was now a family man with a Malayan Chinese wife and a son, and well liked by both planters and locals.

"Did we know each other well?" Mark asked breaking the silence. He leaned forward planting his elbows on his thighs and clasping his fingers together.

"Of course. We were in Tanjong Malim together, you as a planter and I with the military then. My unit was based in a wing of the Agricultural College not very far from your residence. It was such a small community. Everyone knew everyone else."

"What happened to me? I mean did they find out the motive behind my capture?"

"To instil fear I suppose. You were not the only planter to be persecuted. Your predecessor lost his life. Surely someone must have told you about it."

"Yes! I hear the same things from almost everyone I ask. My former firm gave a similar account. Yet I have flashes of memory, of faces that I could not quite place. Since my arrival I seem to recall in particular a certain face." Mark smiled sheepishly. "A beautiful Chinese girl. The image comes and then goes, like a phantom that has no shape. The other day, I saw a lovely Chinese woman with long hair. I went up to her. I often get this feeling when I see a Chinese lady with long hair that it must be this missing face that I could not quite place. I alarmed her."

Mark's voice dropped. He leaned closer towards Hugh. "I should not be asking this," he said feeling guilty even as he voiced his question. "Was I involved with a woman?"

Hugh stared at Mark's red face, aware that they were broaching dangerous ground. "Not as far as I know," he said cautiously. He paused, weighing the situation. His face was bland of expression; his heart, however, was beating wildly. May, May he wanted to cry in anguish. There was no way he could hide her without creating greater suspicion. "Perhaps you remember my wife. She worked for you. She is certainly beautiful." He gave a snort of laughter. It sounded false, even to his own ears. "As long as you don't mistake her for anything else. She is my wife."

Mark fell back to his seat. "Why didn't you mention it before?" He was incredulous that Hugh had not disclosed this previously.

"We didn't have time to talk. Remember?" Hugh laughed. "I was too busy thinking of my speech, my first, to the planters. It was a very important day for me. You know that things are getting tricky out here. My head is full at the moment and it was certainly full on the first day of our meeting. In fact I have been meaning to say this. It is something I tell the others as well. Guthries should worry about the rapidly changing situation for British firms. We are not doing well, even against the Japanese. Imagine that! People seemed to have conveniently forgotten about the Japanese occupation and the atrocities committed during their time here. The Japanese are now winning more contracts than us. They are persuasive. They are willing to impart a greater equity share than we do when they embark on joint ventures with their Malayan counterparts. It is something that you should discuss with your employer. It might have to re-think its position."

"Yes, yes of course I'll mention this to Guthries," Mark replied impatiently, startled by Hugh's change of subject. He didn't want to talk business, not yet. He would not be distracted; at last there was someone else he knew from Tanjong Malim.

"You said that your wife worked for me. What did she do? May I speak to her?"

"My good friend," said Hugh, " I am sorry. We are expecting our second child and she is indisposed at the moment. Maybe when she feels more herself. I'll raise it with her." He felt his heart thumping even as he smiled. There was nowhere to hide May. But Craig! Mark must never know about him.

***

Sunlight streamed down on one side of the narrow street in Chinatown. It lit up the covered five-foot pathway fronting the long line of three-storey terraced shophouses. Baskets and sacks of dried fish and shrimps stacked cheek by jowl in front of the shops. May spotted a sack of dried shiitake mushrooms. She selected some and placed them in a rolled up newspaper bag. Soon her shopping basket was full of little bags of dried provisions. Threading through the sacks and baskets of goods on display she made her way across the road to the Central Market, a cavernous building that housed the biggest array of fresh food stalls in any single outlet in the capital city. The heady scent of fresh fish, vegetables, fruits, meat and flowers hit her the moment she stepped into the market's interior. She bought quickly and efficiently, selecting from the vast display of vegetables, a bunch of watercress, spinach and a green marrow. She headed for the fish stall and bought a grouper. Wrapped in newspaper, the fish stared back at her with glassy reproachful eyes. By the time she had completed her purchases, her arms were aching from the weight of the basket. She headed back to the opposite side of the street and went into a coffee shop.

It was crowded with shoppers enjoying cups of coffee and tea and a late morning snack. Steam rose from a stall plying fresh spring rolls stuffed with fine strips of Chinese turnips, crab meat and prawns. Another stall was churning out flat rice noodles fried with a glistening black sauce, bean sprouts, prawns and cockles. "*See ham char kway teow,*" yelled a lad no older than ten years. He ran barefooted between the packed tables ladling out plates of noodles. The air was filled with the smell of garlic and soya sauce.

May placed her basket by a chair and sat down. She was beginning to feel light headed. She had not been sleeping well. Although Hugh had asked her to leave the food shopping to the maids, she had decided she would do it herself. It gave her an excuse to see Fu Yi. Fu Yi was retired and lived in one of the dormitories above a shop just a couple of doors away. Fu Yi would not allow May to come to her. She was embarrassed by her straitened circumstances. May had only been to see her once in her lodgings when she was ill. All she had was a narrow metal bed with a thin mattress. It was a bed amongst a dozen or so set in a long room. There was hardly two feet between the beds. The dingy room was home to women with circumstances similar to those of Fu Yi. Space was at a premium. Long and narrow, terraced shophouses could only have windows at the front. Hence rooms in such shophouses were veiled in darkness. All these Fu Yi accepted as part of her fate. However, it had disturbed May. May's distress in turn upset Fu Yi. From then on she forbade May to come to her. She insisted that they meet on the neutral ground of a coffee shop.

May placed her hand on her stomach. She felt queasy from the smell of cooking. She gulped down the hot sweet coffee.

"You shouldn't have come," Fu Yi said appearing suddenly from behind. It took May by surprise, even though she had been waiting for her. Fu Yi hovered by May's chair. She noticed the young woman's pinched cheeks. "Master Hugh would be most cross if you were to fall ill," she said, placing one hand on the back of May's chair. Her eyes travelled to May's hand clasping protectively over her tummy. Fu Yi's eyes glimmered and looked questioningly at May. May nodded.

Fu Yi sat down. She had shrunk in the ten months since her retirement. Flesh seemed to have fallen off her, leaving a skull-like face with prominent cheekbones and weathered skin. "It is time. It is good," she said sagely. "I have been praying to the Goddess of Mercy for that to happen. Your husband is a good man; he deserves a child."

May half rose to embrace the older woman. She could not thank Fu Yi enough for looking after her all those years ago. She would have died if it had not been for Hugh and Fu Yi. Memories of the cell came crashing into her thoughts. Despite the years that had passed she recalled it as though it was yesterday the chipped enamel bowl that served as her latrine and the hard cement floor, her bed. The questioning had been relentless. Hunger and thirst had made her ready to admit to anything. She remembered eating ravenously the boiled lump of cold gruel that was pushed through the bars of her cell. If it had not been for Hugh rescuing her, she would have admitted to any guilt forced upon her.

May sat down and took Fu Yi's hand in hers. "Why don't you come to us? You can stay with us."

"And what will happen when you go to England? No. I am okay where I am." Fu Yi's eyes wandered towards the five-foot way fronting the coffee shop. A beggar sat cross-legged on the cement floor. A bowl lay by his side. "There are many worse off than me. I am all right."

"Remember, the invitation is always there. You are always welcome."

"Don't worry about me. There is no need for you to come to see me. Look after yourself, especially now with a little one coming. You had better go. Your driver is waiting." With that, Fu Yi stood up to leave. She didn't think it appropriate that May should spend time with her.

"Wait! We have hardly exchanged a word. At least let me give you these." May fished out the little bags of dried provisions and placed them into a larger bag. "They are for you. I have asked the grocer to deliver a sack of rice to you. He will replenish your rice store when you tell him. Remember too that we have an account with the Chinese herbal shop. If you need medicine, go there. I have told them to bill us."

"Thank you. You shouldn't have. If there is nothing else, go home. This is not a place for you."

May hesitated. She couldn't leave without asking Fu Yi. She needed her reassurance. Yet she felt guilty at asking. If she didn't, she would not be able to sleep. The worry was driving her mad. She could see Fu Yi looking at her questioningly.

"Remember Mark's wife?" May asked. "You were with her for a short while. Did she know that I was pregnant then? Did you tell her?" Embarrassed by her own words, two twin spots of red appeared on her cheeks.

Fu Yi's eyes were reproachful as she looked at May. She shook her head. "I didn't tell her. I don't think she knew. I told you that before. Don't make me repeat." She reached out and grasped May's wrist. Her hand spotted and gnarled against May's smooth and delicate skin. "Remember, Master Hugh is a good husband. He treats your son like his own. Forget Master Mark. He has a wife. Ruth is a good woman. Your first duty is to your husband, especially now with a child on the way. Now go home. Go home to Master Hugh and look after him as he has looked after you."

May's face burned an even brighter red. She reached for her basket.

Fu Yi watched silently May's departing back. Master Mark must be back, she surmised. She prayed that May would not lose her common sense. She knew how much May had loved the first master.

Chapter 20

RUTH WANDERED LISTLESSLY round the house. It was so quiet, she could hear her own breathing. After the rush of activity moving house and settling Libby into a school, the enforced leisure was an anti-climax. She longed for work that would keep her mind occupied. It was impossible to garden; her skin blistered under the hot sun. In any case the gardener would be shocked to see her engage in any manual work. Walking, an activity that could have occupied her, was impossible in the heat and humidity. She was tired of the coffee mornings. She had nothing in common with the other women. It was incredible that they could fill their time with idle chatter. The social rules were as endless as they were mindless. She was told that fraternization with locals was to be avoided. A good hostess, it seemed, served canned peaches and not native fruits. Ruth heaved a sigh of exasperation.

She walked into the dining room. It was large enough to seat twelve or more. Eating in the room on her own made her aware of her solitude. Mark was hardly around. A whirlwind of travel to rubber plantations spread over the entire peninsula kept him busy. When he was away she missed him and fretted. When he returned, she waited with bated breath for him to announce that he remembered, for her world to crash around her. She jumped at every quizzical look he cast at her. She was overwhelmed with guilt. She had held him back all these years, refusing him a chance of recovering his memory. If there were grounds to do so because of his past infidelity, she had forfeited all rights and justification by her own sordid affair with Steve.

Steve! She dug deep into her pocket and clutched at the letter within its depths. She did not know how Steve had found her address. She worried that a letter would arrive one day and it would be Mark who took delivery of it. Steve had threatened that he would write to Mark if she did not reply. If Mark learnt of her entanglement with Steve, would he suspect that Libby was not his? Just thinking of it made her break out in sweat. She brushed away the beads of perspiration with the back of her hand.

By mid-day, Ruth was desperate for anything that could occupy her mind and dispel her worries. She decided she would drive to the British Council to borrow books to fill in her time. If she had known of the scarcity of reading matter, she would have brought with her caseloads of books. There were few bookshops around in Kuala Lumpur and even fewer libraries. The British Council would be her surest bet.

***

At the other end of the town, May was equally unsettled. Fu Yi's insistence that she had to be true and loyal to Hugh made her doubt herself. Was it possible that she still had lingering feelings for Mark? Did it show in her face? What could have prompted Fu Yi's words? Annoyed, she pulled and tugged at her ring. "Of course not," she said aloud startling the driver. It was likely that she would not even recognise Mark. Yet Fu Yi's words made her feel guilty even though she had not done anything. Niggling self-doubt wormed into her being. What if she were to discover when she met Mark that she still had feelings for him? The thought unnerved her. She settled back into the seat. The car accelerated smoothly out of Chinatown, leaving the hustle and bustle behind. She wound down the window. The air had cleared. A warm breeze blew in, bringing with it the scent of lush vegetation. Ahead a building rose by the wayside.

May signalled the driver to turn into the driveway. "Leave me here. Take the shopping back. Tell the *amah* to put it away. Then come back for me." She got out of the car and made her way to the building. She did not wish to go home immediately. She needed time for herself and the British Council's library would afford the quiet she sought. Few people were about at this hour. She would choose a corner in the library to sit and reflect. A couple of women waved when she entered the building. She waved back, rearranging her face to show a brightness of spirit she did not feel. Her mouth tilted up at the corner in a parody of a smile. Once in the library, she wandered down the aisle examining the books. The air was hot and musty. She sneezed and looked up. From across the shelf, over the books lined up in a row, a pair of cornflower-blue eyes stared at her. May stared back. A fleeting recognition registered in the pool of blue.

Unnerved, May stepped quickly round the corner. There was no one there. The woman was gone, leaving behind a faint whiff of the perfume she wore. I see things that are not there, May thought.

She placed a hand on her tummy. Craig, Hugh and the baby came immediately to mind. They would go through whatever life threw at them. They had each other.

***

Ruth dropped the pile of books she had borrowed at the librarian's desk. They landed on the desk with a thud. The librarian glared and mumbled her displeasure. Ruth didn't stop to apologise. She walked quickly away, stumbling out of the building as though someone was pursuing her. She did not look back. Her head was reeling. Was it her? Was it May? She had not seen her before, just her photograph. That had been seven years ago. Surely she would have changed. The face she saw across the shelf had the same finely chiselled cheekbones and large almond eyes. There were no lines, no wrinkles to suggest the passage of time, just the same heart-breaking loveliness that had torn at Ruth's innards and had made her so jealous that she was willing to sacrifice her husband's memory rather than lose him to this woman called May.

She got into the car and drove quickly back home. The car swerved through the wrought iron gates and screeched to a stop, spitting gravel from the driveway on to the lawn. Mark's car was parked by the verge. She had not expected him to come back so early. He was supposed to be in Seremban, some forty miles or so to the south. She tilted the rear mirror and looked at herself. The face that stared back at her was drained of colour. She swung open the door and took a couple of deep breaths to quell the feeling of nausea. It wouldn't leave her. The sourness stuck at the back of her throat and filled her mouth. She saw the gardener looking at her, a scythe held mid-way in the air, his face a picture of concern mingled with curiosity. He wiped the back of his hand over his forehead. Sweat fell like rain drops. She put up a hand and nodded to indicate everything was well. He smiled, white teeth flashing against skin blackened by the sun. She turned away in embarrassment. She must get a hold of herself. Slowly, with measured steps she made her way to the house.

Ruth's heart fluttered wildly. I must tell Mark, she thought. But what should she say? That she had seen May, when she was not supposed to know anything about his affair and, when in all probability, he still did not recall May. She couldn't think clearly. The longer things remained hidden, the more difficult it was to untangle them.

"Mark," she called out loud.

"Father is on his way to Kuala Kubu Bahru, somewhere to the north of us," shouted Libby running into the room. "Teacher showed me on the map. He sent the car back for us to use. He says he is more comfortable with the jeep they supplied him with for work around the estates. The driver could take me to school in his car and that would leave you free in yours for other things. Isn't that great?"

Ruth heaved. She gathered Libby into her arms. She was relieved to be given a reprieve. She would not have been able to deal with Mark's searching questions and looks. She imagined his suspicion. She could no longer distinguish between reality and the imagined. All she wanted was to curl up and sleep, an oblivion that proved tantalisingly impossible.

***

The jeep jolted and rolled. Potholes littered the road. Heavy rain had washed away the soil on the embankment leaving large tracts of the hillside bare with the roots of trees scarcely holding on to the fragile land. Overhead monkeys chattered and swung from branch to branch. The Emergency was almost over. Incidents of attacks were rare, he was told, and they would be safe. Yet Mark was uneasy. During a visit to a plantation, the driver had refused to stop the jeep even when Mark pressed him. "No, *Tuan*," Din exclaimed, forehead furrowed and eyes glistening with fear, "no stop. Danger. Toilet later when we reach office." He had then pressed on the accelerator sending the jeep hurtling along, just as he was doing now. Mark grimaced. The wheel hit a buttress root jutting from the embankment. The car swerved and his shoulder caught the side of the car.

"Will you tell me why we are travelling at such speed?'

""Rumour, sir. Bandits have refused to accept the amnesty offered by the Government. They're not willing to surrender. Hear they would take up arms once more. Their leader Chin Peng is still at large. We must go quickly. Look! Sun going."

Even as Din spoke the sun was fast dropping below the horizon. They skittered past row after row of rubber trees. They turned into a dirt driveway. The jeep came to a stop. A bungalow had been allocated for Mark's visit. It stood before him, a solitary wooden building with no particular features except windows framed by metal-grilles and behind them metal mosquito nettings. Mark got out of the jeep. The door slammed shut behind him breaking the stillness of the evening. The skylight vanished completely throwing the drive into a blanket of darkness. Someone switched on the lights in the bungalow.

The golden rays filtered on to the path. Mark heaved a sigh of relief. He was spooked by what the driver had said. He searched deep into his memory. Bits flashed before him, disjointed but sufficient to cause his heart to pump erratically. This outpost was different from the ones he had visited so far. Those were modern, developed estates with a big labour force. This was a small, isolated plantation, one that Guthries was planning to rid itself of. He was gripped by sudden fear. He turned to motion to the driver to come with him into the house. The man was nowhere in sight. Only the eerie outline of the jeep testified to his existence. Mark hurried to the bungalow. The door had been left open. Someone must know he was coming. He looked round. Not a person in sight. He went straight to the phone by the hallway. He picked it up and dialled. The line was dead. He went into the kitchen expecting to see at least the housemaid. There was no one.

***

The bar in the Selangor Club was packed. Every stool alongside it was occupied, every table taken. Hugh sipped his drink, his elbow resting lightly on the polished counter, one leg crooked as he leaned on it. The room buzzed with life. A group of women arrived to join their partners. He looked away. He was due to meet up with May. Not here. Memories of how May had been treated in the Club still riled. He gulped the last drop of his drink, a virgin Mary without the alcohol but with a stiff stir of Tabasco. They would eat in Chinatown tonight, a quick meal before they headed home to put Craig to bed. He straightened up and dusted his trousers. To his dismay, he saw Reid. The Commissioner was walking to him purposefully.

"One word," Reid called out even before he reached Hugh. "I got a call from that chappie, Mark. I'd like you to have a word with him. He was distraught. Apparently he was fed a lot of nonsense from his driver. To top it all, his telephone line went dead. He rushed off to a neighbouring estate to call me, after failing to get to anyone in his firm. I tried to tell him that telephone lines frequently get cut off. That the disconnection could be due to an arm's length of things not connected with Communist rebels. He was hysterical. Perhaps a word from you would put his mind at rest."

"Right now?"

Reid ordered himself a beer before turning back to Hugh. "Perhaps not right now. In any case, he can't be reached at the bungalow where he is staying. The line is dead. Let him stew for a bit. Tomorrow morning, when he wakes up perfectly safe, he will realise that what we told him is true. That the insurgency is over."

"Where is he now?"

"Near Kuala Kubu Bahru."

"But that is near Katang Bali where our troops allegedly massacred twenty-five civilians. You can't blame him for his reaction, not after his previous encounter."

Reid took another gulp of his beer. "Yes, of course," he said. "Assure him, though, that things are different now. He won't be of any use to us if he falls apart; we would be obliged to tell his employers. Tell him that the insurgents have lost their cause. They formed the Malayan People's Liberation Army to liberate the country from us. By granting Malaya independence, we have destroyed their cause and made a mockery of the rationale for their existence."

***

Mark settled into bed. The mattress was hard and lumpy. It was quiet, so quiet he could hear the hum of mosquitoes hovering around the bed netting. From a distance the faint sounds of animal cries floated in, breaking the silence. The housemaid had left on the strip of flourescent light at the back of the house. The pool of light in the backyard was reassuring. She too was afraid to be on her own. She had confessed that she was in her sister's lodging some fifty yards away when he turned up that evening.

He asked if there was anyone else who could be in the house when he arrived because someone had switched on the light.

"No one sir," she replied, seemingly surprised at his question. "I left the light on in case you arrived. Perhaps the light was not noticeable until darkness came."

Mark recalled the conversation he had with the Commissioner's office. He had been gladdened by their reassurance. Yet now, sitting on the bed, with the silence around him, he was again uneasy. He grappled with his memory. He turned on to his side. He couldn't sleep. His mind wandered. Hugh had said that his wife May had worked for him. Surely this May would be able to tell him a bit more about his past life in Malaya. He spoke May's name aloud. There was something very familiar in the sound of the name; he found comfort in the way his lips moulded round the word. Was it her face that came to mind when he tried to recall the past? How strange that he should think of one woman when there was a whole lot of things that he could not recall. He had thought it prudent not to tell Ruth he remembered a face. He had not told her about his meeting with Hugh either. For some unknown reason, he deemed it wise not to do so. Ruth was not keen to delve into the past. His thoughts went round and round. Finally he drifted off into an uneasy sleep.

Chapter 21

"Have you come back for the books?" The librarian's eyes were cold and unfriendly. She pointedly eyed Ruth up and down. The dark rimmed glasses she wore had slipped down. They perched just below the ridge of her nose. Her eyes rose like twin half-moon darkly pencilled globes. "I have put them away where they belong after you left them in an unsightly heap on my desk yesterday." Her voice was frosty. She turned back to her ledger, dismissing Ruth in that gesture. Moments passed. Sensing that Ruth remained standing in front of her desk, she added without looking up, "You will have to retrieve them from the shelves if you wish to borrow them."

"I am sorry if I caused inconvenience," Ruth mumbled keeping her voice low and apologetic. "I wonder if you could help me. My neighbour, Mrs Drew, said that you are one of the most knowledgeable and helpful people she has met. You are Miss Fong?"

The head shot up and a pair of eyes stared at Ruth with interest from behind the black-rimmed spectacle frame. "Yes, that's me." The surliness disappeared; the voice was inquisitive rather than dismissive. After all, Mrs Drew was a member of the Executive Board. "What can I do for you?"

"Do you have a minute to spare? Is there somewhere where we can have a cup of coffee? I would like to make amends for my rude behaviour yesterday. It would be so kind if you were to say yes."

Miss Fong looked at her watch. "I'll see if I can get someone to cover my desk."

***

Ruth gripped the steering wheel tightly; her knuckles bleached white against the black leather-bound wheel. She had not imagined May. She had prayed all night that it was her imagination that was playing havoc with her mind. In the calm of her own bedroom she had almost convinced herself that she had been mistaken. It was not so. May was very much alive. Ruth rested her forehead on the steering wheel. She could feel her pulse racing. Suddenly she felt overwhelmingly hot. May was here in the same city, not tucked safely away in Tanjong Malim or shipped out to China. She was married. When Miss Fong told her that May's husband was Hugh Anderson, Ruth dropped her teaspoon. She had to bend down in haste to retrieve it from the floor to hide her face.

Ruth took a deep breath and released her grip on the steering wheel. She drew herself up and reached for the ignition key; the engine sprang to life. Ahead of her the dazzling sunlight shifted behind a copse of tall trees. Light filtered through the leaves, sending ripples of silver on the car bonnet.

She wondered if she was worrying unnecessarily. After all, May with a husband and a child surely meant that she, Ruth, had nothing to worry about. As for Hugh, she remembered his kindness. He would understand her plight. He had not told on Ruth; he had kept quiet, allowing her to engineer Mark's quick departure from Malaya. Surely she could trust Hugh. She must try to see him to make doubly sure. For the first time in many weeks, Ruth smiled. It lit up her face and transformed it.

Then, as suddenly as her mood had lifted, it fell. "What if Mark remembered? Would May's marriage be sufficient to deter him from wanting to be with May? If it wasn't, she – Ruth – still faced the same problem. Everything hung on Mark's memory. Ruth switched off the car engine. Mark had been distracted in recent weeks. He had thrashed and turned in his sleep, calling out in Malay. She didn't understand what he said but was quick to realise that Mark's inner self was in torment. Could he be searching for May even if he did not know it? Ruth's doubts and cares came crashing back. "I love Mark too much to lose him now; not after all that I have done; even allowing for what I shouldn't have done," she whispered, her voice dissipating into the engine noise as she restarted the car.

***

A hint of pale silver seeped in through the thin cotton curtains. Shadows shifted; a breeze stirred the hot air of the bedroom. From a distance a cock crowed. Almost on cue the mosque's morning call to prayer broke the silence of the morning. Mark woke up with a start, full of the dreams that chased through his mind. He remembered! He remembered! This very bedroom reminded him of the one he had while in Tanjong Malim. The proximity to a mosque, the early morning prayer that had awakened him each dawn with May by his side. May's face appeared before him. Those beautiful serene eyes that had looked at him with such love. A longing to hold her in his arms filled him. His mind's eye shifted. Another face, Hugh's face, interrupted Mark's reverie. Hugh, his erstwhile friend, now husband to the woman he loved; the woman his mind had been grappling to remember all these years. He had been duped by the two he had trusted more than anyone while he was in Malaya. How long had those two been involved? Were they lovers even while May shared his bed? Were they lovers while he was in captivity? How convenient it must have been for them!

Anger rose like bile, filling him with hatred; jealousy gripped him like tentacles squeezing his heart until he was breathless. Deceived by those he trusted most! They had allowed him to flounder, perpetuating his memory loss and in the process reduced him to half the man he used to be. He had lost so many years of his life. Only Ruth had stood by him, Ruth whom he had deceived for one as faithless as May. He threw aside his thin blanket and pushed apart the mosquito netting. Thrusting his feet into the sandals by his bed, he got up abruptly. He walked up and down the small confines of the bedroom, muttering to himself.

A gunshot pierced through the air. He stopped his furious pacing. The sound triggered yet another memory. He remembered! Amat, his driver slumping forward to hit the steering wheel. The horn had blared. He had tried to help Amat until hands manhandled him out of the car.

With nervous energy, Mark continued to pace the room. His strides grew quicker and quicker. His hands moved in agitation. He stopped at intervals to ruffle his hair until it stood on end. His face was red with anger and agitation. Sweat trickled down his back and his pyjama top clung damply to his skin. Amat! He stopped suddenly. Amat had a brother called Din. His present driver was called Din. Could it be just coincidence? He needed to check it out. He threw off his pyjamas and pulled on a pair of trousers and a shirt. He rushed out of the house, leaving the door open.

Outside everything was still cloaked in a velvety mist. The jungle surrounded him, menacing in its all-encompassing immensity. It blocked out the first glimmer of the sun rising above the horizon beyond. Through the dewy morning shadows, a group of men were coming from the direction of the mosque. Mark was sure that Din would be among them. He jumped into the jeep. He revved the engine and headed towards the men. He stopped when he spotted Din. Din ran towards the jeep leaving his fellowmen behind. Lunging forward, Mark threw open the door. "Hop in," he commanded.

"*Tuan!* Sir! Where are we going? Did you not hear the gunshot? We left the mosque early when we heard it. It is not safe to travel."

Mark reached out and hauled Din into the vehicle. He stepped on the accelerator. The jeep hurtled forward.

***

The jeep went roughshod over the ground sending stones flying in the air and throwing up earth and dust on its way. A trail of red dust bloomed in its wake. Din held on to his seat.

"*Perlahan, perlahan!*" he whimpered. His plead to slow down had no effect on Mark, who drove with reckless speed, like a madman, venting his anger on the vehicle. Almost an hour into the journey, Mark came to an abrupt stop. His shoulders slumped forward. All energy sapped out of him. He turned to Din. "You drive," he said, his voice terse. "Drive to Tanjong Malim."

"Why, Tuan? Why Tanjong Malim?"

"Weren't you from that town? Did you not have a brother called Amat?"

"Yes, sir."

"Was he not the driver that was killed? Was he not the one that drove me that fateful day?"

Din's eyes glittered. Tears brimmed; with effort he held them in check.

"And you did not think it important enough to tell me this information?"

"Sir. I told Ma'am Ruth. She said that I was not to trouble you. That telling you would reawaken your nightmares. That the past was the past."

Mark sank back to his seat. Ruth! Even she whom he thought was the only one he could trust was keeping things away from him. A nervous tic appeared at the corner of his lips. He was furious. "Drive! I want you to tell me everything Amat told you when he was alive. Every single detail."

***

The sound of water woke Mark up. He did not know when he had dozed off. The heat, the lulling motion of the jeep, his physical and emotional exhaustion must have caused him to fall asleep. All he remembered was that they had passed a river an hour ago and had taken the dirt track to the right of the bend in the river deep into the jungle. From the vehicle he could see several tiers of waterfall. Clear icy water cascaded into deep pools carved one above the other in the mountainous terrain. Their spray sparkled like jewelled drops under the shifting sunlight peeping through the leafy canopy above. Din said that the track would lead them directly to the plantation and the bungalow Mark had shared with May.

May, the one Mark had sought to remember during these past years of bewilderment. So much time had been lost. Now she was someone else's. It hurt him to think of May with Hugh, his friend. Friend?! His hurt exploded into anger.

The jeep slowed down. They had arrived at a settlement. Children were playing half naked in a small dusty patch of land. Tufts of grass grew here and there like an after-thought. Goats grazed laconically. They moved from one tuft to another munching slowly, oblivious to the ball sailing high above them as they rendered even greater bare patches of red lateritic soil. Children's laughter filled the air.

"We are nearly there. Tuan can you remember? Fu Yi your maid used to buy milk from an Indian man living in that hut." He pointed to a hut with corrugated walls and a thatched roof. "She told me you made her boil the milk and then later you would complain that it did not taste the same as milk in England. Miss May used to tease you about it."

"Fu Yi?"

"Yes, Fu Yi. She was this high," he gestured with his hand, "like a gnome because she was tiny and quite stooped. But she was strong and a wonderful cook."

"Can I speak to her?"

"She is gone, retired to Chinatown in Kuala Lumpur. Ma'am May would know her whereabouts."

Mark's heart flipped at the mention of May. She was central to all the mysteries surrounding his kidnap. How could he trust such a fickle, disloyal lover?"

"What happened to May when I was captured?"

Din glanced quickly at his boss before turning his attention back to the rough track. "She disappeared. Later they found her in the jungle. She was beaten badly and was left for dead. Initially everyone suspected her of being involved in your capture. It was *Tuan* Hugh Anderson, then a Major, who helped prove her innocence. Fu Yi told me."

Din's eyes slid sideways to examine his boss again. Mark was stone-faced, his lips drawn tight. His jaws were working relentlessly. Perhaps, Din thought, he should not have mentioned *Tuan* Hugh. He gripped the steering wheel hard and fell silent.

Chapter 22

MAY PICKED UP a pebble and threw it into the pond. She watched the ripples grow turning the pond's previous calm into a gentle whirl of concentric circles. Music and children's voices drifted from across the lawn. She made her way back to the house. Feeling queasy, she had taken a five-minute break from the party. The children were playing musical chairs on the terrace. Squeals of laughter were accompanied by the scraping of wood against tiles. She saw Craig and waved to catch his eye. He was perched on a chair, one leg dangling down, and the other set firmly on the ground ready to propel him forward. His fair hair caught the glint of the sun. He looked up and grinned. May's hand shot up to her chest. How could anyone not tell that Craig was Mark's? Craig was the image of him. She looked around almost expecting someone to agree with her.

She smiled back at Craig. How could she be so silly? No one had ever said so. No one knew except Hugh and Fu Yi. They would not divulge her secret. Yet her heart remained troubled.

Fu Yi's warnings continued to haunt her. She had gone to Hugh's arms every night to seek reassurance that she did not love Mark. She loved the way Hugh held her; the way he treated her with reverence like a piece of porcelain. She felt safe with him. When she watched him sleep beside her, his face relaxed, his breathing deep and punctuated by gentle snoring, she could hardly refrain from burrowing back into his arms to feel the security of his love. Yet ... Mark's face appeared like an unwanted ghost.

May looked around desperately in search of Hugh. He was late. The music stopped. Someone was bringing a cake out to the terrace and beckoning the children to a long table decked with colourful hats and balloons. Blue, green, red, white, yellow! Victoria sponges, bursting with butter cream, were laid out alongside Chinese buns filled with sweet sesame paste. Malay coconut rice cakes and sweet Indian jalebi stood in between. The birthday candles sparked to life. The children surged forward and May surged forward with them. She caught up with Craig, who was already at the table. The children's rendition of Happy Birthday was loud and enthusiastic. She joined in and forgot, in that brief interlude, her worries. Craig looked up; she winked, and kissed him soundly on the cheek. He squirmed, shook his head and looked at his mother reproachfully. May felt a hand on her shoulder. She reached up and took it, placing it against her cheek. "You're back," she sighed, a smile on her face.

Hugh clasped both her shoulders and turned her around. "I can't stay. I have to leave within the next few minutes."

"Why?"

"There has been an incident. Mark is missing. He might have been taken. I'll let you know once I know more."

***

In the makeshift meeting room, a row of blank faces stared back at Hugh. He had assembled the estate staff as well as those in the bungalow where Mark had spent the night. Over and over again he questioned them about Mark and Din's disappearance. He got nothing from them except that Mark had been extremely agitated the night before. The housekeeper confirmed the account. As for Din, they claimed that he had gone for his morning prayers and had then been later picked up by a jeep. Hugh passed Mark's photograph around. No one seemed able to confirm that Mark was the person in the jeep. They assumed that it was so. It had been dark. They could barely see each other. The dew was thick at five in the morning. Moreover, one of the men sniggered, just as the white *tuan* had difficulties in distinguishing the locals, they too find it difficult to distinguish one white man from another. They pointed in the direction the jeep took. "Jeep *pergi sana*!" From the back row of men, a small voice piped. "Maybe the *tuan* got taken away. Last week, a local Chinese man disappeared. He was later found shot in the neck. When we heard a gun shot that early morning, we all went home and kept low."

Hugh searched out the man who had spoken and asked if he could elaborate a little more. The man shrugged and looked away. Absolute silence followed.

"There goes Reid's theory that the war was won. We have certainly not won people's hearts and cooperation," Hugh muttered. He shook his head in exasperation. There was a distinct dichotomy in views between those at the central office and those in the outlying offices as to the dangers still posed by insurgents. It was true that the threats posed by them had declined. But speaking to men at the grassroots, it was obvious that the danger was diminished, not obliterated. The new Prime Minister's withdrawal of the offer of amnesty five months after its initiation had led to a stalemate. The Prime Minister would not meet the insurgents for negotiations without their complete surrender. The insurgents would not surrender unless they were guaranteed that they would not be punished. They demanded that they be given the privileges of other citizens.

Hugh realised that no more could be gained from continuing the meeting. The more he pressed them, the more reluctant the people would be to divulge any information. They would have to be questioned on their own, free from the presence and pressures of their peers. He made a note of the last speaker. He would deal with him later and in private.

"You may go," Hugh announced to the inscrutable faces staring back at him. He turned to an accompanying officer and pointed to a box filled with films. He was reminded of Reid's instructions. "Before I forget. These are for them. Pass it also to the people in the village. These films should keep them entertained and out of mischief."

"Sir?" The man looked confused.

"They are a series of ten films called the *Adventures of Yaacob*." Hugh smiled apologetically. "We have been instructed to distribute them. They are anti-bandit stories modelled on Tarzan films that Malayans seemed inordinately fond of. The films apparently had a positive impact on efforts against insurgents. The tactic was used in the war against the Mau Mau in Kenya. They persuaded people to join the counter insurgency movement and to make heroes of themselves. So the instruction is to introduce them here."

"You think it will work?"

Hugh kept his doubts to himself. "It is good entertainment for the villagers and keeps them happy. He leaned closer and lowered his voice. "After they have disbanded, I should like you to question each of them separately. Perhaps someone would tell us more about Mark's disappearance. Make it casual. Get your local counterpart to accompany you. They might tell more on their own when I am not around."

He watched the people disperse. He had lost a day. How could Mark disappear without a trace? If Mark had driven the jeep, he must have been instrumental in his own disappearance. Hugh made his way back to his own vehicle. Where had Mark gone, he wondered. Did Ruth know that Mark was missing? Had she been told? Should he speak to her?

Chapter 23

WAVES LAPPED ON to the sandy seashore leaving a trail of bubbles on the golden sands. Over and over again they came to shore, only to withdraw back into the deep sea, each time scattering seashells in their wake. Ruth bent down to pick up a shell; she held it to her ear and then popped it into the little cloth pouch she carried. She would give it to Libby. Libby was with a friend, a one-night sleepover that had extended to the entire weekend. With Mark away, Ruth decided that she would take the opportunity to get away from Kuala Lumpur. Libby was growing up fast and did not want her constant fussing. The two days spent apart would be a good thing for the both of them. She had not been good company for her daughter. She knew her anxiety coloured her behaviour, often prompting Libby to look at her with brown eyes full of unspoken questions.

She drove to the one place that she knew and had found comfort in when she was last in Malaya – Port Dickson. She had not told anyone where she was, not even Libby. Let them worry about her for a change. In any case, she doubted that anyone would miss her. Mark was not due back until next week and Libby was too wrapped up with Nina, her new friend. Nina's mum had promised to keep a close eye on the two girls and Ruth had promised to call. She did not have a contact telephone number to leave behind. She didn't know where she would be staying. "Go! Do what you need to. The girls will be fine with me," Nina's mum had assured her.

Ruth walked barefoot, relishing the feel of the warm sand slipping between her toes and the sun on her bare shoulders, arms and legs. Sun kisses! A sun that warmed her skin and reminded her of hot toast dripping with honey. The wind whipped up her hair. She closed her eyes in bliss. Coming to Port Dickson was a good thing. For the first time since arriving in Malaya, she felt at peace. She quickened her footsteps and walked inland, up a slope of fine white sand riddled with runners of exotic blooms, the colour of violets. Beach Morning Glory, they call it here, and they were indeed glorious. Ahead of her, wedged between two rows of hibiscus plants with nodding blossoms of scarlet, was the hut she had been loaned. She had driven to Port Dickson on impulse. It was uncharacteristic of her. She was not an impulsive person. Perhaps acting on impulse was something she should do more often. Already her spirit was lifted. She smiled. She had gone straight to the coffee shop where she last met Hugh and asked for Fatty, the proprietor. He emerged from the coffee shop attired just as before, in white cotton shorts and a singlet stained with black sauce. The aroma of fried garlic mingled with the salt-scented air. Not much had changed from when she was last here, just an older Fatty. His welcoming grin and laughing brown button eyes were the same. He remembered her. She asked where she could stay. He replied instantly that he had a fisherman friend who owned a hut adjacent to his own. He let it to backpackers. It was basic. The fisherman's wife would lend a helping hand in the kitchen if needed. She would take care of Ruth. Ruth did not need further persuasion.

Ruth's feet sank deep into the sand as she neared the hut. An urn of water had been laid out for her. She dipped the coconut ladle into the urn and drew water to wash her feet. She sluiced the cool clear water on to both her feet and then dried them with a rag of old sarong left by the side of the urn. The fisherman's wife Fatimah had explained that it was customary to remove footwear before entering a house. Maintaining clean feet before entering any household was sacrosanct. She walked up the flight of wooden steps that led to the balcony of her little hut. The door was thrown wide open. Through it was the one room that served as kitchen, dining, living and bedroom. A kapok fibre mattress was rolled up in one corner.

Ruth was not ready to go into the hut. It would be an hour or so before darkness settled in the sky. She returned to the top of the flight of steps and sat down, anchoring her feet on the rung below her. From her perch she watched Fatimah. Dressed simply in a sarong tied above her bosom, her brown arms bare and her feet shod in a pair of red wooden clogs, Fatimah was cooking dinner alfresco. A clay pot was bubbling on one charcoal stove and on the other she wielded a deep wok. The aroma of mixed spices wafted to Ruth; shallots, chillies, turmeric, galangal and fermented shrimp paste. Ruth found herself transported to the time she first set foot on these shores. Fu Yi had used the same ingredients, frying the paste until it was aromatic before squeezing tamarind juice into the mixture. Fatimah dropped handfuls of fresh prawns caught that day into the medley of spices, letting it bubble until the prawns turned pink. Then she sprinkled a big pinch of salt and sugar into it. "*Mari,*" she said with a wide smile, her hand waving Ruth over. She took a scoop of rice from the pot and ladled the prawns on to the rice, adding a pile of freshly sliced cucumbers. "*Makan!*" She mimed with her hand scooping imaginary morsels of food into her mouth.

Ruth hurried down the steps stopping to slip on a pair of flip-flops before heading towards Fatimah. By the time she reached her, Fatimah's three little children, a boy and two girls, were already sitting cross-legged on a mat laid out on the grass. All three had plates of rice heaped with cucumbers and a tiny scattering of prawns. They sat, waiting patiently for Ruth to eat before tucking in. Ruth ate, dipping her fingers into the spicy prawns and moulding the rice into little portions before dropping them into her mouth. The children giggled to see specks of rice rolling off her fingers and the tears in her eyes. Her lips burned from the spice. They licked their fingers and Ruth did the same. It made them laugh. Ruth felt at home and at one with this family whom she had just met. Their generosity touched her. No wonder Mark loved Malaya. Mark! She realised that she had not thought of him since she had arrived. She had become obsessive about him, about the wrong he had done and the wrong she had done. If only she was free like the people around her.

She shifted on to her knees and breathed in, deeply inhaling the scented evening air. Everything would be fine; she could feel it in her bones. She looked at her watch. There was no telephone around. She would call Libby first thing tomorrow morning. For tonight, she would be selfish. She would sleep and let the peace of the night and of this gentle family cocoon her.

***

May returned the phone to its cradle. Hugh's message rang deafeningly in her head. Mark was missing! She sat down. How could it be possible? she asked herself, silently mouthing the many questions that sprang to mind. Could it be coincidence? Chun couldn't have been instrumental in Mark's second disappearance. Although Chun's body had never been found May was sure that he was dead, like the many found burnt to cinders in the black crater left from the British army's bombing.

Memories of charred bodies, burnt faceless heads, bodies with broken limbs, some flung far away, tormented her. They had taken her to identify the corpses after the bombings. She couldn't recognise them; she didn't know which of the corpses could have been Chun. She could merely recount what Chun told her and confirm his involvement in the kidnapping of Mark. Yet the nightmare of faceless, limbless charred bodies haunted her. Her mind went blank for days. Then one morning, she felt a stirring of life in her body. She opened her eyes and was temporarily blinded by the shaft of light seeping through the bars in her cell. An omen! The baby! Mark's bequest. A life born of love. She told herself that she must live. And Hugh came to her rescue, a devoted, loyal Hugh who worked day and night to prove her innocence. He had nursed and cherished her, loved her. He had made her what she was now. Above all he loved Craig as his own. Craig was their secret. Fu Yi was wrong to think that she could still be in love with Mark. Her feelings towards Mark were those of guilt. She was guilty of denying Mark his son; she was guilty of stealing Mark away from his wife, Ruth. She had been callous. At seventeen, all she had thought of when Mark wooed her was that she was in love. She had not known about Ruth. When she did, she had still no thoughts about Ruth. She had been too deeply in love. She had justified her love by assuming that Mark was unhappy with his wife and that their marriage was over.

May walked to the French window. Out in the garden bamboos shifted and swayed in the breeze; their bright red stems in stark contrast to the verdant green of the leaves. Now older, she was wiser. Whether it was from the folly of youth or not, she was guilty of causing grief to Ruth. And now Mark was missing again. She must help Ruth.

***

Ruth's eyes fluttered open. For a moment she did not know where she was. She sat up and pushed aside the mosquito net draped around the makeshift mattress on the floor. Last night's dream was still with her. A smiling and indulgent Mark was playing with Libby and Ruth was looking on. It was a wonderful dream; the first happy dream she has had in years. Outside, a cock crowed and birds warbled their morning song. Sun poured into the hut, bathing it in a warm honeyed light. She remembered where she was and what she had to do. She rushed down the flight of steps to the urn of water. There was no one about. Fatimah must have gone to meet her husband; she had mentioned that he would be bringing in the night's catch at the break of dawn. He had gone fishing for squid; they called them *sotong*, fish with just one bone. Hastily she sluiced water over herself as she had seen local women do. That would have to suffice as a wash. She shivered. The water was cold. She must drive into town and borrow Fatty's phone. She would call

Libby. She wanted to let Libby hear her happy self. She would be the mother that she had not been for a while.

The road was clear. Few cars were around and the road-check was brief. The policemen waved her through immediately when they saw her; white people were not under suspicion. Fatty was sliding open the metal door of his coffee shop when she arrived at the town's market square.

"May I use your phone?" she mimed with her hand, dialling an imaginary phone and putting the receiver to her ear. He waved her inside. Once in the hallway of the half-opened premise, she took up the phone and dialled. She was excited. It might be too early to call but the maids would be up. She could persuade them to call Libby to the phone.

The phone rang. To Ruth, the ringing seemed prolonged and infinite. Then a voice answered. An English voice.

"May I speak to Libby?"

"Who is this?"

"Ruth."

"Thank God you called. This is Hazel, Nina's mum. Libby is distraught. We have been looking for you. You have to come back immediately. Your husband is missing. He disappeared with his driver, Din."

Chapter 24

THE BED WAS littered with papers and clothes. Hugh gathered the papers together and packed them into his briefcase. Then he crammed the clothes into a holdall, unmindful of whether they were dirty or clean. With a grunt, he zipped up the bag. He was glad to be heading home to May. From outside, raised voices, excitable shouts of *Tuan, Tuan*, cut through the air. They came nearer and nearer, followed by footsteps. Looking out from where he stood, he saw a group of men marching towards the building. They were pushing someone along. Hugh rushed out of the rest house.

"Din! Din! We found Din!" The man they called Din fell to the ground. He lay there in a heap, chest heaving, his shirt torn and trousers ripped.

"Send for the doctor," Hugh commanded. "Quick!" He knelt down and cradled Din's head. Someone placed a bottle of water in Hugh's hand. He lifted Din and placed the bottle to his lips. Din drank in great gulps, spilling some down his chin and onto his chest.

A motley crowd gathered around them. The babble of voices rose again. Malay interspersed with a smattering of Chinese and a sprinkling of Hindu and English. All venturing their account of how they had spotted Din. Hugh silenced them with a wave of his hand. "Let him speak!" he said in response to Din's hoarse attempt to talk. Hugh placed his ear near Din's lips. "Where is *Tuan* Mark?" he asked.

"*Tuan* Mark," Din whispered through cracked lips. Fine lines of blood mingled with dry white scabs. "I don't know where he is. We drove to Tanjong Malim. He asked me to drop him off and to drive back on my own to Kuala Lumpur. He didn't say where he was going. I think he was going to take a train."

"What happened? Where is the vehicle?"

"I met with an accident during my journey here," Din replied, his face ashen with fatigue. His lips twitched nervously. "I drove into a ditch and lost a wheel. I tried to get a lift; no one would stop. People are too frightened to stop for strangers. I walked all the way here." Din prayed that no one would ask him why he had not used the spare wheel or why he had abandoned the vehicle. He had failed to check the jeep before they left Kuala Lumpur. He had not remembered that the spare wheel had been taken out for repair. He would probably lose his job for this negligence.

Oblivious of Din's worries, Hugh rose and stepped away. "What could Mark be up to? Has his memory returned? Why did he decide to travel by train? Where did he go?" Hugh asked himself. He grimaced. He returned to his room and picked up his holdall. The driver had given little away so far. This did not mean, he thought to himself, that he had no more to tell.

The telephone rang. He picked up the phone. He listened intently, nodding at intervals, his forehead creased by a web of lines. He placed the receiver down. Mark was back in Kuala Lumpur. He had turned up at his office as though nothing had happened. Well not entirely, Reid had explained. Apparently Mark had regained his memory.

Hugh rushed out to his car. He must hurry back to May.

***

Hugh was lost in deep thought as he drove. He normally loved driving through the Malayan countryside. He loved the neat plantations interspersed with clusters of Malay wooden houses on stilts with brightly coloured washing hung out to dry in the front-yards. Often, villagers would display fruits from their garden on wooden stalls. The smell of jackfruit, ripe papayas, rambutans and even durians, the thorny fruit that smelt of sewage to some and glorious richness to others, would permeate the air. Often he had to wind up his window to stop the car interior from being flooded with their hot heady scent. This time he saw nothing. The trees whizzed passed. Miles and miles of rubber trees, planted in straight lines like a never-ending grid. Plantations he had helped to develop. All he could think of was May and what they would have to do if Mark were to come to see them. Would Mark suspect that Craig was his? He could no longer push such worries aside. The return of Mark's memory was a reality, not a possibility.

Darkness fell and still he drove at reckless speed. It was nearly midnight when he turned into the driveway of his house. The lights were still on. May must be waiting up for him. He stopped the car and switched off the ignition. He sat for a while staring at the lit-up windows. He saw May standing in one, her slender silhouette dark against the glow of light. She put up a hand to wave and then she was gone. He could imagine her footsteps running down the stairway and out to the front porch to greet him. He had called before he left for Kuala Lumpur; he had not been able to reach her. He had left a brief message. Hugh got out of the car and, sure enough, May was already by the front door, her long skirt billowing in the breeze. He went to her and gathered her in his arms. "May," was all he could say. They stood locked in embrace, each feeling the tenseness of the other.

"When Mark comes to see us," he said after a while, his arms still around her, "we will tell him the truth; we got together after he left Malaya. That is the only thing to do. He should understand. I had wanted to tell him about you. Ruth didn't. She loved him and didn't want to lose him to you. She was persuasive. I felt sorry for her. I had not planned to fall in love with you. I certainly did not connive with her to keep you from Mark for myself. You do believe me don't you?"

May remained still in his arms. Her silence troubled Hugh. "Do you still lo.... still have feelings for Mark?" he asked.

She shook her head and nestled deeper into his chest. Hugh tilted her face towards him and looked deep into her eyes. He was perturbed by what he saw. "Do you wish to tell him about Craig?"

"No," she whispered. "The past is finished. I love you."

Hugh heaved a sigh of relief. He was so tense, he could feel the knots in his neck building up. Yet a niggling of worry remained; he kept it to himself.

***

A week passed. They did not hear from Mark. During that time, May stopped almost all her normal activities. She accompanied Craig to school every morning and would wait outside the gate. The driver would park the car by the school entrance while she remained inside the vehicle until it got too hot. She watched anxiously for visitors at the school gate. Then reluctantly, she would go home to have lunch before returning to the school to collect Craig. She kept close to Craig, unwilling to let him go and meet his friends without her by his side. Craig complained to Hugh. The driver, observing May's odd behaviour, told his master that he had cleaned and polished the car so many times while standing outside the school that there was nothing else to clean. "*Mem sakit*?" he asked fearing that May might be ill.

The weight fell off May. She lost her appetite for food. She was restless at night. She spoke little. By the seventh day, Hugh took her aside after Craig went to bed. They were in the sitting room. It was a warm sultry evening. Above them, the ceiling fan whirred slowly stirring up the heavy air.

"May," said Hugh gently, "what is troubling you? Sorry, let me rephrase. I know what is troubling you. You are worried that Mark would somehow guess and claim Craig. But is there anything else?"

May's lips trembled. She was exhausted and fought for control of herself. She couldn't speak. She didn't know what was troubling her; she didn't want to know for fear of discovering something she wished didn't exist. Both Fu Yi and Hugh had asked her repeatedly if she had any lingering love for Mark. They had questioned her so many times that she had begun to feel that perhaps she harboured such feelings and had buried them deep within her heart. She began to doubt herself. She didn't want to possess those feelings; she wished with all her heart that she could say unreservedly that she no longer loved Mark. She only knew that she loved Hugh; she did not know if she also loved Mark. She was frightened of meeting him; feared that it might rekindle feelings she didn't know still existed. She despised herself. She thought of Ruth. For Ruth's sake, for Hugh and Craig, she must be strong. "I am just exhausted," she replied. "Yes, I worry that he might take Craig from me, from us."

"I know." Hugh knelt in front of her and took her in his arms. She rested her head on his shoulder inhaling deeply, finding comfort from his closeness. "He has not been in touch," continued Hugh, "perhaps he never will. Perhaps like us, he wants to be free of the past and start anew. He left today for London. Guthries sent him there on business."

Hugh could feel relief coursing through May's body. He held her tighter to him. "You have to look after yourself. Think of our baby." He pushed her away at arm distance and, gently, with one hand, traced her tummy. "It will be all right. There is nothing to connect him with Craig. Ruth doesn't know; no one does other than you and me."

May went still. There was one who knew. Fu Yi. But she wouldn't tell.

***

After Mark left Din, he took the train back to Kuala Lumpur. He didn't wish to involve Din, didn't trust him to keep silent. He did not return home. After his visit to the office, he went to Chinatown.

It was nightfall. The street was busy. Although most of the grocery stores were shut, stalls offering a range of hot food had opened up for business. They lined the street, spilling out into side streets. Wooden tables and stools filled every nook and corner. Light from kerosene lamps lit the way and the aroma of cooking filled the air. Pans sizzled, pots bubbled. Tables were filling up. People were dropping in for a quick meal before heading for home. Others were eating out before going to the cinema. Chinatown never slept. There were always people doing business, talking, eating and wandering amongst stalls looking for bargains. They came out in shorts and vests, some even in pyjamas. Amidst this festivity, a group of old women sat on low wooden stools taking in the warm night air. Mark walked up to the group. "I am looking for Fu Yi," he said. "Do you know her? She used to work for me."

The women stared blankly back at him with rheumy eyes. Mark switched to Cantonese. The heavily accented words rolled off his tongue. They looked away, flicking their fans, their faces bored. "Don't know," one volunteered. Mark peered closely into the group. A movement caught his interest. There was one amongst them who seemed to physically shrink away. "Is that you Fu Yi?" he asked her. The rich smell of cooking drifted through the air. Without warning, a picture of Fu Yi flashed through his mind: Fu Yi, small, thin with black hair drawn back into a tight bun with a tortoise shell to hold it in place. This woman was even smaller, hunched and skeletal in frame. There was something familiar in the way she held herself. "Fu Yi?" he asked again.

The woman raised her head. "Yes, Master," she replied.

"Can we speak?"

"What about? I have nothing to tell you. I am old and forgetful. It has been a long, long time."

"Come. Come with me. I just want to talk, to refresh my memory. I lost it, you know, and have only just started to recall. Help me. Please. I need you to fill in the blanks."

"No, Master, Leave me be. I am tired. I am old and forgetful. I can't remember."

"I just want to talk, please."

Fu Yi relented. She did not like to see her former master so reduced as to plead with her in front of the other women. It just didn't seem right. Perhaps a few words would not matter. She would have to be careful when speaking about May. She would guard her tongue. "Just for a little while. I don't feel well and will need to go to bed soon."

"Come this way. We'll find a quiet corner." Mark helped her up and guided her by the elbow to a table set up by the roadside. He sat her down gently on a chair and ordered tea. The other women looked on in wonder; they nodded and talked amongst themselves. What had Fu Yi done to deserve this treatment, they wondered. They had never seen a white man come to visit a servant.

Chapter 25

A DOOR BANGED shut. Ruth woke up with a start. She had only just dropped off from sheer exhaustion. Hastily she shrugged on a silk wrap and hurried downstairs barefooted. Halfway down the stairs she met Mark coming up. For a moment, they stared at each other; like two adversaries preparing for battle. The previous night's anxiety turned rapidly to anger when Ruth saw a perfectly safe and unharmed Mark.

"Where have you been?" Ruth screeched, eyes flashing. Her hair was dishevelled and her skin blotchy with tears. "I have been worried sick. We thought you were kidnapped, killed even." Seeing Mark safe wiped away her fear, sadness and dread in one fell swoop. She was furious at Mark's audacity in turning up at home without attempting to call earlier to say that he was fine. Overwrought by anger and fatigue and relieved at the same time, she began to tremble; she sat down on the stairs.

For a split second, Mark was contrite. He moved to take her in his arms. Then he recalled Din's words. It was Ruth who had stopped Din from telling him about May. He stopped; his arms fell to his side. His heart hardened. What else had she done? When had she found out about May and was that why she had whisked him away from Malaya after he was rescued? He recalled her reluctance to let him return to Malaya. At times he had even suspected that she was happy about his memory loss. She was vague and evasive when he questioned her about Malaya. He recalled asking her if she had packed all his possessions from the bungalow in Tanjong Malim. He had thought that they might give him a clue as to his previous existence. "Nothing, there was nothing in the bungalow," she had told him many a time. Suddenly, the sight of her filled him with distaste. He was willing to ignore her adultery. She didn't know that he knew about her affair with the schoolteacher. He had blamed himself when he discovered it. He had not been a good husband; he wasn't able to provide for the family. He thought he deserved what she had done even when he read the letter from Steve Fisher. The letter had been delivered not long after their arrival in Kuala Lumpur. He had opened it inadvertently, not expecting the letter to be for Ruth. Since coming to Kuala Lumpur, he had tried hard to be a good husband, to make amends. He knew he was responsible for making her unhappy and that it was unhappiness that had driven her to this man. But what he could not forgive was that she had kept his memory from him.

Without bothering to answer her, Mark brushed past Ruth. He didn't care that he nearly knocked her over. He ascended the stairs and on reaching the landing turned. The ceiling light lit up Ruth's upturned face. Her eyes were swollen.

"I am going to shower," he said coldly, as though nothing was amiss, "and change. Then I am going to the office. We shall talk when I come back." With that he turned and strode away.

Taken back, Ruth exploded. She didn't know this new Mark, this callous Mark with anger repressed into a coldness she had not known possible. It riled her. She had spent a sleepless night fretting over his disappearance and he had not even bothered to explain. She got up and ran after Mark.

"You cad!" Ruth stabbed his chest, pushing him. "You owe me an explanation! Where have you been? Have you no decency? Don't you realise the worry you caused me? Have you forgotten that you have a child? A family? What will your employers think? Are you out of your mind to disappear and then reappear as though nothing has happened and no explanation is necessary? You could well get the sack! This post would be another one of your short-lived jobs."

Mark turned livid with anger. "Get out of my way. I say we'll talk this evening."

Furious beyond control, Ruth slapped Mark. He raised his hand to return the blow and then stopped. He held her eyes for a moment. Then, without a word, he strode away.

***

The meeting room in the Consulate was filling up. Planters vied with tin miners to get a good seat. They were to discuss future plans to ensure the British stronghold in the Malayan economy. British firms and their various business associations were traditionally given privileged representations in the colonial legislative and executive councils. These arrangements were expected to come to an end when Malaya's fully-elected legislature came into force. Hugh watched intently. Small groups formed and dispersed. The conversation was animated. He knew the importance of this meeting. Britain's investment in Malaya was greater than that in India. Seventy per cent of these investments were still in rubber and tin. However, the time had come for them to branch into other areas. British trading houses wanted to bring UK manufactured goods into Malaya's fast expanding economy and export Malaya's commodities not only to the UK but also to Europe. They were confident that they were well set up for it. The Malayan dollar was linked to sterling, easing the international financial transactions that went with such businesses. Everything should go well for Britain's investments in Malaya, that was, if they could cultivate the right contacts. Already within the few months of independence, Malaya had become the second most profitable destination for British investments after Germany. Their main threat was again the Japanese. The Japanese were also busy courting Malaya.

From across the smoke-filled room, Hugh caught the Commissioner's eye. Reid was motioning him over.

"I want you to meet Lord Hill," Reid said nodding towards a gentleman with a thick bushy moustache and side-burns. "You will work with him when you are in London."

Surprised, Hugh looked questioningly at the Commissioner. He had not been told about a London assignment.

"I apologise. I have not had time to broach the subject with you. Things keep piling up on my desk and I have been distracted. I am not sure if you know that Mark Lampard from Guthries is in London on business. Apparently other companies have also sent their men to the City. A team of important Malay, Chinese and Indian government officials from the Federation's Ministry of Commerce and Industry will be visiting the United Kingdom. So these business conglomerates have despatched their representatives to, well let's say, make the lives of these visitors comfortable in the United Kingdom. I would like you to go to London to oversee things. You are the planters' representative. I don't want any unpleasant undercutting and lobbying. *Ummph!* No scandals. See that they behave. You will liaise with Lord Hill."

"How long will I have to be in London?"

"As long as it takes. So I leave you with Lord Hill. He will fill you in with the information you need. You leave in two days time. One more thing. Check up on Mark Lampard. He is a loose cannon. According to Guthries, his local knowledge of the Malayan people is indispensable. They have faith in him." Reid's face showed the opposite. "Yes, keep an eye on him. I don't want him to upset the boat."

***

Hugh took the pile of shirts from May and stuffed it into the suitcase.

"Let me do it." Patiently May refolded the shirts and placed them neatly in the suitcase. Then she packed his underwear, socks, trousers and wash bag. She was troubled by Hugh's trip when he told her that he would be working with Mark. "What will you say to him?" she asked.

Hugh took some time before he answered. "I don't know. I will wait for him to broach the subject. Like we agreed, I'll tell him the truth except that concerning Craig." He went to her and held her at arms' length. "There is nothing he could do to us. It may become unpleasant if he feels we betrayed him. I can handle it. I'll explain. Don't worry."

***

There was little that Ruth could do except to sit it out and wait. She was sorry for losing her temper and for the unkind words that had poured out of her mouth. It was wicked, intolerable and unforgivable. She could not retrieve them. She had no opportunity to apologise to Mark, to explain that her anger stemmed from her anxiety and fear for him. He did not come home after that fateful evening; he left without a word. He didn't even pack a suitcase.

With a heavy heart, Ruth walked around the grounds of her house. It felt like a cage despite the luscious greenery. The owners had built high walls all round for privacy. What had seemed beautiful when she first arrived now looked big and soulless. It was all in her mind. But she had never felt so utterly alone. She could not confide in anyone, not even Libby, especially not Libby. To think that only a few days ago she had found peace and been so sure that she could mend her relationship with Mark.

She wandered to a wooden bench and sat down. The thick canopy of leaves overhead shielded her from the sun. She took hold of her hat and squashed it between her hands. She wondered at the person she had become. She had progressed from a young wife enamoured of her husband to a jealous woman willing to sacrifice anything to keep him to, finally, a lying, deceitful adulteress. She had wronged Mark. To top it all, she had sneered and insulted him. No wonder he looked at her with such disgust. Had he regained his memory? Was that why? Had he remembered May? Ruth had learnt nothing about Mark's state of mind when she called his office. She could not bring herself to ask about Mark's memory. His staff would expect her to know more than they did. Neither could she reach Din. He had been sent away, posted elsewhere.

The gardener watched his mistress with interest. His scythe moved rhythmically in an arc across the lawn. He inched forward, scarcely paying attention to what he was doing, watching and observing Ruth. He saw the tears coursing down her cheeks. Why would she be crying? She who had everything: a big house, servants, beautiful clothes, a rich husband and a child. He shook his head in despair. If he had half of what the white memsahib had, he would be very happy. She was a strange lady. The kitchen staff had told him that the mistress had not been eating or sleeping. Even the neighbours knew. Gossip passed from one household to another in the market place. Gossip was like money. It changed hands quickly; people enjoyed receiving it and giving it.

Ruth sensed she was being watched. She dabbed her eyes dry and smiled across at the gardener. She pretended that she had grit in her eyes. She got up. She would call Hugh. He was the only person she knew in Malaya who knew of the past. Perhaps he could tell her more.

She went into the house. It was cool and dark inside. The shutters had been partially closed to keep out the bright sunshine. She was glad. She shook off her sandals; the marble floor was cool under her feet. She went into Mark's office. His desk was neat. She tried a drawer, and then the next drawer. They were all locked. She sat behind his desk and took up the phone. She found Hugh's telephone number in the directory and dialled. She waited anxiously for the incessant ringing to stop, for someone to pick up the phone.

"Hello," a woman's voice answered.

Ruth couldn't speak. She held the phone tight to her ear, her lips almost brushing the receiver. For a few seconds, there was only the sound of her breathing.

"Hello. Who is this? Please speak up."

Ruth placed the phone down. What a fool she was to think that Hugh would pick up the phone. More likely it would be May or a maid. It could not be a maid; the English was too good. She sat still, not knowing what to do.

The phone rang. Mark! Could it be Mark calling? Ruth snatched up the phone. "Mark?" she said.

This time it was the other side that remained silent.

Chapter 26

MAY PUT THE phone down. She was sure that it was Ruth. After the mysterious call she had immediately contacted the telephone operator and obtained the number of the caller. From there it was easy to trace the call to Mark's house. But Mark was in London. He couldn't have called. Unable to stop herself, she dialled the number. Even without ever having had direct contact with Ruth, she knew instinctively that it was her. It was an English voice, totally different from English spoken with a Malayan intonation.

May wondered why Ruth had called.

The sky was overcast outside. Great rolls of dark clouds formed and dispersed. A storm was brewing. The air was thick. Her chest felt tight, as though the weight of the atmosphere was pressing on her. It was quiet in the house, its silence adding to the oppression. With Mark away in London, she had not stood watch outside Craig's school. Instead she went to see Fu Yi after she had dropped Craig off. May learnt that Mark had been to see Fu Yi. He had no idea that Craig was his son. However, all was not well with his marriage. Ruth, she learnt, was unhappy. At the market stall, over cups of hot steaming coffee, maids exchanged gossip about their employers. The gossip filtered through to Fu Yi who knew the coffee lady, and she in turn, repeated it to May. They talked about the tears Ruth shed when she was alone; her unaccompanied trip to Port Dickson and the sharp words exchanged between Ruth and Mark before he left for London. He did not return home after that quarrel; he left for London without a word to his wife or child.

May was stricken with guilt. Whether it was intentional or not, she had taken Mark away from Ruth in the past. She wanted to atone for it. She wanted to reassure Ruth that she had nothing to fear from May. Ruth needed a friend and May wanted to be that friend. Fu Yi's account touched her. May pushed aside the niggling doubt in her mind that she might still love Mark. She would not put that to the test; she would avoid seeing him. She reminded herself that she loved her husband.

Yet, the thought of pushing herself forward and engineering a meeting with Ruth worried her. What if Ruth spurned her efforts? At least I would have tried, she countered. She fretted just thinking about it. What could she say to Ruth? How could she even start a conversation? Her thoughts switched one way and then the other. She could not reach a conclusion. All she knew was that she wanted to make amends. She wanted Ruth to be happy. She felt guilty. She had found happiness and was blessed with a husband who loved her, while Ruth and Mark were estranged. Hugh was going to do his part with Mark. She must do hers with Ruth.

Unable to shake off her thoughts, she decided that she would drop in at Fu Yi's again, this time unannounced. There were still a couple of hours before she had to collect Craig from school. Talking to her would clear her mind. Fu Yi was like a parent to her and would not mince her words.

***

May climbed the narrow dark stairway to the second floor. It was hot and close in the building. She stepped into the dormitory, Fu Yi's home. Light filtered through the front window. She could see washing hung out on lines thrust out through the window. Fu Yi was sitting on her bed with her back towards May. The confined airless dormitory, narrow beds packed close together and the old women on them struck her again. May felt her throat catch. She longed to take Fu Yi away from such surroundings.

"*Aiyah!* You are very popular, Fu Yi. So many people come to see you. You are lucky. Twice in one day!" said an old lady who was sitting facing the doorway. She had on a pair of black trousers hitched up to reveal a pair of legs that were so thin, that matchsticks might not be an inappropriate description. Fu Yi turned round immediately. She saw May.

"You here again! Is something wrong? You should not have come," she admonished. "This is no place for you. Remember who you are. Let us get out, away from prying eyes." Fu Yi glared at the woman who had spoken. Eight pairs of eyes watched them as they slowly made their way out of the dormitory.

May helped Fu Yi climb down the stairway. Sacks of dried

fish stood cheek by jowl on the landing. At the bottom of the stairwell, an earthen vat of *kiam chye* stood with its lid open. The smell of salted fish and pickles rose to meet them as they descended the stairs.

"It is smelly here, May. You should not come. What would Master Hugh say?"

"He would not mind. He is Malayan at heart. You know that. He has eaten enough fermented fish paste and dried shrimps not to worry about such matters."

They made their way into the bright sunshine outside. "Why have you come again? Why didn't you warn me that you were coming?"

"You don't have a telephone. In any case, if I had asked beforehand, you might not have let me see you."

May steered Fu Yi to the coffee shop next door. They took a table further in. A young boy came and took their order. "So!" exclaimed Fu Yi after the boy left, "I hope you are not hankering after Master Mark. Is that what is troubling you that you need to see me twice in one day? Your first loyalty is to your husband and to your children."

"I am not hankering after Mark. I told you! Lots of times. Don't you trust me? I am worried about his wife, Ruth. Ever since you told me about her, I have felt guilty. For a period, that guilt was buried by my fear that Mark would find out about Craig. Now that I know that he does not know, my feelings of guilt have resurfaced in a different form. Particularly after I learnt from you this morning about how unhappy she is. Is there nothing I can do for her?"

May was bright red. She was indignant. She was not yearning for Mark. She wished Fu Yi would stop putting such thoughts in her head. No one but Hugh and Craig mattered to her.

"You should leave things be."

"I want to make it up to her."

"You must be mad. She won't want to talk to you." Fu Yi stirred condensed milk into her coffee and watched the brew change colour to a muddy brown. She slurped the hot coffee before returning the cup carefully to the saucer. "Listen. You can't do anything. Salving your conscience might just make things worse for her."

"I am not trying to salve my own conscience." May was stung by Fu Yi's sharp remark. "I want her and Mark to be happy, just as I have found happiness with Hugh."

"The only way you could help her is to make sure that you let go of Master Mark. He still has very strong feelings for you. When he comes to see you, send him back to his wife."

Fu Yi took May's hands in hers. They were cold and small in Fu Yi's gnarled ones. "I know you mean well. I am just telling things as they are. I don't wish you to be hurt, nor your husband to be hurt, nor Master Mark and Ma'am Ruth. Don't meddle."

***

May left Chinatown and went straight to Craig's school. She weaved the car through the congested narrow High Street before turning off into the leafy green suburbs towards the west. She wound down the windows. Warm air rushed in. She allowed it to dry her wet cheeks. Craig would be alarmed to see her that way. She had become very emotional; the doctor had explained that it was perfectly normal and had to do with her hormones. She placed her hand over her little bump. It had grown. A little tight hard round, not quite obvious except to the discerning eye. She found comfort in its presence.

Unlike Ruth, at least she and Hugh had something joyful and wonderful to look forward to. She must do something for Ruth.

She parked at a side lane. It was congested with cars and children coming out from the schools. Boys marched out from the building to the left and girls from the building to the right. The two international schools stood side by side catering for the two genders. Craig was with a group of boys. They were talking to some girls from the adjacent school, distinguished by their blue and white uniforms. She looked on; she didn't wish to interrupt. Craig was chatting animatedly to one of them when a woman arrived to take her away. The girl waved and the woman, slender and very blond, turned. May gasped. Ruth! She had not seen her since that fateful night when she had hidden in the fence and spied Ruth on the terrace. May saw her take the girl's hand. They walked to a green MG Magnette parked some distance away.

May walked rapidly up to Craig. "Who is that little girl?" she asked.

"You mean Libby? She is new here. That was her mother."

"You know her well?"

Craig looked embarrassed and wrinkled his nose. "No! Our schools are holding a joint concert for parent's day. That is why we were talking to the girls. We have to practise with them."

"But she is a friend, isn't she? Do you like her?"

Craig rolled his eyes; he blushed. "She is just a girl. She wants to join in our games. She is too young, much younger than me. I suppose she is quite fun, for a girl. She doesn't fuss even when she falls and grazes her knee."

May concealed a smile. Craig looked so smug and superior. He was only seven going on eight.

"She says she is used to fending for herself. Her father was very ill at one time. She says her parents are not friends any more. They quarrel a lot."

May took Craig's hand; he pulled away. "Mummy! Stop! I know how to cross the road. I am a big boy. I am not two, you know."

"Shall we invite Libby for tea. Do you think she'll come?"

Craig shrugged. He turned and waved to the other boys. May was shocked by what she had heard. From a babe's mouth! If only she could do something to help Ruth. Poor Libby!

***

"Shall we go somewhere nice for tea?" Ruth asked Libby as she manoeuvred the car on to the main road. "There is a new American snack bar quite close by. We could have an ice cream if you like. They have one of those soft ice creams." She threw a sideway glance at her daughter. Libby was very quiet, quite changed from the happy smiling child she saw at the school gate. "What is wrong?"

"Is Daddy going to divorce you?"

"Of course not. What put that into your head?"

"Nina said that would surely happen. Daddy left without saying goodbye and I heard you quarrelling with him."

"Well Nina should keep her views to herself. I shall have a word with her mum."

"Daddy doesn't love us any more. He doesn't talk to me; *you* don't talk to me either."

"I am sorry darling. Adults are sometimes silly. We are kids at heart really. We quarrel just like children do but we make up later. So don't worry. We are not getting a divorce."

"If Daddy leaves us, if he doesn't come back, what shall we do? Will I still go to school? Nina says that I would probably have to stop school because it costs a lot of money for me to attend school."

Ruth turned quickly to look at Libby. She saw the bewilderment on her daughter's face. She reached out and took Libby's hand in hers and squeezed it before guiding the car to a side lane. The car came to a halt. "My poor sweetheart. Nothing of that sort will happen. I won't let it happen." She pulled Libby into her arms and kissed the top of her head. How could she have allowed Libby to be reduced to such fears? "Don't you worry," she said, "and don't listen to Nina. What made her say such horrid things? I love your daddy very much and he loves me. We are not going to get a divorce."

"I told her about your quarrel with daddy. Her mum asked me about you when I stayed over. You went off on your own to Port Dickson. Do you remember? Then Daddy disappeared only to go off again without even saying hello to me." Libby's voice caught. "Why doesn't he love me anymore. Why? Am I naughty? Have I been a bad girl?"

Ruth held her tight. "Of course he loves you." She placed a finger under Libby's chin. "Believe me. Everything is fine. He is busy at work. When he returns, we will have a holiday together. What do you think?"

***

That night, after Libby went to bed, Ruth went out into the garden. She wrapped a cotton shawl around her. The air was heavy with the scent of gardenias and jasmine. She went over Libby's words in her mind. "My poor, poor darling," Ruth whispered aloud, "to be so encumbered by worries. In trying to protect her I have inadvertently cut her off by not speaking to her. No wonder she feels unloved and unwanted. What a heavy burden for a child to carry. I have been such a stupid mother. I have been very selfish, wrapped up in my own unhappiness."

She walked up the narrow path that led to the edge of the garden where a grove of palm trees grew. She wondered what Mark was doing. Was he still angry? She must do all she could to fulfil her promise to Libby. She retraced her steps back to the house. She would send him a telegram. He had not left a telephone number but a telegram to Guthries in London would surely reach him. She would say sorry; she would tell him that she missed him, that she loved him.

Chapter 27

Buckinghamshire

MILE UPON MILE of low undulating green woodland stretched out as far as the eye could see. Beyond the woodlands were farms and fields divided like miniature postage stamps in vibrant greens and yellows. The view and colours were breathtaking.

"So is everything ready for their arrival?" Lord Hill cocked his eye and looked quizzically at Hugh, sizing him up. He liked what he saw. He perceived drive, energy and great empathy behind Hugh's unassuming manner.

"Yes! The delegation from Malaya is expected later today. Most of them will be arriving around teatime. A traditional cream tea has been arranged followed by a walk around the immediate vicinity of the estate. Dinner will be a formal event.

There are twelve of them in total. We will keep it a very English affair. The ministers will expect a certain level of pomp. Many of them have studied in this country, though I imagine not many would have had access to country estates such as this while they were here as students."

"Good, good. From what I hear, they are uncommonly fond of show and display. What about representatives from our firms?"

"Only representatives from the our bigger companies including Guthries, Sime Darby and Boustead will attend this evening's banquet. They will stay on for tomorrow's shoot. Some of the ministers are coming with their wives. We have made separate arrangements for the ladies' entertainment."

They walked on back to the manor house. The formal garden with its maze of box hedges and rose beds provided a beautiful backdrop to the magnificent Georgian manor. To the west of the house was a lake with a fountain at its centre. To the east stood a topiary of yew trees. Hugh slowed down his stride to match Lord Hill's. "Thank you for lending us your estate and allowing me such a free rein with your staff. Without your help, I would not have been able to make all the arrangements in time."

"Don't thank me. Reid is a good friend. Tell me, how are you getting on with the business side of things?"

"I have had a preliminary discussion with the three firms I mentioned earlier. Everything is in hand. No formal business meetings will be held this weekend. We want to keep the delegates relaxed and happy. We have, however, coordinated our own positions. We will talk business. Only it will be done in a way that is painless. We don't want to be too obvious and pushy. We'll try to lead them in our direction. HSBC and Chartered Bank will be sending their people along tomorrow to join the party. They too have been briefed."

"Good! My late wife always maintained that to get the best out of your business associates, one has to keep them happy. And you, I understand from Reid, have been in Malaya through the pre and post independence era and know how to deal with them. You know their sensitivities."

"Yes, things are rather delicate. Many of the delegates are still smarting from the way they have been treated in the past. We have to make sure that we do not rub them up the wrong way. On the other hand, we must not show any weakness."

"Yes, indeed. I see we are in good hands. Let's return to the house."

A silver Mercedes swept into the grounds. A man emerged from the car. "Excuse me," Hugh said to Lord Hill. "I see someone I need to talk to urgently."

He walked quickly in the direction of the new arrival. "Mark," he called even before he reached the car. He was nervous. He did not know how Mark would react. It was their first meeting since Mark had recovered his memory. He covered his nervousness with a broad smile.

Mark turned around. "Hugh," he replied, his voice flat.

"Welcome! I hope you had a good journey."

Mark ignored Hugh's proffered handshake. For a fraction of a second, Hugh's hand remained suspended in the air. Then he dropped it to his side before putting it in his pocket. As the planters' representative in Malaya, Mark would need to talk to him sooner or later. Sooner, however, might be better to clear the air before the others arrived. "Shall we take a turn in the garden?" Hugh asked. "The butler will see to your luggage."

Mark looked straight at Hugh. His eyes were ice cold. "If we must. Just keep the conversation to the business in hand. I have nothing else to say to you. Nor do I wish to hear what you want to say to me outside that which concerns business. Our friendship is over. I know everything." He turned away.

***

Hugh waited for Mark's luggage to be sorted. His smile remained fixed on his face until the footmen left. He had gone through various scenarios of this meeting. He had not expected such a curt opening. It gave him so little opportunity to make any overtures or to explain. Mark's jaw was clenched and his hands balled up in a fist as he waited for his luggage to be unloaded. His anger was bottled up, ready to explode at any minute. Any moment now, thought Hugh, he would turn on me. He imagined having to duck a fist thrown in his face or giving one back in turn. It would be a scandal that would find its place on the front page of every tabloid newspaper. He needed to release the stopper on Mark's bottled-up anger and let it fizz away before the other guests arrived. Perhaps it might only do so partially. Even that would be better than a full explosion later in front of the others.

"I do not know what you have been told or remembered," Hugh said, getting straight to the point. "I can only guess. But can we not talk it over, man to man? We cannot allow our personal issues to affect the outcome of this weekend which has such implications for British firms."

Mark spun round. His eyes were fierce. "Is that all you can think of? The firms!"

"No! But they are part of it, an important part. The lives of many people depend on them. More importantly, I believe your anger may not be justified. At least hear what I have to say."

"Why are you in such a hurry to talk? You tried putting off talking before."

"That was my mistake. You had no recollection of the past then. I thought that if you did not remember, then the problems would somehow fade away. I was wrong. I am sorry."

Hugh was aware of several pairs of eyes upon them. "There is a pub nearby. We could talk there. You tell me what you think you know and remember or been told. I tell you my version. I promise it will be the truth. You can decide then what you think. You might still think badly of May and me. I will take that chance."

***

The pub was almost empty. It was a workman's pub, not the sort that people from the manor would visit. They sat opposite each other like two adversaries. Two empty tankards stood between them. They had drunk quickly, each seeking courage as much from the act of downing their beer as from the beverage itself. A stack of photographs was fanned out on the wooden table stained with age and spilled ale. The dank sour smell of beer permeated the air. Behind the bar, the television was switched on to a cricket match. The commentator's voice drifted across the room.

Mark picked up the photographs one by one from the table. They were pictures of May injured and in detention and photos of her recovery and finally a photo of her marriage to Hugh. He flipped the last photo face down. He didn't want to look at it. He had listened unwillingly to Hugh's account. Could he believe him? That May and Hugh had got together only after he, Mark, returned to England?

Hugh saw the angry way Mark handled the photograph and the rapid throb of the veins on the side of his forehead. It had been a mistake to bring the wedding photograph along. He had hoped that it would force Mark to come to his senses, to realise that May was beyond his reach.

Hugh pushed a picture of Ruth towards Mark.

"Your wife was distraught when you were captured. She found out about your affair with May. She was frightened of losing you. She did not tell you of her discovery because she loved you. Surely you can understand that?"

Mark took the photograph of Ruth. She was sitting by his bed nursing him. She looked wan, thin and worried. Fu Yi's account of Ruth as a devoted wife corroborated with Hugh's. Ruth had nursed him back to health. Images of the hospital room and her face, filled with concern, came to him. He was the one that betrayed Ruth's trust. For a tiny second guilt crept into his heart.

A man came into the pub. He had with him a blond woman. She reminded Mark of Ruth. The couple sat at the far end; their movements were furtive. They kept glancing at the door as if they were expecting someone to burst in on them. Then, after a couple of minutes, they threw caution to the wind. They kissed passionately. The man's hand slipped down to the woman's buttocks. The woman giggled and pressed closer to the man. The pub's landlord winked at Mark when he caught him staring at the couple. Mark thought of Ruth and her affair with Steve. How could he give credence to the story that Hugh had fed him? Hugh and Ruth must have connived to keep May away from him, Hugh because he coveted May and Ruth because she wanted to keep him for herself. And May? What was her role in this?

Mark stood up, toppling the chair. "Don't worry," he snarled, "I will not jeopardise your precious business negotiations. Don't," he stressed, "don't speak to me ever again unless it is to do with business."

***

It was dark outside. The only lights were those coming from the manor. The other guests had retired. Mark stood in his bedroom by the window. He watched as one by one the lights in the manor went off, throwing the grounds into even greater darkness. An owl hooted. It sounded loud in the quiet of the night.

He lit a cigarette; its tip glowed red. He drew deeply on it. Smoke spiralled and the air turned instantly pungent. Something did not click when he went over Hugh's account. He could not figure out what it was. He walked up and down the room. Could he believe that May had not double-crossed him when she was still his lover? Her child. Craig! How old was he?

Mark stopped abruptly. There lay his answer.

He walked over to his desk and took out Ruth's telegram. He read it again. Then he crushed it into a ball and dropped it into the wastebasket. He looked at his watch. It would be morning in Malaya. He picked up the phone. "Operator, can you connect me to the Department for the registration of marriages, births and deaths in Kuala Lumpur?"

***

The bed was soft, yielding to Mark's form like liquid. He buried his face in the nape of May's neck and wrapped his arms around her, breathing her sweet scent. Her naked body was like satin and warm against his own. He turned her around to kiss her, reaching out to hold her face to him. Her lips were warm and her breath moist as their tongues made contact. He opened his eyes. It was not May! It was Ruth! How had she wedged herself between May and him? He struggled and pushed Ruth away; he couldn't. His arms were paralysed. No sound came out when he shouted; his arms remained heavy, inert, and lifeless. Hugh rose from behind Ruth. He had a rope in his hand, a rope tied into a loop. He swirled the loop round and round like a lasso. Then suddenly Mark felt himself in the sea. Water surrounded him; he fell deeper and deeper into the blue void. May's face appeared; beautiful May with her hair streaming behind her, swirling, swirling in the blue, blue sea. She smiled and slowly, ever so slowly, she waved her hand. Goodbye, her lips mouthed. Goodbye! She grew smaller and smaller, carried away by the tide. No! No, he wanted to shout. Nothing came out of his mouth, except water. He couldn't breathe.

Mark woke up. Sweat poured from his brow. His pyjamas clung to him like a wet sponge. He was out of breath, panting as though he had sprinted for miles, his heart bursting with the effort of it. It was a bad dream, just a bad dream.

Chapter 28

Kuala Lumpur

THE DAYS PASSED very slowly for Ruth. Mark had not replied to the telegram she had sent him. She sat at his desk fingering the pens that lay before her. Listlessly, she picked up a glass paperweight and watched the flecks of snow rise and disperse within it. She had bought it for Mark when they first holidayed in Brighton. She placed it down carefully. She wondered if she should send him another telegram. Perhaps the last one hadn't reached him. She could not believe that he could be so cruel. An image of his face, red with anger and, worst of all, disgust rose before her. Her throat caught. Ruth got up and shook her head to dispel the image. She went to the window. It was another hot and humid day outside. The trees stood absolutely still. Not a leaf stirred. It was too hot to be in the garden. How should I spend the hours until I pick up Libby, she wondered. She moved to the next room. How could she have ended up so friendless? Only Mary, the Headmaster's secretary, had written to her once. The letter was full of news about the school. Mary wrote about the other teachers, bits of gossips gathered during tea breaks in the staff room. She mentioned Steve in particular. Ruth deliberately skipped reading that section. She didn't want anything to do with him. She had thrown the letter away. She hadn't replied either. Since that last communication, no others had come. So what could you expect, she scolded herself, except to have no friends. She hurried up the stairs to fetch her keys and bag. She passed the console in the hallway. The sultry seductive scent of tuberoses caught her attention. Beside the vase of flowers stood a letter. It was addressed to her. The maid must have left it there.

She tore it open. It was short and to the point.

Ruth,

I am writing to seek a divorce. You could divorce me citing my adultery with May as grounds. This would allow you to preserve your reputation. However, if you refuse, I shall divorce you on the grounds of your adultery with Steve Fisher. I have his confession at hand. Please let me have your decision before my lawyers draw up the divorce documents.

Mark.

Shock went through her like a thunderbolt. The letter slipped from her hand. Mark knew of her affair! That was the reason for the revulsion on his face. She sank slowly to the floor. Her bag fell, spilling the keys and other contents within it. An overwhelming sadness and shame took hold over her. She pressed her face into her hands; her shoulders shook as she sobbed her heart out. She cried for her love of Mark, a love that had been battered over the years by his neglect and his affair with May, a love that had been battered by her own misconduct and infidelity, a love that she had tried to retrieve and mend these last few months. It was over. It seemed so final in black and white.

Nurin heard the sobbing. Alarmed, she came out into the hallway. She stood with a confused look on her face. After a while, she retreated back into the kitchen. Afraid she would embarrass the mistress if she made her presence known, she stood behind the kitchen door instead. Minutes passed. She tiptoed out again into the hallway. Ruth lay prostrate, her head turned with a cheek resting on the black marble floor. Tears streamed unchecked from the corner of her eyes. Her eyes were open but unseeing. At the end of the hallway, the grandfather clock ticked rhythmically. Nurin retreated once again back to the kitchen. She called the cook. Together the two women lifted Ruth up and took her to bed. *"Jangan menangis, jangan menangis,"* they pleaded with her not to cry. After a while they left the room. It was best for the mistress to weep out all her pain.

***

Ruth remained inert in the bed long after the women left. She buried her head into the pillow to stifle the sobs that threatened to break out again. Gradually her thoughts switched to Libby.

Mark had not mentioned Libby. Did he know that Libby was not his? It did not matter now. She would fight to keep her daughter, no matter the consequences. But how would they live? She recalled the difficulty she had when she tried to find a job in Malaya in the past. Could they stay on in Malaya? What should she say to Libby? Would Libby hate her? From across the hall, the clock chimed three o'clock. Libby was at school. It was her school concert that evening.

Ruth sat up. She swung her legs to the ground. She went to the bathroom and turned on the shower. She took off her clothes and threw them aside on the floor. She stepped into the shower and allowed the hot water to cascade over her. She soaped and lathered, scrubbing herself clean, hoping to wipe away the hurt, sadness and worry. The cubicle steamed and clouded. All was silent except for the sound of water. Later towelled and dried, she sat in front of the dressing table and carefully blow-dried her hair, brushing it until it was shining and bouncy. Then, carefully, she made up her face, just a touch of colour to her cheeks and lips and a lick of mascara. She went to the cupboard, dropping the towel on the way. The mirror showed her slender figure: pale with a narrow waist and long legs. She straightened herself to throw her shoulders back. She needed to hold herself together. She chose a slim skirt and a silk blouse amongst the garments hung neatly in a row. Libby had told her that Craig's mother wanted to meet her. She had ignored the invitation. She would see her now. She would attend the joint school concert. She would tell Libby about the divorce after speaking to May. She knew May would be at the concert.

***

Ruth stood at the entrance to the school hall. People were streaming into the hall. She searched the room, looking from one end to the other. She couldn't see May nor Craig. Clutching Libby's hand firmly in hers, she moved aside to let people enter. The seats were rapidly taken; still no sign of May. Ruth could feel her heart beat. Perhaps May would not be here; perhaps she was not feeling well.

"Here they are, Mummy," cried Libby. She tugged Ruth's hand and pointed. Ruth turned. May was standing behind her. They looked at each other. Neither spoke. Ruth held on tight to Libby. Her hand was clammy and Libby was trying to extricate herself from her mother's clasp. The children were desperate to join the others to prepare for the start of the concert.

"We have to go," they cried, freeing themselves from the restraining hands of their parents and dashed away.

"Shall we sit together?" asked May. Ruth nodded in reply. They made their way towards the front and squeezed in through a row of seats already occupied by excited parents. They sat down, both self-conscious, both tense and each very aware of the other. Though masked somewhat by the chatter and excitement in the hall, their protracted silence grew awkward. Minutes passed. Unable to stand the tension, May turned and extended her hand and took Ruth's in hers. "Please, I would like us to be friends."

Ruth was completely thrown by the gesture. Unable to speak, she found herself pressing May's hand in return. A friend, thought Ruth, from such an unexpected quarter. She swallowed hard. She needed a friend. She had not come expecting friendship. She had come to do battle, to ask for help against the biggest of odds.

They settled back in their seats. Unconscious of Ruth's stream of thoughts, May was delighted. Ruth had not withdrawn her hand and had not turned down her offer of friendship. Perhaps everything would be fine after all. She wondered at what she could do to seek forgiveness from Ruth, to make Ruth happy. The concert began. Midway, just after the children took their bow, Ruth whispered fiercely to May. "I want to talk to you in private. It is urgent."

"Of course." May threw an anxious glance at Ruth. Ruth's lips were drawn tight and the sinews on either side of her neck stood out. Her eyes remained fixed ahead on the stage. May realised that all was not well and she had been too precipitous in her conclusion. A flush spread from her face to her neck. She told herself that if Ruth were to harangue her with accusations, she would take it. She would not, should not offer excuses. She could only offer her sincere regret for causing Ruth hurt in the past. It was naive of her to think that Ruth would accept her friendship so easily. May felt a flutter in her stomach. Instinctively she placed a protective hand over it. "There will be a fifteen minute interval before the next act. Perhaps we could go out into the garden and talk in private."

***

Ruth and May walked across the football field to a bower at the far end. Behind the bower stood a netball court, which marked the boundary of the girls' school. May sat down on the wooden bench below the bower and Ruth sat beside her. They could see, across the field, long files of people moving from the hall into the adjacent room set up as a temporary refreshment room. Their voices floated across to them.

"First let me say thank you for seeing me," said May, "I don't deserve your kindness."

"Don't thank me," Ruth retorted. She turned fiercely to direct her gaze at May. "Mark wants a divorce."

"No!" May looked at Ruth with horror and shock. She grasped Ruth's hand. "It cannot be."

Ruth shook away May's hand. "Yes. He wrote; he says he wants me to divorce him citing him and you as the guilty party. Did he come to you? Did you agree to this?"

"No! I must warn Hugh. I will call him tonight." Suddenly May felt ill. She stood up. Her head swam and she sat down again, cradling her tummy.

"You could stop Mark from taking this route."

"How?"

Ruth searched May's face. What makes her more worthy and more lovable than me, she wondered. Why does she have such a hold over my husband? It must be something more than loveliness, though lovely she is, Ruth admitted to herself. For a split second, her old jealousy rose. She quelled it. "Mark still loves you. He would be open to what you say to him."

"But Hugh has already tried to explain."

"Hugh is not you. Mark would view Hugh as a rival, an opponent and an enemy even. But you ... it might be different. Can you not even try?"

"What do you want me to say to him? Not to pursue the divorce? I can't dictate to him. I have not seen or spoken to him for over seven years."

"Tell him you don't love him. Tell him that you have never loved him. Tell him anything that will stop him from thinking that he has a future with you. If you can convince him, he might at least drop his pursuit of the divorce. He might come back to me."

May stared wild-eyed at Ruth. She couldn't think clearly.

"Don't you see? Mark thinks he has a chance of winning you. I am sure that is why he wants a divorce." Ruth's face flamed red with embarrassment. To have to plead with her husband's former lover! She was appalled at her lack of pride. Still she had to try to keep her family together for Libby's sake if not her own. She would prostitute her soul if needed. It might not work. She had no alternative. She cursed herself for her own infidelity. There was nothing she could do to undo it. She could only hope that Mark would believe that Steve had meant nothing to her. If only he would give her a chance to explain.

May saw the desperation in Ruth's face. "I will try to help. I don't know if your suggestion would work. I must talk with Hugh. You must know that it is not only me; Hugh is involved too."

Chapter 29

May was still awake long after everyone in the household had gone to sleep. She lay on her side listening to her heartbeat. Ruth's revelation and request frightened her. She stared at the photograph on the dressing table. Hugh had his arm around her shoulders. He was gazing at her with such adoration that May had to swallow hard to stop the emotion coursing through her body. She thought of the consequences for Hugh's career and social standing if she was cited as the 'other woman' in Mark's divorce. It would destroy Hugh's career. The media would make a meal of it. Divorces were rare in Malaya and a triangular affair involving two Englishmen of standing would hit the front page. Malayan politics would have a field day of it. It would reinforce the new nation's view of the morals of its former colonial master. And Craig! He would suffer at school. Perhaps even the baby might be tainted by her one youthful blunder in the past. She too would be marked for life. Asian women would never let her forget it. She imagined the disparaging remarks that would be made. Then she thought of Ruth. She owed Ruth. But would telling Mark that she had never loved him make him return to Ruth? Was it a price she should pay to make it right for Ruth? Her head felt tight with the juxtaposition of conflicting thoughts. She could not think.

The clock struck midnight. It would be late afternoon in the UK. Hugh would be back in the flat he called his temporary home. She picked up the phone and placed her call.

***

Hugh was stunned by the news. For a moment he held the phone some distance from his ear staring at it as though it was guilty of some profanity that he could not quite bring himself to believe. Mark had not given the slightest indication that he was going to divorce Ruth. Quite the contrary, he had been affable and charming with all the guests the following morning. The shoot was a resounding success. A row of dead pheasants, carefully laid on the lawn, was testimony to that. Amidst much chatter, laughter and backslapping, the weekend had ended with a successful business agreement for the British side. Their Malayan counterparts seemed equally pleased. Both parties felt that they had the better deal. Hugh was glad that Mark had at no point raised any questions regarding Craig. And now this bombshell! It could only mean one thing; Mark had not believed him and thought that he had been cheated on by May and his best friend. He was out for revenge. He was out to smear Hugh and May's reputation even at his own expense.

Hugh, however, did not understand why Mark was divorcing Ruth. What did he hope to gain from that? Surely he could not have believed that he had a chance with May. Didn't Mark know that he was a lucky man with such a devoted wife, willing to forgive him even when he was the guilty one?

"Let's think carefully about Ruth's suggestion." Hugh's voice rasped over the phone. The line was breaking up. He moved his lips closer to the mouthpiece. "Telling Mark that you don't love him is one thing. It is the truth," Hugh crossed his fingers and squeezed his eyes shut willing himself to believe it, "but never having loved him is another. Mark is a driven man, driven with hate and suspicion. I don't know him any more. That might be the final straw for him. It would clinch his suspicion that you and I cheated on him while you were still with him."

May's silence was palpable. "May, are you there?" Hugh asked. The phone crackled and buzzed.

"Look, sweetheart. The line is breaking up. Can you hear me?" Hugh waited but the line remained disjointed. "I am coming back in two days time. I have to finish some business here. We'll talk then. We need to think it through carefully. Don't do anything until we have discussed it. I love you."

The phone clicked. The line was cut. May placed the receiver down. The realisation hit her like a thunderbolt. So much so that she hardly heard Hugh in the last few minutes of their conversation. She did not love Mark, not any more. When Ruth told her of Mark's intent to divorce her, May had not, for a single moment, rejoiced. She would have if she had still been in love with Mark. Instead all her thoughts were for Hugh and her family. She smiled and the joy lit up her eyes. She had been plagued by doubts about her own feelings these last months, especially with Fu Yi putting the thought in her head and Hugh's continued questioning about her feelings. She was free. She could face Mark and tell him to his face that she did not love him. If he pressed her, she would even tell him that she had never loved him. It would be a lie she was willing to tell to compensate Ruth. Perhaps he would go back to Ruth. Perhaps then the divorce would not be initiated. She, May, would not be named and shamed.

***

The air hostess stopped next to Mark. "Anything for you sir?" she asked. She pointed to the row of bottles sitting on the trolley. "We have red and white wine. There is gin, brandy, whisky, vermouth or perhaps a glass of sherry." She smiled, flashing dazzling white teeth.

"Whisky, straight," Mark replied.

"And you sir?" she asked the man seated next to Mark.

"Gin with a dash of tonic and a slice of lemon, please." The man eyed the quick way Mark downed his whisky.

"Trouble?"

Mark did not want any conversation. He closed his eye and feigned sleep, his hand still clasped round the glass of whisky. It did not stop the man.

"The tropics do get a man down after some time. Drinking becomes one's passport to bliss. We have our Government to thank for that. We might be short of many things when posted out to the Colonies but never gin and tonic. As Winston Churchill once said, gin has saved more Englishmen's lives and minds than all the doctors in the Empire. When I was in Germany just after the Second World War, the NAAFI ensured gin was available even when other essentials were not. It was the same in Ceylon."

Mark shifted in his seat. It was clear that the man would not stop his chatter. Moreover, he could hear the trolley returning. He wanted a refill. He sat up straight and opened his eye. The trolley was just a yard away. The bottles glittered like jewels. He could feel his lips twitching. A surge of longing for another drink rose from the pit of his belly to his throat. Beads of sweat sprouted on his forehead and upper lip. Impatiently he wiped them away with the back of his hand. He had promised to curb his drinking when he got his appointment with Guthries, the drinking that had been his downfall. Until the past few weeks, he had been successful. He released his glass and pushed it away. The man next to him was staring. Mark met his eye.

"Another drink sir?" The trolley and the whisky bottle were tantalising close. The whiff of alcohol hit his nostrils.

"Thank you. I don't need another." Mark busied himself, searching for the newspaper he had tucked in the pouch in the front seat. His hands shook.

"Good man." His portly neighbour eyes twinkled with amusement and respect. "I am sorry for the impertinence. When you get to my age, you say things you wouldn't when you were younger. You showed all the signs I had when I was about your age." He pushed his own full glass away. "I stopped drinking for many years. I test myself by ordering one and having it in front of me. I drank to drown my problems but the drinking only magnified them. I learnt the hard way. But, you, young man, have a life before you."

Mark turned away. He did not want a conversation. He certainly did not need a lecture from a stranger. He flipped open the newspaper and turned to the page of personal advertisements. He had put a notice in the paper for anyone who had known him in Tanjong Malim to get in touch.

"I lost my son. He would be thirty now. I saw the papers you were riffling through earlier. Divorces are nasty business. One should avoid them where possible. I believe that marriages are for better or for worse. Believe me, they are never a clear ride. If you want to talk, I am here. After all who better to talk than to a stranger whom you will probably never see again?"

"Will you bloody well mind your own business?" Mark rounded on the man, teeth bared, head jutting forward ready for a full confrontation. The commotion caused some of the passengers to turn. Mark saw an air hostess making her way towards them.

Mark settled back into his seat and closed his eye. The air hostess retreated. Quiet once more descended the cabin. Not for long.

"I am a dying man. I have only a few months. I see you in me. I mean it. If you wish to talk, I am here. I will be in KL for the next month or so. I have affairs to tidy up before the final event." He laughed mirthlessly. "I am Robert Haskin. People call me Bob."

Reluctantly Mark grasped the extended hand. It felt dry, the skin mottled like a mosaic of faded brown spots against thin pale skin. He looked into the man's eyes. They were hooded. Loose flesh hung over pale blue eyes; eyebrows once bushy were mere strands of sparse sandy-coloured hair. Yet the eyes themselves, despite their pallor, were still bright with intelligence. Mark felt himself drawn to Bob. Perhaps it was the burning need to talk to someone, perhaps it was being thirty odd thousand feet above ground level in a confined cabin filled with strangers, perhaps it was the burring therapeutic mechanical sound of a running engine, perhaps it was tiredness, perhaps it was sitting on a reclining chair with a captive audience, but suddenly Bob didn't feel like a stranger.

"When I was twenty, I joined the army," Bob continued. "I was posted to Burma. I loved Burma. I had never met young maidens with skin the colour of mulled honey, skin that smelt of cloves and cinnamon in a land of sunshine and smiles. At least that was what I thought. I fell head-over-heels in love with one. I gave up my English girlfriend and the army. I took up with my Burmese girl. She had expectations; she insisted that I bring her to England. For her I was a ticket out of hell while I viewed her as my beauty in paradise. We never spoke much; I was too eager to be in her arms." Bob tapped his head; his lips curled in disdain at his own recollection of himself.

"What happened?"

"Within a year we broke up. I returned to England and married my old girlfriend. Then I had another posting, this time to Ceylon. I was unfaithful to my wife. I blamed her for my infidelities. I thought her cold. You see, it is always easier if the fault lies with someone else." Bob chuckled and again tapped a finger to his temple. "I didn't appreciate my wife. I confused physical desire with love. She came out to join me. Our son was born in Ceylon. I went from affair to affair. Each time she forgave me and I grew to expect forgiveness as a matter of course. When our son died, the source of forgiveness dried up. She divorced me and went back to England."

Bob's voice broke. Mark saw a glimmer in his eye and a tear rolled down his wizened cheek.

"Until then, I did not know how much I loved her, depended upon her to right my wrongs, depended upon her for comfort and support, depended upon her for love. Now it is too late. She passed away last year."

"You are where you are," continued Bob. "Whatever happened in the past is not important. It is the future that matters. Give your marriage another chance."

Chapter 30

"HERE, HAVE MY ice lolly," Craig said pushing the fast-melting stick of pink ice into Libby's hand. Libby hesitated for a moment before taking the stick. Then closing her eyes, she licked, sticking her tongue out like a scoop. A dribble of pink stained her chin.

"Are things really bad at home?"

Libby thought of her mother's tear-stained face. Her own glistened. A swell of emotion, like soured limes, rose from her chest to her throat. Her nose filled. "Pretty bad," she replied mustering a nonchalant shrug that belied her face.

"So what's going to happen?" Craig asked.

They were sitting on a low wall separating the two schools. The late afternoon sun was scorching. Clusters of children lined the pavement vying for a space under the two huge trees that stood on either side of the gate. They were waiting for their parents to collect them. Libby was told to wait with Craig. Her mother would be coming with May to collect both of them.

"I don't know. Even my mum doesn't know, although she tries to tell me otherwise. My dad didn't say goodbye to me when he left. I must have done something bad. He doesn't love me. He never talks to me. Maybe that is why he wants to leave us. It is my fault."

Libby swung her legs letting the heels of her shoes hit the wall before bouncing forward. Both her knees were grazed. Tiny spots of blood oozed from broken skin to trail down to her ankles. She didn't care. Nothing could match what she felt inside her. She sniffed, stifling the snot that threatened to roll down from her nose. She threw the lolly stick away and crashed her heel on the wall even harder, catching the back of her calf.

"My mum lied to me. Nina told me that my father is going to leave us. My mum denied it. But I can see from her face that it is true! I don't trust her any more."

Libby looked away. She didn't want Craig to see her. She rubbed her nose. A trail of mucous appeared, milky white and slug like, on one cheek. Craig pushed his handkerchief into her hand. He felt responsible for Libby. His mother had told him to look after Libby like a sister. "Don't worry," he said. "My mum will help. She is always helping people. She likes your mum."

***

Ruth eased her foot away from the accelerator as she approached the roundabout. She was not comfortable going to May. Yet, where would it be safe to meet? May couldn't risk coming to Ruth. That would be reported to Mark immediately.

She took the first exit leaving the busy main road. She was late. They were to talk and then to collect the children. Trees and houses whizzed by. Her mind was elsewhere. She paid scant attention that she was passing through Kampong Baru, a small village that sat smack in the centre of a burgeoning city. A man on a bicycle with a child on the bar in front of him was suddenly ahead of her. He was meandering unsteadily in the middle of the road. She swerved narrowly missing the bicycle. The man waved, revealing yellowed stumps of teeth. The temporary lifting of his hand caused the bicycle to veer sharply to the verge. He smiled as though it didn't matter that he and the child were nearly killed. His basket filled with papayas and bananas toppled over. The fruits spilled onto the road, covering it with bright orange flesh, clumps of shiny black seeds and stems of yellow, mashed to a pulp.

Ruth's car screeched to a stop, juddering violently as it did so. Ruth fell forward. She hit the steering wheel setting off the horn. It blared straight into her ear. A crowd gathered around her car. Somehow, dazed and disorientated, she clambered out. A hand guided her to the wayside and sat her down on the grass edge. Someone pushed a sweet syrupy drink that smelt of roses into her hand.

"Are you hurt?" The accent was clipped and precise above the melodic rabble of sounds and words still unfamiliar to Ruth.

"No," she replied, glad not to have to struggle in Malay. "I am all right." Ruth looked around for the man with the bicycle. "Did I hurt anyone?" Her voice sounded strange to her, almost disembodied, hollow and hoarse.

"No harm done, except for some fruits mashed to pulp. His fault. I have taken care of things. He has left."

She tried to rise. Her legs gave way with the mere effort. She looked at her watch. She was late! "I have an appointment. I have to go." The words came out in a tumble as she tried to muster strength in her wobbly legs.

"Take it slowly."

For the first time Ruth looked at the man who had spoken. His eyes were chocolate brown with lashes that were almost too pretty to belong to a man. His brown arms were extended towards her. Ruth took his hands and drew herself up from the grass. She reached just above his shoulder. She was suddenly very aware of her dishevelled state, her wind-blown hair, her creased skirt and the height of the man. Two months into her stay and she had got used to people being smaller and shorter than her. "Where am I?" she asked, her hand straying to pat a wayward curl in place.

"Kampong Baru. Where do you wish to go? I shall drive you. You are in no state to drive after that excitement." His voice brooked no dissent.

"I am fine. Really." Ruth took an unsteady step. He stopped her. She was conscious of his firm grip on her bare arm.

"I insist. I'll drive you. You can pick up your car later. Or I can deliver it back to your house." Without waiting for her reply, he propelled her forward to his car. "I am Omar." He didn't ask for her name.

Ruth allowed herself to be led. Exhaustion from sleepless nights paralysed her. She resigned herself to being taken care of, even if by a stranger. She was past caring. She was burning. Her head ached and her throat was sore. She didn't want to fight, make decisions and do things. She was done with doing. She was weary; she would grab whatever was offered. In a short time, she realised, she would have to make decisions, plot and plan to survive. But for the moment, she would allow herself to be cared for.

***

May paced up and down the room. Ruth was late. There would not be enough time to talk. She looked at her watch for what must be the tenth time. School would be over soon. She parted the curtains and peered out of the window. The hot sun had created a haze. Trees shimmered and a mirage formed over the tarmac. A Jaguar swept into the drive, its sleek body painted racing green. A flurry of dust rose in its wake. It slowed and then nosed its way to the front of the house. A man stepped out and opened the passenger door. Ruth emerged. May gasped. She recognised him. One had only to open a newspaper and almost inevitably he would be there. Why was he here with Ruth?

May ran down the stairs. Her feet barely touched the floorboards. The front door opened. She heard her maid greeting Ruth and then the roar of a car departing.

She stepped into the front hallway. "The man who brought you here, how do you know him, Ruth?" she asked without preamble.

"I had a slight accident."

"Accident! Are you okay?" All thoughts of the gentleman she had seen flew out of May's head. She took Ruth by the elbow and placed an arm around her waist. "What happened? Shall I call the doctor?"

"Fine, just shaken. He said he was Omar. He kindly gave me a lift."

"Omar! Did he not say anything about himself?"

Ruth shook her head. They had travelled in silence. She could hardly keep her eyes open during most of the journey. Every sinew in her ached and her head felt as though it had been compressed and was now a mass of roaring pain.

"He is the son of Tun Zikri and Toh Puan Siti," May continued, "and one of the most eligible men in town, rich, well educated, Oxford no less. A powerful man. It is rumoured that his parents are busy arranging his engagement. No one apparently is good enough for Omar."

May stole a glance at Ruth. It was strange that he should go out of his way to rescue a stranger. His family was renowned for their snobbery. *Sombong* was the word people used to describe them. She recalled the picture of Omar's mother decked in diamonds in that morning's newspaper.

"Count me out." Ruth was weary. Yet an unaccountable twinge of regret rose in her breast. She attributed it to madness. She would probably never see him again. She wondered at her ability or rather stupidity to let her mind gather such thoughts. He had been kind, masterful and unquestioning. For one mad moment during the journey she had allowed herself to dream. In another life, Omar would be the kind of man she could fall in love with. He was someone who would take care of things. She needed someone to take care of things, an uncomplicated, unquestioning sort of person. He had not even asked her name. But she had never been good at judging people's character. Steve and Mark were cases in point. An overwhelming sense of tiredness descended on her once more. She shivered. "I need to sit down."

"How silly of me, gabbling away. Come and sit down. I'll collect the children and you can rest here. Have dinner with us. Hugh is still away. We'll talk afterwards."

Ruth sank on to the sofa. She felt her body burn. She tried to respond in a way befitting someone intending to wave away the friendly overture of a rival. Instead her lips quivered, not quite doing what she wanted them to do. Everything became too much for Ruth. She had come to press her case, had imagined last night that she might have to resort to threats. May's kindness and attentiveness disarmed Ruth. The conversation they just had could have been between two friends. Yet she did not count May as a friend. How could she? She wondered if the day's events were real. Meeting a celebrity and having what she had once considered her arch-enemy fuss over her. Was May for real? Her eyelids felt heavy. The weeks of sleeplessness took over. Under the oppressive soporific heat, she drifted off into a troubled sleep. A sleep where before her yards and yards of silk rippled through the air; their brilliant colours mingling to form a rainbow shooting through the sky. The colours broke and came together like a coloured stream. She felt herself enfolded into its midst; its softness caressed her skin, making it cool and then warm. If only, if only she could remain in its embrace. The corner of Ruth's lips lifted; she was drifting, drifting in the warmth of the silk. The warmth turned into heat. The silk became flames, bright fiery red licking her skin, turning it into blisters. She was on fire. She struggled. The flames held her, flickering and burning, flickering and burning.

***

"How long has she been like this?" Omar was shocked when he saw Ruth. Her skin was almost translucent, like white muslin with a hint of blue. The hands that peeped out of the bed cover lay limp and lifeless.

"Two days. The doctor has been twice. I have been bathing her with ice water. The fever has finally broken. She is very weak. How did you find out?"

"I brought her car to her house. Her address was in the glove compartment. The staff told me that she was with you. I waited a day before I came, as I did not wish to be too intrusive. I am glad I came."

May adjusted the bed cover over Ruth. The curtains were drawn. A table lamp on a chest of drawers threw a soft light in the room. She took the bowl of water she had been using to wipe Ruth's brow and stood up.

"I'll like to sit with her for a while. May I?" Omar asked. His face was partly hidden, for the light was behind him.

May hesitated, uncertain that it was the right thing to do. So much had happened these last two days. She was glad that Hugh would be back that evening.

"Please," he said.

May relented. It would be rude to say otherwise.

Omar sat down by the bed. He edged closer bringing his face close to Ruth's. He drank in the paleness of the oval face in repose and the soft hair like spun gold spread out on the pillow. Ruth stirred. He took her hand in both of his. He murmured something to her.

From the doorway, May watched in silence and astonishment. She couldn't hear him. Then she closed the door slightly, leaving it partly ajar to maintain propriety.

Chapter 31

MARK BADE FAREWELL to Bob Haskin at the airport terminal and made his way to the car park. His ears were still ringing with the advice of his new friend. He threw his suitcase into the boot and got into the car. He sat in the sizzling heat, his fingers suspended over the ignition key, thinking. Sweat poured off him, trickling into his eyes and down his back. There was a certain truth in the old man's words. Perhaps he had been too hasty in blaming Ruth. Why should her infidelity be a greater wrong than his? The blame lay with May. He thought of the information gathered from the Registrar's office. Craig's birth date showed that he was conceived before Mark was kidnapped. She must have deceived him with Hugh even while professing her love. She could well have connived with her cousin to have him kidnapped and out of the way so that she could be with Hugh. Hugh's role in vouching for her character played a major part in her release. Of course Hugh would vouch for her character. He was her lover. He, Mark, had been two-timed.

He grew more and more agitated in the confined space of the car. Away from the moderating reasoning of his new-found friend, Mark's anger once again imploded in itself. He slammed his fist on the steering wheel. He had lost years of his life because of their treachery.

He started the engine. It roared into life. He revved it hard. Fumes, black as coal spurted out of the exhaust pipe. He reversed, hardly paying any attention to his surrounding or the people in it. The tyres carved sharp treads on the tarmac. He raced out of the car park with his foot pressed hard on the accelerator. The tyres screamed in protest. He drove like a madman. Trees and houses rushed past him in a blur. He overtook a car, and then another, swerving to the left to hit the grassy verge and then accelerating even more to overtake from the left. He did not care that he was breaking the law. People gestured and pointed to the speed limit, cars honked. He saw nothing. Just red!

He drove without knowing where he wished to be. He knew only where he did not want to be. He didn't want to go home. He couldn't go to the office, not like this. He headed to the north of Kuala Lumpur towards Ipoh. Rubber estates whizzed by. Between the estates, open cast tin mines dotted the landscape. They too flashed by in a blur. He overtook every vehicle on the road, cars, big trundling lorries, unwieldy motorcycles, anything and everything. Oncoming vehicles veered to avoid him. The single carriageways were not made for speed. The heat in the car became oppressive. Mark wound down the windows. Hot wind rushed in. His hands on the burning steering wheel became clammy with sweat. Then, suddenly the sky changed. Black clouds gathered; huge cauliflower-shaped cotton wool, dark as soot, blotted out the sun. Lightning struck. Jagged shafts of white light lit up the sky. A flock of birds shot out of the trees and dispersed like black flecks. Then the heavens opened. Rain spattered fast and furious on to Mark's windscreen. It came through his open window. He released his grip on the steering wheel to wind up the window. His fingers slipped. The wheel spun free. He panicked. He stepped hard on to the accelerator. The car veered to the other side of the road. An on-coming lorry loomed, its light shone straight into Mark's face. Mark's car shuddered with the impact of the lorry. With a deafening bang its body crumpled fold upon fold with Mark wedged inside it.

***

"Does Ruth know?" Hugh asked the minute he stepped into the house. News of the accident had come through when he was at a board meeting. He had hurried home immediately.

"No! Come into the study. She might hear us." May beckoned her husband to follow her. The house was as quiet as a graveyard. The maids were huddled in the kitchen, whispering amongst themselves. They had been warned not to mention anything to Ruth or the children. Craig and Libby were still at school. May had insisted that Ruth and Libby stayed with them until Ruth was fully recovered.

May drew the curtains shut. She could see Ruth seated in an armchair on the terrace under a sunshade. Ruth's eyes were closed and her head was resting on a pillow that May had wedged behind her. She looked pale and tired.

"We have to tell her. She has a right to know."

May's face crumpled. She had no words to express her horror and the compassion she felt for Ruth. "I wouldn't know how to tell Ruth. I wouldn't know what to say to Libby. Poor, poor things."

"We'll have to tell Ruth. Perhaps Ruth would like to speak to Libby herself. We can't hold back the news. It would leak out. We can't trust the servants not to let it slip."

"We must do everything we can for Ruth. I know she has financial difficulties. Mark had not left her with much housekeeping money. I had to pay her servant the wages owed." May had been aghast when she learnt of Mark's cruelty. "She can stay on with us, can't she?" May asked her husband.

"Of course. I'll arrange to terminate the rental contract for her house. We'll cover Libby's school fees, until such time as we can work out a more permanent plan."

May lifted the curtains aside to peer out. Ruth was staring blankly at the shrubs surrounding the terrace. On her lap, lay the shawl that May had given her. Ruth's fingers were listless, making little knots of the soft silk until it formed a crumpled heap.

"We'll tell her now," said May with a sigh.

Part
Three
Port Dickson,
Malaya
1960

Chapter 32

The house stood on the crest of a low hill some hundred metres from a little stream. From where she stood, Ruth could hear water gurgling as it cascaded over stones as smooth as jade into a deep pool of darkness. She made her way to the stream, stopping to gather a posy of hibiscus and long grassy seed heads. Her feet sank into the grass, still damp with the morning's dew. When she reached the water's edge, she turned and looked up. The house was a silhouette of dark wood against the bright rays of morning sunshine. Memories of another life crowded in. Impatiently she shook them away. She must not dwell on the past. Today she would see her daughter. Sunday was her day of respite. Slowly, she lowered one foot and then the other into the stream. The water was crystal clear, so clear that the motley of stones in the riverbed looked like coloured gems. Water swirled between and around her toes. She sat on an outcrop of rocks letting the bottom end of her sarong dip and billow in the water. Then, carefully she placed the flowers down on the rock and waded into the pool. It was ice cold. She gasped with the impact and swam swiftly. Her arms looped wide and pulled, her legs fanning out behind her. Her sarong with its swathes of browns, blues, yellows and crimson swelled like a balloon. Then, turning face upwards, she floated. Her hair streamed behind her like seaweed in an intricate dance. She closed her eyes and allowed the sunshine to warm her face, revelling in the contrast of warm and cold. A bird broke into a song. From the corner of her eye she saw a kingfisher land on a branch by the stream. All was quiet except for the gurgling of the water, the chirping of birds and swishing of bamboos. Peace and solitude. That was what brought her back to Port Dickson, the one place that gave her solace. She thought of Libby. She would be here soon. Ruth flipped over and swam back to the outcrop of rock. She stood up. The sarong moulded to her wet body outlining her slim muscled form. She retrieved the bunch of flowers and headed up the hill.

Water dripped down her back leaving a trail of wetness as she strode up the slope. Her bungalow, built above the ground and on stilts, was only a short walk from the school. The villagers had helped build it, as they did the little pre-school that she ran. Both were simple wooden structures with wide verandas and carved banisters round them in the style of Malay houses in the vicinity. While the school was a new construction, her bungalow was a vintage fisherman's hut revamped to provide her with a postage stamp sized shower and a small galley kitchen. Hugh and May had provided the funds for the purchase of the land and the materials for the buildings.

Home! Yes, she thought of this as home. It gave her such immense pleasure and peace. She had May and Hugh to thank for it. They had cared and looked after her for almost a year before she found the will to be human again. They would be here soon with Libby. She must hurry.

***

A rich smell of lemon grass, galangal, turmeric and coconut wafted through the air. Ruth blended the spices in her granite mortar and pounded them to a fine paste. She tipped shallots and chillies into a clay pot and added the paste, frying the mixture until it turned a russet brown. All she had to do was to stuff it into the red snapper, wrap the fish in banana leaves and place it on the barbecue. Then a sauce made up of lime juice, a sprinkling of fish sauce, a dash of palm sugar, and perhaps some sliced chillies would be all that was needed to accentuate its flavour. She was pleased with her menu: a salad of pineapple, cucumber, sweet onions and bean shoots and rice to go with fish. On Fatimah's instructions she poured coconut cream and tucked a bunch of the local aromatic *pandan* leaves into the soaked rice grains. Soon the rice was bubbling and a fragrant aroma filled the air, a tantalising sweet and savoury combination that would have appalled her in the past. She thought of Mark and how his changed palate had filled her with surprise. Now, they too were flavours she and Libby loved.

A little nudge of regret rose in her breast whenever she thought of Libby. She could not share everything with her daughter. Some things must remain hidden. Perhaps, in the years to come when Libby became an adult, she could tell her. She shut her eyes to still her rebellious mind. Silently she mouthed the word *aman*. Fatimah had taught her to repeat the word peace ... until the threat of tears dissipated.

She filled a tray with cutlery and plates and went down the steps into the garden to set the table. She wanted the day to be perfect and had decided to serve lunch under the huge tree by the side of the house. Now she was uncertain if it was a good idea. The sun was sizzling hot. She gathered the cutlery and plates and took them back into her bungalow. The table on the veranda might be a better idea. She flung a brightly coloured batik cloth over the table's rough wooden surface. Diagonal swathes of vibrant browns and blues sprang to life. A clock struck twelve. She was running late. She dashed into her bedroom to change. She brushed her hair until it shone and then looped it up into a ponytail. She smiled at the image in the mirror. The white tee shirt and blue slacks suited her tan. A car purred into the driveway, shortly followed by another. She was puzzled. Two cars! Who could the other one be? she wondered.

By the time she ran down the flight of wooden steps, Libby was already running towards her followed by Craig, May and Hugh with a toddler cradled between them. Libby hurled herself into her mother's arms, talking non-stop. Ruth's eyes travelled beyond Libby's shoulders. May was waving frantically. Beyond her, standing by the car was Omar! Their eyes met.

May hurried over. "I couldn't stop him from following us. He wants to see you and would not take no for an answer. Libby told him we were coming today."

"It's fine. He is here. I can't turn him away." Ruth felt her whole body tingle. She hugged Libby tight and kissed her before turning to embrace May and Hugh. "Do join us," she beckoned Omar. She mustered a smile to quell her fast-beating heart. She hoped her invitation sounded natural and nonchalant. She had tried to stop him from seeking her out. She didn't want any involvement. She didn't need any complications in her life. She had found peace here. Yet her treacherous heart was telling her something else. Its words came unbidden and unwanted. "Has peace always to be twined with loneliness? Are you at peace or are you lonely?"

"Mummy, did you hear what I just said? Can we go to the beach later this afternoon?"

"Yes, dear, I heard," she murmured in her daughter's ear. "We'll talk about it later. I am sure May and Hugh will need a rest and their lunch. Many days lie ahead of us. You don't have to rush. I had better check on the tide before saying yes."

Over Libby's shoulder, Ruth could see Omar approaching, his feet lightly treading the bed of Casuarina pine needles on the driveway. She panicked. She deliberately turned away to look for May but May had wandered off with Hugh to the other side of the garden. When she turned back, Libby was gone. Her voice floated down from the bungalow. She must have gone to check on the food and was now running from room to room with Craig trailing behind her. Their carefree laughter filled the air.

Suddenly Omar was inches away from Ruth, filling her entire space.

"Thank you for letting me stay," he said.

Ruth found her hand in his.

"Gosh, your hands are cold." So saying Omar took both her hands in his, squeezing them gently.

Ruth stepped back and withdrew them. "I am fine. Do take a walk in the garden. I need to check on the food. Excuse me." She sounded unnaturally clipped and formal, even to her own ears. She ran up the steps into the kitchen. For a brief moment she hovered over the kitchen sink to catch her breath. She must put a stop to this madness. He must leave after lunch. He must be discouraged from coming again. They had managed to keep her whereabouts away from him until now. Why had Libby told him? She dropped her head in despair. She felt a hand on her shoulder.

"Are you all right?" asked May.

Ruth shook her head; her body still slumped forward over the sink, her hands clutching the rim of the basin.

"It's Omar, isn't it? Do you want me to send him away? He has been coming almost every week for the past year. We didn't let on that you were here until Libby accidentally revealed that we were coming to see you. He followed us. He is very persistent."

Ruth ran the tap and sloshed water on to her face. "I am all right. I just have to get hold of myself. I'll tell him myself after lunch. We owe him at least a lunch for his effort, don't we?" she said, summoning up a smile.

May stood on tiptoe to put her arms around Ruth, the taller of the two. "We are here if you need us. You know that, don't you?"

Ruth hugged her friend. "Thank you," she said. "Let me get on with the food. Everything is almost ready. I'll join you in a minute and will call for help if I need it. But," she said to May, her eyes swimming with unshed tears, "it is better if I do it on my own. I need some space to clear my thoughts."

***

From the top of the steps May could see the two men talking. Their heads were close, one chestnut brown with streaks of sun-bleached gold and the other almost jet-black. Over the past year or so, the two men had become good friends. However, as far as Ruth was concerned, Hugh had kept to his word.

He had not interfered nor given any hint to Omar on Ruth's whereabouts.

With her eyes still keenly fixed on the men, May sat down on the step and rested her elbows on both knees and her chin on her upturned palm. She wondered what they were talking about. From the corner of her eye, she could see Craig and Libby engaged in a game of their own invention under the dappled shade of the big flowering angsana. Her eyes wandered over to her baby Lin. She was still napping on the mat after the tiring journey. Soon she would wake and demand May's attention. For the moment, May had time to herself. It was such a peaceful scene, palm trees swaying gently in the breeze, flowering bushes, the sound of a stream gurgling, and the aroma of spices drifting through the air. Her thoughts wandered back to the day when they received the news of Mark's death. She could not think of it without feeling guilty. His death had spared May and Hugh from the ugliness of a divorce suit. Mark's death, however, had shaken Ruth to the core. She had sunk deep into depression and despair.

Overhead, white clouds chased each other against a backdrop of pure blue sky. May's eyes glazed over as she stared into space. She thought of the tumultuous events of the past two years.

Two years ago, 1958

The two attendants in white locked their arms around Ruth. They half-carried her back to the bed. She struggled to break free, kicking her legs until her hospital gown rode high up on her bare thighs. She wailed, her voice soaring to bounce off the white washed walls like a siren. The two men thrust her down on the narrow cot and pulled up the side rail. Then with a flurry of practised moves, they took out a syringe, tested it and then injected the pale liquid into her arm. Within seconds, she fell silent. The energy leached out of her. Her arms went limp and her head flopped unresisting on to the pillow. With a sigh, the two men locked the rail in place.

May crept closer to the bed. Ruth's eyes were closed. She looked like a rag doll or a half-starved child. Pinholes dotted the crooks of both arms, that were as pale as pale as could be. Tears rolled down May's cheeks; two drops like translucent pearls spilled on to Ruth's white gown when she bent over the cot. She remembered the arms before, firm, strong, golden. Tremulously she placed a hand on Ruth's cold damp forehead. With the utmost tenderness, she stroked it, pushing the damp hair off her face. "Ruth, if you can hear me, don't do this to yourself. We love you. Let the past be. Come back to us. Libby needs you. You are not alone. We are here for you."

"Madam, she can't hear you. It is best you leave her be. Go to the canteen. Have a coffee. We'll call you." The nurse, slim and bespectacled, ushered May out of the room.

"What happened this time?" May asked.

"She tried to harm herself in the bathroom. We caught her with a blade."

May felt a rock pressing into her, twisting her insides until she felt physical pain.

"Oh yes! I almost forgot," the nurse added. "A gentleman, Omar, is here to see the patient. We have put him in the waiting room. He wanted to speak to you when we told him you were here. Come with me." Leading the way into the corridor before May could reply, she pointed to the waiting room. Then she pushed open its blue door.

May didn't want to speak to Omar. All she wanted to do was to curl into a ball and cry her heart out. Ruth had tried to harm herself again! Poor Ruth, poor Libby. But Omar had already seen her. He was striding towards them. The nurse saw him and walked briskly away, her rubber-soled shoes making soft squelching sounds on the polished floor. May stood rooted to the floor. The room swam and the people sitting in the hard-backed chairs behind Omar swayed and blurred and then crystallised to normal. By then Omar was in front of her.

"Can I see her? They wouldn't allow me because I am not a relative. They referred me to you."

Distraught and unable to speak, May shook her head.

"What happened?"

May turned on her heels and walked away. She went faster and faster, moving away from the white washed walls and the intense smell of disinfectant. Omar hurried after her. She burst out of the building into the bright sunshine. Gently Omar led her to a wooden bench. "Tell me," he said.

"She tried to kill herself when she learnt of her husband's death. We didn't know she blamed herself. She was so calm when we broke the news to her. Later that night, she took an overdose of sleeping pills. We brought her to this hospital. She tried to harm herself again today."

May paused to catch her breath. A trolley pushed past. It held a body, inert, and covered. Suddenly the image of the sick, the stench of disinfectant and the cold bleak hospital corridors and rooms seemed too much to bear. "We have to take her out of here." she said. "Ruth does not need chemicals pumped into her in this sterile environment. She needs love and care, a reason to live again. She needs her daughter, people who love her. She needs to come home with me."

Omar's voice dropped to a soft murmur. "Let me help."

***

It was almost a month into her convalescence at May' house. Ruth sat in a reclining chair with a hat on her head, a hat that May insisted she wore to protect herself from the sun. Ruth spoke little and smiled even less. She was lost in her own thoughts, still blaming herself for Mark's death. Her body was physically in May's house, her thoughts, however, were elsewhere, in an unreachable place. May watched her like a hawk, terrified that she might still harm herself.

Somewhere from within the house, the clock chimed. May checked her watch. Soon she would have to do the school run. Both Craig and Libby had to be collected from school. Omar generally came during those hours to take over from May. He was gentle with Ruth and May was comforted by his presence. It was getting increasingly difficult to do all the things she normally crammed into a day. Her body was getting bigger as the months went by. Instantly the baby kicked, as though it knew that it must make its presence known before its mother's attention was too diverted from it. The kicks came one after another. May felt her stomach contort as a foot or a fist push from within. A week, the doctor had said. "Just one more week to go. Take lots of rest, especially with this heat."

May felt a shot of pain in her lower back and grimaced. She clenched her teeth and bit her lip. Her face was white. She rose from her seat, clasping her under belly. Omar was immediately by her side.

"I am not sure if the contractions have started. It can't be. The doctor said I had another week. Call Hugh. He is at his office."

"Let me help you into the house." Omar held May and supported her into the house. "Shall I call the maids?"

"*Shhh!* Yes! Let's not trouble Ruth," May said as another shot of pain went through her body.

Omar glanced over his shoulder. Ruth seemed unconscious of what was happening. The hat that May had so gently placed on her head was on the ground, fluttering with every gust of wind. Any moment it would be blown away and Ruth would still have not noticed. She sat very still with her shoulders rounded. Lifeless, uninterested, all joy sucked out of her. She was no longer skeletal, just painfully thin.

"Don't worry. I'll take care of Ruth. I'll take her away so that you have some time for yourself and the baby. You need to rest."

"Where? Where will you take her?" Alarmed May clutched Omar's arm. "She is not ready. She is still hurting."

"I know she is still hurting. But she is slowly opening up. I catch some words she says to me when we are alone, and when I prompt her she adds to them. I am beginning to know her."

A sudden surge of jealousy rose in May's breast. "She talks to you?"

"Not much, but she does. A few words here and there."

May was happy yet jealous that it was Omar and not her that Ruth had broken her silence to. Another sharp jab of pain broke through. May broke out in perspiration.

"Send for Fu Yi," she said as her waters broke. "Call Hugh."

Chapter 33

"LUNCH IS READY," shouted Ruth.

May looked up slightly dazed from her deep thoughts of events in the past two years. She got up and made her way from the top of the stairs where she was sitting to the veranda where the table was laid out for lunch. The men and children were already there. She sat down. Ruth took the chair next to May, putting distance between her and Omar and avoiding Omar's overtures that she should sit next to him. For one split second, Omar opened his mouth as though he was going to say something. He checked himself but he looked hurt. No one noticed except May. The children's laughter and everyone's enjoyment of the lunch Ruth had prepared masked the under current of tension at the table.

***

"That was wonderful," Hugh said pointing to the empty plate before him. "I am going to take May and the kids to the beach. A bit of exercise would help to keep this trim," Hugh pointed to his midriff. "Omar, Ruth, are you coming? We can help clear up after."

"You go ahead. I'll help Ruth clear up," Omar replied quickly. "Don't go," he said turning to Ruth. He had followed her into the narrow galley kitchen. "Can we talk? Not here, somewhere no one can intrude." He placed the dishes he had helped clear from the dining table on to the worktop by the sink. Ruth felt his closeness. In the confined space of the tiny kitchen, and with her heart beating fast, she felt overwhelmed by his proximity, the heat of his body, his scent, the memory she had of him. She took a deep breath.

"It is best that you leave. There is nothing more to be said." Desperately, she looked out of the window at the fast-departing group that had helped fortify her through the lunch.

Omar caught hold of her waist and drew her to him. "Please, we have to talk."

She pushed him away. "We can't be together. Can't you see? Can you really not see that I want you out of my life?" she hissed; her voice grew louder with each word. She threw down the dishcloth and fled. She ran out of the kitchen, down the steps and into the garden. She paused for a moment to seek out May. She saw her and raced down the path, past the flowering bushes and on to the track that led to the beach.

May heard Ruth. She had been uneasy leaving Ruth with Omar. Hugh had insisted that they should be left together to sort out matters and May had conceded unwillingly. The flurry of footsteps, the urgency of Ruth's cry, alerted her that not all was well. She hurried back slipping on the pebbles in her attempt to reach Ruth quickly, Ruth whom she had grown to love and felt protective over despite being the younger and the smaller. The two women met.

"What happened?"

Ruth shook her head. "I told him to leave. I shouted at him."

They heard Omar's car, the roar of its engine as it started to life and then the sharp swish of tyres. They could imagine the cloud of dust and the scattering of pebbles that followed his departure.

May stood on tiptoe and hugged her friend. She pushed a handkerchief into Ruth's hand. "Wipe your eyes. We'll join the others. We'll talk later this evening. I'll make some excuse and ask Hugh to look after the children. We'll find a way to go to Fatimah's without arousing questions. You've told her we are coming haven't you. She will be expecting us?"

"Does Hugh know?"

"No. I haven't said anything. I leave it to you to decide when and whether you wish to tell. It is not my place," said May. She kissed Ruth on the cheek. "Come!"

***

The moon was full, filling the night sky with its buttery mellow light. It was a sultry night, relieved only by the gentle sea breeze blowing in from across the Straits of Malacca. The two women held a torch each. Hand in hand they trod the roughly hacked path towards Fatimah's house. Bushes whispered and swayed in the breeze. Their shadows lengthened and waned on the path.

"I want him with me all the time but I can't. I feel I have abandoned him. Am I a bad woman to leave him with another family?" Ruth asked.

"No!" May squeezed Ruth's hand. She thought of what she herself had done in the past. She didn't know what she would do if she were to be in Ruth's position. In life, circumstances dictated one's actions. Sometimes it was difficult to distinguish between right and wrong.

Fatimah's hut was lit up. The door was thrown wide open and the sound of children's laughter floated across to them. Then a deeper cackling chuckle joined in the merriment.

"That is Fu Yi. I know her laugh a mile away. She is very happy here. I am glad I suggested she came to help. This is so much better than the maid's *kongsi* where she had to share a stuffy dormitory with many others."

"Yes! I too am so glad she came. She is invaluable. Her presence has allowed Fatimah time for her own children and to earn a little extra money for housekeeping. Fatimah makes Malay cakes for sale in the open market every Sunday. You had some of them this lunch. Without Fu Yi, I wouldn't have been able to spend today with Libby." Ruth quickened her footsteps, almost dragging May along with her.

"*Selamat petang. Dia tidoh*," called Fatimah from afar when she saw the two women. She mimed the action by placing both hands together and resting her cheeks and closing her eyes.

Fu Yi scolded in Cantonese. "I wait whole day for you. Come, he asleep." She held up the little bundle in her arms. "See how peaceful."

Ruth took the baby in her arms and held him close, pressing her nose to the little face, inhaling his scent. Her heart did several flip-flops. A yearning rose from the pit of her stomach, a yearning to press him to her and never let go. The baby opened his blurry eyes. He smiled showing his toothless gums and his dimples. May reached over and stroked his dark head and the down on his cheeks. "He looks like him," she whispered.

The baby whimpered, pushing his little fist out of the sarong that swaddled him and immediately put his thumb into his mouth. His lips closed over the thumb and he sucked. Instinctively Ruth felt her breast ooze. She held the baby close. "He is weaned but my body still responds to him."

"It will do. Fu Yi says he has taken to the powdered milk well. At least you don't have to worry about his feeding. Have you decided on what you should do?"

Ruth glanced quickly at Fu Yi and Fatimah. She indicated that they should walk on. "It is more private over there," she pointed. They went to a tree trunk hacked out into a horizontal bench. They sat down close together, as though keeping close gave them strength. May saw how Ruth clung to the baby. She placed an arm around Ruth and hugged her close.

"I will adopt him," Ruth replied. "Then Libby, the baby and I can be a family together again. I will have to talk first with Libby. She has to agree to the adoption. If I did it without consulting her, she would be hurt. She would find the proposal strange. I will tell her that the baby belongs to Fatimah's niece. That she wants to give him up for adoption because of her family circumstances. I have spoken to Fatimah and she has agreed to my story."

May looked hard at Ruth. "Are you sure?" she asked. "One lie leads to another; it becomes difficult to untangle them."

Ruth turned to face May. "I can't give him up. I just can't. Leaving him here with Fu Yi and Fatimah hurts me even though I see him every day. I hate not being able to tell the world he is mine or to tell Libby she has a brother. I worry that if Libby knows the truth, she might inadvertently disclose it to a friend. After all she is still a child." She buried her face in the baby and held him close. "Then, he would know. And I would lose the baby."

She looked up, her eyes filled with sadness. "I am mortified that you have to lie for me and to keep things from Hugh."

Fatimah and Fu Yi looked on at the two women huddled close together. They knew and shared their secret. They looked at each other. Fu Yi got up and walked over to the two young women. "Better go home. You not want Master Hugh come look for you. Here let me have the little one. Go now! Master will be worried you venturing in the dark. He sure come searching."

Reluctantly, Ruth handed the baby back but not before she had kissed him and inhaled his scent as though she wanted to bottle it inside her. May took her hand and squeezed it. "Come," she said, "Fu Yi is right. Hugh will be worried and it will be difficult to spin too many stories. There is also Libby. She will look for you; you have to spend some time with her as well."

"You are right. Poor Libby! I have neglected her. I am grateful that she is settled and has a good friend in Craig."

"Yes, they are good friends," replied May. Ruth did not see the flicker of worry in May's face, a worry that May kept close to her heart. Of course they would be good together, she thought, for weren't they half-siblings? May had considered telling Ruth that Craig was Mark's child. She held back. Telling would be betraying Hugh who claimed Craig for his own. Moreover, it might rekindle Ruth's old animosity. At this stage, as long as Craig and Libby were just good friends, she told herself, there was no need to dig up the past. It would be necessary only if their friendship developed into something more when they grew older. Yet she worried. What if they were to fall in love in the future, she asked herself. A sigh escaped May. Hugh had warned her not to chase after worries and problems that might never occur.

"Are you okay?" asked Ruth.

"Yes. I was just wondering whether Lin would be asleep. She likes me to read to her and tonight, it will be Hugh doing it."

"I am sure she'll be fine. Hugh is wonderful with children."

They retraced their steps, up the path towards the bungalow. The lights were still on and voices rang from within.

Just yards away from the bungalow, Ruth stopped. "I shall name him Michael Solomon. Michael is my father's middle name," she explained to May, "and Solomon, the Christian equivalent to Suleiman. I wish him the wisdom that I never had. It will be his connection to a father, whom he will never know." Ruth paused. She took May's hands in her own. "Yet how can I regret what happened in the past year despite everything if I have Michael?"

"Yes," May agreed, "no regrets. As one wiser than me said, 'A regret now is for the regret tomorrow for having felt regret today.'"

One year ago, 1959

In the mellowed golden light of the family room, May leaned back in the crook of her husband's arm and stretched out her legs. They had the whole house to themselves. Except for the ticking of the clock utter silence surrounded them. It was bliss. The maids were away; Lin was asleep in her cot; Craig and Libby were on a school trip and Ruth had gone out with Omar. Such moments were rare.

"I am so happy for Ruth," May whispered, breaking the silence. "She had been poorly for such a long time."

Hugh drew May closer to him until her head was on his chest. "Yes! She is a different woman from what she was when Mark died. I still see traces of melancholy every so often, though. Let's hope they disappear completely. You have done such a wonderful job with her."

"Not just me. Everyone, particularly Omar, don't you think?"

"I was suspicious of his intentions initially. I am slowly getting round to the idea that he loves her."

"Of course he loves her. Ruth is meeting his parents today! That could only mean he is very serious. I am keeping my fingers crossed. His parents are old-fashioned. It is well known that they wish him to marry someone of standing, of their own culture and religion, someone who would enhance his ability to rise to the very top in politics. I had never expected this day. To take Ruth to see his parents must surely mean that Omar is certain that they will accept Ruth."

A frown appeared on May's face. She pushed herself up and sat bolt upright. "Oh Hugh, I hope everything goes well for them. It would be disastrous if the meeting went badly. Ruth was so excited. She changed five times. I just don't want her to be disappointed."

Hugh crushed May to him and kissed her soundly on the forehead. "I worry about Ruth too. However, this is our evening and I would like to have my wife back. You can't fret all the time. We'll know soon enough."

***

When the car swept into the grounds, Ruth caught her breath. The house was huge. She reached out and placed her hand on Omar's arm. "You didn't say," she accused him, "that it was so grand." The car whizzed past the long line of trees and entered into a parking area near the front portico.

"It is not mine, it is my parents'. If I had my way, I would not live here. For me it is a monstrosity. Look at the architecture!"

Omar took Ruth's hand in his. "I had better tell you a bit about my parents to prepare you. The house is their status symbol. They built it to impress. They want to show the world we have done well without our former Colonial masters. My father, you see, was closely involved in the nationalist movement. As for my mum..." he shrugged with an apologetic grin, "she is a bit of snob."

"It does not sound like they are likely to accept me. I am English! Perhaps you have forgotten."

"Be on guard!"

"What?"

He smiled at Ruth, his eyes softening at her shock and discomfort. "I am teasing. I don't see you in that way. I see you as the woman I love, the one I want to spend my life with."

"Have you told them that?"

"I have had a long talk with my parents. I confess they were not pleased initially."

Ruth recoiled. He held her fast. "Don't worry," he said quickly, "I won't let their objections stand in my way. They know. After my talk with my mother, she seemed reconciled to the situation. It was she who suggested I bring you here. She would like to meet you. My mum can be difficult. But generally her bark is worse than her bite."

"You didn't tell me they weren't pleased. You should have done." A shadow of doubt crossed Ruth's eyes and she looked at Omar reproachfully.

"Then you wouldn't have come. In any case, my mother promised she would behave. She is slowly coming round to the fact that I will not change my mind where you are concerned."

They sat in the car. Ruth took a deep breath. "Can we leave? I don't think I am ready to face them."

"Come! It will be fine. I am here with you."

"How do I look?" She smoothed the skirt she was wearing. It showed off her elegant legs.

"Beautiful," he replied and reached over to open the door.

They got out of the car. From behind the curtains of the tall window on the upper floor in the west wing, Siti stood watching in silence. Her lips curled as she saw a flash of bare legs and then a head of blonde hair followed by a slim body emerge from the car. "So this," she said to herself, "is the woman my son wants!"

***

The interior of the house was even grander than its facade. Ruth saw her reflected image in the polished black marble floor. Behind her the reflection of Omar shifted as he came alongside. The hallway opened up to another room. Chandeliers hung from high ceilings and the furniture was gilded. She walked in with Omar by her side. Her high-heeled sandals made a loud clacking noise; it resonated across the room. It made her self-conscious. She turned to Omar, uncertain if she should have taken them off. May always walked barefoot at home. Ruth had attributed it to a wish for comfort. Now she wasn't sure. She suddenly remembered what Fatimah said about not wearing shoes. She looked across the room and saw maids similarly barefooted. She looked down and saw that Omar was wearing socks. When had he taken his shoes off? Panic-stricken, she bent down to take off her sandals. It was too late.

Omar's parents were already upon them, a strained smile on their faces as she stood one foot bare with the other sandal in her hand. They were dressed formally. Omar's mother was covered from top to toe. Ruth felt under-dressed; her skirt, just skimming below her knees, seemed too short and her neckline too exposed. Omar was oblivious.

"*Ibu*, mother. This is Ruth."

"I am Siti," Omar's mother said, "and my husband, Zikri," indicating the short portly gentleman next to her. She smiled but her black currant eyes held no warmth. "Come! Leave your shoes on. You are not expected to know our custom."

"I am sorry I didn't tell you," whispered Omar. "It is the custom of Malay households to take off their shoes because wearing shoes in the living room would soil the floor, making it unbefitting for prayers. In May's house, I see you barefoot and therefore it did not occur to me to tell you. Mother wouldn't think anything of it. As she said, you are not expected to know." He grinned. "In any case, we do not normally pray in the living room and our western guests do not take their shoes off."

Ruth turned bright red. She sensed what Siti was really saying. Ruth was not expected to know because she was a foreigner and didn't belong. She saw Siti's eyes on her. Ruth tried hard to keep her smile in place but the tightness in her chest and face made it difficult.

Omar placed his lips close to her ears. "We do not call an older person by their names, even though my mother told you hers'. It would be a sign of disrespect if you did. It is specially so when they are titled. So call my father *Tun* and my mother, *Toh Puan* until, of course, we are engaged. You'll soon get to grips with our customs. We do it without thinking." He squeezed her hand. "You are doing fine."

This piece of information unnerved Ruth even more. May had primed her with basic Malay etiquette. She had not come to grips with it, especially the arm length of titles that people in Malayan high society might hold. Everything, even the little that she had grasped, had flown from her head. Her tongue was dry. It stuck to her palate

They sat down. A maid pushed in a trolley laden with silverware and fine porcelain and with it an array of cakes and dainty sandwiches.

"For you my dear. Omar has said how much you like English tea." Siti gestured to the maid to pour the tea.

"Thank you. You are most kind."

"I fear that you might not like our cakes. I have instructed the kitchen to make English pastries. I assume that this is what you normally have." She pointed to the vast array of delicately iced cakes, éclairs and sandwiches.

"Oh this is more, much more than what we have." Ruth thought of the steaming mugs of tea and crumpets she shared with her father at the farm and the shop-bought cakes when she was teaching. She wished she were back home in England, sharing tea with her father. She found the grand formal drawing room stifling. She crossed her legs and, conscious that the hem of her skirt had slid above her knees, uncrossed them again. She tugged at the hem. A faint film of moisture appeared above her lips. Suddenly it felt overwhelmingly hot.

"Oh!" exclaimed Siti, her face seemingly incredulous. "What do you have for tea then? Toast?" She turned to her husband, stretching her lips in a parody of a smile. He, silent throughout the meeting, met her eyes and nodded imperceptibly.

"Mother!"

"It is all right." Ruth stared straight back at Siti. She was aware of the undercurrent hostility, of the frostiness behind the smiles and of being examined and found lacking. Suddenly she was not nervous. She was not going to try to please. She would be herself; she would not make herself out to be what she was not. "We do not have help in the house. I do all the housework. Tea is usually served in mugs with a biscuit or two, or a cake if we have time or when there is something to celebrate. I do not come from a well-off family. We have always to count our pennies."

"My dear, do have a cake, then," Siti said handing a plate of delicately iced fairy buns to Ruth. Once again she glanced at her husband. Her expression was one of satisfaction. She was right about her perception of Ruth's background.

Ruth bit into the bun. Siti seemed to be examining her relentlessly. Nervous, her teeth caught the corner of her lips and tears sprang to her eyes.

"I believe you were previously married and your husband passed away not long ago. It must be hard for you. I am so sorry for your loss, as you must be."

Ruth dropped the cake onto the plate shocked by the sudden personal observation sprung out of the blue. Icing scattered on to her skirt to cover it with a dusting of white.

Siti continued without any preamble or change in tone. "I do not wish to be rude but do you not think that people would gossip if you were to remarry so quickly? Would it not reflect badly on my son? You know that he has a brilliant future..."

"Mother! Stop it." Omar jumped to his feet. "This is not an inquisition. You promised! We will leave now if you continue in this way."

"I am merely stating the obvious. Surely you cannot object to that? She should know what she would have to confront should she continue to pursue you." Siti said all this without looking at Omar. She directed her gaze only at Ruth, hoping that Ruth would see the folly of her behaviour. If she could not get her son to stop seeing Ruth, perhaps Ruth could be stopped instead.

Ruth, speechless, held on to her plate, suspended in time. The plate tilted and crumbs spilled onto the floor.

"Well I can object and I am objecting. Remember this. I will marry Ruth whatever you say." Omar stood up and stretched out his hand to Ruth. "Come!" he said.

Siti's face crumbled wiping away her previous show of confidence. She rose to her feet; her breath came in quick gasps. She had not expected this response from her son whom she had nurtured and had placed such hopes. "But Omar, I say this only out of love for you and to protect you. You have no future with her. Tell him, Zikri," she pleaded her husband.

"I don't care!" Omar pulled Ruth to her feet. Together they left the house and headed for the car. Ruth tried to walk with her head held high. She stumbled and Omar caught her by the elbow. She was numbed with shock. The minutes before were like watching a nightmare being played out. What began as a tea had quickly deteriorated into a battle. How had it happened? They were there for less than fifteen minutes. Once in the car, Omar gathered Ruth in his arms. She was shivering from both anger and bewilderment. She did not know which was worst.

"Listen to me. Nothing matters except for you and me. Nothing! We'll marry with or without their consent."

"And your future?"

"My future will be of my making. Not theirs."

'But."

Omar kissed Ruth to stop her from protesting. "Listen. It will be all right."

Chapter 34

IT WAS QUIET except for the night sounds of the jungle. In the spare bedroom in Ruth's bungalow, the wooden windows were thrown wide open to allow in breeze. The air under the mosquito nettings, however, remained stubbornly warm. May couldn't sleep. Seeing Ruth and baby Michael earlier that evening had unsettled her. She knew how hard it must be for Ruth to leave him with Fatimah. May pushed aside the thin cotton covering. Her skin was damp with perspiration. She could hear Hugh's deep breathing and the little snuffling noises Lin made in the cot. Gently, she parted the netting and swung her legs to the floor and got out of bed. She tucked the netting back in place and, quietly, tiptoed out of the room, into the sitting room. Here in this larger area, the air was cooler. Craig and Libby were bundled up in their bedding fast asleep. They had no nets. Instead, Ruth had lit coils of incense to keep mosquitoes away. The scent hit her nose and May sneezed. The children remained oblivious; their chests rose and fell in a steady rhythm. She walked across the sitting room into the tiny hallway; then gently she pushed open the front door. She placed one foot gingerly in front of the other, worried that the wooden planks would squeak and wake the household. The planks held firm. A sigh of pleasure escaped her. At least, out in the open, the night air was cool. She sat on top of the steps that led down to the garden, the same steps she sat on earlier that afternoon before lunch, before Ruth had sent Omar away.

Ruth did not explain why she had sent Omar away. In fact, Ruth had never given any specific details about her breakup with Omar, just generalities. May hoped that they would make up. She wondered if she should ask. She hadn't because she knew Ruth valued her privacy. She hoped that with time Ruth would confide in her. She couldn't begrudge Ruth keeping information away from her. She too, had not told Ruth everything. Craig was her big secret. Fu Yi's words came immediately to her mind. "*Nei mn ho kah yeem, kah choh,*" telling Ruth about Craig, Fu Yi said, would only add salt and vinegar to her wound. Ruth had been distraught when she found out about Mark's infidelity with May. Telling Ruth about Craig would rekindle Ruth's hurt and jeopardise their relationship, one she had worked so hard to establish. Yet May felt uneasy. That was then. Things had progressed. Perhaps the time had come for her to tell Ruth. The longer she kept it a secret, the more difficult it became to tell the truth. Craig and Libby were inseparable. The two confided that when they grew up, they would marry. May was alarmed. Hugh, however, laughed. "They are just children playing. It will pass." Still the idea took root in May's mind. The worry ferreted and grew. She couldn't shake it off.

The only way was to separate them. Yet how could she send Libby away? Libby could not stay with Ruth in this tucked-away place, a little *kampong* without even a secondary school for older children. This little hamlet had little to offer in terms of education. She couldn't ask Ruth to return to Kuala Lumpur; Ruth wouldn't be able to leave baby Michael. This place was Ruth's sanctuary.

An owl hooted startling a flying fox gorging fruits on a nearby tree. May shivered. The morning dew was heavy dampening her skin. She drew her feet closer and hugged her knees, resting her head on them. She saw a pair of bare feet standing by her. She looked up.

Hugh sat down by her side and put his arms around her. She felt his warmth. "I was woken by your absence. Not worrying are you? Do you want to tell me?" he asked.

May snuggled into the crook of his arms. "It's Craig and his attachment to Libby and she to him. They do not know that they are half-siblings. I worry that their attachment might grow into something more."

"Craig is only just coming up to ten. Boys of that age say all sorts that they forget. Soon he will be going to school. Remember, we spoke about the possibility of his going to a boarding school in England?"

May caught her breath. She remembered the conversation well. She thought that the idea had been shelved until they returned to England as a family. Hearing its imminence was a shock.

"We have to prepare ourselves. The political situation in this country is changing fast. The emergency is over. However, I hear of new developments on the horizon. An idea is growing that Malaya could expand from just a peninsula to one beyond its present boundaries to include Singapore, Sabah and Sarawak. Sabah and Sarawak are rich in resources, oil and timber, just what Malaya needs. This has caused alarm and resentment amongst the neighbouring countries. There is most likely to be a period of unrest. Also we are needed less and less. Malaya is flexing its muscles. I do not know how long my post will continue in this country."

"What about Ruth and Libby? Can they stay?"

Hugh sighed, "It is my belief that Ruth should not stay in this little hamlet on her own forever. She is not a Malayan, no matter how much she likes it here."

***

Ruth lay still in her bed. She too was restless. Bits of Hugh and May's low murmuring floated in through her open window. Her room overlooked the veranda and her window shutters were also thrown wide open. She wondered if she should tell May that Libby was not Mark's. It would allay May's fear. May had been wonderful to her. Yet Ruth held back. Telling meant revealing her shame. More importantly, she didn't want Libby to find out. She could not bear Libby's hurt knowing her mother was an adulteress and that Mark, the person she had looked up to as a father, was not her father. A time might come when she should tell May. This was not the time.

Ruth buried her face in the pillow, smothering her desire to scream. She wanted to rail at herself, inflict pain on her own body. How else could she absolve herself from the hurt she had caused to all those she loved. No wonder Omar's mother had seen through her. The tension in her head became unbearable. She shut her eyes tightly. Tears welled up behind her swollen eyelids but they did not flow. With infinite care, she rolled to one side and got out of bed. She tiptoed to the chest of drawers by the side of the window. She looked out. May and Hugh were getting up, readying themselves to return to their bedroom. Ruth ducked under the window and held her breath. She waited until all was quiet and the soft murmuring of May and Hugh were no more. Then she rose to her feet and drew open the top drawer. She rummaged under the pile of neatly folded clothes. She drew out a small box. She slid down to the floor, her back against the chest, and opened the box. Inside was a razor. It gleamed, a metallic grey. With shaking hands she placed it against her forearm. It felt cold, a whisper against her flesh. Gritting her teeth, she cut herself. Relief rushed into her body. She watched the blood gush out on to her lap, turning her white night dress crimson. This was punishment for all the wrong she had done. She hadn't cut herself for a long time. She should have, for she was no good. Siti's words rang in her ears.

One year ago, 1959

Ruth stepped out of the bedroom on to the terrace. The sunlight felt good on her face after the cool damp morning air. She undid the band that held her hair in a ponytail and shook her head. Her blond hair glinted gold in the sunlight. Everything was wonderful. Somewhere a bird sang. A light breeze stirred the blossom on a tree sending shafts of sunshine through the dappled shade. She felt every movement, heard every sound, saw every colour with a clarity and sharpness that brought joy to her soul. Her whole being was alive and she tingled with the memory of the night before; she could still smell the scent of Omar's body on the bed sheets. He had left early in the morning with the promise that he would return in the evening and they would plan for their future then.

She twirled in her nightdress and laughed at her own joy. For it was sheer joy that coursed through her veins. She didn't want to go back into the house. She didn't want to be cooped up. The sun shifted and the heat reflected off the terrace tiles. Ruth sank down on to the ground and her nightdress spilled softly around her to cover the tiles. She inhaled the scent of the jasmine flowers and closed her eyes.

"Madam, someone to see you."

A lopsided smile still on her face, Ruth rose to her feet. She asked in stumbling Malay if the visitor was really for her and not for May.

"Yes!" the maid replied in Malay. "A grand lady. Smartly dressed. She says she is Toh Puan Siti."

The joy Ruth had felt just moments ago left her. An overwhelming fear descended in its place. She could hear her heart palpitate, *boom, boom*. Suddenly the heat was unbearable.

Horrified by Ruth's white face, the maid took Ruth by the elbow and tried to guide her to a seat.

"Shall I send the lady away?" she asked.

Ruth didn't hear. Whatever it was that Omar's mother came to say she must meet it face on. Without a word, she returned to the bedroom and pulled on some clothes. Hastily she brushed her hair. She rubbed her face to bring colour to her cheeks. A wild-eyed image on the mirror stared back at her. This behaviour would not do, she scolded. She took a deep breath. Then, carefully, more calmly she put lipstick on her lips. She needed to be calm.

She would hear Siti out. She would not be persuaded to leave Omar. She loved him and he her. Together they could, would, see through all obstacles in their way. Wasn't that what Omar had said to her over and over again? Remembering his words calmed her. She went out of the bedroom holding her head high to meet Siti.

***

Siti took in her surroundings; the pale cream sofa, the dark teak armchairs with matching cream covers, the crimson rug and the duck-egg blue Chinese porcelain scattered round the room. Her eyes narrowed. Possibly antique ware, she told herself, and expensive! They had done well in this country.

She settled back on the chair. Carefully, she crossed her legs. She would be patient. A whole day lay ahead of her. Omar would not be back until evening. She had checked with his office. His calendar was full for the day.

When Ruth entered the sitting room, Siti's face was in repose; it gave no clue as to what was going through her mind.

"You came to see me?" Ruth asked with a tremulous smile.

Siti returned the smile and indicated that Ruth should sit.

For a moment, Ruth allowed herself to think that perhaps, she was mistaken. Perhaps Siti had come to make amends. She sat down, her heart lighter. She must be more positive.

"I see that Mr and Mrs Anderson have taken it upon themselves to accommodate my son. Such generosity!"

"Yes! Hugh and May have been very kind."

A gleam of pure hatred flashed in Siti's eyes turning them almost pitch black. She had lost many nights of sleep over her son's misdemeanour with this *angmoh*. She had prepared many days for this meeting. She schooled her face and it fell again into repose.

"And you, of course, benefit most from their kindness." Siti's voice was honeyed. "For with their generous help, you are able to steal our son from us. Don't you realise that you have turned him against his family and have ruined his chances of a glorious career in politics? You have made us a laughing stock."

"Please do not blame May and Hugh for Omar being here. Do you not see? We love each other. All we want is to be together and have your blessing. Omar is very sad that he has hurt you. I too am so sorry..."

"Love?" Siti snorted, not letting Ruth complete her sentence. "Not love. Maybe lust for white skin. I suppose he has not had many experiences with white women. You are a novelty. A lust, my dear that I guarantee will not last. I know my son. Omar is a Muslim. With three words, *I divorce you*, he could cast you aside, even if he married you. If he does not cast you aside he is still entitled to four wives. And, my dear," her voice still like liquid honey, "are you sure you know what marrying a Muslim entails? You have to take our faith. Are you willing to forsake yours?"

Ruth felt her heart constrict. She opened her mouth to speak; she couldn't. Her throat was completely dry. Omar had assured her that they would find a way round the many obstacles in their path.

"If you marry a Muslim you have to take up Islam. This is the rule. Omar cannot renounce his faith." Siti's sharp words cut into Ruth's thoughts as though she had read Ruth's mind.

"If I have to become a Muslim to marry Omar, I will do it. I love him. He is everything to me. Please give us a chance."

"He is everything to you?" Siti mocked. She raised one eyebrow in question. "You mean like your husband Mark was everything to you? Does Omar know about your lover, Steve? That was a pretty story was it not? Cheating on your husband, stealing someone else's husband. Mr Fisher had an invalid wife, did he not?"

Siti rummaged in her handbag and took out an envelope. "I managed to track him. He wrote me this letter. We had the detectives on your trail the minute we found out about Omar's involvement with you."

Trembling, Ruth stood up. "If you have come to blackmail me, let me tell you that I am not afraid. Omar loves me. I will tell him about Steve. I had planned to tell him. I am not proud of my actions. I was lonely and Mark was unreachable. I know that it is no excuse for my failings. I failed my husband. I failed myself. And I am ashamed."

"Shame? You have no shame! Do you think my son would forgive such a squalid affair? Do you think he would still think of you the same way once he knew about your past? You are in Asia. We value chastity. How do you think Omar's social and political standing would fare if he was encumbered with someone the likes of you? My dear girl, Omar would not forgive you if he knew your past. We brought our son up to believe that women must be chaste. I know my son. You! How long have you known Omar?"

Ruth sank back onto the seat. Her teeth were chattering so much she could not speak. She hunched over and clutched her middle. Shame, fear and bewilderment chased through her.

Siti walked over to the window and stared out into the garden. No one spoke. Minutes passed. The tension in the room was palpable.

"If you do not care about my son," Siti said, "think about your daughter. School children can be cruel if such information is let loose. Think about your friends. One word from my husband to the appropriate circles and Mr Anderson might find himself ostracised. The British Commission is hardly going to retain him in his present capacity if his Malaysian counterparts do not like him. Is that how you wish to repay their friendship?"

Without waiting for Ruth's reply, Siti gathered up her handbag and left the room. She did not look back. She had done all she could to save Omar from the terrible fate that would surely be his if he were to marry this woman. He was her only son, one whom they have placed all their hopes.

Ruth's head swam. The coffee table and sofa swelled and retreated. She pictured herself as how Siti described her; a wanton, lustful, selfish woman. She stood up and rubbed her sweaty palms on her dress, creasing the cotton and leaving it with damp patches on it. She returned to the bedroom and shut the door. She couldn't kill herself. Her hands went to her belly protectively. She was with child. Omar didn't know. She had wanted to be sure before she told him. Now she was glad that she hadn't. Siti was right. The barriers were too insurmountable for them ever to be together. She could not bear the shame of Omar knowing about Steve. She was a wicked woman to have had an affair with a man with an invalid wife. She could not bear to inflict that shame on Libby. She couldn't let Hugh and May down by her own selfish pursuit of happiness.

She went into the adjoining bathroom. It was dark inside. She didn't switch on the lights. She knew where Omar kept his razor. She deserved to be punished.

Chapter 35

MORNING CAME. THE sun rose, ascending in the sky like a huge ball of fire. Within minutes the morning dew on the leaves and grass evaporated and the air turned humid. Only the gentle sea breeze from across the Straits of Malacca brought welcome relief.

May let herself out of Ruth's house with Lin by her side. It was the last day of her stay with Ruth and she was going with her to visit baby Michael. May yawned. She was tired. By the time she and Hugh returned to their bedroom after their chat, it was almost five in the morning. While Hugh was able to sleep immediately, she did not.

May went down the steps. Ruth could not be found in her bedroom or in the kitchen. She hitched Lin on to her hips and walked down the path towards the river. Ruth might be there.

The water supply to the house was erratic. Sometimes the water would gush out in full force; at other times it trickled to a drip. Ruth had said that she had taken to washing in the upper stream of the river, where it was clean.

She passed a flock of hens with their chicks. Someone had scattered rice husks on the ground. They were pecking furiously and paid May scarce attention as she walked by. Up and down their heads went, clucking incessantly.

May turned a corner. Here the ground descended more steeply. Tall grass grew on the verge. She could hear the gurgling of the stream. She hitched Lin more securely on her hip and brought a hand over her brow to shield from the glare of the sun. She spotted Ruth at once, bent over the river edge dipping a cloth into the water and applying it to her arm. The water turned crimson.

Alarmed, May hurried down, unmindful of the sharp blades of *lalang* that scratched her legs and feet. Lin had nodded off. The weight of her little body bore May down. She shifted Lin to the front and wrapped both her arms around her tiny body, hugging her close, one hand protectively on her head. Halfway down, she saw Ruth straightened up to bandage her arm. Slowly with infinite care Ruth pulled her sleeves down to cover the bandage. May stopped. She guessed what happened. She remembered the day when she had first discovered Ruth inflicting cuts on herself. She must be doing it again. When did it restart? Was it Omar's sudden appearance that had sparked it? Had Ruth overheard her with Hugh?

Ruth looked up. She saw May and the concern in her face. "I cut myself. It was an accident. Just a scratch. Let's go to Fatimah's. The children will be there soon."

Ruth hurried over to May. May examined Ruth's face for any telltale signs of distress. Ruth looked absolutely normal. In fact her eyes were sparkling with excitement, the blue in her eyes reflecting the iridescent gold from the sun.

"The children will meet us at Fatimah's. I want Libby to see the baby and to fall in love with him before I come up with this proposal to adopt him. Do you think it will work?"

May's eyes were fixed on Ruth. How could she look so buoyant and normal?

Ruth looked away. She tugged at her sleeve for it had ridden up revealing her bandaged wound.

"It was an accident. Help me with Libby. Please. She must like baby Michael. So much depends on it. We can't be together like a family if I don't get to adopt him."

***

Ruth and May arrived at Fatimah's at noon. They knew because the sun was directly above and the tops of their bare shoulders were turning pink from the heat. Libby was already there. Fatimah had hung a sarong beneath a tree, looping its end over a low branch. It was the shadiest bit of the garden. The tree was huge. Its branches sprawled wide to cast shade over the open stretch of straggly couch grass. The baby was curled inside the sarong, its little body snug and cocooned within its confines.

Ruth waved to Libby. She beamed when she saw her mother.

"Look mummy! A baby. Fatimah taught me to jiggle the sarong gently to send it to sleep. It is her niece's baby. He is sweet, almost milky chocolaty in colour, with long lashes. Just like Uncle Omar."

May looked quickly at Ruth, whose face had turned pale.

"I too would like to have long eyelashes," Libby continued, blissfully unaware of the sudden tension. She was sitting cross-legged on a brightly coloured straw mat next to the suspended sarong.

"Where is Craig?" May asked. She saw him before Libby could answer. Craig was kicking a rattan ball. He was clearly bored. A cloud of dirt rose and then settled to colour the ball a dusty brown. He did not know why Libby was fussing over the baby when they could be exploring the beach. There was a little rock pool nearby which he would like to visit.

May walked briskly to her son. "Come," she said linking her arm through his, "let's take a walk. I am sure Ruth would appreciate some time with Libby. They have had hardly any time together since we arrived."

Ruth watched them leave. She went to Libby and sat down by her. She placed one arm around her daughter. Together hand over hand, they jiggled the sarong. It was quiet in the garden, except for the sounds of chickens clucking and the occasional bleating of a goat tethered to a rough fence at one end of the plot of land. Ruth buried her nose in Libby's hair. She inhaled the lemony shampoo of Libby's hair. "Would you like to hold him," she whispered. "Fatimah is preparing lunch and she has given us permission to hold him if we wish."

"Can we?" Libby was excited and jumped up immediately.

Ruth rose to her feet. "I'll take him out of his sarong cradle." Gently she reached into the sarong and brought the baby out. She held him tightly to her before kissing him. He smelt of milk and talcum. He stretched, kicking out his sturdy little legs, and brought a fist to his mouth. "There,' she said placing the baby in the crook of Libby's arm. "Be careful!"

Ruth looked on as Libby swayed and crooned over the baby. Her heart swelled. "Do you like him," she asked.

"He is sweet. Not when he cries though. You should have seen him earlier. His face was all crinkly and red. Before you came he wailed so loudly that I thought he was ill. Fatimah changed his nappy. I had to hold my nose. I didn't realise that baby's poo could be so stinky. When he is quiet like this he is fine." Libby grinned. "I wouldn't like to be around when he is throwing tantrums."

"Would you like it if we adopted him," asked Ruth casually. "His mother is not able to look after him and is considering putting him up for adoption." Her heart was pounding as she waited for Libby to answer.

"Is it because she has no husband? My friend Nina said that was what happened to her neighbour's daughter."

"It would not be right to discuss Fatimah's niece. It is a private matter. But would you like to have him as your brother?"

Libby grew very quiet. Ruth searched for a clue on Libby's face.

"Perhaps not," Libby frowned. "It is not that I don't like him. We don't have enough money do we? We are always short. Auntie May pays for my school fees. Would she have to pay for the baby as well?"

Ruth was dumbstruck by her daughter's answer. She hadn't realised that Libby was so aware of and troubled about their straitened circumstances.

"Also would the baby live here with you while I have to live with Auntie May?" Libby asked solemnly. A look of apprehension and suspicion crossed her face. She looked intently at her mother.

Ruth nodded mutely. She could not help the tears that sprang to her eyes nor could she stop them rolling down her cheeks.

The tears upset Libby. She became furious. Why was her mother crying over the baby? She never cried over me, thought Libby.

"Here, you have him," she said thrusting the baby back to Ruth. "I don't want him. I think you will love him more than me. You'd rather he lives with you than me!"

"That is not true. Libby! Libby!"

But Libby had turned away and was already half way down the path to the beach. Ruth ran after her but with the baby in her arms she couldn't make speed. Woken by the commotion, the baby began to wail. Fatimah rushed out. Ruth handed the baby back to her and ran.

***

The sand was bleached white on the beach. Coloured pebbles and seashells lay scattered at random, washed in by the tide. They gleamed under the bright sunshine. Many were caught in a tangle amidst the twining stems of Morning Glory that grew wild in this part of the beach. Craig picked up a piece of driftwood lodged between the purple blooms and hurried over to May and Fu Yi. The two women were talking softly with Lin sitting between them on a towel.

"Can I take this home?" he asked. "I can use it for my school project."

"Of course. I'll look after it while you wander around." May looked fondly at her son. His hair was wind-blown and stood on ends. She reached out with one hand and flicked away the sand on his face. "Go on! We'll be here."

"*Aiyah!* It is too hot! Wear a hat! Why you let your boy roast in the sun? Look at the freckles on his face! All of us want to have white skin and you let him go brown!! Craig-*ah*! Wait! I make this for you. Eat! Eat!" Fu Yi reached into a tote bag. She drew out a bun filled with sweet roast pork. "*Char siew pao!*

Your favourite." Fu Yi grinned with pleasure. "May! You don't feed your boy enough. Look he so thin!"

"Yes, Mum doesn't feed me enough," shouted Craig cheekily as he hurried away grinning, his mouth full of the bun.

"You very lucky, May. Craig good boy. Hugh wonderful husband. Now this beautiful girl. *Ho choy!* Look how things turn so well for you. That is why you have to do good," Fu Yi said with a sage expression on her face. "Buddha says life a cycle, what you do to others, you will also reap yourself. Do bad things, next life you reincarnate into a cockroach."

"I wish that things would turn out well for Ruth. I am worried about her. I am sure she has started to inflict harm on herself again. She denies it. I do not know what to do."

"Love and security. That is what she needs. I go to the temple tomorrow and pray for her."

"Ruth likes and trusts you, Fu Yi. Would you move in with her? You could keep her company and look after Michael. If she can have Michael with her, I am sure she would put him first and not contemplate harming herself. But he can only be with her if she has someone to look after him when she is teaching."

"What would people say? The reason why the baby is with Fatimah is to prevent any gossip that the baby is Ruth's."

"Well that might not be a problem. Ruth is planning to adopt Michael if she can get Libby to agree."

Chapter 36

"DAMN!" OMAR SLAMMED the report on the desk and walked to the window. The street was packed with people and cars. Ever since independence, the country had been expanding its support for rice farmers in the quest for self-sufficiency. Today's report showed that they were nowhere near their goal. Malaya was still heavily reliant on its neighbour Thailand to provide the grain. Far from growing more rice, farmers were migrating to the cities. If it were not for the successful diversification to palm oil and the modernisation of its rubber industry, the economy would have faltered badly. The price of natural rubber had fallen in the world market. He shook his head. He could not bear the thought of the consequences if planters had not replanted with higher-yielding varieties. Replanting had at least allowed the country to match its natural rubber prices to synthetic varieties. But now, it must look further afield to strengthen its coffers.

Omar returned to the desk and picked up the report, flipping to the last page, which contained a list of proposals. Manufacturing and electronics offered one possibility. That on its own, he believed, would not be enough. Malaya needed to expand its borders. The formation of a bigger entity with Sabah and Sarawak, with their oil, gas and other natural resources would be better; it would provide the country with the catalyst it needed. He will have to make the case for this tomorrow when Parliament met.

He placed the report back on the desk and buzzed his secretary. It was well past six o'clock. He remembered that he had given the secretary permission to leave early. Omar picked up his jacket and briefcase and made his way out of the building. The driver would be waiting. Tonight he would see his parents. He had not seen them since that fateful day when he had brought Ruth to meet his mother. He was willing to sacrifice everything for Ruth. Why had she sent him away? He was sure she loved him. With a heavy heart he went out of the main entrance of the building and stood at the top of the flight of steps.

He hoped the meeting with his parents would not be confrontational. He knew they had his interests at heart. Obviously that did not include his wish to marry Ruth. His mother had sent him a letter some months ago. She had suggested he took Ruth as a mistress if he must have her but on no account was he to marry her. She had not minced her words. She called Ruth a string of names. He had not replied. He wondered what Ruth was doing? What could he do to convince her of his love? Something must have caused her violent reaction to his visit to Port Dickson. He had been upset when she rounded on him.

Yes, he had been angry at the rejection and had driven away in fury. He regretted it. If he had stayed on, shown some patience, could he have coaxed her to tell him what was bothering her? Was it his mother's doing?

A car slid smoothly into the drive. He got into it. "My father's house," he said.

***

"I don't like leaving Ruth on her own." May turned on her side to plump up the pillow. "Something is troubling her. She must be lonely all on her own. Libby wouldn't speak to her. Didn't you not notice the tension between Ruth and her daughter before we left?"

Hugh turned over. "Stop worrying. Ruth is a grown woman. You've done all that you can. You can't follow a person twenty-four hours a day."

May wished she could tell Hugh about baby Michael. She longed to unburden herself, to tell him that Ruth had cut herself deliberately. She daren't. Mentioning Ruth's recent self-harm might lead Hugh to insist she seek medical help. As far as May knew, there were no such facilities in the country. There were only asylums for lunatics and even those were scarce. In fact she knew of only one. Ruth would be considered insane. She would be pronounced unfit to teach. Ruth was not insane. May was sure that Ruth was not a danger to anyone. She just needed love.

"Come here," Hugh said, drawing May into his arms. "Can we talk about something else? I only get to speak to you at bedtime. I have been so busy with affairs in the office."

***

The dinner with his parents went more smoothly than Omar expected. Throughout the meal, no mention was made of Ruth. Lulled by the convivial atmosphere, Omar loosened up. They adjourned to the family room. He knew his parents were hurt by his long absence and neglect of them. He wanted to make amends. He complimented his mother for the wonderful dinner she had arranged. Pleased, she responded with alacrity on how she had ensured that the meal had included all the dishes he liked.

"Come home," Siti said. "The house is empty without you." She touched her chest as though in pain; she missed her son terribly. She did not understand how he could place Ruth above his own family.

Omar shifted in his chair. He could tell from the tone of his mother's voice and the expression on her face that the conversation would take a turn for the worse. He was not wrong.

"Are you going to allow an *orang putih* to come between you and your family?" Siti also, lulled by her son's genial smiles, could not help herself. An only child herself, she was too used to getting her way.

"Siti!" Omar's father uttered sharply. They had agreed that they would not do anything to jeopardise the reunion. And here was his wife doing exactly what she should not do. Would the woman not learn?

"Son, you do what is best, " he interrupted. "This house is yours, your home. We would like you to come back of course. We are getting old and life can be lonely. I enjoy discussing things with you, my son, and there is much to discuss with the pending formation of Malaysia."

Tun ignored his wife's blazing eyes. If looks could kill, I would be dead, he thought to himself. He wished Siti would stop being so confrontational. She would do much better with a softer approach.

"I miss our discussions too, father. I am, however, a grown man, too old to remain at home."

Siti sniffed and glared at her husband. "I told you not to send him to England to study. His head is filled with strange ideas!" She rounded on Omar. "Here in this country, we think differently. We believe in extended families. When I married your father, we lived with his parents. It is normal. When they were old, we had them with us. You should be proud of yourself. Remember, we are the indigenous people of this country. Why do you wish to dilute our race by marrying a foreigner?"

"Mother, my great-grand father was from Sumatra. One of our ancestors came from the Middle East. I am like most people in this country, mixed in some ways. Of course I respect and value our culture. Marrying Ruth does not mean I don't value our culture and traditions. Not remaining at home does not mean that either."

"You do what is best, son. As long as you come back to see us." Tun Zikri tried to stop Siti from saying more. He flashed her another look of warning. "Times have changed," he said sharply to his wife.

Omar could see his mother fuming. He had had enough. "I have some work to complete this evening. It was good to see both of you." He stood up to leave.

"Wait! I have something for you." Siti hastened out of the room and was back within minutes. She thrust an envelope into Omar's hands. "Read it! Open your eyes!" Then, suddenly, she burst into tears. "We love you so much and this is what you do?" She clutched at her heart, her chest heaved as she sobbed and wailed. "*Tidak bersyukur!*" Ungrateful!

But Omar had already left, banging the door behind him.

***

The silence was so compelling that Omar fancied he could hear a fly buzzing, a gecko chirping on the wall and his own heart. It was pounding hard, just like the pulsing in his temples. He had not meant to upset his parents. He knew they loved him. He knew their disappointment and was filled with regret and guilt. But he couldn't give in to his mother's incessant criticism of Ruth. He wouldn't have her dictate whom he married. Was it his education and the time he had spent abroad that made him what he was?

Omar switched on the light. The room was simply furnished, a contrast to his parents' house. He had wanted to set up home with Ruth here and had not bothered to furnish it. He wanted Ruth to do it; had waited for her to do it. He had waited months to no avail; he had not been able to find her until last week in Port Dickson.

He went over to the lone armchair in the living room. He sank down in the seat. Ruth! A picture of her came into his mind. He closed his eyes. He saw her blond curls, the freckles on her cheeks, the way she smiled with her lips curling up and her blue eyes sparkling with joy. Then a bleaker image took over, a Ruth immediately after her husband's death, a Ruth, so ill and sad that she was like a ghost. He remembered holding her. Her arms were stick thin and could have belonged to a half starved child. It was her fragility that clutched at his heart. Then the recent Ruth, a calm, self-contained Ruth. A woman who sent him away. What had made her change?

He shrugged off his jacket. An envelope fell out of its pocket. He picked it up. He had forgotten it. Slowly with infinite care he opened the envelope and took out the sheaf of papers within. The words, 'Confidential Report' blazed on the top sheet. He settled back in his seat and read.

***

All afternoon Ruth cleaned. It was strange how empty the house felt after May's departure. She returned the chairs to their original position and unfolded a mat that had been rolled and pushed aside to make way for Libby and Craig's makeshift sleeping bags. She picked up the bedclothes that were strewn to one side. Then she swept and mopped. May had wanted to tidy up before she left. Ruth had refused her help. She needed to keep busy. The mundane jobs kept her occupied. She sang a bar from a song she heard on the radio. It echoed and bounced off the walls, emphasising the emptiness of the house. She started again. The song and her voice sounded free. Her chest swelled and she sang even louder. She hit a warble in her throat and stopped. She bundled up the bed sheets and dropped them into a basket. Fu Yi insisted that she sent the washing to the Chinese 'dhobi man' who had recently set up a laundry in the village. Fu Yi assured her that he would do it for very little because his child went to Ruth's school. It was a one-man laundry. Any one going into the village would not fail to see the multiple rows of starched white sheets hanging around his compound. Fu Yi claimed he was doing very well. A small hotel, sprung up a couple of miles to the north, was keeping him well supplied with dirty bed sheets. Soon more shops would open up. More shops meant more Chinese traders. Fu Yi was very happy that there would be more shops, more Chinese people in this otherwise predominantly Malay kampong. At the moment, she felt outnumbered and she longed to speak Cantonese.

Ruth missed Fu Yi's chatter. It helped to distract her. She broke into a different song. Her voice soared. She forced herself to think randomly. Fu Yi! The dhobi! White sheets! Anything, except that which was troubling her most. Her head spun. She sang louder still. But she could not contain her sadness. Her voice broke.

"You don't love me," Libby had accused her. Ruth wanted to reassure her that she did. But Libby had turned and run away. Libby had been unapproachable after that incident.

No matter how much she tried, Ruth could not shut away her worries. She could not leave Michael with Fatimah for ever. She had to bring him back even at the risk of hurting Libby. Then what? she asked herself. The small income she received from teaching could hardly cover her own maintenance, let alone Fu Yi's wages. Libby was right. May had helped out with everything. She couldn't possibly expect May to help out indefinitely. She must go back to England. Yet there was nothing in England to return to. She had no one, no job and no savings.

She began to panic. She told herself to breathe deeply. Someone tapped her arm. She turned.

"Here, hold him," said Fu Yi handing baby Michael to Ruth. She had witnessed Ruth's maniacal singing and cleaning.

Ruth did not hear Fu Yi enter the room. She wondered how long Fu Yi had been in the kitchen. She looked beyond Fu Yi and saw the kitchen back door open. She looked at the baby in her arms.

"You will feel better. May told me to come and stay with you. Tomorrow school starts. You go teach. You feel better. Hold him. He yours, make you feel good. You make him feel good also. May will talk to Libby. Everything will be fine."

Ruth took the baby and buried her face in his little body. Fu Yi made things sound so simple. If only they were so.

"You sit there with baby. I make tea." Fu Yi grinned showing a gap in her front teeth and a mass of wrinkles like little grooves that radiated from around her eyes. "Chinese tea!"

"I can't pay you a wage you know and I can't allow May to pay on my behalf."

"I am retired. I don't need pay, just food. I help grow vegetables, get cheap fish from Fatimah. No worry."

"Oh Fu Yi. What can I say? How can I thank you? I don't deserve such kindness. I am not a good woman. I have done beastly things."

"You are a good woman. I saw how you loved Master Mark. Everyone makes mistakes. Stop blaming yourself. You just like May. She say my fault, I am guilty all the time. I go to the temple and pray. You be fine."

Chapter 37

MAY STEPPED INTO the hotel's foyer. She was meeting Hugh for lunch. He had warned that he might be late. She stood for a moment on the large expanse of marble floor in search of him. She looked from one corner of the lobby to the other. There was no sign of him. She didn't want to loiter around the lobby or the reception area. A lone woman's presence could be misconstrued. A man in a western suit tried to catch her eye. She turned hastily away and headed for the Dragon Court. The restaurant was famous for its afternoon dimsum. Hugh would know she would be there.

The waiters showed her to a table. They brought her Chrysanthemum tea. It was her favourite brew. She loved the flowery aroma. She took a sip and toyed with the menu. The restaurant was fast filling up. Waitresses in long cheongsams pushed trolleys of dimsum around. The aroma of sweet and savoury dumplings wafted through the air. Families gathered around tables, chopsticks poised in the air. Businessmen discussed deals between mouthfuls of dumplings. It was a typical Chinese restaurant. Snatches of conversation floated by. A woman was comparing the merits of the dumpling she was eating with the one she had in another restaurant. Someone began talking about his mother's cooking. May settled back to listen and watch. It always amused her that conversation at a Chinese meal would always focus on food, food that had been eaten previously and food that was about to be consumed. Perhaps it could be traced back to the years of poverty and famine that most families had experienced in the past. She took sips of tea, letting the steam warm her face. The trolley had stopped by several times and each time she had to wave it away. "I am waiting for my husband," she apologised. She looked at her watch. Hugh was half an hour late. She knew it was an important meeting. If he did not arrive in the next fifteen minutes she would be obliged to order some food. She looked at the queue of people waiting for a table. Many were looking her way, impatient for her to leave.

She grew uneasy. From across the room, a man waved. Hugh! He was smiling.

"Sorry I am late," he said giving her a kiss on her lips when he arrived. May blushed and glanced quickly around. Chinese people were not demonstrative and kissing in public was still rare although she knew from Hugh that it was a common form of greeting in England.

"I am ravenous." He waved a waitress over. He gave her a disarming smile. "One each of everything that you have. Perhaps two of those," he pointed to a bamboo casket of steamed prawn dumplings.

"How did the meeting go? What was it about? You didn't say, just that it was important."

"I didn't say because I knew you would be worried."

"And not telling me helps?" May smiled indulgently at her husband. He was popping a whole crab and pork dumpling into his mouth.

"It is official. We are cutting down our office here. We are to return to England."

May dropped the dumpling she was about to eat. She felt ill, light-headed.

Hugh took her hand in his and brought it to his lips. "We've talked about returning to England frequently. It is just that recent events have precipitated the decision."

"Why? I don't understand." May was very pale.

"The reason is we are not doing well in Malaya and we are cutting our losses. Our firms have tried to support the Malayan government's objective to expand the local manufacturing sector. However, we are just not able to compete with the US and especially Japan. They too are intent on setting up joint ventures with our Malayan counterparts. The red tape and bureaucracy frustrate our companies. They complain of the lack of consistent criteria for the award of pioneer status. The Malayan government in turn criticises the British for their slowness in making investments. So it has been hellish, a vicious cycle. This is not helped by the Japanese being always at the side, ready to take up virtually any project suggested by the Malayans. Our chaps are just not willing to take the risks. Of the hundreds of investment projects proposed by the Malayans, we have only taken up a handful. The Japanese have won the contest! The Malayans are now fast looking to the east to bolster their economy.

So as I said, we are cutting our losses. Our office here will be significantly diminished."

"And you? Do you still have a job?"

"Of course! You are not to worry. " Hugh saw the creases on May's forehead. He leaned over and smoothed them. "Here," he said picking up a morsel of food with his chopstick and placing it on May's lips. "Eat, as Fu Yi would say. You need your strength. Leave all the worrying to me. We'll break the news to Craig this evening."

"Yes," she said, her face still pale.

***

After Hugh left for his office May returned home. She wished Fu Yi was around. She needed to talk to someone. She was apprehensive about going to England. She had never been outside Malaya. Would she be able to integrate with English people? she asked herself. Would they accept her? How would Craig fare? The treatment she had received at the Selangor Club years ago still lingered in her mind. Would it be worse in England? It was all happening too fast. Yet she should have been prepared. They had talked about the possibility frequently enough. Hugh assured her that there would not be discrimination in England. "We are a hotchpotch of different races, a melting pot. You would be just one amongst the multitude settled in England," he had said, "you'll do just fine."

May wandered from room to room, her fingers lingering on the furniture she passed. She loved her life here with Hugh and Craig. Each room in the house, each piece of furniture held such memories. Then of course there was Ruth, Libby and baby Michael. She couldn't leave them here just like that.

Who would take care of Libby after they left if Ruth stayed on in Port Dickson? How could Ruth support herself without May's help?

She sat down and reached for the phone.

***

Fu Yi fed the baby and placed him back in the crib. Out in the garden, a breeze picked up sending the washing billowing on the clothesline. Bringing the baby to Ma'am Ruth had been a good decision. May was right. In the week since she had moved here with the baby, Ruth was already looking happier and more settled. Fu Yi made sure that Ruth was never alone but constantly with people who loved and respected her. So far, there had been no further incidences of self-harm. Yet the worry was always there. She had to keep vigilant.

Fu Yi stepped out into the garden and began folding up the washing. Night after night, she sat with Ruth and heard her unburden herself. Through a mishmash of Malay, a smattering of Chinese and English, they made themselves known to each other. In truth, Fu Yi did not understand all that she was told, but the telling seemed to help Ruth and so she allowed the words to flow over her, nodding sagely from time to time to provide encouragement for the outpouring from Ruth. More often than not, Ruth would fall asleep, exhausted by her emotional telling. Fu Yi would then cover her mistress with a blanket and leave her to sleep.

Fu Yi hitched the basket of washing on to her hip. There was a time, she recalled, when she was young. A smile broke out on her sun-browned face, deepening the creases on her cheeks. It was hard to imagine herself young. She looked at her hands.

They were lined and spotted. Once these hands had caressed a young man and loved him as Ruth had loved. She was glad she was no longer of an age where such loves were important. They brought too much pain. Now she loved like a mother and a grandmother. She would have done anything for May; she loved her like the daughter she had never had. Transferring some of the love to Ruth was not hard. She had seen how Ruth suffered. Master Mark was a charming man but he was selfish, putting himself before others. Then who could blame him? Who could blame him for falling in love with May?

Fu Yi grinned again. *"Aiyah!"* she chided herself out loud. She would, of course think that. She was biased when it came to May. It was all to do with fate. You couldn't change fate. It was meant to be.

With the basket of laundry still on her hip, she went into the kitchen to prepare the evening meal. There was the *ikan kembong*, a mackerel, to gut and fillet, then just some greens and boiled rice.

From a distance, the school bell rang followed by the sound of children. "I am glad I am here and not in the airless dormitory that was my retirement home," she muttered. "Work and caring for others has given me new life."

***

Ruth waited until all the children had left. The classroom looked abandoned without them. She picked up the exercise books left on the desks and stacked them up in a pile. The children had been copying out the alphabets. She would mark them later in the evening. She sat down and took a piece of paper.

Dear May,

I am coming to you this weekend. I have to speak to Libby. Baby Michael is with me. Fu Yi brought him and is staying on to look after us. Thank you. He brings me such joy. I still want to adopt him as my own, a farce, I know, as he is mine. I can't let the world know. I can't let Omar know. I fear he will take him away from me. Even if he didn't, his parents would probably try. I must convince Libby this weekend. I hope she will agree.

I love Libby and just do not know how she could be persuaded to believe it.

Love,
Ruth

Chapter 38

ANGER, DISAPPOINTMENT AND jealousy! Omar felt them all. They rushed through his blood and fired him with disgust, disgust for Ruth and disgust for his mother who had commissioned the report. He wanted to choke the lifeblood out of the person who had written those vile words. Was Ruth the Ruth painted in these pages? He flung the papers away from him as though they were hot coals. They scattered on the floor. A photograph landed on his foot. He kicked it away. He clasped his head. Could it be, could it be, he asked himself. Was this what Ruth had wanted to tell him when he stopped her, each time saying that he did not care about her past, just what lay ahead for them? Yet the past was indicative of the future. Would he have brushed the past aside if he had known what lay in it? Confronted by the allegations in the report, he found himself in a quandary. He was a hypocrite! He scolded himself. Nothing should change if he really meant that he was only interested in the future. Yet ... yet! He was suffused with jealousy. The sordid accounts of their trysts burned in his mind. The Ruth he knew should have known better, behaved better, for the man had an invalid wife.

Omar rose to his feet. He growled, a growl that became an agonised howl. He felt his heart ripped out of him. This was how jealousy felt, a burn that turned his insides out. Was this man the reason why Ruth had rejected him? He walked furiously up and down the room. He had harboured such hopes even after his failure to win her over when he visited Port Dickson. He wanted to hit out at someone, something and anything. His fist crashed into the nearest wall.

He strode into the bathroom, knuckles bleeding, and turned on the shower. He stepped into the cubicle without undressing. He allowed the steaming hot water to gush over him. It fell like a torrent, its roar hiding his roar of anger.

***

May sat patiently in the car listening to Omar. Her heart went out to him. She had never seen a man so utterly distraught. Where was the Omar the public knew, the confident, magnanimous man who was always on the winning side? The media projected him as the most eligible man in town. She had assumed that he must have had many affairs, many women, and many loves. In fact she had been afraid for Ruth because of the stories surrounding him.

"Did you know about this? Did Ruth tell you that she had another lover, someone of whom she is still enamoured? Was this why she sent me away?"

May shook her head. "I didn't know. I don't believe it. I think you should let Ruth tell you herself."

'The report had photographs."

"As there are photographs of you and other women. It is what you read into them. They are what you make them out to be."

Omar looked unconvinced.

"I never knew you to be judgemental."

"I am not. I try not to be." He reddened. He knew he was. "My first reaction might have been. I have had time to think it over since. I am more jealous than judgemental. According to the report, they are still lovers. It drives me crazy."

"If that is what is bothering you, then I can assure you that Ruth has not loved anyone but you since Mark died. No matter what she says, she is still in love with you."

They were parked in a lay-by. "Imagine if someone saw us together today and tells Hugh," May continued. "Imagine if they were to take a photograph. It would not look good would it?"

"I am not saying," she continued, "that Ruth was not acquainted with this man, which obviously she was, nor that he was not her lover when she was in England." May took a deep breath. Her heart was beating fast. This was her opportunity to help Ruth.

"Ruth has had a very hard time. Mark was unfaithful to her. This is not hearsay. Don't imagine that it is Ruth telling stories to justify her actions. I know because I was his lover when he was first posted here. I was young, impressionable, and he was handsome. He swept me off my feet. I didn't think of Ruth. It is a guilt I have to live with. People make mistakes."

Omar blinked. May looked away. Her ears were burning and her face was red with embarrassment. He realised how hard it was for her to tell.

"Hugh knows?" he asked.

"Yes, he helped me. He was my pillar. Without him, I would not be what I am." She smiled and her eyes lit up with the thought of her husband. "I was a frightened young girl with no money. My parents were placed in a settlement. It was the time of the Emergency. They died. I didn't speak English as I do now. I love Hugh. And my love for him grows with every trust he places in me."

May looked him in the eye. "I didn't call you to talk about this. I didn't know of the report or the information in it when I made that call. I came to tell you that Hugh and I are returning to England. Ruth will need a friend. She loves you. After you left, she started self-harming again."

***

When May returned home, she found Ruth's letter waiting for her. She read the short missive several times in her bedroom. Carefully, she folded it neatly and placed it in a little box in her dressing table. She walked over to the window and sat down on the ledge. It was her favourite place. It looked out into the garden. She was just in time to see a host of sparrows land on the grass. Since Hugh had told her of their imminent departure, every moment spent in the house was poignant. They had had so many happy years in this house, her first real home with Hugh. The future was a big unknown. She stretched her hand out of the window to let the sun touch her arms, feeling its heat caress her. She would miss it. She would miss Ruth. She would miss Libby, as would Craig. She feared that it would be difficult for him to adjust to England. If Libby returned with them, may be...

No, she scolded herself. Libby couldn't possibly go back with them. Ruth would not agree. Her place was with her mother. It would be unhealthy for Craig and Libby to be so attached.

May was fired with the need to mend the despair in the lives of those her past actions had touched. She must mend the rift between Libby and Ruth before she leaves. If Ruth was able to adopt Michael and the three could be together, it would make such a difference.

Hugh's car turned into the driveway. He had collected the children from school. She ran out of the room and down the stairs. Her heart felt as though it would burst with love when she saw her husband and son. Her meeting with Omar showed how lucky she was to have Hugh. It seemed unthinkable that she had once loved another. She went quickly to her husband and kissed him. He was taken back by her passion.

"What brought that on?" He held her close. "Not that I am complaining."

"She swallowed. "The heat," she replied, red-faced. The children sniggered and rolled their eyes.

"I need you to do some shopping. Take Craig with you." She held Hugh's eye before glancing quickly at Libby.

He understood. "Come on then," he said to Craig.

***

Talking to Libby proved more difficult than May had anticipated. She had gone over it many times in her head. Yet when the crunch came, she was nervous her intervention would worsen things. May poured a glass of orange juice and handed it to Libby.

"Is everything all right at school?" May sat down and drew Libby alongside her.

"Yes! Fine!"

"I spoke to your school mistress. She said that you seemed distracted." The teacher's words were stronger: naughty and disobedient was how she described Libby.

"I am fine." Libby sipped her orange juice and avoided May's eyes. She stared straight at the wall in front of her and swung her legs up and down before dropping her gaze to the floor. "We had sport practice all afternoon. I am tired. That's all."

May placed an arm around Libby's shoulders. "You know, we are very fond of you. If you have any problems or any issues at all, you will come to us, won't you?"

Libby swiped the back of her hand over her mouth. She didn't answer, nor did she look up.

May leaned over and kissed Libby lightly on her forehead. "We are worried because you look out of sorts. You can talk to me about anything," she repeated. "I will keep your confidence."

Libby mumbled something under her breath and turned away. A tear splashed down her knee.

"My dear, come here." May wrapped her arms around Libby and held her close. "I know something happened between you and your mother when we visited her; something that made both of you sad." She could feel Libby's body trembling. Soon May's blouse was wet with Libby's tears.

"Nothing is as bad as it seems once you talk about it." The poor child should not have to bear a burden on her own, May thought. She knew from Ruth that Libby was jealous of Michael. She needed to expel the jealousy. Yet she must not mention Michael. It would have to come from Libby herself.

"When I was a child, there were many occasions when I rowed with my mother. This is normal and part of growing up. You must not worry about it and let it eat you up. Your mother loves you. "

Libby shrugged away May's arms. Her face was red with anger. "That is the problem. My mother does not love me. She does not have time for me. She is always preoccupied with something or other. Yet she wants to adopt Fatimah's niece's baby! Have him live with her while sending me to you. She gives him time. She has none for me."

Libby stood up and put the glass down on a table nearby with force. Orange juice splashed over; a puddle of yellow collected on the table. She turned to head towards her bedroom. May caught hold of her hand.

"Your mother loves you with all her heart. I know because she told me. She talks and worries about you all the time. She is proud of you. There are times when adults find it difficult to express themselves."

Libby tugged her hand free. "I don't believe you." She spat out the words with vehemence.

"Your mum is coming to see you this weekend. She wants to explain. Believe me, there is a good reason for everything. Give your mother a chance. Give yourself a chance. Your mother loves you like I love Craig."

Libby stood still, head bowed. May was glad that she did not bolt away

"She was heart-broken when she left you here with me. She did it only to allow you a better education. It was not an easy decision for your mother. Without you she is lonely. She is willing to subject herself to loneliness for you. Not having you with her is her way of saying how much she loves you."

Gingerly, May took Libby into her arms again. She stroked her hair. "Talk to your mother when she comes. Be generous with her. She has had a very hard life. You will understand when you are older."

May could feel Libby's body relax.

"Everything will be fine. You'll see."

Chapter 39

RAIN PELTED DOWN thick and fast. The bus was packed. The central aisle had no standing room. People stood like tin soldiers, hip to hip, swaying with the motion of the bus. Inside the vehicle, with bodies in close proximity, the damp heat was unbearable. Within minutes of departure from Port Dickson, the air in the bus became musty. Moisture condensed on glass. The windscreen misted over. *Tick tack* went the windscreen wiper. The driver leaned forward to peer. His chest brushed the steering wheel. He reached out to wipe away the condensation on the windscreen but moisture collected almost immediately.

Ruth sat squashed next to a Malay farmer. He had a rattan basket on his lap. Inside it were several fluffy little chicks. From time to time, he jiggled his foot. *"Untuk cucu saya,"* he explained. "For my grandchild."

She smiled in answer before turning to look out. She could see little. She rubbed the windows with the heel of her palm. Huge black clouds loomed and trees bent and swayed. The wind was strong. She was glad that baby Michael was safe at home with Fu Yi. The bus lurched to the left. Someone screamed. The farmer's basket fell, caught in time by the man standing next to him. The bus righted itself. The passengers heaved sighs of relief. Everyone began to talk.

"*Alamak!* Bound to flood-*lah*. The last time I was in KL floodwaters reached my knee. Is this your first trip to the city?" asked the man in the seat in front of her. He stood up and turned to look at Ruth.

"I lived there for a few months. I have not known it to flood."

"You are lucky-*man*. Floods very common *one* you know. Monsoon-*what*. Maybe you lived in good area. All depends on where you are." He rubbed his thumb and index finger. "You rich; all white people rich. Money counts."

Ruth smiled politely and looked away.

The man glared at her, clearly offended and sat down. "Stuck up," he muttered.

Embarrassed, Ruth looked apologetically at the farmer who was sitting next to her. He was observing the exchange with interest. He pointed at the man's back and whispered leaning into Ruth's ear, "*Jahat! Penyibut,*" making a face to indicate that the man in front of them was a busy body and was to be avoided. The bus continued to plough through the rain. More and more cars overtook them. Each time the bus swerved to the verge to make way. The road was narrow. The heat, the mingling of odours in a confined space, became unbearable. Ruth felt nauseous. She placed her forehead against the window to get some coolness. A car sped by perilously close to the bus, its metallic grey body a blur as it overtook. Harsh lights shone into Ruth's eyes from an oncoming car, its body indiscernible under the pelting rain. A loud bang followed. The bus swerved and rolled over in slow motion, down the side of the road into a parallel ditch. Ruth could feel her head banging against the window, once, twice, three times. She lost count. Then darkness.

***

"Why is Ruth so late?" May asked. Streaks of lightning lit up the sky but within seconds everything fell back to darkness. May pushed aside the curtains and looked out. Rain lashed down with force, driving diagonal sheets across the lawn and driveway. "I said I would send the driver to her. I begged her to at least take a taxi. She insisted on using a bus. She wouldn't even allow us to meet her at the station. She wanted to make her way here on her own! I couldn't make her see sense. She is *so* stubborn."

"In this bad weather the bus journey could take four hours, more if the traffic is bad. Remember the potholes when we last went to Port Dickson? Shall I drive to the bus station? I tried calling. No one answered. The connection is poor." Hugh could see that May was agitated.

"I'll come with you." May went into the hallway to get some umbrellas.

"No! You stay at home and keep safe and dry." Another streak of lightning lit up the sky, followed by a roll of thunder. Huge drops pelted the windowpanes. "Look at the weather. An umbrella would not protect you against the rain. The wind is gusty. It would turn it inside out within seconds. Umbrellas under such conditions are more a hindrance."

"I want to come."

The phone rang. The sudden succession of rings startled May. She looked at Hugh but he was already striding towards the phone. He picked it up. May watched his grim face as he listened. His hand went up mid-air to stop her from asking questions. Minutes passed: the clock in the hallway ticked. Gently, he placed the phone down. "It is Ruth. There has been an accident."

***

Ruth's eyes fluttered, they moved rapidly from side to side. She saw Buster. He bounded up to her wagging his tail and leaving behind him a trail of flattened golden ripe wheat. It was summer and the sun was shining bright. He jumped, his paws catching the threads on her skirt. Ruth knelt down and stroked his head. The fur was soft and she could smell his doggy scent. She looked up. Mark was calling and waving to her. His voice soared and trailed in the wind. She could see his smile and sense his eagerness for her to join him. He stood in the field with the wheat reaching up his waist. His hair was like the colour of sun-bleached grains. The sky was clear blue. "Come," he gestured to her. "Come to me," he seemed to say, his words lost in the sound of the wind.

Then another voice came from behind her, stopping her. She turned. Green paddy fields inundated with water stretched before her. The water gleamed black. Overhead the sun was red. In the midst of it stood Omar. "Stop, don't go! Stay with me," he shouted. His eyes sought hers. He ran towards her with his arms spread wide. "I love you." He caught her wrist. She sensed a movement behind her. From the corner of her eye, she could see Mark. He was fading away with each backward step he took.

Ruth struggled, hitting out with her hands, her arms flailing.

"Nurse, hold her," a voice commanded. "She will harm herself."

May stood petrified at the bedside. Ruth was twisting and turning in the bed. Her eyes were squeezed tight shut. Yet behind the blue-veined eyelids, her eyeballs continued to dart wildly from side to side. Ruth opened her mouth to speak. No words came out; instead an unnerving agonised howl issued from her lips.

May dropped to her haunches and took Ruth's hand in hers. She stroked it. "*Shhh!* We are all here. You had an accident. Everything will be all right. Libby wants to see you. You won't want her to see you in distress." May's face was wet as she leaned over to stroke Ruth's cheek.

The nurse administered a needle in the crook of Ruth's arm. Ruth stopped struggling and her head lolled to one side She was very pale and her lips were blue. There was a deep gash on one side of her temple, which had been stitched and bandaged.

The nurse pulled a chair to the side of the bed. "There, a seat for you. Let her rest. We will run a series of tests when she wakes up. For the moment sleep is the best thing for her." The nurse went out and came back shortly with a box of tissues. She placed it in May's hand. "She must mean a lot to you. I'll be back soon to check."

***

Omar opened his eyes. Gingerly, he touched his cheeks and felt the rough stubble of two days' growth. He was fully dressed. His shirt, unbuttoned almost to his waist and un-tucked from his trousers, was crumpled. He could smell himself. A necktie lay carelessly half hidden and trapped by a cushion. He must have fallen asleep on the sofa. Since that fateful day when the poisonous documents had been rudely thrust into his hand he had dragged himself to the office and performed like a robot before heading home and drinking himself into a stupor. He looked around the room. It was a mess. Bottles, glasses, half-eaten food lay on every surface. He had given the maid leave. He wanted to be on his own to think. Instead, he drank.

That was until the previous night. Filled with self-disgust, he had emptied a whole bottle of whisky into the kitchen basin and stood listening to the gurgling of the golden liquid as it disappeared down the waste hole. After that he collapsed on the sofa and slept until bright sunshine shone straight onto his face.

He rose to his feet and stamped them. They were cramped and sore. He went into the kitchen and took a bin bag. With methodical care, he cleared up the bottles and mess from the floor and tables until some semblance of order returned. He went to his bedroom and stripped off his stale clothes and walked into the shower. The sensation of hot water pounding his body, the fresh scent of soap and shampoo breathed new life into him. He scrubbed until his body tingled. He dressed with care. He had reached a conclusion about himself and Ruth. He was a hypocrite. She had not told him the whole truth about her past because he had not wanted her to. He had told her that they should look forward to the future and not backwards. How could he blame her for not telling him? Her past was not for him to forgive. He had no right. Yet, the words of the report sprung before him, black on white and vicious. He had no right. But was it a question of right? Could he trust Ruth to be faithful to him, when she had not been faithful in her previous marriage, even though May had tried to explain? A picture of Ruth with

Steve rose in his mind's eye. He could not stop his revulsion. He recalled May's words. Could he be magnanimous like Hugh? Deep down, he wasn't sure.

The doorbell rang. He rose to his feet and walked to the door. He opened it. "Hugh!" he exclaimed in surprise. Behind Hugh another car swerved into the driveway. It was his parents.

Omar pushed open the door and indicated that Hugh should enter. He looked over Hugh's shoulder and saw his mother getting out of the car followed by his father.

Hugh hesitated with his foot suspended over the door's threshold. He followed Omar's eyes. "You have guests. I won't stay. What I have to say won't take long. Ruth is in hospital. She has had an accident."

Omar held on to the doorframe. "Accident?" he asked. "How? Is she going to be all right?"

Siti's voice cut in. She had hurried over the minute she saw Hugh at the door. "Of course she is all right. All this fuss over a little accident." She brushed past Hugh without greeting. "You again," she muttered aloud, "interfering with my family affairs. Isn't it about time you packed up and went home like the rest? You don't belong here. We have had enough."

"I am sorry. My wife is upset," Omar's father said with a curt nod to Hugh before he too brushed past and went into the house.

"Well! I'd better leave you." Hugh, embarrassed by the assault of words, turned to leave. He could hardly blame Ruth for not wanting to be part of Omar's family.

"Omar! Come into the house. We have something to say to you," his mother shouted from within.

Chapter 40

MAY SAT WITH her knees pressed against the hard metal bars of the hospital bed. Her back ached from the long hours spent on the uncomfortable chair. A nurse came in with a cup of coffee. May took it gratefully with two hands. With infinite care, she sipped the hot sweet liquid, savouring the heat and the taste of it. She watched the nurse take Ruth's blood pressure and change the drip.

"You should eat something," the nurse advised. She looked at May over her glasses. She was a stout robust-looking lady with a no-nonsense look about her. Her eyes were, however, kindly and they now stared straight at May. "Take a little rest yourself." She adjusted the bed sheets and wrote on the board hung at the end of the bed. "I'll come back in a little while," she said taking the empty cup from May.

May rolled her shoulders, for they were tense and rigid. She was about to stand up when Ruth's hand moved agitatedly on the bed sheet as though she was in search of something. May took her hand and stroked it gently. "I am here," she whispered. Ruth responded by gripping May's hand back in return. May was surprised by the strength in her fingers.

"May!" Ruth left the name hanging in the air; her eyes were still tightly shut. Despite the strength of her fingers her voice was weak. She had tried to speak many times previously. She had failed each time. This was her first clear discernible word. May's heart leapt. It was a good sign.

May bent closer. Ruth's grip tightened.

"I know that Craig is Mark's son."

May straightened up with a start. She pulled her hand away, her body poised to run. Ruth stopped her. "It is all right. I am not angry. I am glad in a way because I have not borne him a child. It is good that some part of him lives on." Tears rolled down from the corner of Ruth's eyes, leaving streaks on her cheeks.

May placed her cheek against Ruth's, mingling her own tears with Ruth's. "Don't say that," she said, "Mark lives on in Libby as well."

"Libby is not Mark's. She is the fruit of my indiscretion. I do not want her to know. I am ashamed of myself. That is why I cannot be with Omar. His mother found out and threatens to tell him if I do not give him up. I cannot bear his scorn and anger when he learns what a bad woman I have been." Ruth opened her eyes and looked straight into May's. "Should something happen to me, please take care of Libby. I know you were worried that Craig and Libby are siblings and that their attachment to each other will lead to incest. They are not related at all. You have nothing to fear."

Ruth released May's hand. She turned away for a few minutes before returning her gaze to May. "In the eyes of the world, Craig will be yours and Hugh's and Libby, mine and Mark's. That is if my indiscretion," she continued, her eyes tired and her voice weak, "is kept secret. If Omar's mother were to disclose this, people would gossip. The international community here is small. I don't mind it for myself. I mind the stigma on Libby."

"Surely no one would blame Libby. Not in this day and age. We are in the Sixties."

"Yes, in this day and age even in England and particularly if I were to stay in this country. Think, however, of all the things we cannot do without men's consent. Moreover, society generally views a man's adultery more kindly than it does a woman's." Exhausted by her exertion, Ruth slumped back on to her pillow.

May held Ruth's hand tightly in hers. "I promise we'll look after Libby. Nothing is going to happen to you. I won't let it." She kissed Ruth's palm. It was clammy. "Please don't fret. We'll work things out. Omar..."

But Ruth had already drifted off.

"Omar," May wanted to say, "knows about Steve." Her unfinished sentence hung in the air.

***

When Omar stepped into his house after seeing Hugh off, he found his father standing by the kitchen door with both hands clasped behind him. He stood with legs firmly apart and heels dug in as though he needed the strength and support of the floor. He didn't turn round at Omar's entry. Omar could hear the sound of clinking bottles from the kitchen. His mother must have found the empty bottles he had carefully bagged. He waited for the torrent of accusation that would ensue. He was caught wrong-footed; his intention to confront his parents for their ill manners temporarily evaporated at the sight of his mother rushing out from the kitchen. She pushed a bottle into his face and shouted.

"What could you be thinking of? Do you think bagging the bottles will conceal your wrongdoing? Do you not know that alcohol consumption is a sin and illegal for Muslims? Anyone, and that includes the rubbish collector, could report you. How could you? Madness! You would be publicly flogged if anyone found out. Your political career would be in tatters!"

"Where did you get those bottles? Siti screamed in frustration when Omar didn't reply. "We have to make sure no one else knows."

"For once I agree with your mother," his father said. He wagged his finger at Omar. "This must not get out, especially now. We came today because I received news, good news. You are being considered for the post of Second Minister of Finance. I cannot emphasise enough the importance of this appointment and what it opens up for you in the future. To get this offer at your young age is no mean feat. There can be no scandal. And it includes this! Especially this!"

Tun Zikri slapped down a stack of papers onto the coffee table. The gesture was so violent the pages flew and dispersed about the floor. Omar retrieved them. There were a couple of photographs of him and Ruth. In one her head was resting on his shoulder; in the other they were kissing. They must have been taken without them being aware. A caption underlined in red caught his attention: *Omar's secret love involved in an accident. Is there more to the story?* He read quickly. It gave a brief account of

Ruth's background, the recent loss of her husband, her daughter Libby, the sighting of Omar and Ruth together not long after Mark's death. Then the insinuations and speculations...

"Are these out?"

"No! I stopped it. *Alhamdulillah!* Thank God! Your cousin saw this at his editor's desk and alerted me. It cost me. A lot," stressed Tun Zikri, " and now we are indebted to your cousin. So no more silly antics. Forget the woman! She is not good for you."

"Omar, I am your mother. I have only your interest at heart. Her past will leak out sooner or later. You cannot be involved with her if you wish to have a political career. She has shown herself to be heartless. She stole the husband of an invalid woman. She did this when her own husband was ill."

"Stop! Stop! I don't want to hear anymore. Let me think for myself. Leave me alone!" Omar went to his bedroom and slammed the door shut. His head was bursting.

***

Fu Yi placed baby Michael firmly into Libby's arms giving her no chance to withdraw. Libby stiffened, unused to the little floppy body. It seemed so tiny and vulnerable. She didn't want to hold him, didn't want any connection with someone that competed with her for her mother's love. She handed the baby back at Fu Yi. "I don't want him."

Fu Yi stared sternly back at Libby and walked out of the room. "I don't have four hands. You have to help."

Libby ran after her. "I don't want to hold him."

Fu Yi went into the bathroom and locked herself in. "Talk to him, take him for a walk round the house, sing to him. Anything.

I need to go to the toilet," she answered from behind the door. She waited for further protests from Libby and when none came, Fu Yi smiled.

Libby held the baby gingerly. He squirmed and opened his mouth in a big yawn. Then he smiled revealing toothless gums and two little dimples on either side of his cheeks. Libby held him closer; his soft warm body smelt of milk. She looked around, saw that no one was about and bent down and pecked him on the cheek. She began pacing round the house. It was quiet. May was at the hospital and Craig was still at school with his tennis coach. The baby began to blow bubbles, gurgling and smiling at her. His eyes seemed to recognise her. With one free hand she wiped his mouth and with the other she jiggled, imitating the movements she had observed when Fu Yi carried him.

Libby was sorry for the things she had said to her mother. She didn't dislike the baby. In fact she liked him very much. It was just that she was jealous. She was also worried about the pending departure of Craig and his parents. If they returned to England, where would she stay if she couldn't be with her own mother in Port Dickson? She knew it was not the baby's fault. Filled with remorse, she kissed the baby again.

"*Aiyah! Ho lah! Ho lah!*" Good! Good! You can give him back to me," said Fu Yi appearing suddenly. She put out her hands out to receive the baby.

"Didn't you say you don't have four hands and need to do something else? I'll hold him if you wish," said Libby.

Fu Yi had seen Libby kissing the baby. "Okay! You hold! I make lunch. You and I eat. Then go hospital. Your mother wants see you. She thinks of you all time. Mother's love."

"What about this baby? Perhaps she loves him more than she does me."

Fu Yi glared sternly at Libby. "You too jealous. Not good *hap choh!* Baby small. Everyone loves small babies. You too. Not mean your mother love one more than other. All equal, *a yeong, a yeong!* She cry every night for you." With that she turned and went into the kitchen with a huff.

Libby listened to the banging and chopping sounds from the kitchen. "Perhaps I was wrong. Perhaps mother does love me. May thinks so and I believe in May." She cuddled the baby and kissed him. "I'll tell mother that she can adopt Michael. He is not bad at all, when he is not crying."

***

The nurse propped Ruth up on the bed. "Will you try to get out of the bed and walk to the bathroom? I'll help you. A wash would do you good."

Ruth shook her head and closed her eyes. She slid down again burying herself in the hospital bedclothes.

The nurse muttered under her breath and looked disapprovingly at her patient. "You need to move. The X-rays have come back. There are no broken bones or fractures, although you are very bruised. Come! I'll help you."

Ruth turned over on to her side. She didn't want to move. What was the point of it? She didn't want to go on. She felt very tired, not only in her sore body but also in her chest and head. She was vaguely aware that people were speaking in hushed tones around her. She was detached from it all.

Suddenly she felt a hand on her arm. "I'm here," May said. "The doctor said you could come home."

Ruth didn't reply.

"Here! We have a surprise for you." Gently May helped Ruth to sit up, surprised at how light Ruth had become. May could feel her ribs as she helped her friend to sit upright.

"Mummy! Please wake up! Look at us! Look at Michael." Libby held the baby to her mother's face. "I am sorry for the spiteful things I said. I didn't mean it."

Ruth opened her eyes. For the first time that day there was a flicker of interest in them.

Libby edged closer with Michael. Ruth took him in one arm and with the other she hugged Libby. A tickling sensation hit her nose. She held back the prickling in her eyes. They were her reasons for living.

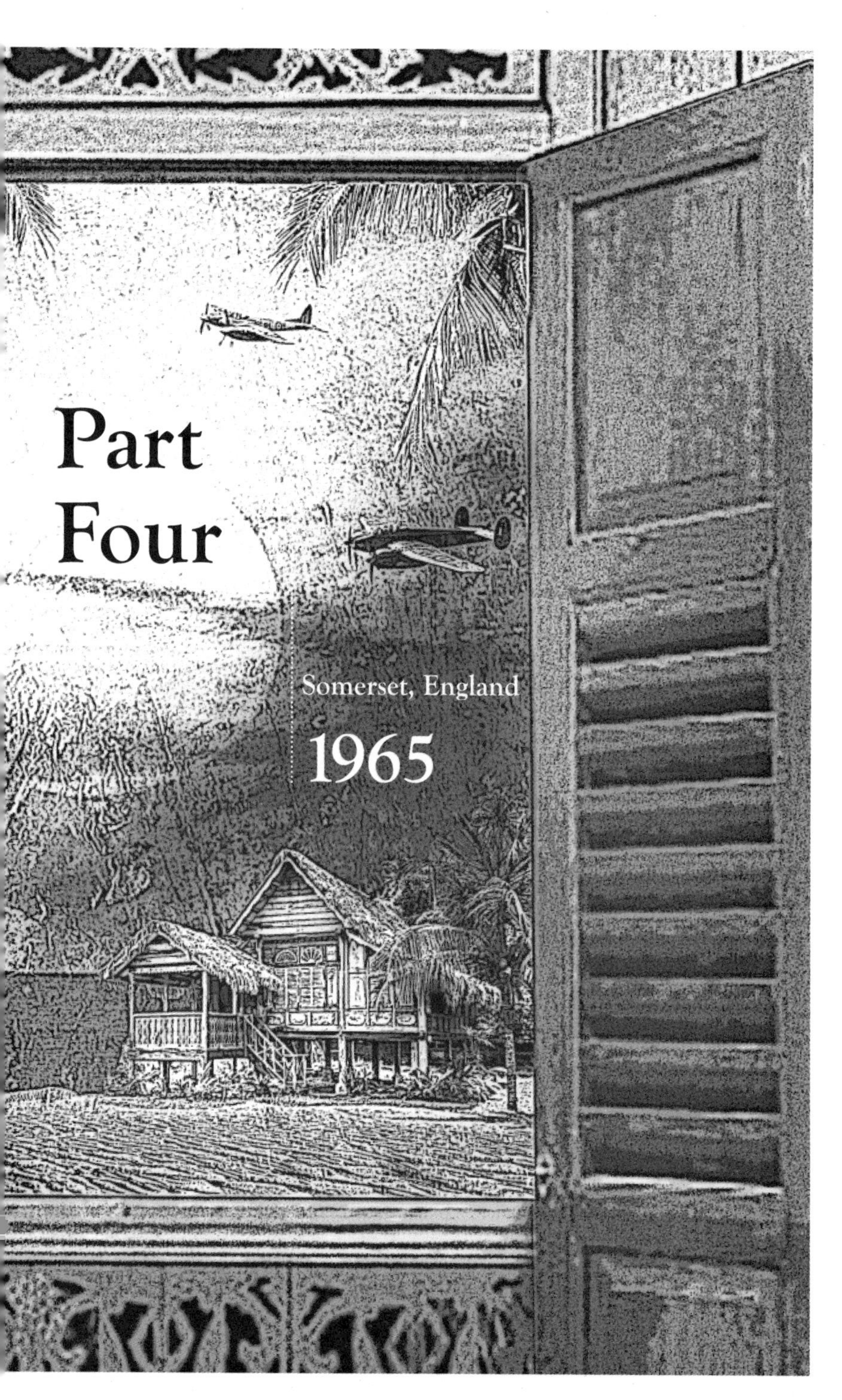

Part Four

Somerset, England

1965

Chapter 41

RUTH MADE HER way down the hill scrunching the grass under her feet. It had been a dry summer and the grass had taken on a yellowy hue. A few metres down she stopped and peered into the distance. The hillside rolled gently down before her and at the bottom a river ran as far as her eyes could see. Tall rushes by its side swayed with the wind. To the right of her she could see a narrow stone bridge. In medieval times, horse carts used it as a main thoroughfare into the village on the other side of the river. Beyond the bridge, a church steeple rose high above a scattering of cottages with tiled roofs.

The hill and the surrounding countryside reminded her of her father's farm. She had not been there since her return to England. It would bring back too many memories and memories were not what she sought.

Ruth dug her hands deep into the pocket of her dungarees and stood for a few more minutes on the hill slope. A wind picked up speed and the branches on trees swayed and rustled. Their soft whispers reminded her of coconut palms. Another country, another life, she told herself, one which she should not dwell on. Afraid that any more time spent on such thoughts would awaken the sadness she had buried within her, she resumed her descent, picking her way along the dirt path. Puffs of dust rose, for it had not rained for many days, the driest and hottest summer in a decade some said.

"Slow down!" James shouted as he ran after Ruth.

Ruth spun round. "Where is Michael?" Her voice was sharp, anxious.

"He is fine, at home with my sister. You know how much Sue loves Michael. So the minute she saw that I was alone with him, she volunteered to take over and shooed me out of the kitchen. So here I am." He smiled sheepishly at Ruth.

Ruth made an apologetic gesture for being sharp with him and smiled back in return. They walked down the hill in step with each other. James would have liked to link his arm around Ruth. He gave her a sideways appraising glance and held back. He gauged that she would recoil. Ruth had a sad look about her. At times, caught unaware, she would stare into space with a wistful expression. He wished he could make her smile more. It had taken him a long time to break the ice and even longer still to persuade Ruth that she could call on him for emergency help. She did it rarely. Mentally, James counted. Perhaps only three times, when desperate for help she had asked him and Sue to look after Michael.

"How did it go?" he asked.

"Fine. Mrs Bennett liked what I did. I am to go to her to collect more of the same to be typed. She paid me handsomely in cash." Ruth drew out a wad of notes from her pocket. "I can pay some of my rent now."

James's face grew a bright red. "You don't have to pay me now. Keep it until you have the full amount."

"I mustn't impose on your generosity. You have helped me so much. I would not have been able to work from home otherwise. And I do need to work from home so that I could be with Michael."

"Think nothing of it." Embarrassed, the colour on James's cheeks deepened even more.

"You gave me my first job, introduced me to clients, gave me this idea that I could earn a living by freelancing and typing." Ruth would not be put off. She had wanted to thank James many times and each time he had shrugged it off. She was sure that the rent he charged for the cottage was nowhere near a commercial rate.

James stopped at the bottom of the hill and turned to Ruth. He placed both hands on her shoulders. He sensed her freezing at his touch and dropped them hastily. "I did what any decent chap would do. Moreover, you made a marvellous job of my report. So I should thank you instead."

Ruth fell silent. Living a reclusive life these past years had lost her the skill of light chatter. Her previous attempts at thanking him had come out garbled. They walked on past the village and turned on to a narrow road that led to a cul-de-sac. A very large stone house stood at the end. Behind the house, the sun was beginning its gradual descent, its rays lingering to touch the house with a golden glow. The change in light was slow, almost imperceptible. Ruth thought of a sun that was fiery red, a place where the skies would darken in a flash, a place where the sunrise was a burst of red. She sighed. She must stop doing this to herself.

"Come in," said James breaking into her thoughts. "Michael and Sue will be in the kitchen." The sound of children's laughter and voices could be heard from within.

"*Hah!*" he exclaimed. "Libby must be back from school. You must come in now that both your children are at our place."

"I won't stay long. Thank you for looking after them."

"Come in and thank Sue. She is the one doing the baby-sitting. Mind you, she doesn't consider it work. Listen to them! Why not stay for supper? Sue normally cooks far too much and you are not living that far from us to have to risk a long journey back." James grinned and nodded towards Ruth's cottage. His white teeth gleamed against his dark tan. Ruth's house was a mere stone's throw away from James's. It had been a footman's cottage in the past, before the entire estate was parcelled out and sold.

"Go on! Come in," James said and strode towards his house before Ruth could protest.

***

James dried the last of the dishes and flicked the tea towel over his shoulder. "That was a lovely meal, Sue."

"Do you think Ruth enjoyed it? She was awfully quiet." Sue's coppery hair caught the light as she tossed her head and blew at a wayward lock of hair falling over her eyes. "I worry about her. She seems distracted."

"I guess she has a lot on her plate. I think she worries about the children and not having enough to cover her outgoings." James looked out of the window towards Footman's Cottage. A single light shone from a room on the ground floor, a room where he knew Ruth did her work. He could almost imagine hearing the clacking of the typewriter.

Sue observed her brother. His concern over Ruth was etched all over his normally cheerful face. She knew he was fond of Ruth. She remembered the day when Ruth had first arrived at the village. She had come alone on a bus. Sue and James had seen her looking lost and had gone up to her. She had told them that she was looking for accommodation, anything small that could house a family of three. With a face turned bright red, she confessed that she could not afford much. Sue could tell even then, how much her brother was taken with Ruth. He offered Ruth Footman's Cottage immediately, waiving the deposit normally due on rentals.

"Why don't you ask Ruth out for a meal or a drink? I'll baby sit."

James leaned against the washbasin. "She might refuse."

"You don't know until you try. You could get to know her better. There is a mystery about her. She doesn't say much. We hardly know her background, what she did before, except that her husband had passed away and that they lived for a while in Malaya. Libby told me something interesting though."

James looked sharply at his sister. "I hope you have not been prying."

Fine lines radiated from the corner of her eyes. They twinkled at her brother in jest. "I was curious. Surely you must have noticed that Michael is Eurasian? He is dark and has the loveliest head of strong black hair. Libby, however, told me her father was English."

"Oh Sue! You shouldn't. It is none of our business."

Sue looked at him with a triumphant smile. "Libby told me today that Michael is her adopted brother, adopted after her father passed away. I just find it fascinating. There must be an interesting story behind this. I am curious."

James placed the tea towel onto a rail and gave his sister a disapproving look. "You shouldn't pry." He looked reproachfully at his sister.

"Libby told me that they stayed in London with May and Hugh when they first returned to England. She called them her aunt and uncle though, as far as I know, they are not related, just a term that is apparently used in that part of the world when the young address the old. Not that May and Hugh are old. May is certainly not old! She is quite young and lovely in fact. You must have seen them. We must invite them over the next time they visit. I often wondered at their connection with Ruth. Apparently Ruth had some problems in a London park. She had Michael with her. She was called hate names. That was why they moved here."

"Did you dig up this information from Libby? You are incorrigible!"

"I am fond of all of them. It is just that my curiosity was aroused. Ruth has this sadness about her that whets my interest."

James walked out of the kitchen. "I don't want you digging any more information. Hear!"

"But James you like Ruth! Surely you are interested in knowing about her."

James came back to face Sue. "When she is ready to tell me," he said more gently.

***

James sat down in an armchair and flicked open a newspaper. The sitting room was large with white-washed walls, beautiful honey coloured flagstone tiles and a big open fireplace. Persian rugs peppered the floor and the table lamps scattered round the room lent it a warm comforting glow. It was a place he adjourned to each evening to read and listen to music. Overhead he could hear Sue moving in her bedroom. This evening he could not concentrate. After supper, he had walked Ruth back to her cottage. James carried Michael, who was already asleep. He recalled the child in his arms, the satisfying weight and warmth of his body. "I'm getting old, too old to think of fatherhood," he mused. He wondered if he should ask Ruth out. He shook his head in answer to himself. She would think I am too old for her, he thought. Yet a longing persisted in his heart. "Really!" he chided himself.

Chapter 42

London

May spotted the empty bench and immediately hurried towards it with Lin skipping by her side. All round them, people were settling down on grassy banks or on benches to take in the sun. She guessed that the bench was empty because it was under the shade of a silver maple. Hugh would have pulled her leg for seeking out the shade. Everyone else seemed to be making for the sunniest spot they could find.

"Mummy, can I have an ice cream?"

"Yes, of course. Let's have our picnic first." May sat down and unloaded her little basket. Out came a round of ham sandwiches, a roast chicken leg, two slices of chocolate cake and lemonade. She could not help but compare it with what she would have filled the basket with if they had been in Malaysia. Coconut rice wrapped in banana leaves with *sambal* on the side would have been *must* items for a picnic.

"Sit down next to me here." She patted the space beside her. Lin clambered up and stretched out both her sturdy legs with their white ankle socks and black shoes. She pointed and flexed her feet in play.

"Sandwich or chicken?" May asked. She hid a smile. Lin was looking round-eyed at the roasted drumstick that May held up. Without waiting for a reply, May placed it in Lin's hand and sat watching her daughter munch and tug at the drumstick with relish. "Slow down, no one is going to take it from you."

May had no appetite. She sat on the bench, one arm stretched out along its back, the other still holding on to the basket. A flock of pigeons landed in front of her, tempted by the crumbs of food on the ground. She watched them peck, their tiny heads bobbing up and down. She thought of her new life in England. It was so different from that in Malaya. Even the air smelt different.

Lin slid down to the ground and pushed the drumstick licked clean into May's hand. "Finished," she announced with a happy grin. "Can I go there?" She pointed to the play area a few yards away. Before May could answer, she was already running towards it. May sighed and followed her. She was wary about meeting other mothers in the playground, especially after Ruth's experience.

The playground was crowded. There were children playing, young mothers chatting and grandmothers knitting. It was literally a whole community of women of all ages charged with minding kids. She saw a bench and went to it. "May I?" she asked of the two women seated there. They nodded and returned to their chatter, cigarettes in hand. May perched herself at the seat's corner. She was conscious of being alone in a crowd. Ruth had told her that London could be a very lonely place, revealing bits of her previous life when she was with Mark. May agreed. She stared at the women around her and wondered if the person who had shouted abuse at Ruth was among them. She had not suffered racial discrimination like Ruth. Neither Craig nor Lin looked typically oriental. Their light complexion and hair helped and she would probably be mistaken as their nanny.

She recalled the day when Ruth came back from the park with Michael in her arms. She was furious. Her face was pinched white and her freckles stood out like tiny specks the colour of sea sand. "You know what they called Michael? Black! All because I intervened when a bunch of kids harangued a Jamaican lady and her little girl. They obviously thought that Michael's father was West Indian. I will not stay a moment longer in London. "

They couldn't stop Ruth. "Let her go," Hugh had advised May. "Ruth needs to find her feet, be more independent. She will feel more useful if she finds work. Leaving London might do the trick. We can help her set up home, find a local school for Libby, give her some seed money to get her started. Anything. I think it is time we let her go." So May let Ruth leave and felt a part of her wrenched away.

Hugh was proved right and for that May was thankful. Ruth seemed revitalised. Work gave her a sense of self-respect. That was possibly what she needed.

For want of something to do, May took out a sandwich and bit into it. The two ladies on the bench turned. "Have I seen you before?" one asked. "Do you work in that Chinese eatery round the corner, the one with the hanging ducks and roasted meats in the front window?"

May shook her head. "No! I..."

"Well then, ... Sorry!" Their interest waned as fast as it was aroused and they returned to their chatter leaving May little chance to say anything else. The woman who had asked the question shrugged. "Difficult to tell them apart. I wanted to ask her the recipe for the roast duck," May heard her say.

***

The door clicked shut. "I'm back," Hugh called.

May switched off the gas stove and placed aside the wooden spoon she was using to stir the rich sticky sauce in the saucepan. She could hear him taking off his shoes. She hurried out to the hallway.

"That smells wonderful. What is it?" Hugh wrapped her in his arms and gave her a resounding kiss.

"Duck roasted with five types of spices; cinnamon, cloves, fennel seed, star anise and Szechuan peppercorns, roasted and ground to a fine powder. And of course salt. I did it on the spur of the moment, prompted by ... something I heard today." May thought of the comment made by the woman in the park. "It is in the oven and I have a rich plum sauce to go with it."

"*Yum!* How did you learn to cook this way?" Hugh looked ruefully down at his middle and patted his belly.

"Fu Yi." May returned to the kitchen with Hugh in tow. "A cup of tea?' she asked. "Lin is having a nap. I will wake her up soon or she'll not settle down this evening." She busied herself with the kettle and teapot.

"Good day?" he asked. He stood behind her and slipped both arms around her waist.

"The same. We went to the park and had a picnic. Lin played. And you? Any news of what is happening in Malaysia?"

Hugh released May. His face became grave and his voice serious. He had been following news from Malaysia. "From today, Singapore is no longer part of Malaysia, just two years since its formation. It is now an independent and separate sovereign state."

May gasped. The teaspoon she was holding fell with a clatter on the table.

"This has taken everyone by surprise. I suppose if we think about it, it is inevitable. I must confess that I had found it hard to believe that Singapore would accept the conditions set for her inclusion into Malaysia. Apparently the tiny island would have to foot thirty-five percent of Malaysia's Federal budget and contribute forty to sixty percent of its revenue. And of course, with its predominantly Chinese population, Singapore is viewed by its mainland neighbour as a potential threat to the balance of political power. This is probably the reason for Malaya's ready agreement to have Singapore leave. Some say that Singapore was actually booted out."

May set the saucer and teacup down carefully on the table. She sat down. "Will there be implications..."

"Yes! Things are already a bit unstable as they are with Indonesia and the Philippines still protesting at the formation of Malaysia. So this breakaway will certainly add to uncertainties as the balance of the population becomes re-arranged. I think a lot of Chinese in Malaya might move to Singapore."

Hugh dragged his chair closer to May and took her hand in his. "I am glad we are here until things sort themselves out. Craig is very happily settled in his boarding school. He seems to have taken to boarding life despite our anxiety. And Ruth. She is doing well, as is Libby. I know you miss your home country. We will go back to visit if nothing else. I promise."

"It is just that I am lonely at times when you are not here."

"I know," said Hugh sitting down, "things are different from when we were in Malaysia. We had a big house and you had domestic help there."

"I don't care about a big house or having help. They are not important to me." May slid on to Hugh's lap and laid her head on his shoulder. How could she tell him of the loneliness she sometimes felt in this busy vibrant city?

***

James stood in front of Ruth's door. He took in the tangle of weeds by the gatepost. At the far end, an overgrown buddleia with its spikes of violet turned brown, leaned heavily on one part of the wooden fence causing it to sag. Apples littered the ground and dandelion seed heads blew hither and thither in the wind. He could hear Ruth's typewriter early in the morning. She was typing at great speed, drowning the sound of chirping birds. She had been working late into the night. He knew. From his bedroom window, he had seen the solitary light in the little front room she called her office. He tightened his hold on his fork and trowel and pressed the doorbell.

Ruth opened the door. Her hair was tied up into a ponytail. Some had escaped to fall in soft trails around her face. "Oh!" she said, "I thought it was the milkman come to collect his money. I am sorry. Come in."

James could see that she was anxious. He wanted to brush away the frown lines on her forehead.

"Is it about the rent? I shall have it by the end of the week."

"No! That never crossed my mind. Sue sent me over." James turned a bright red at his lie. "She said I should give you a hand with the garden. So here I am with my fork and trowel." His eyes crinkled at the corner as he broke into a grin. "She also said that you are welcome to come over and pick whatever vegetables you wish from our garden. There is an abundance of French beans, carrots, parsnips and beet, all begging to be harvested. We can't eat them all."

At least that part of it was true. James felt the tip of his ears grow hot, a telltale sign of his embarrassment. Sue had told him that she could always tell from the colour of his ears. He wondered if Ruth had noticed.

Relief shone on Ruth's face. She could not express her gratitude for his kindness. She thought of the many times she had been late in payment. Impulsively, she stood on tiptoe and kissed him on the cheek. "I ... I can't ... thank you enough," she finally stuttered, suddenly shy from her bold act.

James's ears deepened to crimson. Two bright spots appeared on his cheeks. "My pleasure. Shall I get on with it?" He lifted his fork, mentally noting that he would probably have to return home for more tools. He had noticed that the gate needed mending as well.

"Yes, yes of course, that is if it is not too much trouble. I am sorry I am not keeping the garden as well as I should. I will, I promise, make a better job of the garden when I have finished my assignment. Mrs Bennett is paying extra to have her manuscript typed by the end of the week. I have to concentrate on that."

"Don't worry about it. It is no trouble at all."

Ruth watched James retreat into the garden. She saw his solidity, his broad shoulders, and remembered his dependability. She recalled his soft brown eyes, shy and caring always when he looked at her. Perhaps he was like this with everyone. All the villagers spoke well of him. The words of the postmistress stuck in her head. 'The poor dear has never married. His fiancée left him many years ago. He never recovered from it. He had no eyes for anyone except for her. A pity that. Any girl would give a tooth and an eye to catch him.'

Ruth closed the door behind him and went back to her table She sat down but did not type. Her hands remained poised above the typewriter. She looked out of the window. She could see James. Once again, she could feel the hammering beat of her heart. "What is wrong with me?" she wondered. "How many times have I to be bitten before I realise that I am better off alone." She resumed her work, typing furiously. James could hear her from the garden.

Chapter 43

THE BUS TRUNDLED to a stop. May stepped off it with Lin by her side. Ahead of her a narrow cobbled pedestrian street led straight to the centre of the village. The street was lined on both sides by quaint little shops that might have come off a chocolate box. At the end of the street was a square with a pretty, disused well, a reminder of times when people had to draw water for their daily needs. Radiating like a carriage wheel from the square were three lanes, each with tiny picture postcard cottages bordering it. To the east, she could see the church steeple. To the west was the hedge-bound lane leading to Ruth's cottage.

The first time Ruth told her of the village, May thought she was pulling her leg. "Puddleway?" she had repeated. "That is the name of the village?"

"It is beautiful," Ruth affirmed with eyes shining with emotion.

Standing on the pavement with her eyes glued to the village ahead of her, May understood why Ruth had fallen in love with it. The contrast between this village and those in Malaysia could not be greater. She thought of Ruth's *attap* house on stilts in Port Dickson with its dark brown wooden walls and the palm leaf thatching on its roof.

"No one from my past would find me here! It would be my sanctuary," Ruth said and May had agreed.

"Come, let's go find Aunty Ruth. She is expecting us," May said to her daughter.

They walked up the High Street. People stared at them discreetly, dropping their eyes when she stared back at them. Unabashed, May smiled holding Lin's little hand firmly in hers. A woman with a ponytail came out of a store carrying a basket filled with groceries. A loaf of bread hung precariously out from its corner. She stopped to stuff it in and lifted her head. She caught sight of May.

"May?" she squealed, her eyes wide with surprise. "Remember me? I'm Sue, Ruth's neighbour."

"Of course I do." The smile that Sue gave her was so heart-warming that May responded immediately.

"I assume you are here to see Ruth." Sue fell into step with May, her sandals crunching on the cobbled path. She reached into her basket and took out a bun. It was popping with black currants and had a dusting of sugar on the top. "May I give this to Lin? I have a soft spot for children," she confessed.

May remembered the last time she visited; Sue had taken charge of both Michael and Lin, leaving Ruth and May to talk. She smiled. "You are very good with them," she said. They walked companionably towards the square and then turned into the lane that led to the Manor House and Footman's Cottage. Hollyhocks and delphiniums lined the lane. "You have a beautiful house." May stood for a moment to admire the stone house. The sunshine had warmed its walls to a pale gold.

"It is not mine. It is James's. It is his and all these," Sue threw an arm out in a wide arc, "are his as well. I am taking a sabbatical, shall we say, from my work up north. I teach. I am doing a bit of research and helping out generally in the house. James is quite absent-minded when housework is concerned although you would not have guessed it if you had met him in his previous and even present *other* capacity. He is meticulous when it comes to his proper work."

"What does he do?"

"Besides being a landlord you mean?" Sue smiled. "He was a barrister and had a firm in London. He gave all that up when my mum died to take over the family's business. He runs this from home now."

"I didn't mean to be nosy. James has been very kind to Ruth."

"Mummy, I've finished," interrupted Lin thrusting up her sugar coated hand. May stooped and cleaned the streaks of sugar around Lin's lips and hand.

"Can I run ahead?"

"Yes!" May watched Lin run up the lane towards the cottage, her little legs pumping fast. "Careful!" she shouted.

"I cannot help but notice from your last visit that you are very close to Ruth," said Sue in a matter-of-fact voice. "How did you both meet?"

Sue could see a flash of apprehension or was it embarrassment cross over May's eyes. Then it was gone. In its place was a bland look, as if she had drawn a veil firmly in place.

"I am sorry. This time, I am the nosy one. It is just that ... well ... Perhaps when we know each other better, you'll tell me."

They walked on until they reached Ruth's cottage. Lin was already at the gate.

"I shall say good bye here," said Sue. "Pop around for drinks."

"Thank you. Hugh, my husband will be here later this evening with our son Craig. We'd like that very much."

***

"So do you like Sue and James? "They have been very good to me, especially James." Ruth threw a sidelong glance at her friend before she pulled the plug out of the bath. It was eight o'clock in the evening and they had just bathed Lin and Michael and put them to bed. The two women watched the bubbles disappear down the drain.

"I think James has a soft spot for you, Ruth."

"No. He is just being nice, that's all. I am glad that Hugh likes him, at least enough to go to the pub with him this evening. It was tactful. It leaves us time to catch up. Ruth straightened up and reached out for a towel. She began drying the bath, buffing it to a shine before putting the array of bath toys back on the shelf.

"Let's go down and have a cup of cocoa. I believe the children are asleep." Ruth paused a second to listen for sounds from the bedrooms flanking the bathroom. When none were heard, she beamed. "Come!"

They linked arms and walked down the stairs. Ruth pointed out the spots on the steps that made the loudest creaking noises. They giggled, muffling their laughter with their hands over their mouths like a pair of children as the stairs creaked and groaned. "It is an old house," Ruth explained.

"I miss you so much. London was pretty lonely for me after you left." May lowered her voice to a whisper. They entered the kitchen. She pulled a stool from under the kitchen table. Ruth took one next to her. They sat companionably in the tiny kitchen with its flagstone tiles, an Aga in the corner and a sink by the window overlooking the garden.

"I couldn't stay in London. It doesn't hold good memories for me. I was afraid of bumping into Steve. Every time I went to the park or turned a corner, I feared he would be there. I jumped each time I heard footsteps behind me. I disliked the racial discriminating notices I see in some parts of London. *No coloureds or Irish!* Imagine! There was a serious racial riot in 1958 in Notting Hill you know. It was all over the papers. The image is still firmly ingrained in my mind and when that awful woman began abusing me when she mistook Michael for a West Indian, I just lost it."

"I understand." May leaned over and placed her head on Ruth's shoulder for a second. "Hugh is sure that things will improve." She recalled the words of the woman in the London Park. "Some people find it difficult to tell one Chinese from another. They say we look the same."

Ruth looked at May, her eyes round with mirth. They giggled. "Will you go back to Malaysia?" Ruth asked.

"England is my home now. My home is where Hugh is. With Fu Yi gone, I have no one in Malaysia anyway. I miss her so much."

"Me too! I couldn't believe the suddenness of it all. Her death took everyone by surprise."

"Yes, it was sudden, a heart attack that came out of the blue. None of us knew that she had a heart condition. But I am glad she did not die alone in that horrible dormitory above a shop. She was happy with Fatimah and by the time we left she had also found new friends. Remember the man who ran a laundry near you? His children wrote to tell me that Fu Yi spent most days with them when Fatimah was out and about selling her cakes. They were with her when she died."

May brushed away the tears that rolled down her cheeks.

"Fu Yi was happy that you came back with us. She would want to see you settled and remarried. She told me before we left."

"No chance. I am just happy as things are. My work and the children take up all my time. I don't reflect too much on things. Anyway, who would want me? I carry too much baggage with me."

***

In the dim light of the pub, beer tumblers and wine glasses sparkled. The Fox and Hounds was doing a brisk trade, for the locals had taken to having a pint or two in the pub on a Friday night. Hugh and James took their drinks and found themselves a seat in a corner from where they could watch people drink their brew.

"Have you lived here long?" asked Hugh. He took a gulp of his beer and sighed with pleasure. "Nothing like a strong warm beer." He appraised his companion openly. James seemed a good chap, friendly without being overly so. Hugh liked what he heard about him. Hugh was protective of Ruth, a trait he had adopted from his wife. Ruth had made such progress. He couldn't stand the idea of her being hurt again.

"I was born here. The family home has always been here."

A man's voice cut in. "James is just modest. His family practically owned most of the land and houses in this village and beyond. He is descended from a long line of lords and ladies." He guffawed and raised his tumbler of beer, the colour of golden liquid honey, and toasted James. "To your lordship."

Hugh turned to look at the man but he was already busy chatting to someone else, nodding his grey head vigorously at what the other person was saying.

"Don't listen to him," James said. "He is just pulling my leg as they are wont to do whenever I come to the pub. He has known me since I was this high." He gestured with a hand to his waist. "This pub used to be the local for workmen from the farm that was part of our estate. It used not to welcome what they considered the lords and ladies. Mind! My parents and theirs before them had never been lords and ladies. It is just that the folks around considered them the gentry. That was then. Now we are all the same." James was red with embarrassment having to explain.

"What happened to the farm?"

"We lease it out."

"You are not married?"

James shook his head. "I had a fiancée once. She left me. It is a long time ago. I have been too wrapped up in my career since but," he smiled, "I am in the process of winding down. I am almost fifty. Before my mum died she asked me to settle down and to stop my hectic pursuit of work as she called it. I must admit I was that way inclined. She gave my father's early death as a caution. My mum was a very strong-minded woman. She had to be. My dad died very young. She was left to carry on the management of the estate and family business on her own. I didn't help much. I was in London practising law."

It was the longest speech James had made for some while. He ruffled his hair and looked ruefully at Hugh. "Perhaps it is too late for me."

"It is never too late if one meets the right person."

***

May pulled up the sheets until she was fully covered. She edged closer to Hugh who had his back to her. She was cold despite it being summer. She was always cold. She rubbed the goose bumps on her arms. "What was he like?" she asked, her mouth close to his ears.

Hugh could feel her warm breath on the nape of his neck. "Nice," he replied without turning around.

"Nice! That is not a description! Tell me," she demanded. "I am curious about him, just as his sister Sue is curious about Ruth. She asked me questions about Ruth's past. I think her brother is enamoured of our Ruth. Is he?"

"He didn't say. He thinks it might be too late for him to look for a wife."

Hugh turned and took his wife into his arms. "Let's not talk about James," he murmured.

"*Shhh!*" May giggled. "It is an old house. Everything creaks."

Chapter 44

"ARE YOU SURE it is her?" Steve held the phone tightly against his ear. He listened intently. A frown gathered on his face. Outside, a red double-decker bus stopped alongside the kerb in front his house. Three women got on it. One was very old and almost bent double. She had to be helped on to the bus. The other was a mother with a teenage daughter dressed in a short bright yellow mini skirt that revealed a long expanse of pale thin legs. The daughter clambered on to the bus. The mother following behind tugged at the girl's skirt. She said something sharp to the girl. It was lost in the roar of the bus engine.

"Wait a moment. Can you repeat the name of the school again?" He pulled open a drawer and took out a pen and notepaper. He wrote, biting his lower lip hard as he did so. "Thank you. I owe you," he said. He returned the phone to its cradle taking care to be as quiet as he could be.

"Who was that?"

"A crank call. Nothing of importance." Furtively, he folded the piece of paper and pocketed it.

"Come in and finish your tea."

Steve could hear his wife's wheelchair manoeuvring around the room. "I am coming." He hurried back into the small sitting room. He stood at its entrance, one foot in, the other still out. He could hardly bear to be in the room. It was crammed with little mementos that Margaret had collected when she was young and mobile, all of them holding special memories for her. She would not relinquish any of them, so they covered the mantelpiece, the nest of tables in the corner, even the surround of the gas fire. He eyed the gaudy ceramic shepherdess with what was akin to hatred.

"Is everything all right, love? You look out of sorts." Margaret looked anxiously at her husband. He had been very tetchy of late.

"I am fine, just a headache building up. It is so hot in this room." Steve willed a smiled on to his face. It wasn't Margaret's fault that his situation had deteriorated in the last few years. Things had turned for the worse ever since Ruth had broken off their relationship. Their trysts had been the only thing that made the boredom of his terrible life a little better. People just did not understand how he felt having to care for a disabled wife. He did not love Ruth. He loved Margaret or at least felt beholden to her. Didn't everyone say what a noble and caring husband he was? He was proud of that image. How could Ruth expect him to spoil this picture of the caring husband by leaving Margaret for her? He was sure that Ruth had broken off with him because he wouldn't leave Margaret. He took the teapot and winked at his wife. "I'll put the kettle on and refresh the tea."

Steve went into the kitchen. A pile of plates was waiting to be washed and the sink was cluttered with mugs and saucepans. He used to be house-proud. Not any more. He filled the kettle and put it on the stove. "Selfish bitch!" he muttered. He remembered bitterly the scene in the headmaster's office after Ruth resigned. He was given a month's notice to leave and no reference. He was out of a job for months and had to scrape and borrow just to keep afloat. Who could blame him, he asked himself, if his feelings for Ruth turned to hate? So when, out of the blue, a private detective contacted him about Ruth, he had willingly cooperated with him. He acknowledged that he had embroidered on the account of their affair. Finding someone to doctor the photographs of them was a stroke of genius. This was what they wanted, wasn't it? And he was paid handsomely for it. The money, however, was soon gone and no more, it appeared, was forthcoming from that source. It was sheer bad luck coming at a time when he was again unemployed.

"The two-timing bitch. Cavorting with the natives. Now she is back!" He crashed his fist against his other palm. "I'll make her pay for getting me the sack."

***

The table groaned with the weight of food on it. Two large quiches, several types of cakes, a potato salad, a green salad, French beans laced with sliced plum tomatoes and boiled eggs, and platters and platters of barbecued meats sat snugly against each other. Sue came out with yet another dish, her crowning glory she claimed. "It is my own special summer pudding made from berries fresh from the garden. May, with an apron tied snugly round her waist, followed with a huge jug of cream. "More cream, in case there isn't sufficient," she grinned cheekily nodding at another jug of the same already in place at the other end of the table. "I have my instructions," she explained. "Blame Sue. She'll have us all fattened, if we are not careful."

"James, you can stop now," said Hugh sauntering to the barbecue. "I think there are enough burgers, sausages, chicken, and steaks to feed an army. Go on. Take a rest." Hugh took the fork from James. He gave a desultory poke at the smouldering fire and went back to the table. He was relaxed, more relaxed than he had been for months. He looked at May and saw how happy she was. Perhaps they should also consider living in the country.

James was wary of leaving the barbecue as the fire was still smouldering away. He took a bottle of water and dashed some of its contents onto the barbecue. Smoke billowed. He wiped his forehead with the back of his hand leaving a streak of black on his cheeks. He sensed Ruth turning up beside him. They didn't speak. There was no need for words. During the course of the day they seemed to have settled into a companionable silence that he found comforting. She handed him a glass of lemonade. He took it with a smile. He looked tenderly at her. Her hair was blowing wildly round her face. James brushed a lock away from her face. Taken back by his own actions, he stammered an apology.

"I don't mind." She knew he was shy and wanted to allay his embarrassment. "Come, let's join the others." She walked ahead, the soft folds of her skirt brushing her tanned legs. James followed her with his eyes.

"Did you see how he looks at Ruth?" May nudged her husband. "I think he loves her."

"Don't meddle! You should not try to be a matchmaker!"

"He seems a lovely man despite your nondescript characterisation of him. Let's hope something good will happen for Ruth. She deserves it."

***

The wind whipped up speed. Craig and Libby had run all the way down the hill and were breathless. Libby doubled over, her face red with the exertion. Craig held a hand to his side. "I won this time," he said jubilantly.

"Only by this much." Libby held up her thumb and index finger and narrowed them until only a miniscule gap lay between them. "I am just out of practice, because mum doesn't like me wandering out on my own and certainly not up the hill."

"Are things better?" he asked, a serious note in his voice.

"Yes! Mum is happier. She likes it here and Uncle James has been very kind to us. I like him." Libby noticed that Craig had changed. His voice was deeper. He spoke differently and had also grown significantly taller. The easy companionship they had when they were younger was diminished. In moments like this, she felt shy.

They stood on the narrow stone bridge that led back to the village, each wondering about the other. Craig picked a stone and skimmed it across the river. "Then we'd better get back to the party before anyone misses us. I am ready for a glass of lemonade."

They began running again. A cloud of dust followed them. From across the river, a man waved at them. "Stop! Wait!" he yelled.

They stopped. The man broke into a jog towards them. He was clutching a hat. Sweat dribbled down his face. He took a handkerchief from his pocket and wiped his face before setting the hat back on his head. Libby thought him vaguely familiar. He was good looking in a kind of smarmy sort of way. She had learnt the word from Gracie, her friend who had used that description of her stepfather. Gracie explained that her stepfather had a shifty look about him and a permanent insincere smile plastered on his face. The man in front of them fitted that description.

"Can you tell me the way to Footman's Cottage?" he asked.

The children looked at each other. The man smelt of alcohol. Tiny veins of red spread like a spider's web on both his cheeks. His eyes were, however, intent and watched them like a hawk.

"Who do you want to see?" Craig stared at the man. He had taken an instant dislike to him.

"Ruth Lampard. We used to work in the same school when she was in London. Her husband died in Malaya. She has a daughter."

Craig turned to Libby. She leaned into his ear. "I think I have seen him once at mum's school."

"So shall we take him to your mum?"

Libby hesitated and then nodded. He must know her mum if he knew so much about her.

"Follow us, sir."

***

The hot sultry summer afternoon had settled to a warm eventide as the sun began its decline. Bees hummed and buzzed amongst the lavender bushes. James and Hugh made their way to the reclining chairs under a big cedar tree. Ruth watched the two men sit themselves down, drinks in hand.

"They certainly look comfortable with each other," said May. "Hugh likes James. He said he was nice and for Hugh that is a big compliment. "

"It has been such a beautiful day. Look at the sky, not a cloud in sight." Ruth threw up both her arms. If she could, she would embrace the world. "For the first time I can confess that I am truly happy. What with you and Hugh here, Craig, Lin, Libby and Michael."

"You forgot to mention James and Sue. He is keen on you. I see how he looks at you." May winked mischievously at Ruth.

"He is not. He is attentive to everyone. It is just his way." Ruth patted her hair self-consciously. She had found herself thinking about James quite a lot these past few weeks. She stole a glance in the direction of the cedar tree. James was smiling at something that Hugh had said. He looked solid, dependable and above all kind, a description that sprang to mind every time she saw him. There was no affectation in his behaviour. When she first met him, she thought he was the local farmer, well-spoken and somewhat posh, with a spare cottage to let. He spoke with genuine respect and kindness to everyone, young, and old, rich and poor. If only she could allow herself to think that he might like her. But how could she with her background? She blushed. She could not forgive herself for what she had done in the past. How could she expect anyone else to do so? She thought of Omar. She had not heard from him. The only news she had got was from May when she showed her the news article about his wedding and his rise in politics. Ruth was glad that he had found someone else. It would never have worked; Siti, his mother, had been right.

She went across to the table and began clearing up the plates and glasses. May had placed little netted food covers over the uneaten food and was now folding them away before transferring the food on to a huge tray to be taken indoors.

May sighed. "I wish I could stay in a place like this, away from the city. London is wonderful but I would rather be in the country."

"I wish you were nearer to me too. It would be wonderful to..." Ruth looked up. Craig and Libby were running towards them. Right behind them was...! She dropped the plate she was holding. It crashed onto the table, knocking a glass down, and broke into smithereens. It can't be, she thought. She shivered despite it being warm.

May reached out and took Ruth's hand. "What's the matter?"

"It is him!" She wanted to run, to hide. There was nowhere she could hide. Libby! What had Steve said to her? Had he somehow found out that Libby was his? She could feel her knees buckling underneath her. She gripped the table tight.

"The children seem to have brought another guest," Hugh called from his reclining seat.

Ruth saw James rise and walk towards the children, his hand extended in welcome. She couldn't speak. Horrified, May put an arm around Ruth. "You mean he is *the* Steve?"

Ruth could not remember her reply. She somehow managed to walk towards them. Her legs were wooden and she, a robot in automatic motion. She had to forestall James. The children looked at her in expectation. They sensed that something was wrong and were scared. "Mummy, he said he knows you from your school when we lived in London."

"It has been a long time," Steve stepped forward. He looked her up and down with insolence and familiarity before placing both hands on her shoulders. He leaned forward to kiss her. Ruth shook him off.

"What do you want?" Ruth's voice was low. She could see James from the corner of her eye. He stood frozen, a bewildered look on his face. The hand he had extended in welcome fell limply to his side. He was looking at them, his eyes full of unasked questions. He hated the man's familiarity. He saw the fear in Ruth's face.

May went quickly to James. She didn't want James to catch what Steve was going to say. "Perhaps we should leave them to talk," she said to James. She bid Libby and Craig over. The children went reluctantly. James hesitated.

"If you want me, I am just over there," he called out to Ruth. Reluctantly, he went back to the reclining chair, shifting it so that he could have Ruth in sight. He was worried for her. He had never seen her so upset before.

"What do I want?" Steve snarled. "What do you think I want?"

"Can we do this some other place, some other time?"

Steve looked over to James. He sniffed, his nostrils flared. "New boyfriend? Don't you think he would want to know as well? Bet he doesn't know about us."

Ruth didn't know what to say. She was filled with horror and disgust. How could she have taken this man as her lover? The buzzing of the bees seemed to grow louder. Her head drummed with incoherent thoughts. She drew herself up. She couldn't hide from Steve forever. She couldn't hide from her shameful past. She would just have to see it through this time.

"I have nothing to hide from my friends. You can't harm me more than you have already done," Ruth looked across at James, anguish in her eyes. She saw the way James looked back at her. She realised then that he loved her! She regretted that he was here to witness her shame. She turned away, unable to bear the pain of losing him, for she was sure that he was as good as lost to her. How could she not have known that he loved her after all the care that he had given her this past year. His face said it all. Now it was too late. He wouldn't after this.

"Do what you want?" she said softly to Steve.

Steve sneered. He pushed his face close to hers. She could smell his breath and recoiled.

"I came to offer you a lifeline. All I want is compensation for losing my job, my reputation and my life. But I see that you are still too high and mighty. You think you are better than me?" Steve tossed his head in the direction of James, his eyes narrowed to a slit. "You think he would still want you after I tell him the sort of person you were, still are?"

"Tell him, if you wish. I won't succumb to your blackmail."

"Maybe your new man will if he loves you. He might pay to keep your good name. If he doesn't, then you know where you stand with him."

Steve spun round and walked purposefully towards James. May ran to Ruth. She wanted to stop Steve. She couldn't hear the conversation but the evil on Steve's face left her in no doubt that he meant harm. "Stop him!" she begged Ruth. Ruth shook her head. Her shoulders were slumped in defeat. May looked across at the horrified and bewildered faces of the children. At least, she thought, Steve had no inkling of Libby's parentage. He would say if he did. She caught Hugh's eyes. Stay calm, they seemed to say to her.

***

James watched Steve striding towards him.

"He is here to make trouble again," Hugh said to James under his breath. "Ruth had a relationship with him when she was married to Mark. She ended it a long while ago. But he won't give up. He wants to hurt her and blacken her reputation. I thought you should know that before you listen to his lies." Hugh leaned back on his chair, his eyes intent on James. He hoped he had said sufficient to help Ruth.

James got up. He took two steps towards Steve. Before Steve could speak, he took him by the collar with both hands and lifted him off his feet. He held him suspended in the air and then he dropped him down like a sack. "Get out! I do not want to see you here or near Ruth ever again. If I ever see you trying to contact her or me, for that matter, I will get the police on you. Now scram!" James gave Steve a shove.

"You think she is so pure! She might look as though butter wouldn't melt in her mouth but she is a slut! Look at these photographs!" Steve pulled out a wad of pictures from his jacket and waved it at James.

"I don't want to. I don't have to." James looked across at Ruth. She was trembling. "I believe in her." He wrenched the pictures from Steve's hand and tore them up.

"I have copies." Steve's eyes bulged. He was mad with anger. Sweat poured from his forehead.

"And I will hound you to the ends of the earth if you ever bring these up again. Blackmail is a very serious crime and I have you recorded here." James patted the bulge in his shirt pocket. His voice was deadly calm. "I always carry a recorder around, part of my training in dealing with criminals. Now go!"

Hugh got up and went to stand next to James to give him support. James could feel Hugh's eyes on him because Hugh knew that he did not have a recorder. He had a big box of matches left over from lighting the fire.

Sue came running out. "I have called the police. They will be here any moment."

Steve hesitated. He glared at Ruth. He spat landing a gobbet at her feet. "You'll pay for this. All of you! Particularly you! Slut!"

Chapter 45

IF SHE COULD have burrowed herself into the earth like an earthworm, she would have done so. Ruth could not stop trembling. She could feel the hammering of blood in her temples. Most of all she could not stop her shame. Libby was running to her. She bent forward, opening her arms to receive her daughter. She wondered what she should say. She caught sight of May carrying Michael; May was staring at her with concern and sympathy from across the lawn, where just minutes ago such a joyous gathering had taken place. She turned to look at James. He locked eyes with her. She could not tell from his face what he was thinking. Had he really meant what he had said? she wondered. Did he believe in her? She blinked her tears away. His grim face told her *no*. With an overwhelming sense of loss, she swept Libby into her arms and buried her face in Libby's neck. "Mummy will explain," she whispered, her hot tears soaking into Libby's neck. "Come home with me."

They turned and walked away, back to the cottage watched by everyone in the garden. Ruth pushed open the blue gate and then the front door. Libby followed her into the cottage. "I am so sorry I brought the man back. Who is he? Why did he call you a slut?"

Ruth closed the door. She stood in the tiny hallway. Coats, jackets and scarves hung from a line of hooks on one side. On the opposite wall was a painting of a cottage similar to Footman's Cottage with hollyhocks and delphiniums in its front garden. It was a normal everyday scene in someone's normal, everyday life. Totally unlike her own. How could she explain to her daughter? How could she tell Libby that she had cheated on Mark, whom Libby believed to be her father, with that man?

"I am sorry." Ruth dropped her face into the palms of her hands; her voice wobbled. She stayed in that way, unable to speak. All was quiet outside the house. She forced herself to lift up her head and look at her daughter. Her lips quivered. "... Steve, the man who said all the vile things, taught in the same school as I did many, many years ago. I was very lonely then. Your father and I were not getting on. He was depressed from his inability to find work and recover his memory. He drank. I began to resent it. Steve came along and we became close. We had an affair. It was wrong of me to do that. You see, when your father and I came back to England, I was filled with hope that our life would return to normal. When that did not happen, my disappointment turned to resentment. I took matters into my own hands. I tried to find happiness elsewhere." Ruth saw the horror in her daughter's face. She could not bring herself to make it worse by telling her that Mark had himself been unfaithful and that part of her actions was in retaliation for his neglect and involvement with May. What good would it do to dash her daughter's faith in people whom she loved and loved her. Libby's view of May would change forever if she knew. At such a tender age she would never understand. She caught hold of Libby's wrist. "Please. I broke up with Steve a long time ago, before we went to Kuala Lumpur. He harbours a grudge against me and wants revenge. He wants money."

Libby pulled her hand away. Ruth tried to gather her into her arms. "Grown-ups make mistakes too. I made a mistake. I have no excuse for my past behaviour. Will you forgive me?"

"I want to go to my room," Libby said in a strangled voice. She wouldn't look at Ruth. She stared doggedly at her feet.

"Let me come with you."

Libby flung Ruth's arms away. She ran. The stairs echoed with the impact of her footsteps. "I hate you. I am so ashamed!" she cried.

Ruth followed. She heard Libby draw the bolt on her door. She pressed her face to the door. "Please let me in. It is not your shame. It is mine."

"Go away. Leave me alone."

Ruth slid down on to the floor, her back pressed against the door. Evening was slowly turning to night. Still she sat with her back against the door begging Libby to let her in.

***

"I think we should all go back into the kitchen and have a cup of tea." Sue believed firmly in the restorative effect of a nice strong brew. "Thank God that the two small ones are asleep." She was utterly shocked by what transpired in the garden just minutes ago.

"We should do as Sue says. Ruth would appreciate some time with Libby on her own." May could see James over Hugh's shoulders. He was still rooted to the same spot in the garden. He was looking at Ruth's cottage. "Hugh, get James to come in."

"Could you throw some light over what happened?" Sue asked with a nod towards the garden as soon as May entered the kitchen. Outside in the garden, the trestle table still held remnants of the party they had held. It looked sad and forlorn as though its heart and soul had been torn out.

"Have you seen Craig? May asked in reply.

"He has gone for a little walk about," Sue pointed towards the river. "I think he was embarrassed by it all. He said he felt guilty because he brought that awful man back. So are you going to tell me about this afternoon?" Sue was not going to be so easily sidetracked. She raised her eyebrows, challenging May to answer.

"I don't know whether it is my place to tell." May did not hear Hugh and James enter the kitchen.

"I have told James the gist of it. So you had better know what I said," interrupted Hugh with a quick glance at his wife. "Ruth had an affair with Steve when her marriage was on the rocks. She ended it a long time ago. He wants to blackmail her and tarnish her reputation."

"The thing is," added May, "he has done it before, threatening her I mean. Ruth is only just recovering from the trauma of recent years. I hope this incident is not going to set her back." May was very worried. It took all her resolve not to rush to the cottage. She thought of the times when Ruth had tried to punish herself by self-harm.

A furrow of lines appeared on Sue's forehead. She looked at James who had not said a word. She suspected that there was a lot more to the story. She prayed that James would not be hurt.

***

May went in search of Craig. She found him sitting by the river. She sat down on the grass beside him and watched him pluck at the grass round him. The sun was gradually sinking below the horizon, softening the light in the sky to a sweet mellowness that she had grown to appreciate and love. "Are you okay?" she asked.

"I shouldn't have brought that man back. Libby is very upset. Why does her mother give her so many problems? Remember the time we were in Kuala Lumpur? Libby thought that she was unloved. I hate it when she is upset." He plucked another long blade of grass and chewed it. "Is her mother really a slut?"

"Don't ever repeat that word. Of course she is not. She made a mistake. Everyone makes mistakes. As I have made mistakes. In life, we have to put what is bad behind us and work for the future. Ruth loves Libby. They were all so happy until today's episode. Can you not try to tell Libby that no one, none of us, thinks badly of her mother?" May crossed her fingers and prayed that was true for James and Sue. "If anyone can, it's you. It is better coming from someone of her age. It would help if you could convince her. Remember that everyone makes mistakes."

Craig shrugged. He was unsure.

May put her arm around Craig and hugged him. "Let's go back. It is getting dark. We are going to have a very light supper at Sue's and James's."

"If you think that would make Libby feel better, I'll talk to her," Craig said after a while. "I'll talk to her before supper. I don't want her to be sad. I will go to her now."

***

Ruth tied the belt snugly around the waist of her dressing gown and made her way down the stairs in the dark. She held on to the banister to ease her way. The floorboards creaked in protest, their noise magnified tenfold in the quiet of the night.

"I am right behind you," whispered May. "I couldn't sleep either. It is almost two o'clock in the morning."

They padded into the kitchen. Moonlight crept through the window, turning the kitchen into a maze of shadows. Ruth perched herself onto a stool. May did the same on the one next to her.

"Have you told Libby?" May asked placing a hand on Ruth's.

Ruth nodded. Her eyes swam with tears. "She is disgusted with me. I am disgusted with myself." She lowered her voice and May bent her head closer to hear what she had to say. "I haven't told her everything. She must not know that Steve is her biological father."

"That is wise."

"Promise me that you will not tell anyone. Not Hugh, not Craig, not James, not Sue, not anyone."

"Of course."

"I can't stay here. I can't face James and Sue."

"But you must. You love it here. What about James?"

Ruth stared out of the window. The moonlight had turned the trees to pale silver. She had found such peace here. Yesterday in the garden where everything fell apart, she had realised that she had fallen in love with James, a process that must had been so slow and imperceptible that it had taken her by surprise. She swallowed hard, overwhelmed by a sense of loss. It was not the love she had felt for Mark when she was a young girl, nor was it the passionate, defiant love she had for Omar when she was on the rebound. It was much more than all that put together. He wouldn't want her after today. She could see his grim face and imagined his eyes boring into her back when she walked with Libby to the cottage. How could he not be disgusted? How could he trust her after what he had heard?

May stood up and wrapped her arms around Ruth. She was worried, very worried that Ruth would return to self-harming. "Then you must come back with us to London. We leave tomorrow morning. You know you will always have a home with us."

Chapter 46

THE FIRST THING James saw when he came down the stairs the following morning was the envelope on the mat. He picked it up, trepidation in his heart. It was too early for the postman. He opened the front door. Hugh's car was gone. Hugh and May had bidden him farewell the previous evening. Even then he had not expected them to leave so early. He stood on the doorstep. A trickle of sunlight was struggling through the morning mist. He had not spoken to Ruth since yesterday. She had not reappeared after she had left with Libby. Should he go to her now? He looked at the envelope. He recognised her writing. Slowly he tore it open, reluctant to read what was inside. He had hardly slept the previous night. Instead he had stood by his bedroom window and watched Ruth's house. He slipped the piece of paper out of the envelope.

Dear James,

I am sorry for all the trouble and distress I caused you and Sue. Please accept my apologies. Do not think badly of me though I could hardly blame you if you did. I have done many unforgiveable things in my past. I am ashamed.

I thank you for standing by me yesterday and for the trust and help you have given me in the past year. I have been happy in Footman's Cottage. However, I cannot stay on. I will return to pack and pay my rent once I have a clearer idea of what I should do.

Ruth

James rushed out of the house. He pushed open the blue gate with a clang and knocked on Ruth's front door. He knocked and knocked again. There was no answer. He peered through the front windows. No one was there. He went to the back and peered into the kitchen window. Empty milk bottles lined the windowsill. The kitchen was empty. Deserted! James growled in frustration. He should have acted faster. Now she was gone. He blamed himself. He walked at a furious pace back to his own house. Sue was standing by the front door.

"She's gone!" The pain in his face was like an open wound for all to see. A moan escaped his lips.

Sue had never seen her gentle steady brother like that, not even when he lost his fiancée. "She must have left with May."

***

May saw James even before he rang the bell. She had been standing by the window when she spotted him walking towards the house. She ran to the front door and opened it. He stood before her with his hair uncombed and face unshaved. He looked as though he had put on his clothes in great haste. A corner of his shirt had come un-tucked. He gave her a nervous smile. "Hello!" he said. The dark shadows under his eyes spoke of worries and sleeplessness. "May I see Ruth?"

May nodded, glad that he had come. "She's upstairs in her room. She has not eaten nor slept nor spoken since we left the cottage. It is good that you are here."

"I'll go to her." James took a step into the house. May placed a hand on his arm to stop him.

"Please don't say anything that will hurt her. She blames herself for everything. That is why she left you a note instead. She is," May hesitated, "delicate."

"I know." James went into the house.

"She is in the first room on the left by the landing. It is unlocked."

James walked up the stairs. May stood at the bottom. She watched him. She prayed silently that everything would go well. She had hidden everything that Ruth could possibly use to hurt herself despite Ruth's assurance that she would not do anything silly. She had even taken the key to Ruth's door, worried that she would lock herself in. At the top of the stair, James turned. May gave him an encouraging smile.

***

James paused in front of Ruth's bedroom. All the way to London, he had practised what he should say. Now his thoughts were a jumble. He pulled his shoulders back. It was now or never. He had procrastinated long enough. He knocked and went in without waiting for an answer.

Ruth did not turn around. She was sitting on the ledge by the bay window with her knees up and her arms clasped round them. Her thin cotton dress fell round her like wisps of inconsequential petals. She looked so desolate that James wanted to take her in his arms and comfort her.

"Ruth," he said softly, a catch in his throat.

She spun round and rose to her feet. Tears welled up in her eyes. He took two steps towards her and gathered her in his arms. "I love you," he said, his lips on her head. "I don't care about your past. I don't care that you have had previous lovers. I only care that you should love me." He placed a finger on her chin to tilt her face towards him. "Can you love me a bit?"

Her lips trembled. Tears coursed down her cheeks and her eyes were bright with the wetness of them.

"If you don't, might you give me a chance?"

She buried her face in his chest, soaking it with her tears. "You won't want me if you know all the things I did in the past."

"I don't need to know." He hugged her close, his arms wrapped round her waist. "Look at me. I love you. It is the present and the future that I care about." His heart felt as though it was going to burst. Then he kissed her. Her lips were soft and moist against his. She kissed him back. Her arms went up and encircled his neck. They did not know how long they stood there, locked in each other's arms. Somewhere a clock struck. Ruth stopped suddenly. "I want you to know everything," she said, her hands against his chest to keep some distance between them. "I don't want any secrets between us. I want to tell you about Libby and Michael."

They sat and talked, he holding her hands in his. He listened. At times he would comfort her. Ruth saw no censure on his face. Dusk came and still they sat, their heads closed together. "Ruth," he said, "I shall love Libby as my own, as I would Michael. A time might come when you would need or wish to disclose to them their true parentage or they might ask you. You will know when or if that time comes. Do not make any precipitous decision. They are very young. For me, Libby and Michael are yours and that is all that matters to me."

***

It was a bright sunny day in August. The sky was a clear blue with not a cloud in sight. The village had come out in full force for the wedding. The air was filled with the scent of blossom. People gathered outside the church to wait to see the couple. A loud cheer rose from the crowd when the couple appeared from the church. James leaned over to kiss his bride. The eager crowd gave a sigh. Libby smiled and turned to Craig standing next to her. "Mum doesn't know," she whispered, "but I had often wished that James would be my father. Now my wish has come true."

Hugh and May stood well back and watched on. "I am so, so happy that everything has turned out well for Ruth," said May. "At last, I feel at peace."

"Yes. It is time for us to move on." Hugh gazed fondly at May. He stooped to whisper into her ear. "I have found a house in the country. I want you to see it. It could be ours if you like it."

May smiled and squeezed his hand. "I would like that very much," she said. She looked across at Ruth. Their eyes met. The sun was high up in the sky. She squeezed her eyes tight and breathed in deeply the perfumed air. She remembered another sun, one that was fiery red. Yes, she thought. It was time to move on.

Historical Background

On 8 December 1941, the Japanese Imperial Army landed in Kota Baru on the north east coast of Malaya and began its advance to the south. One by one the various states and cities in Malaya fell to the Japanese. Its conquest of Malaya took two months. On 16 February 1942, the Allied troops surrendered to the Japanese, marking the start of full Japanese occupation of the entire country. The Japanese remained as the occupying force until their surrender to the Allies on 4 September 1945.

During the period of Japanese occupation, tension between the different ethnic groups in Malaya intensified. Before leaving Malaya, the British military trained the Malayan Communist Party (MCP) to conduct guerrilla warfare against the Japanese. Most of the MCP members were ethnic Chinese. This resistance movement came to be known as the Malayan Peoples' Anti-

Japanese Army (MPAJA). In retaliation the Japanese conducted a massive programme of repression, torture and massacre against Chinese civilians. An estimated 50 000 or more ethnic Chinese were killed. Many Chinese fled the cities to live as squatters around forests and jungles. In return for protection against the Japanese, the squatters provided food and assistance to this anti Japanese army.

To win local support, the Japanese launched a propaganda programme '*Asia untuk orang Asia*' or 'Asia for Asians' and projected themselves as saviours of Malaya. Their policy was to favour one ethnic group against the other, in part by incorporating many pre-war civil servants into their administration. This divided the people and fostered friction between the different sectors that comprised the Malayan population.

When the Allied forces returned to Malaya, the economy of the country was in disrepair. Rubber plantations and tin mines had been abandoned and rice planting had ground to a halt during the war. As a result, the immediate post war years witnessed soaring food prices, wide spread food shortages and hunger, unemployment and low wages. Labour unrest grew to a peak. But perhaps more significantly was the awakening of politics and nationalism in Malaya.

On 1 April 1946, seven months after its return, the British Government established the Malay Union. This was a union of nine Malay states and the British Straits Settlements of Penang, Malacca and Singapore under a single administration with Sir Edward Gent as its governor. Up until then, only Penang, Malacca and Singapore came under direct British administration. With the Union, the powers of the nine Malay sultans were to be diminished. All those born in Malaya or living in British

Malaya in the previous ten years were to be granted citizenship irrespective of their ethnicity.

A huge outcry by the sultans and their subjects against the Malay Union forced the British Government to retract. The negotiations that followed resulted in the establishment of the Federation of Malaya on 1 February 1948. Under this the rights of Malays and the positions of the sultans were guaranteed. The conditions for the automatic granting of citizenships to other ethnic groups were tightened and modified. Only those born in and had lived continuously for fifteen years (or whose fathers were born in and had lived fifteen years continuously) in the country qualified.

Discontent in the country rose. The Malayan Communist Party organised hundreds of strikes. Three hundred strikes were recorded in 1947 alone. In response, the British authorities arrested and deported the strikers. The MPAJA, initially hailed as heroes after the Second World War, went back to the jungle.

On 16 June 1948, three European plantation managers were killed, precipitating the introduction of Emergency laws. The Malayan Communist Party was outlawed. Chin Peng, its leader, formed the Malayan People's Liberation Army (MPLA) and began a guerrilla campaign against the Establishment. Many of its supporters came from the former MPAJA. Rubber plantations and tin mines were specially targeted because they formed the backbone of the economy.

To counter this, General Sir Harold Briggs developed what came to be known as the Briggs Plan. Squatters and farmers living at the edge of the jungle were rounded up and forcefully relocated into New Villages. Some 450 New Villages were established and just under half a million people were placed in them. These villages were surrounded with barbed wire fencing and police guards and were floodlit at night. Long curfews were imposed. Food supplies to these villages were severely rationed. Collective punishment was meted out to villagers. Its aim was to cut off support for the outlawed Malayan People's Liberation Army. In 1952, Sir Gerald Templar took command of the British forces. Commonwealth troops from Australia, New Zealand, Southern Rhodesia and Fiji were brought in. The British army also began a campaign to win the hearts and minds of people to turn them against insurgents.

The Emergency, often referred to as the Forgotten War, was to last until 1960. In terms of human cost, over 6,000 guerrillas were said to have been killed as opposed to an estimated 1,300 Malayan troops and police and about 500 Commonwealth soldiers. Civilian casualties amounted to about 2,500 and an additional eight hundred were recorded missing.

On 31 August 1957, Malaya became independent. Six years later, on 9 July 1963, the Agreement for the formation of Malaysia, which comprised the Federation of Malaya, Singapore, North Borneo and Sarawak, was signed. On 9 August 1965, just two years on, Singapore separated from Malaysia to become an independent and sovereign state.

Between 1963 and 1966 Indonesia's opposition to the formation of Malaysia resulted in the outbreak of violent conflict between the two countries. This was known generally as the Indonesia-Malaysia Confrontation.

About the Author

Born in Kuala Lumpur, CHAN LING YAP was educated in Malaysia and the UK. She has a PhD in economics and was Associate Professor of Economics at the University of Malaya and then Senior Economist in the Food and Agricultural Organization of the United Nations in Rome. She now lives in the UK. Her novel *New Beginnings* won the Readers Popular Choice Award in 2014 in Malaysia while both *Sweet Offerings* and *Bitter-Sweet Harvest* were shortlisted for the award. Her fourth novel, *A Flash of Water*, was published in 2015. For more information visit www.chanlingyap.com.

Also by Chan Ling Yap

SWEET OFFERINGS

ISBN: 978-981-4328-44-9

Set in the late 1930s and 1960s, this is the story of Mei Yin, a young Chinese girl from an impoverished family. Her destiny is shaped when she is sent to Kuala Lumpur to become the companion of the tyrannical and bitter Su Hei who is looking for a suitable wife for her son Ming Kong ... and ultimately a grandson and heir to the family dynasty. *Sweet Offerings* is not just a fictional story of the events that ripped one family apart, but a taste of Malaysia's historical, political and cultural changes during its transition from colonial rule to independence and beyond.

BITTER-SWEET HARVEST

ISBN: 978-981-4351-68-3

Set in a Malaysia emerging from the outbreak of racial conflict in 1969, *Bitter-Sweet Harvest* tells of the difficulties and tensions of a marriage between a Malay Muslim and a Chinese Christian. Atmospheric, dramatic, action-packed and intriguing, this novel is peppered with local flavour evoking the heat, colours and sounds of Southeast Asia.